# THE ELSON READERS—BOOK SEVEN
# A Teacher's Guide

---◆---

## Catherine Andrews

B.A. English Education, National Board Certified, Teacher of English, International Baccalaureate/Bartow High School

## Mary Jane Newcomer

B.A. English Education, Teacher of English, Frostproof Middle-Senior High School, Frostproof, Florida

**L**OST **C**LASSICS
**B**OOK **C**OMPANY
Lake Wales, Florida

# PUBLISHER'S NOTE

Recognizing the need to return to more traditional principles in education, Lost Classics Book Company is republishing forgotten late 19th and early 20th century literature and textbooks to aid parents in the education of their children.

This guide is designed to accompany *The Elson Readers—Book Seven,* which was reprinted from the 1921 copyright edition. This guide contains all the original questions and exercises from the reader along with suggested answers. It also includes new "Extended Activities" that reinforce and enhance the original study sections.

We have included the same glossary and pronunciation guide of more than 2100 terms at the end of the book that is included in the reader, and which has been updated with pronunciation notation currently in use.

*The Elson Readers—Book Seven,* which this volume is meant to accompany, has been assigned a reading level of 1190L. More information concerning this  reading level assessment may be attained by visiting www.lexile.com.

© Copyright 2005
Lost Classics Book Company
ISBN 978-1-890623-31-9

Designed to Accompany
*The Elson Readers—Book Seven*
ISBN 978-1-890623-21-0
Part of
*The Elson Readers*
Nine Volumes: *Primer* through *Book Eight*
ISBN 978-1-890623-23-4

On the Cover:
Priscilla, The Courtship of Miles Standish, 1885 (oil on canvas)
by Laslett John Pott (1837-98)
**Harris Museum and Art Gallery, Preston,
Lancashire, UK/Bridgeman Art Library**

# TABLE OF CONTENTS

# PART III: OUR INHERITANCE OF FREEDOM

# PART IV: LITERATURE AND LIFE IN THE HOMELAND

## A Note about This Guide

Teachers and students alike may notice a difference in punctuation, capitalization, and spelling between the prose and poetry sections in the reader. Rules concerning these matters have changed since the original reader's publication, and we have decided that in the prose sections it would be in the best interest of the student to update these items so they will learn these rules as practiced today. However, the stories remain completely unabridged. We have exercised constraint, and typical changes consist of, for example: commas used in place of semicolons when appropriate, lowercase treatment of words not personified, or hyphenated spelling of words being contracted to modern spellings. We have, however, followed the traditional editorial practice of not changing these items in works of poetry, leaving these matters to the prerogative of the poet.

Language is always changing, and when the student notices these changes it is often a good place to start a discussion on topics such as: personification, comma usage, "up" or "down" style of capitalization, etc.

We have used *The Chicago Manual of Style*, 14th Edition, published by the University of Chicago, as our primary reference for these changes.

The reader was originally published just after World War One and many discussion questions refer to this great event. These questions can often be used to start discussions on that war and conflicts that occured after it. See the "Appendix" for a brief description of World War One.

Finally, we have provided references to Internet sites that may be useful for some of the exercises. These sites are the property of their creators, not Lost Classics Book Company, and we take no responsibility for their content. Considering the very changeable nature of the Internet, these sites may or may not exist by the time of printing and should only be considered a starting point for research.

# THE ELSON READERS—BOOK SEVEN
# A TEACHER'S GUIDE

## HOW TO USE THIS BOOK

This *Teacher's Guide* was developed to provide teachers with a guideline for appropriate, grade-level, student responses to the questions found in the "Notes and Questions" sections of the reader. Some extended activities have been added to those discussion questions in this manual and may be used at the teacher's discretion to reinforce comprehension and appreciation of the work in question. Unfamiliar vocabulary terms have also been added at the end of each discussion guide in the *Teacher's Guide* to encourage students to broaden their use of language.

Teachers may wish to have students begin with "Part One" and read the book in order, or they may pick and choose the works that fit their classroom goals. The parts are not sequential; however, skills introduced in one part may be reinforced in later parts allowing students to practice and master the various literary skills as outlined in the objectives found at the beginning of each part in the *Teacher's Guide*.

These questions and activities were designed to give the students a greater understanding of the world around them and a deeper appreciation for the contributions of those who have helped to build that world. In addition, students will receive instruction in the qualities so essential to their development as future productive citizens in the world they will inherit.

*Prediction*—It is important that students are able to make predictions about a text based on evidence from the story as well as from prior knowledge. Many of the selections in *Book Seven* are lengthy and are divided into sections. Have students discuss at the end of each section, based on what they have read and what they already know, what they think is going to occur next. Also at the end of each section, have students discuss whether their predictions were correct. It may be helpful to have students write their predictions and explanations in a reading journal.

*Words in Context*—Most of the selections in *Book Seven* have a list of glossary terms. Before students define the term from the glossary, have them identify the word in context and "guess" what they think the word means. Have students create their own definition of the word before they use the glossary. Students tend to be better able to apply and use the word if they can put the definition in their own words. It is also suggested that the students use the terms in their own sentences. Make sure when students do use the word that they are using it correctly. Have students look for context clues. These may be: 1. antonyms 2. synonyms 3. appositives.

*Instructional Aids*—Additional aids have been provided for instructing and evaluating students' progress in the "Appendix."

# PART I:
# THE WORLD OF NATURE

## In This Section—

## *Objectives—*

THE WORLD OF NATURE

By completing "Part I," the following objectives will be met.

1. The student will use effective reading strategies to construct meaning and identify the purpose of a text including:
   a. using illustrations
   b. defining unfamiliar words
   c. retelling and summarizing
2. The student will determine the main idea or essential message and identify relevant supporting details and facts of a text.
3. The student will read and organize facts from the text and other sources to make a report, outline, and perform an authentic task.
4. The student will prepare for writing by focusing on the topic and organizing supporting details in a logical sequence.
5. The student will draft and revise writing.
6. The student will produce final documents that have been edited for correct spelling, punctuation, and grammar.
7. The student will write for a variety of audiences and purposes.
8. The student will write in a variety of genres including narration, exposition, and poems.
9. The student will use reference materials (dictionaries, encyclopedias, maps, charts).
10. The student will use speaking strategies effectively such as eye contact, gestures, and visuals that engage the audience.
11. The student will identify the development of plot and how conflicts are resolved in a story.
12. The student will identify and understand similarities and differences among the characters, settings, and events presented in various texts.
13. The student will identify the author's purpose and point of view.
14. The student will identify and use literary terminology such as personification, simile, metaphor, foreshadowing, and alliteration.
15. The student will identify and use poetic terminology such as lyric, couplet, blank verse, iambic pentameter, rhyme scheme, and slant rhyme.
16. The student will respond critically to fiction, nonfiction, and poetry.
17. The student will recognize cause-and-effect relationships in literary texts.
18. The student will respond to a text by explaining how the motives of the characters or events compare with those in his or her own life.
19. The student will use context clues to understand words and ideas.
20. The student will predict events that may occur in the text and explain the reasoning behind the prediction.
21. The student will understand the qualities necessary for people to become good citizens and apply those qualities to his/her personal life.
22. The student will understand the qualities necessary to develop good character and apply those qualities to his/her personal life.

# THE WORLD OF NATURE

## *ANIMALS*

### THE BUFFALO, p. 23

In "The Buffalo" Francis Parkman takes the reader on a buffalo hunt through the wild, undeveloped plains of Nebraska. After four days on the trail, Parkman with his fellow rider, Henry, left the wagons to hunt for antelope when they saw in the distance their first signs of buffalo. Riding through ravines and over hills, they finally came up on the herd. Sneaking up on them, Henry killed two buffalo which they dissected, loading the meat on their horse, and returned to camp in a driving rain.

The next day the men set out to hunt again, but the hunt was forgotten when they encountered human life: trappers heading down river with their furs and hides. Parkman, wishing to send out a letter, gave up the hunt to meet with the trappers and give them his letter for delivery.

Bored with camp life, Shaw, Henry, and Parkman set out once more to hunt buffalo. In the thick of the hunt, Parkman became separated from his fellow hunters and soon discovered he was lost. Using his compass, he headed toward what he thought was the Platte, but after hours of riding, he saw no signs of the river. Deciding that the buffalo might be his only hope of finding the river, he followed their trail which eventually led to the river. Exhausted and ill, he laid down beside the river and waited for his wagon party to pass by and find him.

1. **Locate on a map the Platte River and the region mentioned in the story.**

   The Platte River is located in Nebraska. The North Platte and the South Platte Rivers join in western Nebraska to form the Platte River, which flows generally eastward until it empties into the Missouri River (*see map on page 14*).

2. **What picture do you see as you read the fourth paragraph?**

   The fourth paragraph describes the view of the plain through the eyes of the author. "… far on the left rose the broken line of scorched, desolate sandhills. The vast plain waved with tall rank grass that swept our horses' bellies; it swayed to and fro in billows with the light breeze, and far and near, antelope and wolves were moving through it, the hairy backs of the latter alternately appearing and disappearing as they bounded awkwardly along, while the antelope with the simple curiosity peculiar to them, would often approach us closely, their little horns and white throats just visible above the grass tops as they gazed eagerly at us with their round, black eyes."

3. **Briefly relate the incident of the first afternoon's hunting trip.**

   Henry and Francis were searching for antelope when they spotted what looked like black specks in the distance. Assuming they had spotted buffalo, they headed for the sandhills where they hoped to find a herd. Riding rapidly through ravines and around dunes, they finally discovered "a long procession of buffalo were walking in Indian file." Harvey took both rifles and crawled through the undergrowth toward the herd. Finally, he shot twice and the buffalo disappeared over the hills. Thinking he missed the buffalo, the two men followed the herd and came upon two buffalo that Henry had shot through the lungs from "more than a hundred and fifty yards." They dissected the animals, tied their meat to the horses, and returned to camp in a driving rain.

4.  **What do you learn of prairie animals from this story?**

    Prairie animals mentioned in this story are: the antelope with "little horns and white throats;" "squalid, ruffian-like" wolves; buffalo "with their enormous size and weight, their shaggy manes, and the tattered remnants of their last winter's hair covering their backs in irregular shreds and patches;" prairie dogs "which sat, each at the mouth of his burrow, holding his paws before him in a supplicating attitude and yelping away most vehemently, energetically whisking his little tail with every squeaking cry he uttered;" "various long, checkered" snakes that lived among the prairie dogs; and "demure little gray owls, with a large white ring around each eye."

5.  **Read the description of the prairie dog found on page 31; why is this description a good one?**

    See the description of the prairie dog in question 4. It is a good description because it appeals to the reader's senses of sight and sound, which help the reader visualize the prairie dog.

6.  **How does this description prove that Parkman was a close observer of nature?**

    He did not give a general description as a passing rider may have, but described in detail the prairie dog's behavior including his paws and his "whisking little tail."

7.  **What insects that differ from those found farther east does the author mention?**

    "Gaudy butterflies fluttered about my horse's head; strangely formed beetles were crawling upon plants that I had never seen before; multitudes of lizards, too, were darting like lightning over the sand."

8.  **Point out lines that show Parkman to be excellent in description.**

    Numerous lines can be identified. Encourage students to find the lines that appeal to their senses and create visual images in their minds' eye as they read.

9.  **Compare travel at the time the author made this trip with travel at the present time.**

Travel was exclusively done by horse and wagons overland or by boat on waterways. Today, travel includes rail, air, land, and waterways.

10. **You read in the "Introduction," page 21, that nature brings adventures to those that love her; mention some adventures that Parkman had on his journey up the Platte.**

His adventures included wild game hunting, animal encounters, riding through rough and dangerous ravines, and getting lost in the plains.

11. **Notice that Parkman adds interest by means of fanciful expressions, such as "skirting the brink" (page 27, line 3); explain this phrase and find other similar fancies.**

"Skirting the brink" is defined in the glossary as "running along the edge" of a deep ravine.

Answers may vary but students are encouraged to find other expressions such as "scantily clothed" (page 24, line 22), referring to the bare hills. "Hugged close to the shore" (page 27, line 19), refers to the boats as they tried to keep from being swept away by the current.

12. **In what simple way did Henry determine the direction of the wind?**

"He tore off a little hair from the piece of buffalo robe under his saddle, and threw it up, to show the course of the wind" (page 24, line 27).

13. **You will enjoy reading "The Bison, or American Buffalo," Roosevelt (in *The Wilderness Hunter*); *In Texas with David Crockett* and *In Kentucky with Daniel Boone*, McIntyre; *The Boy Immigrants*, Brooks.**

14. **Find in the glossary the meaning of: melancholy, ravine, contemplating, languid, apprehension, declivity, furlong, canter, impetuosity, aspect, squalid, fastidious, futility, picketing.**

15. **Pronounce: butte, alternately, minute, bourgeois, robust, circuit, leisurely, intricacies, vehemently.**

## *Extended Activities:*

1. Parkman describes the buffalo using terms such as enormous brutes, enormous size and weight, tremendous weight and impetuosity, huge shaggy head. Have students list all the descriptions of the buffalo they can find in this story that refer to its size, weight, physical appearance, and general attitude. Using this information and other resources, students should research the actual size of the full-grown bull

of which Parkman writes. Using masking tape, rulers, and their research, have them design an outline in a large open space that would show the actual shape and size of a full-grown bull buffalo.

2. Parkman's story is taken from his experiences traveling the Oregon Trail, the longest overland route in the westward expansion of America. It began in Independence, Missouri, and extended to the Willamette Valley in Oregon. Using a map of the western part of the United States and other research, have students outline the trail as it wound through the mountains and deserts of the great western lands. Have them identify where on the outline this story by Parkman occurred.

Helpful Internet resources to begin their research may include:
http://www.pbs.org/opb/oregontrail/teacher/trailmap.html
http://www.ukans.edu/kansas/seneca/oregon/

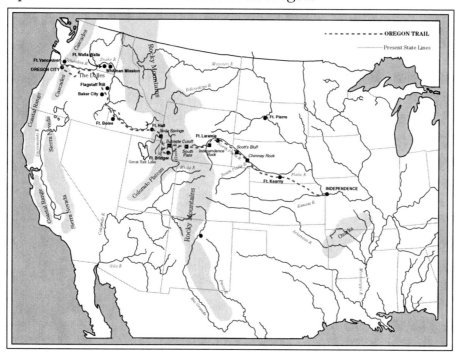

3. Help students experience some of the dangers on the Oregon Trail through a software program entitled "The Oregon Trail." For information regarding this program contact: http://www.mecc.com/ or call mecc at (612) 569-1500.

4. Francis Parkman probably wrote this story after his exploration in 1846. In the *Elson Reader—Book Five,* students will find another story of a buffalo hunt written by Theodore Roosevelt entitled "Hunting the American Buffalo." In this story, Roosevelt described his adventure on an 1889 hunt. While these authors share similar adventures with the buffalo, one can conclude from their narratives that the herds were greatly diminished in the 43 years between Parkman and Roosevelt's hunts. Have students read the Roosevelt adventure and compare it to the Parkman adventure. Have students discuss what may have caused the devastating loss of these magnificent animals.

NAME_____CLASS_____DATE_____

## THE BUFFALO, P. 23

1. Parkman describes the buffalo using terms such as enormous brutes, enormous size and weight, tremendous weight and impetuosity, huge shaggy head. List all the descriptions of the buffalo you can find in this story that refer to its size, weight, physical appearance, and general attitude. Using this information and other resources, research the actual size of the full-grown bull of which Parkman writes. Using masking tape, rulers, and your research, design an outline in a large open space that would show the actual shape and size of a full-grown bull buffalo.

2. Parkman's story is taken from his experiences traveling the Oregon Trail, the longest overland route in the westward expansion of America. It began in Independence, Missouri, and extended to the Willamette Valley in Oregon. Using a map of the western part of the United States (*see map on next page*) and other research, outline the trail as it wound through the mountains and deserts of the great western lands. Identify where on the outline this story by Parkman occurred.

   Helpful Internet resources to begin your research may include:
   http://www.pbs.org/opb/oregontrail/teacher/trailmap.html
   http://www.ukans.edu/kansas/seneca/oregon/

4. Francis Parkman probably wrote this story after his exploration in 1846. In the *Elson Reader, Book Five,* you will find another story of a buffalo hunt written by Theodore Roosevelt entitled "Hunting the American Buffalo." In this story, Roosevelt described his adventure on an 1889 hunt. While these authors share similar adventures with the buffalo, one can conclude from their narratives that the herds were greatly diminished in the 43 years between Parkman and Roosevelt's hunts. Read the Roosevelt adventure and compare it to the Parkman adventure. Discuss what may have caused the devastating loss of these magnificent animals.

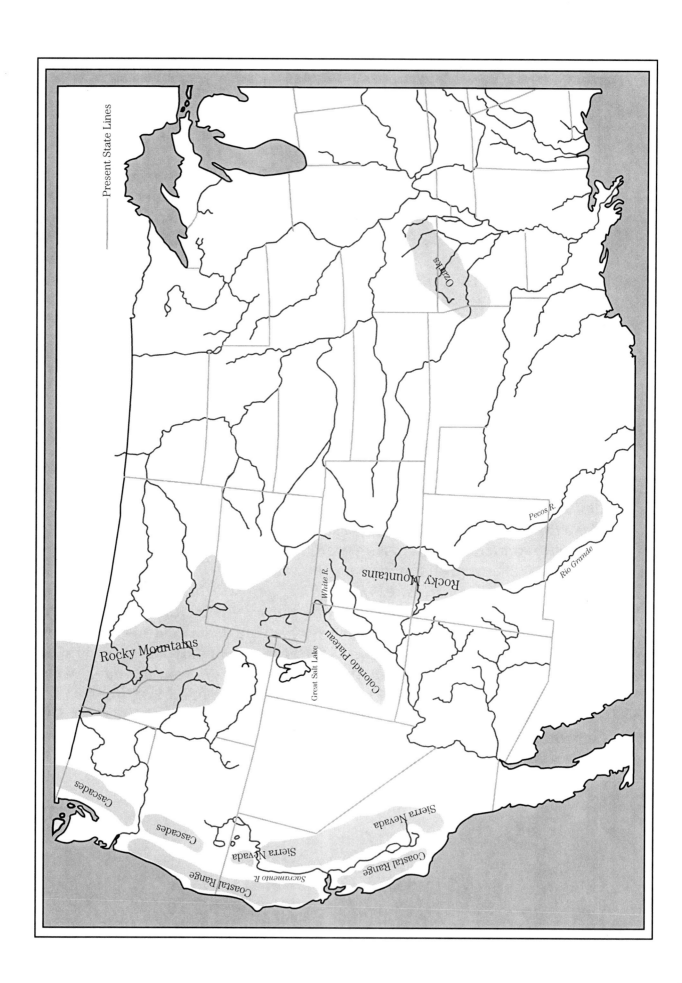

Present State Lines

Ozarks

Pecos R.

Rio Grande

White R.

Rocky Mountains

Rocky Mountains

Colorado Plateau

Great Salt Lake

Cascades

Cascades

Sierra Nevada

Sierra Nevada

Coastal Range

Coastal Range

Sacramento R.

## Hunting the Grizzly Bear, p. 36

1.  **Locate the region in which the author was hunting at the time of the adventure he narrates.**

    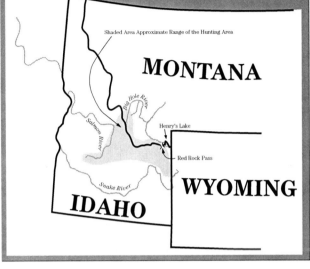

    The author identifies the region as: "the headwaters of the Salmon and Snake in Idaho, and along the Montana boundary line from the Big Hole Basin and the head of the Wisdom River to the neighborhood of Red Rock Pass and to the north and west of Henry's Lake."

2.  **Describe his outfit and tell what must be considered in providing such a hunting outfit.**

    Roosevelt's hunting outfit consisted of "only my buffalo sleeping bag, a fur coat, and my washing kit, with a couple of spare pairs of socks and some handkerchiefs." In addition to his clothes, he took along "A frying pan, some salt, flour, baking powder, a small chunk of salt pork, and a hatchet" along with a rope, a packing cinch, cartridges, knife, compass, and matches. These items provided warmth along with basic food and hunting supplies, a hunter's main concern.

3.  **What moments in the encounter with the grizzly were most exciting and dangerous?**

    Students should be encouraged to identify the parts most dangerous to them, but undoubtedly the description of the grizzly's charge holds high excitement for the reader.

4.  **For what purpose does the author say the grizzly has been hunted?**

    The grizzly "has been hunted for sport, and hunted for his pelt, and hunted for the bounty, and hunted as a dangerous enemy to livestock."

5.  **What habit has bitter experience taught the grizzly bear?**

    "Bitter experience has taught him caution." (See page 39, line 22.)

6.  **What shows you that Roosevelt was a close observer of nature?**

    Roosevelt, like Parkman in the preceding story, uses vivid imagery that appeals to the senses of sight, sound, and touch to help the reader visualize the scene. Phrases such as "scarlet strings of froth" and eyes "like embers in the gloom" show that he was a close observer of nature.

7. **What qualities must a hunter of the grizzly bear possess?**

   A hunter must be cautious, skillful, and hardy with "steady nerves and a fairly quick and accurate aim," acting "warily and with the utmost caution and resolution, if he wishes to escape a terrible and probably fatal mauling."

8. **What conclusions does the author give as a result of his experience in hunting "this chief American game"?**

   "The most thrilling moments of an American hunter's life are those in which, with every sense on the alert, and with nerves strung to the highest point, he is following alone into the heart of its forest fastness the fresh and bloody footprints of an angered grizzly; and no other triumph of American hunting can compare with the victory to be thus gained."

9. **What impression of the author do you gain from this story?**

   Students are encouraged to identify the traits that the author exhibits in this story: bravery, courage, responsibility, etc.

10. **On page 21 you were told that nature sometimes gives us two kinds of adventures; which kind is told of in this story?**

    Nature brings us adventure through "unusual experiences" like "hunting wild animals or exploring strange lands" or through "familiar or common things" around us. This story is an adventure of the "unusual experience" of hunting a grizzly bear.

11. **You will enjoy reading *The Boys' Life of Theodore Roosevelt*, Hagedorn, and "Blackbear," Scoville, in *St. Nicholas*, August, 1919).**

12. **Find in the glossary the meaning of: emergency, coulie, trophy, prone, provocation, redoubtable, pelt, quarry, fastness.**

13. **Pronounce: obliquely, foliage, wound, wary.**

**Questions for testing Silent Reading.**

1. **Where did Roosevelt spend the fall of 1889?**

   He spent the fall of 1889 "hunting on the headwaters of the Salmon and Snake in Idaho, and along the Montana boundary line from the Big Hole Basin and the head of the Wisdom River to the neighborhood of Red Rock Pass and to the north and west of Henry's Lake."

2. **What can you tell about his companion?**

   His companion, called "Hank" or "Tariff" was a crabby, honest, old, moody, surly, skillful hunter with a bad temper. One day while Roosevelt was out of camp, Hank found his whiskey and drank it all.  Roosevelt returned to a very drunk companion, so, after some heated words, Roosevelt left him.

3.  **Of what did Roosevelt's outfit consist?**

    He had a "buffalo sleeping bag, a fur coat, and my washing kit, with a couple of spare pairs of socks and some handkerchiefs." In addition to his clothes, he took along "A frying pan, some salt, flour, baking powder, a small chunk of salt pork, and a hatchet" along with a rope, a packing cinch, cartridges, knife, compass, and matches.

4.  **Describe the place he chose for his camp.**

    He made camp "in a little open spot by the side of a small, noisy brook, with crystal water.  The place was carpeted with soft, wet, green moss dotted with the kinnikinnick berries, and at its edge, under the trees where the ground was dry, I threw down the buffalo bed on the mat of sweet-smelling pine needles."

5.  **What was his object in leaving the camp?**

    He left camp to hunt a grouse for his supper.

6.  **Tell of his stroll.**

    Roosevelt walked through the silent forest in search of game as the sun disappeared behind the mountain.  Finally he decided to return to camp when he spotted the grizzly "walking slowly off with his head down."

7.  **What were the actions of the bear after the first shot?**

    After the first shot, the grizzly "uttered a loud, moaning grunt and plunged forward at a heavy gallop."  He plunged into a thicket where he stayed while Roosevelt skirted the edge, trying to get a glimpse of him.  Suddenly the grizzly ran out the opposite end of the thicket and headed for a nearby hillside where "He turned his head stiffly toward me."

8.  **Give an account of the bear's charge.**

    Roosevelt aimed and fired, shooting the grizzly in the heart.  The grizzly turned and charged.  Roosevelt shot again as the grizzly approached him shooting him in the chest, but he kept coming. Just as the grizzly was upon him, he fired again, hitting him in the mouth and jumping aside as the grizzly swept past him.  The grizzly fell to the ground, jumped back up and tried to go further but "his muscles seemed suddenly to give way, his head drooped, and he rolled over and over like a shot rabbit."

9.  **Why is the grizzly not so dangerous now as he once was?**

    "He has learned to be more wary than a deer, and to avoid man's presence almost as carefully as the most timid kind of game."

10. **What is the chief danger of hunting these great bears?**

    When "fairly brought to bay, or when moved by a sudden fit of ungovernable anger, the grizzly is beyond peradventure a very dangerous antagonist." "It is always hazardous, however, to track a wounded and weary grizzly into thick cover." He may "charge again and again and fight to the last with unconquerable ferocity."

## Outline for Testing Silent Reading.

A note to the teacher: these topics have been covered in detail in the discussion questions and/or the "Questions for Testing Silent Reading" listed above. They are copied here for quick reference should you choose to use only this section of the review.

(a) The part of the country in which the hunt occurred—He spent the fall of 1889 "hunting on the headwaters of the Salmon and Snake in Idaho, and along the Montana boundary line from the Big Hole Basin and the head of the Wisdom River to the neighborhood of Red Rock Pass and to the north and west of Henry's Lake."

(b) Roosevelt's outfit and camp—He had a "buffalo sleeping bag, a fur coat, and my washing kit, with a couple of spare pairs of socks and some handkerchiefs." In addition to his clothes, he took along "A frying pan, some salt, flour, baking powder, a small chunk of salt pork, and a hatchet" along with a rope, a packing cinch, cartridges, knife, compass, and matches. He made camp "in a little open spot by the side of a small, noisy brook, with crystal water. The place was carpeted with soft, wet, green moss dotted with the kinnikinnick berries, and at its edge, under the trees where the ground was dry, I threw down the buffalo bed on the mat of sweet-smelling pine needles."

(c) His discovery of the bear—Roosevelt was returning to camp after seeking a grouse for supper when he spotted the grizzly "walking slowly off with his head down." Roosevelt shot him after which the grizzly "uttered a loud, moaning grunt and plunged forward at a heavy gallop." He plunged into a thicket where he stayed while Roosevelt skirted the edge, trying to get a glimpse of him. Suddenly the grizzly ran out the opposite end of the thicket and headed for a nearby hillside where "He turned his head stiffly toward me."

(d) The encounter with the bear—Roosevelt aimed and fired, shooting the grizzly in the heart. The grizzly turned and charged. Roosevelt shot again as the grizzly approached him, shooting him in the chest, but he kept coming. Just as the grizzly was upon him, Roosevelt fired again, hitting him in the mouth and jumping aside as the grizzly swept past him. The grizzly fell to the ground, jumped back up and tried to go further but "his muscles seemed suddenly to give way, his head drooped, and he rolled over and over like a shot rabbit."

(e) The danger in hunting the grizzly—When "fairly brought to bay, or when moved by a sudden fit of ungovernable anger, the grizzly is beyond peradventure a very dangerous antagonist." "It is always hazardous, however, to track a wounded and weary grizzly into thick cover." He may "charge again and again and fight to the last with unconquerable ferocity."

## *Extended Activities:*

1. Students may want to research the full-grown grizzly bear as they did the buffalo in the previous story and use tape and rulers to draw a life-size replica of Roosevelt's grizzly. See "Extended Activity" #1 under "The Buffalo" for directions.

2. Roosevelt describes his encounter with the grizzly with striking images. Have students list all the phrases that describe the grizzly in this story. Have them create a piece of art that illustrates the grizzly as Roosevelt described it in the charge. Images may include: "scarlet strings of froth hung from his lips;" "eyes burned like embers in the gloom;" "blowing bloody foam from his mouth;" "gleam of his white fangs;" "crashing and bounding through the laurel bushes;" "smashing his lower jaw;" "his head drooped, and he rolled over and over like a shot rabbit."

3. What might the background music of the grizzly's charge sound like if this were a movie? Have students choose or create a soundtrack to accompany the part of the story that describes the charge of the grizzly. Reread the story using the soundtrack to enhance the mood and excitement of the charge.

Name_____Class_____Date_____

## Hunting the Grizzly Bear, p. 36

1. Research the full-grown grizzly bear as you did the buffalo in the previous story and use tape and rulers to draw a life-size replica of Roosevelt's grizzly. See "Extended Activity" #1 under "The Buffalo" for directions.

2. Roosevelt describes his encounter with the grizzly with striking images. List all the phrases that describe the grizzly in this story. Create a piece of art that illustrates the grizzly as Roosevelt described it in the charge.

3. What might the background music of the grizzly's charge sound like if this were a movie? Choose or create a soundtrack to accompany the part of the story that describes the charge of the grizzly. Reread the story using the soundtrack to enhance the mood and excitement of the charge.

## Moti Guj—The Mutineer, p. 46

1. **Read all that tells you of the time and place in which this mutiny occurred.**
   The story takes place on a coffee plantation in India when the British were still in control of the country.

2. **Read all that gives you a picture of life on the clearing.**
   Moti Guj, a powerful elephant, belonged to Deesa, a drunken owner who often beat Moti Guj on his tender forefeet. Deesa used him to clear the land of stumps so planters could enlarge their lands.

3. **Who is the principal character in the story?**
   Moti Guj is the principal character.

4. **What caused the mutiny?**
   Deesa wished to become very drunk, so he asked the coffee planter for permission to attend his mother's funeral, thinking he could escape for a time to get drunk. However, the planter caught him in his lies and refused permission. After several more lies, none of which persuaded the planter to let him go, Deesa finally promised that he would return after ten days. Moti Guj was left in Chihun's care, a man from Deesa's village, while Deesa left on his journey. However, after ten days, Deesa did not return and Moti Guj quit working for Chihun. No amount of begging would change his mind. Instead, "Moti Guj put his hands in his pockets, chewed a branch for a toothpick, and strolled about the clearing, making fun of the other elephants who had just set to work."

5. **What ended it?**
   Deesa returned from his orgy and called Moti Guj who had gone in search of him. Moti Guj returned at once where "he fell into Deesa's arms, trumpeting with joy" and they returned to the "coffee clearing to look for difficult stumps."

6. **What is the most interesting point in the story?**
   Students' responses will vary.

7. **Read parts that convince you that Kipling knows the characteristics of the elephant.**
   Answers may vary but should reflect examples of the elephant's great power in stump removal, his love and devotion to his master, his rate of movement, his sleeping patterns, and the conversations that showed his ability to understand humans.

8. **Find instances where he exaggerates the intelligence of the elephant, giving it human characteristics.**
   Giving non-humans human characteristics is known as personification. Kipling gives several examples of personification.

For example: "Moti Guj put his hands in his pockets, chewed a branch for a toothpick, and strolled about the clearing, making fun of the other elephants who had just set to work." "He slapped old friends on the back and asked them if the stumps were coming easily; he talked nonsense concerning labor and the inalienable rights of elephants." Students may identify other passages that reflect their observations.

9.  **Does this add or take away from the interest of the story?**
    Generally students will agree that it adds interest to the story since it gives the elephant human characteristics.

10. **On page 22 you read that a close acquaintance with nature makes us see our kinship with animals; do the instances you find show companionship between Deesa and the elephant?**
    Kipling gives several examples of the companionship between Deesa and Moti Guj.

11. **Read parts in which humor is shown in dialogue or incident.**
    Students will find various examples of humor. Encourage students to explain how their choices are humorous.

12. **Tell in your own words the main incident.**
    Moti Guj stages a mutiny because his master, Deesa, goes away with the promise to return after ten days but does not come back. Moti Guj refuses to work any longer without Deesa, so he wreaks general havoc in the clearing until Deesa returns.

13. **What do you like about this story?**
    Answers will vary.

14. **Tell what you know of the author.**
    If students have read the "Biography," they will have at least a minimal understanding of Kipling. Born in India in 1865, he was educated in England. At seventeen, he returned to India where he wrote tales of Indian life. He became known for his poetry as well as his stories. He died in 1936.

15. **Find in the glossary the meaning of: dissipated, congested, devastating, inspiration, delectable, caste, inalienable, demoralized, soliloquy, salaam.**

16. **Pronounce: therefore, orgy, adieu, amateur, deign.**

## *Extended Activities:*

1.  Students will note that Moti Guj is given several different descriptive titles to endear him to the reader. Have students make a list of all those titles. They are as follows: Pearl Elephant; Light of my heart; protector of the drunken; mountain of might; fussy old pig; warty toad of a dried up mud puddle; hog of the backwoods; beast after mine own heart; Oh,

my lord, my king; jewel of all created elephants; lily of the herd; misborn mountain; splendor of the hillsides; adornment of all India; devil-son; wild elephant; my son and my joy. A caricature describes a character with exaggerated features to bring out the humor in his appearance. Have students choose several of their favorite titles for Moti Guj and create a caricature of Moti Guj that encompasses those images.

2. While Kipling describes the elephant in a humorous vein using personification to describe its intelligence and importance to humans, elephants have been useful to humans for thousands of years. Have students research the facts about elephants and create a class compilation of their findings. The topics to be researched may include but are not limited to: body description and size, life span, kinds, importance to people, intelligence, foods, travel, reproduction, what is being done to protect them. When the research has been completed, have students identify the elephant traits described by Kipling that were factual and those that were exaggerated.

3. In the *Elson Readers—Book Six,* students will find another story of the elephant as told by Samuel White Baker entitled "A Furious Elephant Charge." Have the students read his story and, based on their research (see activity #2), identify the ways in which Baker was right in his description of the elephant. Have students discuss which description, Kipling's or Baker's, was more entertaining.

NAME_____CLASS_____DATE_____

## MOTI GUJ—THE MUTINEER, P. 46

1.  You will note that Moti Guj is given several different descriptive titles to
    endear him to the reader.  Make a list of all those titles.

_____

_____

_____

_____

_____

_____

_____

A caricature describes a character with exaggerated features to bring out
the humor in his appearance.  Choose several of your favorite titles for
Moti Guj and create a caricature of Moti Guj that encompasses those
images.

2. While Kipling describes the elephant in a humorous vein using personification to describe its intelligence and importance to humans, elephants have been useful to humans for thousands of years. Research the facts about elephants and create a class compilation of your findings. The topics to be researched may include but are not limited to: body description and size, life span, kinds, importance to people, intelligence, foods, travel, reproduction, what is being done to protect them. When the research has been completed, identify the elephant traits described by Kipling that were factual and those that were exaggerated.

_____

_____

_____

_____

_____

_____

_____

_____

_____

_____

_____

_____

_____

_____

_____

3. In the *Elson Readers—Book 6*, you will find another story of the elephant as told by Samuel White Baker entitled "A Furious Elephant Charge." Read his story and, based on your research (see activity #2), identify the ways in which Baker was right in his description of the elephant. Discuss which description, Kipling's or Baker's, was more entertaining.

_____

_____

_____

_____

# BIRDS

## ROBERT OF LINCOLN, p. 55

1. **Read the lines that imitate the song of the bobolink.**

   The lines that imitate the bobolink are the same in all stanzas: "Bob-o'-link, bob-o'-link, Spink, spank, spink;…Chee, chee, chee!"

2. **Describe the dress of Robert of Lincoln and that of his "Quaker wife."**

   "Robert of Lincoln is gayly dressed,
   Wearing a bright, black wedding coat;
   White are his shoulders, and white his crest.
   Robert of Lincoln's Quaker wife,
   Pretty and quiet, with plain brown wings."

3. **Why does the poet call the bobolink's wife a Quaker?**

   She was quiet, as well as "modest and shy," "passing at home a patient life." These are often considered characteristics of the early pioneer Quaker women.

4. **How does her song differ from his?**

   She makes only "one weak chirp." He, on the other hand, is "pouring boasts from his little throat."

5. **What are the work and the care that make him silent?**

   The work and care of raising his family make him sober and silent.

6. **How does the poet account for the bird's changed appearance as the season advances?**

   Time and hard work have taken a toll on him:
   "Summer wanes; the children are grown;
   Fun and frolic no more he knows;
   Robert of Lincoln's a humdrum crone."

7. **Where does he go for winter? When will he come again?**

   He goes south for winter and comes back in the spring, traveling "from Canada to Paraguay." (See "Note" under "Notes and Questions" in the reader.)

8. **On page 16 you read that the poet awakens our fancy, enabling us to picture things that the eye alone cannot see; what fancy does Bryant leave with you, by the last two stanzas of this poem?**

   He fancies that Robert of Lincoln, like humans, grows older from his toil and care. Children grow up and leave, and the excitement of youth dims.

9. **Find in the glossary the meaning of: mead, brood, braggart, knave, wane, crone, pipe, strain.**

## NEWSPAPER READING

In 1825, when William Cullen Bryant became editor of the New York *Evening Post,* there were comparatively few newspapers in our country; but during the century since that date, the number has grown steadily until today there is hardly a town or village in the land that has not its weekly or even its daily newspaper. Besides the thousands of papers printed in the English language, there are daily papers printed in our country in the French, Italian, Spanish, German, Dutch, Norwegian, Polish, Russian, Yiddish, Japanese, and Chinese languages.

The editors who have the power to decide what shall and what shall not appear in their papers exert a tremendous influence in shaping the opinions of the millions of newspaper readers. Who is the editor of the paper that you are in the habit of reading? Bring to class copies of your local newspaper and show that there is a regular place for general news, editorials, society news, sports, market reports, jokes, cartoons, and advertisements; of what advantage to the busy reader is a definite place in the paper for each of these departments? *Headlines* in large type call attention to the story, and *leads* in smaller type directly under the headlines give a brief summary of the story. How do these, also, help to save the reader's time?

When was the first newspaper started in your community? Have you seen copies of newspapers printed one hundred years ago or printed during the Civil War? If you can, bring to class copies of old-time newspapers and compare them with those of today.

Keep a class scrapbook for current events and for interesting newspaper mention of literary men and women and their works. Note especially accounts of local visits by authors. A committee of pupils may be chosen to be responsible for pasting the clippings as they are handed in from time to time by members of the class.

NAME_____CLASS_____DATE_____

## NEWSPAPER READING, p. 58

In 1825, when William Cullen Bryant became editor of the New York *Evening Post,* there were comparatively few newspapers in our country; but during the century since that date, the number has grown steadily until today there is hardly a town or village in the land that has not its weekly or even its daily newspaper. Besides the thousands of papers printed in the English language, there are daily papers printed in our country in the French, Italian, Spanish, German, Dutch, Norwegian, Polish, Russian, Yiddish, Japanese, and Chinese languages.

The editors who have the power to decide what shall and what shall not appear in their papers exert a tremendous influence in shaping the opinions of the millions of newspaper readers.

1. **Who is the editor of the paper that you are in the habit of reading?**

_____

2. **Bring to class copies of your local newspaper and show that there is a regular place for general news, editorials, society news, sports, market reports, jokes, cartoons, and advertisements; of what advantage to the busy reader is a definite place in the paper for each of these departments?**

_____

_____

3. ***Headlines*** **in large type call attention to the story, and** *leads* **in smaller type directly under the headlines give a brief summary of the story. How do these, also, help to save the reader's time?**

_____

_____

4. **When was the first newspaper started in your community?**

_____

5. **Have you seen copies of newspapers printed one hundred years ago or printed during the Civil War? If you can, bring to class copies of old-time newspapers and compare them with those of today.**

6. Keep a class scrapbook for current events and for interesting newspaper mention of literary men and women and their works. Note especially accounts of local visits by authors. A committee of pupils may be chosen to be responsible for pasting the clippings as they are handed in from time to time by members of the class.

## THE MARYLAND YELLOW-THROAT, p. 59

1. **What bird does the poet celebrate in this poem?**
   The poet celebrates the Maryland Yellow-Throat.

2. **What picture does the first stanza give you?**
   The poet paints a word picture of spring when trees begin to bud and flowers bloom beside streams.

3. **What does the Yellow-Throat seem to say?**
   The Yellow-Throat seems to say, "Witchery-witchery-witchery."

4. **Make a list of all the names by which the poet speaks of the bird.**
   The poet calls her: the small bird, a living sunbeam, a spark of light, a prophet, merry bird.

5. **Read again what is said on page 22 about poets who awaken your imagination and fancy; what fancy does the poet express in the third and fourth stanzas?**
   He fancies that Yellow-Throat knows the way to Mary-land where Mary's garden grows, referring to the nursery rhyme, "Mary, Mary, Quite Contrary." He asks Yellow-Throat to invite Mary to leave her garden and return with Yellow-Throat.

6. **What does the poet say is wanting to make the day's charm complete?**
   Mary and the song of the "merry bird" would make the charm complete.

7. **Why is the bird called a prophet?**
   The bird's name, Maryland Yellow-Throat, reflects the poet's fancy that the bird knows the way to Mary-land, "the way that thither goes Where Mary's lovely garden grows."

8. **What is the name of the "woodland maid"?**
   The "woodland maid" is Mary, leaving her garden and joining the Yellow-Throat.

9. **Find in the glossary the meaning of: bedeck, witchery, lay.**

10. **Pronounce: mossy, beneath.**

## *Extended Activity:*

The Reader suggests that students read other poems by Van Dyke. More information about Henry Van Dyke can be located on the Internet at:

http://www.everypoet.com

http://www.ccel.org/v/vandyke/otherwiseman/

## THE SANDPIPER, p. 62

1.  **The poet and the sandpiper were comrades; in the first stanza, what tells you this?**
    "Across the lonely beach we flit, One little sandpiper and I," infers that they were alone on the beach, comrades running together across the sand.

2.  **Which lines give you pictures that might be used to illustrate this poem?**
    The poet sprinkles her poem with many word pictures. Encourage the students to choose the lines that best capture the poem from their perspective.

3.  **What did the poet and the bird have in common?**
    They were both "God's children."

4.  **Give a quotation from the poem that describes the sandpiper's habits.**
    Lines 17-18 describe his habits. "I watch him as he skims along, Uttering his sweet and mournful cry."

5.  **What effect on you have the repetitions of the second line of the poem, at the end of the first and second stanzas and the variations of it at the end of the third and fourth stanzas?**
    The repeating line, along with its variations, is, "One little sandpiper and I." It reinforces the image of the two comrades.

6.  **Which lines express confidence in God's care for his children?**
    Page 63, lines 5-8 express the confidence that no matter how stormy the winds, God will protect them. "I do not fear for thee, though wroth The tempest rushes through the sky. For are we not God's children both, Thou, little sandpiper, and I?"

7.  **What classes of "God's children" do "little sandpiper" and "I," respectively, represent?**
    The "little sandpiper" represents the class of birds and "I" represents the class of humans that are "God's children."

8.  **On page 22 you read that Celia Thaxter learned a lesson of faith and courage from the little sandpiper; which lines tell you this?**
    Page 62, lines 19-22 describe the sandpiper's faith and courage. "He starts not at my fitful song, Nor flash of fluttering drapery. He has no thought of any wrong, He scans me with a fearless eye."

9.  **Find in the glossary the meaning of: bleached, rave, close-reefed, fitful, scan.**

10. **Pronounce: stanch, loosed, wroth.**

## THE THROSTLE, p. 64

1. **Which lines in the first stanza represent the song of the bird?**

   Lines 1-3 represent his song. "Summer is coming, summer is coming, I know it, I know it, I know it. Light again, leaf again, life again, love again!"

2. **Which lines give Tennyson's answer to the throstle?**

   Lines 4-6 are his answer: "Yes, my wild little Poet. Sing the new year in under the blue. Last year you sang it as gladly."

3. **Point out the words in the poem that represent the bird's song.**

   Line 7 is the theme of his song: "New, new, new, new!"

4. **Which lines tell you that Tennyson did not share the little bird's hope?**

   Lines 11-12 indicate Tennyson's doubts. "And hardly a daisy as yet, little friend, See, there is hardly a daisy."

5. **What do the last two lines show that the bird did for the poet?**

   "Summer is coming, is coming, my dear, And all of the winters are hidden." These lines suggest that the bird has brought hope to the poet.

6. **On page 22 you read that we treasure some poems for their musical quality; is this such a poem?**

   Yes, have the students read the poem aloud to experience its musical rhythm.

## To the Cuckoo, p. 65

1.  **Why does the poet call the cuckoo "a wandering voice"?**
    The cuckoo's voice is hard to locate. "From hill to hill it seems to pass, At once far off and near."

2.  **What other names does the poet call the cuckoo?**
    He calls him: a blithe newcomer, bird, darling of the Spring, invisible thing, a voice, a mystery, a hope, a love, blessed bird.

3.  **To what habit of the cuckoo does this poem call attention?**
    The poem calls attention to his voice that seems to be everywhere at once, calling us to seek the hope of which it sings.

4.  **What "golden time" is mentioned?**
    That "golden time" refers to the poet's childhood when he heard the voice and went in search of it.

5.  **Why does the poet say a "fairy place" is a fit home for the cuckoo?**
    A "fairy place" is a fit home because his voice is so illusive, "an invisible thing," "a mystery."

6.  **On page 21 you read that we are sometimes influenced by nature because we cannot understand its mysteries; how does Wordsworth make you feel that much of the charm of the cuckoo is due to the fact that it is "an invisible thing," "a mystery"?**
    Student responses will vary, but should reflect the concept that the bird's illusive call lures us in a way that other sounds in nature do not. The mystery draws us to follow it.

7.  **Find in the glossary the meaning of: vale, pace, unsubstantial.**

8.  **Pronounce: blithe, blessed.**

## A FAMOUS BIRD CLUB, p. 67

1. **How did Theodore Roosevelt practice what he preached in the cause of bird protection?**

   He became the first president of "The Bird Club of Long Island." He actively encouraged the club's growth and protection of birds through his example. He encouraged people to protect the birds from man and/or animals that abused them, work to make their existence easier, and "war against their natural foes."

2. **What organizations in your locality look after the protection of birds?**

   Answers will vary. Many communities have local chapters of the Audubon Society, an organization whose primary goal is the protection of birds and their habitats.

3. **Some cities have passed laws making it necessary for owners to take out licenses for their cats or to see that the cats wear bells; has your city any such regulation?**

   Answers will vary.

4. **Find in the glossary the meaning of: forward, economic, inveterate, sanctuary.**

5. **Pronounce: illustrated, molestation.**

## THE WORLD OF NATURE—*BIRDS*, PP. 55-71

### *More Extended Activities:*

Note to the teacher: Students should be encouraged to research various birds and become familiar with their habitats. Research information related to some of the specific birds mentioned in these entries is available on a wide variety of Internet sites. Several of the sites have educational materials for students and teachers that will aid them in their exploration of the bird kingdom. The following sites were available as of this printing.

National Audubon Society http://www.audubon.org/

Yellowthroat http://www.mbr.nbs.gov/id/framlst/i6810id.html

The following activities can be adapted to any of the entries in this section.

1. Have students choose one of the five entries in this section. Students should rewrite the piece on poster board then, drawing their own pictures or using magazine pictures, illustrate the poem based on the images they find in it.

2. Birds identified in this section cover a variety of bird types from various places and habitats. For example, the sandpiper has a very different habitat from that of a Yellow-Throat. Students should research two birds with different characteristics described in these pieces. Learn about their nesting habits, migration patterns, habitat, and coloring. Then complete the following diagram describing what they learned.

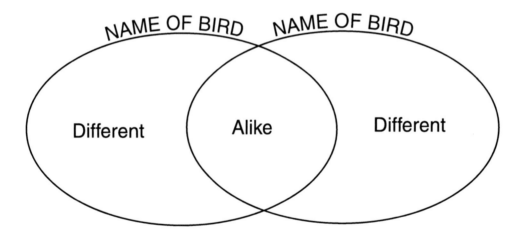

3. Poets frequently use a term called alliteration in their poetry. Alliteration repeats beginning consonant sounds as in "cool and crisp." Have students scan the poems and identify all the examples of alliteration they can find.

Obvious answers may include:

"Robert of Lincoln"—spink, spank, spink; snug and safe; bright black; hear him call in his; nice new; passing at home a patient life; catch me, cowardly knaves, if you can; life is likely; sober with work, silent; fun and frolic.

"The Sandpiper"—wild waves reach; wild wind raves; sullen clouds scud black and swift across the sky; fast we flit; fitful song nor flash of fluttering.

"The Throstle"—light again, leaf again, life again, love again; here again, here, here, here, happy year.

4.  As students will read in the "Note," "To the Cuckoo" is a lyric poem, a short poem that expresses the poet's personal feelings about his subject. In this case, the poet recalls his response to the call of the cuckoo and reflects on the "golden time" of his youth.  Other lyrics written by Wordsworth and mentioned in the "Note" can be found in *Elson Reader, Book Six*—"My Heart Leaps Up," and "March."  "The Daffodils" is found on page 76 of this Reader.  Students may want to read them to better understand a lyric poem.  Have the students complete the following web on a topic about which they feel strongly and then use it to write a lyric poem.  Be sure to use precise words and paint strong word pictures as Wordsworth did.

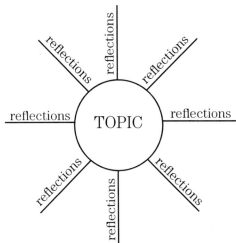

Note that this author's rhyme scheme was ABAB CDCD, etc. Challenge the students to create their poems using a predictable rhyme scheme.

5.  See the "Suggested Problems" on page 71 of the Reader for additional activities that could enhance this section.  The activities could be done separately or be included in a bird day program as suggested.

(a) A bird exhibit showing houses, baths, and/or feeders that students have made or have at home;

(b) Short speeches describing bird encounters;

(c) Sharing a poem about birds;

(d) A bird contest to see who can recognize the most birds from a series of pictures;

(e) Recordings of bird sounds;

(f) Available bird books/resources for students to browse;

(g) Promotional ads designed by the students to invite guests to their program.

NAME_____ CLASS_____ DATE_____

## THE WORLD OF NATURE—*BIRDS*, EXTENDED EXERCISES, pp. 55-71

1.  Choose one of the five entries in this section. Rewrite the piece on poster board then, drawing your own pictures or using magazine pictures, illustrate the poem based on the images you find in it.

2.  Birds identified in this section cover a variety of bird types from various places and habitats. For example, the sandpiper has a very different habitat from that of a yellow-throat. Research two birds with different characteristics described in these pieces. Learn about their nesting habits, migration patterns, habitat, and coloring. Then complete the following diagram describing what you learned.

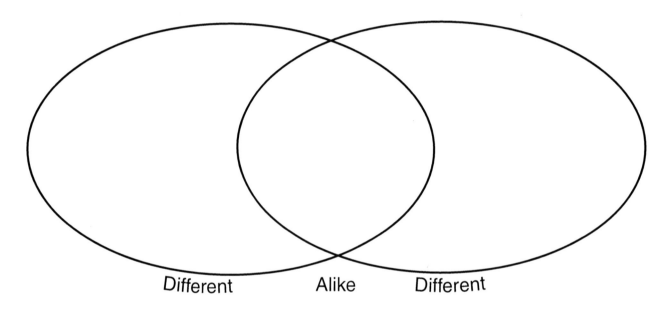

Different                    Alike                    Different

3.  Poets frequently use a term called alliteration in their poetry. Alliteration repeats beginning consonant sounds as in "cool and crisp." Scan the poems and identify all the examples of alliteration you can find.

_____

_____

_____

_____

_____

_____

_____

_____

4.  As you will read in the "Note," "To the Cuckoo" is a lyric poem, a short poem that expresses the poet's personal feelings about his subject. In this case, the poet recalls his response to the call of the cuckoo and reflects on the "golden time" of his youth. Other lyrics written by Wordsworth and mentioned in the "Note" can be found in *Elson Reader, Book Six*—"My Heart Leaps Up," and "March." "The Daffodils" is found on page 76 of this Reader. You may want to read them to better understand a lyric poem. Complete the following web on a topic about which you feel strongly and then use it to write a lyric poem. Be sure to use precise words and paint strong word pictures as Wordsworth did. Create your poem using a predictable rhyme scheme.

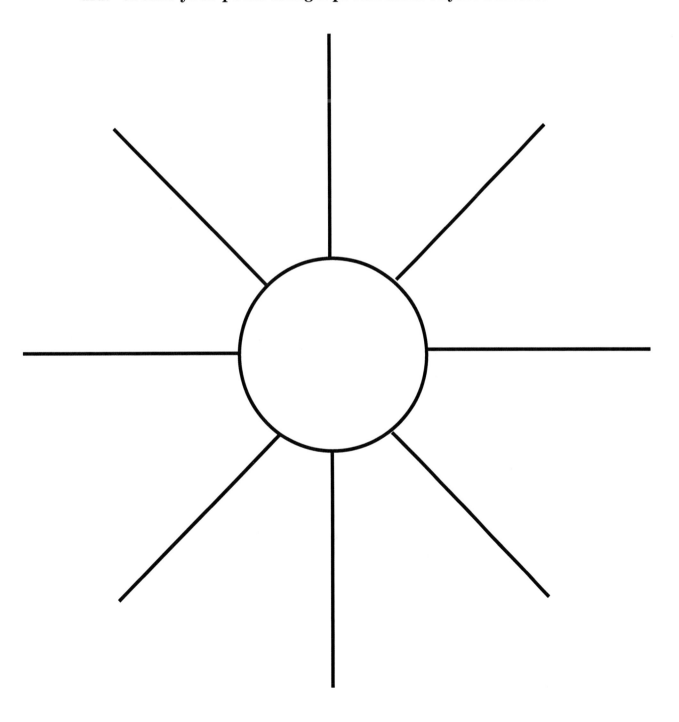

_____

_____

_____

_____

_____

_____

_____

_____

_____

_____

_____

_____

_____

_____

_____

_____

_____

_____

_____

_____

_____

_____

_____

5. See the "Suggested Problems" on page 71 of the Reader for additional activities that could enhance this section. The activities could be done separately or be included in a bird day program as suggested.

(a) A bird exhibit showing houses, baths, and/or feeders that students have made or have at home;

(b) Short speeches describing bird encounters;

(c) Sharing a poem about birds;

(d) A bird contest to see who can recognize the most birds from a series of pictures;

(e) Recordings of bird sounds;

(f) Available bird books/resources for students to browse;

(g) Promotional ads designed by the students to invite guests to their program.

# FLOWERS AND TREES

## TO THE FRINGED GENTIAN, P. 72

1. **To whom is this poem addressed?**

   This poem speaks to the gentian.

2. **In what poetic way does the author tell you the time of year that the fringed gentian blooms?**

   The gentian comes in the fall. "Thou blossom, bright with autumn dew."

3. **What words does the poet use to tell the color of the gentian?**

   The gentian is "colored with the heaven's own blue."

4. **When does the gentian open?**

   It opens "when the quiet light Succeeds the keen and frosty night."

5. **What word does Bryant use for "early morning"?**

   Bryant refers to the "early morning" as the "quiet light" that follows the night.

6. **When do violets come, and in what kind of soil do they grow?**

   Violets usually come in the spring and grow best in well-watered soil.

7. **What words in the poem tell you this?**

   The poet says the violets "lean o'er wandering brooks and springs unseen."

8. **What does the poet tell you about the violets when he says they "lean," and about the columbine when he says it "nods"?**

   He is using personification, human characteristics, to describe the flowers' actions.

9. **What signs of approaching winter does the poet mention?**

   He mentions the bare woods, the birds that have gone south, and "frosts and shortening days."

10. **Why does he repeat "blue" in the third line of the fourth stanza?**

    He uses repetition to emphasize the gentian's color.

11. **Of what is this color a symbol?**

    It is a symbol of the sky that "let fall a flower from its cerulean wall." The glossary defines cerulean as "sky-blue."

12. **To what in his life does Bryant compare the end of the year?**

    He compares the end of the year to "The hour of death" that draws near him.

13. **In this comparison what does the little flower represent?**

The little flower represents "Hope, blossoming within my heart."

14.  **Music for this lyric appears in the *Laurel Song Book*.**

15.  **Find in the glossary the meaning of: portend, cerulean.**

## TO THE DANDELION, p. 73

1. **In which stanzas does the poet express his love for the dandelion?**

   The poet expresses his love for the dandelion in the first three stanzas and in the last stanza. In stanza 1 the poet says, "Dear common flower;" in stanza 2 he says, "'Tis the spring's largess;" in stanza 3 he says, "Thou art my tropics...;" finally in stanza 6 he says, "Thou teachest me to deem More sacredly of every human heart."

2. **Which stanzas tell why the dandelion is so dear to the poet?**

   Stanzas 4 and 5 describe the childhood memories that the dandelion brings back to him.

3. **Where must he have lived to learn what he tells us in these stanzas?**

   He must have lived in the country since he speaks of meadows, cattle, woodland, lamb, birds, and flowers.

4. **Name some "prouder summer blooms."**

   Answers will vary based on where the students live. Students should be encouraged to identify the "summer blooms" in their environment.

5. **What kind of gold wrinkles the "lean brow of age"?**

   Riches wrinkle the "lean brow of age."

   **How does the dandelion's gold differ from it?**

   The dandelion's gold comes "To rich and poor alike, with lavish hand."

6. **Explain lines 7-9, page 74; and name other common things that we do not value enough.**

   Lines 7-9 state that "most hearts never understand To take it at God's value, but pass by The offered wealth with unrewarded eye." Encourage students to identify things in their lives that they take for granted.

7. **What were you told on pages 21-22 of the value of observing closely if you would not "pass by with unrewarded eye"?**

   If you observe nature closely, you will see "many hidden charms" in "your neighbors, the animals, and birds, or the wonders of the changing seasons." In addition, you "will still further enrich your appreciation of nature by awakening your powers of imagination and fancy."

8. **How can the poet look at the dandelion, but see the tropics and Italy?**

   The warmth of the dandelion reminds him of the exotic "clime" of the tropics and Italy.

9.  **Has a poet more vivid imagination than other people? Give reasons for your answer.**

    Encourage a class discussion of the imagination of poets versus "other people."

10. **What "eyes are in the heart, and heed not space or time"?**

    The "eyes" of the heart are the values and memories we cherish, not the things we see around us.

11. **The dandelion is compared to gold and to sunshine; which comparison did the poet have in mind in lines 6-7, page 75?**

    The poet compares Nature to a prodigal, one who lives foolishly, because it does not value the gold of the dandelion.

    **In lines 8-12, page 75?**

    The poet compares "every human heart" to "living pages of God's book."

12. **The flower reflects its "scanty gleam of heaven" in glowing color; how can human hearts reflect it?**

    Answers will vary. Encourage students to discuss how human hearts can reflect the "gleam of heaven."

13. **Find in the glossary the meaning of: El Dorado, largess, lavish, tropics, golden-cuirassed, ravishment, Sybaris, peer, prodigal.**

## *Extended Activity:*

Bring to class and read "The Dandelions," Cone (In *The Elson Readers—Book Six*).

## THE DAFFODILS, p. 76

1. **What picture do the first two stanzas give you?**

   The poet describes the "host of golden daffodils" that "stretched in never-ending line" beside the lake.

2. **To whom does "I" refer?**

   "I" refers to the poet.

3. **Point out the comparison and the things compared in the first two stanzas.**

   "I" is compared to a lonely cloud, line 1; daffodils are compared to a "crowd," line 3; daffodils are compared to stars, line 7.

4. **Why does the poet use the word "host" when he has already spoken of a "crowd"?**

   "Host" amplifies and reinforces the image of the many daffodils the poet saw.

5. **Explain the peculiar fitness of the word "sprightly."**

   "Sprightly" is defined in the glossary as "lively; gay." It suggests an image of the daffodils dancing gaily in the wind.

6. **What lines particularly express life and gayety?**

   Lines 5-6 on page 77 tell us, "The waves beside them danced; but they Outdid the sparkling waves in glee."

7. **Compare the expression, "that inward eye which is the bliss of solitude," with that of Lowell in "To the Dandelion," page 74, lines 12-13, "The eyes thou givest me are in the heart, and heed not space or time."**

   Wordsworth's "eye" and Lowell's "eye" both recognize beauty beyond that which appears to the naked eye; they have caught "a new vision of life in the outdoor world."

8. **How does Wordsworth show that he has received from the daffodils that thrill of "the beauty of the world that lies about them," mentioned on page 21?**

   Wordsworth says that when he recalls the daffodils, "my heart with pleasure fills, And dances with the daffodils." The daffodils are not just pretty flowers; they bring him comfort and happiness.

9. **Memorize the poem.**

10. **Tell why this is a lyrical poem. For music by Mason see *Laurel Octavo.***

    As noted in Wordsworth's poem, "To the Cuckoo," page 65, a lyric is a short poem that expresses the poet's personal feelings about his subject. In this poem, Wordsworth expresses his appreciation for daffodils. Its sentiment and musical rhythm make it a lyric.

11. **Find in the glossary the meaning of: margin, jocund, vacant.**

## TO A MOUNTAIN DAISY, p. 78

1. **How does the English daisy, which Burns describes in the first line of the poem, differ from the daisy that you know, the American daisy?**

   The English daisy does not grow as tall as the American daisy and is colored differently. Whereas American daisies generally have white or yellow disks, the English daisy has yellow disks with red, pink, white, or purple rays in them. Burns describes them as a "Wee, modest, crimson-tipped flow'r."

2. **Select and give the meaning of words that illustrate Burns's use of the Scotch dialect.**

   Burns uses several words from the Scottish dialect some of which are defined at the bottom of page 78 in the Reader. They include: maun, must; amang, among; stoure, dust; bonnie, pretty; neebor, neighbor; weet, wet; blythe, merry; cauld, cold; wa's, walls; bield, shelter; histie, stubble; alane, alone; snawie, snowie; card, compass-face.

3. **Tell in your own words the incident related in the first stanza.**

   Burns apologizes to the daisy for crushing it in the dust.

4. **What do you know about the lark that helps you to understand why it is called the daisy's "companion" and "neebor"?**

   Answers may vary. Larks and daises are frequently found in open meadows or along streams, making them "neighbors."

5. **What comparison is made between the daisy and the garden flowers?**

   The garden flowers are planted in gardens and protected by walls; the daisy grows wild, protected only by "the random bield O' clod or stane."

6. **What "share" is mentioned in the fifth stanza?**

   The "share" refers to the plowshare that "uptears thy bed And low thou lies."

7. **What characteristic of the flower does Burns seem to like best?**

   Burns seems to like its tenacity to grow and bring cheer even when it will be crushed by the "share," or cold "bitter-biting north." (See "Biography" in the reader, page 79.)

8. **Why is this poem a lyric?**

   It expresses a personal feeling or reflection about life with a lilting musical rhythm.

9. **Find in the glossary the meaning of: glinted, random, unassuming, guise, uptears, Bard, elate.**

10. **Pronounce: humble, rear'd.**

## SWEET PEAS, p. 80

1. **Why does the poet say sweet peas are "on tiptoe for a flight"?**

   Sweet peas come in several varieties, some growing close to the ground and others climbing along trellises. "On tiptoe for a flight" may reflect the variety that climbs upward, as a butterfly preparing to soar.

2. **What are the wings of the sweet pea?**

   The wings of the sweet pea are its petals of blue, pink, purple, or red, with a "gentle flush o'er delicate white."

3. **The poet tells of the perfect stillness of the moving water in the stream; what words does he use in the lines immediately preceding to prepare you for this stillness?**

   The poet encourages the reader to "watch intently Nature's gentle doings; They will be found softer than ringdove's cooings."

4. **What picture does the last sentence of the poem give you?**

   "Blades of grass Slowly across the checkered shadows pass." Encourage students to explain the poet's imagery.

5. **On page 22 you read that we treasure some poems for their musical charm; is this such a poem?**

   Yes, if read aloud its musical charm becomes obvious.

6. **What does the poet say is "softer than ringdove's cooings"?**

   "Nature's gentle doings" are "softer than ringdove's cooings."

7. **Find in the glossary the meaning of: flush, taper, rushy, intently, sallow.**

8. **Pronounce: tiny, minutest.**

## TREES, p. 81

1. **Do you agree with the poet's conclusion given in the first stanza?**
   Answers will vary.
2. **What is the most beautiful poem you have read?**
   Answers will vary.
3. **What fact relating to the tree does the second couplet tell?**
   It describes the roots of the tree that draw their nourishment from the earth.
   **The third couplet?**
   It describes the branches that reach for the sun.
   **The fourth?**
   The tree is home to the birds.
   **The fifth?**
   It draws its moisture from rain and snow.
4. **What does the last couplet tell you?**
   Only God can create a thing as beautiful as a tree.
5. **Point out the rhyming scheme of the poem.**
   The rhyme scheme is: AA BB CC DD EE FF

## THE WORLD OF NATURE—*FLOWERS AND TREES,* PP. 72-83

### *More Extended Activities:*

1. A poem consisting of a pair of lines that usually rhyme and present one complete idea is called a couplet. Kilmer's "Trees" is a well-known couplet. Question #5 helped students to identify the rhyme scheme. Question #3 should have helped them to identify the complete thought in each couplet. Have students choose a theme and write a couplet using Kilmer's first five words as a starter: "I think that I shall...." Remember to include rhyme scheme and complete ideas in each pair of lines.

2. The poems in this section mention a variety of flowers: the gentian, dandelion, daffodil, daisy, and sweet peas. Have students choose one of these flowers, research its colors, growing season, and habitat, and write a short report to present to the class on that species. Create a piece of art that depicts the flower to use as a visual aid when presenting the research. If these flowers do not bloom in the students' area, have them choose a flower familiar to their locale to research.

In addition to encyclopedias, the Internet provides abundant resources for researching specific plants. Helpful research web sites may include:

http://www.NationalGardening.com
http://www.gardenclub.org
http://www.garden.org
http://www.botany.org

3. In the Reader, students are advised to include magazines in their reading. (See "Magazine Reading," page 82.) To teach students how to use *The Reader's Guide To Periodical Literature,* mentioned in the passage, plan a trip to the media center or public library and have students locate an article or poem related to flowers or trees in a recent publication.

4. A clincher statement is the statement that summarizes the point or message the writer wants to convey. It frequently appears near or at the end of the work. Have students read the poems and identify the clincher statements in each one, justifying their responses. Do they agree or disagree with the poet's message? Why or why not? Possible answers may include:

"To the Fringed Gentian"—"I would that thus, when I shall see The hour of death draw near to me, Hope, blossoming within my heart, May look to heaven as I depart."

"To the Dandelion"—"and could some wondrous secret show Did we but pay the love we owe."

"The Daffodils"—"And then my heart with pleasure fills, And dances with the daffodils."

"To A Mountain Daisy"—"Ev'n thou who mourn'st the Daisy's fate, That fate is thine—no distant date."

"Sweet Peas"—"And watch intently Nature's Doings: They will be found softer than ringdove's cooings."

"Trees"—"Poems are made by fools like me, But only God can make a tree."

NAME_____CLASS_____DATE_____

## THE WORLD OF NATURE—*FLOWERS AND TREES,* EXTENDED
## EXERCISES, PP. 72-83

1.  A poem consisting of a pair of lines that usually rhyme and present one complete idea is called a couplet.  Kilmer's "Trees" is a well-known couplet.  Choose a theme and write a couplet using Kilmer's first five words as a starter: "I think that I shall...." Remember to include rhyme scheme and complete ideas in each pair of lines.

_____

_____

_____

_____

_____

_____

_____

_____

_____

_____

_____

2.  The poems in this section mention a variety of flowers: the gentian, dandelion, daffodil, daisy, and sweet peas.  Choose one of these flowers, research its colors, growing season, and habitat, and write a short report to present to the class on that species.  Create a piece of art that depicts the flower to use as a visual aid when presenting the research.  If these flowers do not bloom in your area, choose a flower familiar to your locale to research.

    In addition to encyclopedias, the Internet provides abundant resources for researching specific plants.  Helpful research web sites may include:

        http://www.NationalGardening.com
        http://www.gardenclub.org
        http://www.garden.org
        http://www.botany.org

3.  In your school's media center or in the public library, locate an article or poem related to flowers or trees in a recent publication.

4.  A clincher statement is the statement that summarizes the point or message the writer wants to convey. It frequently appears near or at the end of the work. Read the poems and identify the clincher statements in each one, justifying your responses. Do you agree or disagree with the poet's message? Why or why not?

"To the Fringed Gentian"—

_____

_____

_____

"To the Dandelion"—

_____

_____

_____

"The Daffodils"—

_____

_____

_____

"To A Mountain Daisy"—

_____

_____

_____

"Sweet Peas"—

_____

_____

_____

"Trees"—

_____

_____

_____

# WINTER

## THE GREAT BLIZZARD, P. 84

1. **What distinguishes a blizzard from other violent storms?**

   Blizzards are often characterized by their extreme cold, low visibility, and powerful winds. While other storms may have one or two of those characteristics, only blizzards have all three.

2. **What are the dangers when it comes without ample warning?**

   It catches people unprepared, without adequate food, shelter, and fuel.

3. **What was the manner of attack of this blizzard?**

   It was first noticed as "A vast, slaty-blue, seamless dome silent, portentous, with edges of silvery, frosty light." Eventually, the cloud hid the sun, "the wind from the south ceased—there was a moment of breathless pause and then, borne on the wings of the north wind, the streaming clouds of soft, large flakes of snow drove in a level line." It soon became "a vast, blinding cloud, filling the air and hiding the road."

4. **What caused the early darkness?**

   The blizzard blocked out the sun.

5. **What in the storm "appalled" the boy's heart and "benumbed his thinking"?**

   He was overwhelmed by the "steady, solemn, implacable clamor of the storm. It was like the roaring of all the lions of Africa, the hissing of a wilderness of serpents, the lashing of great trees."

6. **What effect had the blizzard upon other members of the household?**

   Possible responses include: "In the house it became more and more difficult to remain cheerful;" "On the third day the family arose with weariness and looked into each other's faces with a sort of horrified surprise. Not even the invincible heart of Duncan Stewart, nor the cheery good nature of his wife, could keep a gloomy silence from settling down upon the house. Conversation was scanty; nobody laughed that day, but all listened anxiously." "The men's faces began to wear a grim, set look, and the women sat with awed faces and downcast eyes full of unshed tears, their sympathies going out to the poor travelers, lost and freezing."

7. **What was the velocity of the wind?**

   The narrator describes the wind velocity in several ways. He says it was "a terrific blast moving ninety miles an hour." "The house shook and snapped, the snow beat in muffled, rhythmic pulsations against the walls, or swirled and lashed upon the roof, giving rise to strange, multitudinous sounds;" "Looking out, there was nothing to be seen but the lashing of the wind and snow." "It was impossible to see twenty feet, except at long intervals." And when Lincoln ventured outside, "Such was the power of the wind that he could not breathe an instant unprotected."

8.  **How long did the blizzard last?**

The blizzard lasted three days and three nights.

9.  **What name was given it because of its force, fury, and duration?**

It was called the "norther," defined in the glossary as the "storm from the north."

10.  **What results proved the violence of the storm?**

"Tales of the finding of stagecoaches with the driver frozen on his seat and all his passengers within; tales of travelers striving to reach home and families. Cattle had starved and frozen in their stalls, and sheep lay buried in heaps beside the fences where they had clustered together to keep warm."

11.  **What new idea of the prairie did the storm give the boy Lincoln?**

"It taught him that however bright and beautiful they (prairies) might be in summer under skies of June, they could be terrible when the Norther was abroad in his wrath."

12.  **On page 21 you read that adventures may come to one who is snowbound; what unusual happenings and tasks came to Lincoln as a result of the blizzard?**

The narrator makes several references to Lincoln's experiences. The roar of the storm appalled him, and when he ventured outside, "his face was coated with ice and dirt, as by a dash of mud—a mask which blinded the eyes, and instantly froze on his cheeks. Such was the power of the wind that he could not breathe an instant unprotected. His mouth being once open, it was impossible to draw breath again without turning from the wind." "Lincoln attempted to water the horses from the pump, but the wind blew the water out of the pail." "It seemed to Lincoln that no power whatever could control such fury; his imagination was unable to conceive of a force greater than this war of wind or snow."

**Did they seem like adventures to him?**

No. The narrator says when he heard the storm was over, he "sank into deep sleep in sheer relief."

13. **Find in the glossary the meaning of: malevolent, inexorable, portentous, momentum, appalled, multitudinous, impenetrably, prodigious, invincible, interminable, relentless, spasmodic, conception.**
14. **Pronounce: recess, infinite, calm, ferocity, heroism.**

## Class Reading

The height of the storm, page 86, line 4, to page 87, line 11.

## Outline for Testing Silent Reading.

Note to the teacher: some of these responses have been covered in the discussion questions. They have been copied here for quick reference. You may choose to use either set of activities to determine student comprehension.

(a) The approach of the storm—It was first noticed as "A vast, slaty-blue, seamless dome silent, portentous, with edges of silvery, frosty light." Eventually, the cloud hid the sun, "the wind from the south ceased—there was a moment of breathless pause and then, borne on the wings of the north wind, the streaming clouds of soft, large flakes of snow drove in a level line." It soon became "a vast, blinding cloud, filling the air and hiding the road."

(b) Neighbors stop for shelter—"One team, containing a woman and two men, neighbors living seven miles north, gave up the contest, and turned in at the gate for shelter, confident that they would be able to go on in the morning. In the barn, while rubbing the ice from the horses, the men joked and told stories in a jovial spirit, with the feeling generally that all would be well by daylight. The boys made merry also, singing songs, popping corn, playing games, in defiance of the storm."

(c) The full fury of the storm on the second day—When Lincoln awoke on the second day, he "crept to the fire appalled by the steady, solemn, implacable clamor of the storm. It was like the roaring of all the lions of Africa, the hissing of a wilderness of serpents, the lashing of great trees. It benumbed his thinking, it appalled his heart, beyond any other force he had ever known. The house shook and snapped, the snow beat in muffled, rhythmic pulsations against the walls, or swirled and lashed upon the roof, giving rise to strange, multitudinous sounds; now dim and far, now near and all-surrounding; producing such an effect of mystery and infinite reach, as though the cabin were a helpless boat, tossing on an angry, limitless sea. Looking out, there was nothing to be seen but the lashing of the wind and snow."

(d) Attempts to take care of the stock—When the men tried to take care of the cattle, "they found the air impenetrably filled with fine powdery snow mixed with the dirt caught up from the plowed fields by a terrific blast moving ninety miles an hour. It was impossible to see twenty feet, except at long intervals." Mr. Stewart could only reach the barn "by desperate dashes, during the momentary clearing of the air following some more than usually strong gust. Lincoln attempted to water the horses from the pump, but the wind blew the water out of the pail." By the third day, they could only feed the animals by climbing "down through the roof of the shed, the door being completely sealed up with solid banks of snow and dirt."

(e)   The third day—"On the third day the family arose with weariness and looked into each other's faces with a sort of horrified surprise. Not even the invincible heart of Duncan Stewart, nor the cheery good nature of his wife, could keep a gloomy silence from settling down upon the house. Conversation was scanty; nobody laughed that day, but all listened anxiously to the invisible tearing at the shingles, beating against the door, and shrieking around the eaves. The frost upon the windows, nearly half an inch thick in the morning, kept thickening into ice, and the light was dim at midday. The fire melted the snow on the windowpanes and upon the door, while around the keyhole and along every crack, frost formed. The men's faces began to wear a grim, set look, and the women sat with awed faces and downcast eyes full of unshed tears, their sympathies going out to the poor travelers, lost and freezing."

(f)   Signs of the end of the storm—"About midnight Lincoln noticed that the roar was no longer so steady, so relentless, and so high keyed as before. It began to lull at times, and though it came back to the attack with all its former ferocity, still there was a perceptible weakening. Its fury was becoming spasmodic. One of the men shouted down to Mr. Stewart, 'The storm is over,' and when the host called back a ringing word of cheer, Lincoln sank into a deep sleep in sheer relief."

(g)   Activities after the storm—After the storm, "the children melted the ice on the windowpanes and peered out on the familiar landscape, dazzling, peaceful, under the brilliant sun and wide blue sky." "Out in the barn the horses and cattle, hungry and cold, kicked and bellowed in pain, and when the men dug them out, they ran and raced like mad creatures, to start the blood circulating in their numbed and stiffened limbs. Mr. Stewart was forced to tunnel to the barn door, cutting through the hard snow as if it were clay." "The guests were able to go home by noon, climbing above the fences and rattling across the plowed ground."

(h)   Tales of suffering—"Tales of the finding of stagecoaches with the driver frozen on his seat and all his passengers within; tales of travelers striving to reach home and families. Cattle had starved and frozen in their stalls, and sheep lay buried in heaps beside the fences where they had clustered together to keep warm."

## *Extended Activity:*

See "Suggestions for Theme Topics" in the Reader, page 90.

1. The "Suggestions" list several student choices for further reading on winter storms, most of which are currently out of print. However, students will enjoy reading a current fiction story by Gary Paulson, "Brian's Winter." Written in 1996, it is the story of a young boy's survival in the northern woods in winter.

2. A simile compares two unlike things saying one is "like" or "as" the other. For example, the dog was like a meteor speeding across the yard. Dog and meteor are similes in this sentence. Metaphors, like similes, compare unlike objects but do not use like or as to make the comparison. The dog was a meteor shooting across the yard. Hamlin Garland laces his story with similes and metaphors. Have students identify all the similes and metaphors in this story.

Similes—the storm "leaps like a tiger;" wind "howled like ten thousand tigers;" the wind was "like the roaring of all the lions of Africa, the hissing of a wilderness of serpents, the lashing of great trees;" "as though the cabin were a helpless boat;" "his face was coated with ice and dirt, as by a dash of mud—a mask;" the animals "ran and raced like mad creatures;" the drifts were "like the sands at the bottom of a lake;" the winds were "as pitiless and destructive as the polar ocean."

Metaphors—the cloud a seamless dome; the snow a vast blinding cloud, the storm a "war of wind or snow."

3. Foreshadowing is the writer's use of clues or hints about what will happen in the story. Hamlin Garland prepares the reader for the storm through foreshadowing. As the students begin reading, have them take note of the early clues or hints that something terrible lies ahead. Then have them predict what they think might happen before they complete the story. Possible answers include: "A vast, slaty-blue, seamless dome silent, portentous, with edges of silvery, frosty light." "Lincoln felt some vague premonition of a dread disturbance of nature..." When they have completed the story, have them compare their predictions with the story; in what ways were they correct? In what ways were they incorrect?

NAME_____CLASS_____DATE_____

## THE GREAT BLIZZARD, p. 84

1.  The "Suggestions" list several student choices for further reading on
    winter storms, most of which are currently out of print. However, you
    will enjoy reading a current fiction story by Gary Paulson, "Brian's
    Winter." Written in 1996, it is the story of a young boy's survival in the
    northern woods in winter.

2.  A simile compares two unlike things saying one is "like" or "as" the
    other. For example, the dog was like a meteor speeding across the
    yard. Dog and meteor are similes in this sentence. Metaphors, like
    similes, compare unlike objects but do not use like or as to make the
    comparison. The dog was a meteor shooting across the yard. Hamlin
    Garland laces his story with similes and metaphors. Identify all the
    similes and metaphors in this story.

Similes—

_____

_____

_____

_____

_____

_____

_____

Metaphors—

_____

_____

_____

_____

_____

_____

_____

3. Foreshadowing is the writer's use of clues or hints about what will happen in the story. Hamlin Garland prepares the reader for the storm through foreshadowing. As you begin reading, take note of the early clues or hints that something terrible lies ahead. Then predict what you think might happen before you complete the story.

_____

_____

_____

_____

_____

_____

When you have completed the story, compare your predictions with the story; in what ways were they correct? In what ways were they incorrect?

_____

_____

_____

_____

_____

_____

_____

_____

_____

_____

_____

_____

_____

_____

_____

## THE FROST SPIRIT, p. 91

1. **Why does the poet personify "The Frost Spirit"?**
   Personification gives human actions to non-human things. The poet personified "The Frost Spirit" giving him human actions to make him seem more real.

2. **Why is "Fiend" personified?**
   See the response to number 1.

3. **How can one "trace his footsteps" on woods and fields?**
   The frost leaves behind a white coating of frost on everything it touches.

4. **Locate on a map Labrador, the pine region of Norway, and the volcano of Hekla.**

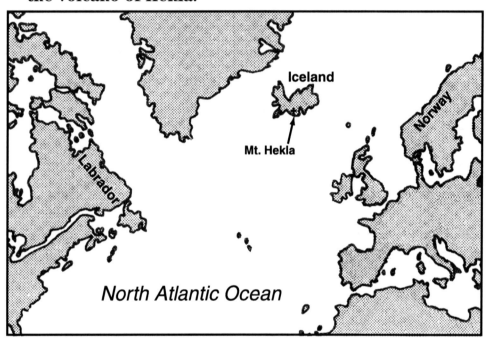

5. **What is the "icy bridge of the northern seas"?**
   The "icy bridge" refers to the frozen waters that link the northern lands for much of the year. The coast of Labrador is only ice-free from June to November.

6. **Why does the poet say, "In the sunless cold of the lingering night"?**
   Sunlight reaches the earth at varying angles and varying seasons. Because of its location, Labrador spends much of the winter season in darkness or semidarkness.

7. **What does the poet mean by the "shriek of the baffled Fiend"?**
   The "baffled Fiend" refers to the Frost Spirit whose cold and darkness is turned away by the "light of the parlor-fire."

**8. Find in the glossary the meaning of: blasted, smitten.**

### Library Reading

"Kathleen," a ballad, Whittier.

## Extended Activities:

1. End rhyme in poetry refers to the words at the ends of two or more lines that have the same sounds. Slant rhyme refers to words at the ends of lines that look similar but do not have exact rhyme, such as wall and soul. Have students identify the rhyme scheme, the end rhyme words, and the slant rhyme words in Whittier's poem.

Answers:

Rhyme scheme is AABB CCDD, etc.

End rhyme words: now, brow; Labrador, o'er; below, grow; blast, past; glow, below; feel, heel; grass, pass; may, away; high, by.

Slant rhyme: forth, earth.

NAME_____CLASS_____DATE_____

## THE FROST SPIRIT, P. 91

1.  End rhyme in poetry refers to the words at the ends of two or more lines that have the same sounds. Slant rhyme refers to words at the ends of lines that look similar but do not have exact rhyme, such as wall and soul. Identify the rhyme scheme, the end rhyme words, and the slant rhyme words in Whittier's poem.

**Rhyme scheme:**

_____

_____

**End rhyme words:**

_____

_____

_____

_____

_____

_____

**Slant rhyme:**

_____

_____

_____

_____

_____

_____

_____

_____

## THE SNOW STORM, P. 93

1. **Picture the scene described in the first five lines.**
   The first five lines describe a snow fall that "Hides hills and woods, the river and the heaven," along with the farmhouse.

2. **Read the first stanza in a way to bring out the contrast between the wild storm and the scene within the "farmhouse at the garden's end."**
   Encourage the students to read with expression, using the punctuation and content to aid mood and meaning.

3. **What is the "tile" with which the poet imagines the "unseen quarry" is furnished?**
   The "tile" is the snow with which the "north wind" decorates the world.

4. **What is meant by "fierce artificer"?**
   The glossary defines the "fierce artificer" as a "harsh workman; here, the wind."

5. **Of what are the "white bastions" made?**
   The "white bastions," according to the glossary, are "fortifications of snow."

6. **Does the use of the word "windward" add to the picture, and does each detail increase the beauty of the poem or detract from it?**
   Encourage a class discussion of the details that enhance the poem. Have students give reasons why they think the details might detract from it.

7. **Who is described as "myriad-handed"?**
   "Myriad-handed" refers to the many hands, or efficiency, of the snow and wind to cover the earth with their beauty.

8. **What is the mockery in hanging "Parian wreaths" on a coop or kennel?**
   "Parian," in the glossary, refers to "Pares, an Island in the Aegean Sea from which beautiful marble came in ancient times." The beautiful "Parian" marble would have been reserved for the palaces of the wealthy, not for dog kennels.

9. **What picture do lines 17, 18, and 19 give you?**
   Common things like thorn bushes, dog kennels, and farmers' lanes are laced in "Parian wreaths" and "a swan-like form."

10. **What does the "mad wind's night work" do for Art?**
    He leaves it "astonished" with his "frolic architecture."

11. **Has this poem the musical charm about which you read on page 22?**
    Encourage students to share their reasons why or why not this poem contains musical charm.

**12. Find in the glossary the meaning of: radiant, projected, proportion, invest, mauger, Art.**

## *Extended Activity:*

This poem by Emerson is an example of blank verse: it does not rhyme; however, it has a distinct meter known as iambic pentameter. The lines are ten syllables long (not every line will have ten syllables) and every other syllable, beginning with the second syllable of each line, is stressed. To help students identify blank verse, have them identify the meter by underlining the stressed syllables. Then have them read the poem aloud to "feel" its rhythm, paying attention to punctuation to help them read with meaning and emphasis.

THE SNOW STORM

RALPH WALDO EMERSON

Announced by all the trumpets of the sky
Arrives the snow, and, driving o'er the fields,
Seems nowhere to alight; the whited air
Hides hills and woods, the river and the heaven,
And veils the farmhouse at the garden's end.
The steed and traveler stopped, the courier's feet
Delayed, all friends shut out, the housemates sit
Around the radiant fireplace, enclosed
In a tumultuous privacy of storm.

Come, see the north wind's masonry.
Out of an unseen quarry evermore
Furnished with tile, the fierce artificer
Curves his white bastions with projected roof
Round every windward stake, or tree, or door.
Speeding, the myriad-handed, his wild work
So fanciful, so savage, naught cares he
For number or proportion. Mockingly
On coop or kennel he hangs Parian wreaths;
A swan-like form invests the hidden thorn;
Fills up the farmer's lane from wall to wall,
Manger the farmer's sighs, and at the gate
A tapering turret overtops the work.
And when his hours are numbered, and the world
Is all his own, retiring, as he were not,
Leaves, when the sun appears, astonished Art
To mimic in slow structures, stone by stone
Built in an age, the mad wind's night-work (exception—only 9 syllables)
The frolic architecture of the snow.

NAME_____CLASS_____DATE_____

## THE SNOW STORM, P. 93

**This poem by Emerson is an example of blank verse: it does not rhyme; however, it has a distinct meter known as iambic pentameter. The lines are ten syllables long (not every line will have ten syllables) and every other syllable, beginning with the second syllable of each line, is stressed. Identify the meter by underlining the stressed syllables. Then read the poem aloud to "feel" its rhythm, paying attention to punctuation to help you read with meaning and emphasis.**

### THE SNOW STORM

RALPH WALDO EMERSON

Announced by all the trumpets of the sky
Arrives the snow, and, driving o'er the fields,
Seems nowhere to alight; the whited air
Hides hills and woods, the river and the heaven,
And veils the farmhouse at the garden's end.
The steed and traveler stopped, the courier's feet
Delayed, all friends shut out, the housemates sit
Around the radiant fireplace, enclosed
In a tumultuous privacy of storm.

Come, see the north wind's masonry.
Out of an unseen quarry evermore
Furnished with tile, the fierce artificer
Curves his white bastions with projected roof
Round every windward stake, or tree, or door.
Speeding, the myriad-handed, his wild work
So fanciful, so savage, naught cares he
For number or proportion.  Mockingly
On coop or kennel he hangs Parian wreaths;
A swan-like form invests the hidden thorn;
Fills up the farmer's lane from wall to wall,
Manger the farmer's sighs, and at the gate
A tapering turret overtops the work.
And when his hours are numbered, and the world
Is all his own, retiring, as he were not,
Leaves, when the sun appears, astonished Art
To mimic in slow structures, stone by stone
Built in an age, the mad wind's night-work
The frolic architecture of the snow.

## SNOWFLAKES, P. 95

1. **What picture does the first stanza give you?**
   The first stanza describes the falling snow from its descent from
   "the bosom of the Air" to its landing on "the harvest-fields
   forsaken."

2. **Compare this picture with that found in the first nine lines
   of "The Snow Storm," page 93.**
   These pictures are different because the snow in "The Snow
   Storm" is announced by all the trumpets of the sky," while
   the snow in "Snowflakes" is "Silent, and soft, and slow."
   They are similar because they both cover the woodlands and
   fields.

3. **To what does "her" refer in the second line?**
   "Her" refers to the Air that shakes the snow "Out of the cloud-
   folds of her garments."

4. **Explain how "the troubled heart" makes "confession in
   the countenance."**
   The poet suggests that when caught in a misdeed, our ashen
   faces, or "white countenance," often reveal our guilt.

5. **How does the poet fancy the "troubled sky" reveals its
   grief?**
   It reveals its grief through the "white countenance" of the falling
   snow.

6. **What is the "poem of the air"?**
   The snow is the "poem of the air."

7. **What is "whispered and revealed"?**
   "The secret of despair" is "whispered and revealed."

8. **This is a lyrical poem; can you tell why?**
   As noted in Wordsworth's poem "To the Cuckoo," a lyric poem is
   a short poem that expresses the poet's personal feelings about
   his subject. Encourage the students to discuss how this poem
   may express the author's feelings about life.

9. **Read again what is said on page 21 about the poets who
   awaken your powers of imagination and fancy; show
   that Longfellow does this in "Snowflakes."**
   Encourage students to explain how Longfellow uses imagination
   and fancy in "Snowflakes."

## *Extended Activity:*

1. *Balance* in writing arranges words or phrases in such a way to give them equal emphasis, resulting in a pleasing rhythm that carries the work along.  Longfellow's poem includes several phrases that show balance and give the poem its rhythm.  Have students identify those phrases that give balance to the poem.

     Answers:

     Out of the...; Over the...; Even as...; This is the....

Name_____ Class_____ Date_____

## SNOWFLAKES, p. 95

1.  *Balance* in writing arranges words or phrases in such a way to give them equal emphasis, resulting in a pleasing rhythm that carries the work along.  Longfellow's poem includes several phrases that show balance and give the poem its rhythm.  Identify those phrases that give balance to the poem.

_____

_____

_____

_____

_____

_____

_____

_____

_____

_____

_____

_____

_____

_____

_____

_____

_____

_____

_____

_____

_____

_____

_____

_____

_____

_____

_____

## Blow, Blow, Thou Winter Wind, p. 96

1.  **Why is the thought of green holly appropriate in connection with the winter wind?**

    We associate green holly and its red berries with wintery holiday decorations which, in northern climates, are accompanied by winter winds.

2.  **What feeling does ingratitude arouse?**

    Ingratitude frequently arouses feelings of pain or anger in those who have been ignored for a service they have rendered.

3.  **Why does the poet say the "tooth" of the wind is not so keen as man's ingratitude?**

    The bitter cold wind does not sting as much as the pain of ingratitude.

4.  **What change of feeling do you notice after line 6?**

    The poet introduces a feeling of lightheartedness and song.

5.  **What do you think caused the change?**

    Answers will vary. Students should be encouraged to define the moods of lines 1-6 and 11-16 and compare them to the other lines.

6.  **In the second stanza read lines that show the poet did not really think that "life is most jolly."**

    Lines 12 and 13, "Thou dost not bite so nigh As benefits forgot," indicate that life for the poet is not jolly.

7.  **Which lines explain the poet's distrust of friendship?**

    Lines 15 and 16, "Thy sting is not so sharp As friend remembered not," indicate that the poet distrusts friendship.

8.  **Which word in the first stanza is explained by line 3 of the second stanza?**

    The word "ingratitude" in the first stanza is explained by "benefits forgot" in the second stanza.

9.  **Find a word in the first stanza that gives the same thought as the second line of the second stanza.**

    "Tooth" in the first stanza has the same thought as "Thou dost not bite so nigh."

10. **What other lyrics do you find in this group of poems about winter scenes?**

    "Snowflakes" is also a lyric poem.

11. **For music by Whiting for "Blow, Blow, Thou Winter Wind," see the *Laurel Octavo*.**

## *Extended Activity:*

1. In the "Biography" on page 96 in the Reader, students read that this poem was set to music and sung in the comedy "As You Like It" by Shakespeare. To appreciate the context of this song, have the students read Shakespeare's play.

2. As noted in the "Extended Activity" for "The Frost Spirit," end rhyme in poetry refers to the words at the ends of two or more lines that have the same sounds. Slant rhyme refers to words at the ends of lines that look similar but do not have exact rhyme, such as wall and soul. Have students identify the rhyme scheme and the slant rhyme words in Shakespeare's poem.

Answers:

Rhyme scheme is AABCCBDDDDD EEFGGFDDDD.

Slant rhyme: wind, unkind; warp, sharp.

NAME_____CLASS_____DATE_____

## BLOW, BLOW, THOU WINTER WIND, P. 96

1.  In the "Biography" on page 96 in the Reader, you read that this poem was set to music and sung in the comedy "As You Like It" by Shakespeare. To appreciate the context of this song, read Shakespeare's play.

2.  As noted in the "Extended Activity" for "The Frost Spirit," end rhyme in poetry refers to the words at the ends of two or more lines that have the same sounds. Slant rhyme refers to words at the ends of lines that look similar but do not have exact rhyme, such as wall and soul. Identify the rhyme scheme and the slant rhyme words in Shakespeare's poem.

**Rhyme scheme:**

_____

_____

**Slant rhyme:**

_____

_____

_____

_____

_____

_____

_____

_____

_____

_____

_____

NAME_____CLASS_____DATE_____

| *Story* | *Find in the glossary the meaning of:* |
|---|---|
| *Reader p. 23* | melancholy_____ |
| | ravine_____ |
| | contemplating_____ |
| | languid_____ |
| | apprehension_____ |
| | declivity_____ |
| | furlong_____ |
| | canter_____ |
| | impetuosity_____ |
| | aspect_____ |
| | squalid_____ |
| | fastidious_____ |
| | futility_____ |
| | picketing_____ |
| *Reader p. 36* | emergency_____ |
| | coulie_____ |
| | trophy_____ |
| | prone_____ |
| | provocation_____ |
| | redoubtable_____ |
| | pelt_____ |
| | quarry_____ |
| | fastness_____ |
| *Reader p. 46* | dissipated_____ |
| | congested_____ |
| | devastating_____ |
| | inspiration_____ |
| | delectable_____ |
| | fastness_____ |
| | caste_____ |
| | inalienable_____ |
| | demoralized_____ |
| | soliloquy_____ |
| | salaam_____ |
| *Reader p. 55* | mead_____ |
| | brood_____ |
| | braggart_____ |
| | knave_____ |
| | wane_____ |

crone_____

pipe_____

strain_____

*Reader p. 59*  bedeck_____

witchery_____

lay_____

*Reader p. 62*  bleached_____

rave_____

close-reefed_____

fitful_____

scan_____

*Reader p. 65*  vale_____

pace_____

unsubstantial_____

*Reader p. 67*  forward_____

economic_____

inveterate_____

sanctuary_____

*Reader p. 72*  portend_____

cerulean_____

*Reader p. 73*  El Dorado_____

largess_____

lavish_____

tropics_____

golden-cuirassed_____

ravishment_____

Sybaris_____

peer_____

prodigal_____

*Reader p. 76*  margin_____

jocund_____

vacant_____

*Reader p. 78*  glinted_____

random_____

unassuming_____

guise_____

uptears_____

Bard_____

elate_____

*Reader p. 80*  flush_____

taper_____

rushy_____

intently_____

sallow_____

*Reader p. 84*   malevolent_____

inexorable_____

portentous_____

momentum_____

appalled_____

multitudinous_____

impenetrably_____

prodigious_____

invincible_____

interminable_____

relentless_____

spasmodic_____

conception_____

*Reader p. 91*   blasted_____

smitten_____

*Reader p. 93*   radiant_____

projected_____

proportion_____

invest_____

mauger_____

Art_____

*Pronounce:*

butte, alternately, minute, bourgeois, robust, circuit, leisurely, intricacies, vehemently, obliquely, foliage, wound, wary, therefore, orgy, adieu, amateur, deign, mossy, beneath, stanch, loosed, wroth, blithe, blessed, illustrated, molestation, humble, rear'd, tiny, minutest, recess, infinite, calm, ferocity, heroism.

# PART II:
# THE WORLD OF ADVENTURE

## In This Section—

*Objectives—*

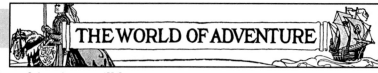
THE WORLD OF ADVENTURE

By completing "Part II," the following objectives will be met.

1. The student will use effective reading strategies to construct meaning and identify the purpose of a text including:
   a. using illustrations
   b. defining unfamiliar words
   c. retelling and summarizing
   d. outlining
2. The student will determine the main idea or essential message and identify relevant supporting details and facts of a text.
3. The student will read and organize facts from the text and other sources to make a report, outline, and perform an authentic task.
4. The student will prepare for writing and for an oral presentation by focusing on the topic and organizing supporting details in a logical sequence.
5. The student will draft and revise writing.
6. The student will produce final documents that have been edited for correct spelling, punctuation, and grammar.
7. The student will write for a variety of audiences and purposes.
8. The student will write in a variety of genres including narrative and expository.
9. The student will use reference materials (dictionaries, encyclopedias, maps, charts, photos, and electronic reference) to gather information.
10. The student will use speaking strategies effectively such as eye contact, gestures, and visuals that engage the audience.
11. The student will identify the development of plot and how conflicts are resolved in a story.
12. The student will identify and understand similarities and differences among the characters, settings, and events presented in various texts.
13. The student will identify the author's purpose and point of view.
14. The student will respond critically to fiction and poetry.
15. The student will recognize cause-and-effect relationships in literary texts.
16. The student will respond to a text by explaining how the motives of the characters or events compare with those in his or her own life.
17. The student will understand the qualities necessary for people to become good citizens and apply those qualities to his or her personal life.
18. The student will understand the qualities necessary to develop good character.
19. The student will analyze and evaluate motives of characters.

# THE DAYS OF CHIVALRY—KING ARTHUR STORIES

## THE COMING OF ARTHUR, p. 105

### SUMMARY

**The Coming of Arthur, p. 105**

The King of Britain, Uther Pendragon, was in love with Igraine of Cornwall. Unfortunately, the love was not reciprical. Uther Pendragon appealed to Merlin, the famous magician, to help him with this situation. Merlin agreed to help Uther, if he would give up his first born child. Uther agreed and he and Igraine were married. They had a son, Arthur, and gave him to Merlin who was disguised as a beggar. When Uther died, he charged all his knights to obey his son. However, disputes arose between the knights. They did not want to obey a boy whom they did not know. During this time Merlin had given Arthur to Sir Ector. Sir Ector raised Arthur as his own son along with his other son, Kay. When Arthur was grown, Merlin had the Archbishop of Canterbury call all the knights together. Who ever could dislodge a sword from a stone would be the true king of England. Sir Ector and Sir Kay, along with Arthur, attended the festivities. In the morning when they rode off, Sir Kay had forgotten his sword. Arthur, not wanting Sir Kay to be without a weapon, went and pulled the sword out of the stone. When people found out they bowed to him and acknowledged that Arthur was the true king of Great Britain.

### How King Arthur Took a Wife, and of the Table Round, p. 109

King Arthur had to fight for his land because eleven great kings opposed him. One of these kings was married to Arthur's sister. With the help of Ban and Bor, kings who ruled Gaul, Arthur was able to overthrow the eleven. Arthur then went about helping others. He helped King Leodogran and fell in love with his daughter Guinevere. The two were married in the great cathedral of Canterbury. As a wedding gift, King Leodogran gave Arthur the Round Table at which 150 men could sit. The table was originally made for King Uther Pendragon by Merlin, "who had meant thereby to set forth plainly to all men the roundness of the earth." At the high festival of Pentecost new knights were ordained to fill the seats. One seat remained unoccupied for Siege Perilous.

### Of the Finding of Excalibur, p. 111

Arthur went out seeking adventure when he came upon the castle of the sorceress, Lady Annoure. She lured him into her castle offering him all her riches if he would stay with her. Arthur refused, so she locked him in a dungeon. Realizing his fortitude, she released him into the hands of a great knight Pellinore. Pellinore and Arthur fought valiantly. Knight Pellinore, when ready to slay King Arthur, was put into a deep sleep by Merlin. Merlin healed King Arthur's wounds and led him to a lake. Deep within its waters rested the palace of the Lady of the Lake. Merlin revealed that she would work for the good of King Arthur, coming to his aid in his time of need. An arm reached out from the lake and held an arm and a sword. Taking a boat, Arthur went to it. He took the sword which was covered with "twinkling gems." Amazed at its beauty, Merlin told Arthur that as long as he kept the scabbard, he would not bleed to death. When Arthur returned to Caerleon, Sir Pellinore, asking and receiving the king's pardon, became a member of the Round Table.

1.  **Is there a historical basis for the stories of Arthur?**

    Yes, there is a historical basis for the stories of King Arthur.

Most historians agree a ruler named Arthur existed. Refer to the "Historical Note" on pages 117-118.

2. **How did they become interwoven with myth and legend?**

   The stories of King Arthur became interwoven with myth and legend when the minstrels blended the tales of King Arthur with the fairy tales of their day.

3. **When Arthur became king, what was the condition of the people of Britain?**

   The people of Britain were arguing and fighting, for each lesser ruler thought he was fitted to be the king of Britain. Those who were poor were taken advantage of and criminals ran wild.

4. **Why did the barons oppose Arthur?**

   The barons opposed Arthur because they did not know him well and did not think the young Arthur was capable of ruling. Each one also thought himself better fitted to be king.

5. **What reforms did Arthur introduce?**

   Arthur introduced reforms of justice. "To all he did justice, righting wrongs and giving to all his dues."

6. **Find lines which show that Arthur thought of the poor as well as of the rich and great.**

   "Thus Arthur was made king; and to all he did justice, righting wrongs, and giving to all their dues." "To all who would submit and amend their evil ways, he showed kindness; but those who persisted in oppression and wrong he removed, putting in their places others who would deal justly with the people."

7. **What was the Round Table?**

   The Round Table was a table given to Arthur as a wedding present from King Leodogran. One hundred and fifty men could sit around the table. It was originally made for King Uther Pendragon by Merlin, "who had meant thereby to set forth plainly to all men the roundness of the earth."

8. **Find the lines that tell of the vows made by the knights.**

   The vows made by the knights were "...to obey the king; to show mercy to all who asked it; to defend the weak; and for no worldly gain to fight in a wrongful cause."

9. **What did the knights promise first?**

   The knights' first promise was to obey the king

10. **Why do you think Arthur put this first?**

    Answers will vary. Arthur probably put this first because in society it is necessary to have a leader.

11. **What reason did Arthur give the sorceress for not wishing to remain longer in her castle?**

    He told the sorceress that he had to leave to "render service" to those whose knight he was sworn.

12. **Find a word in this speech that explains Arthur's life.**

    The word in the speech that explains Arthur's life is "service". Arthur spent his life helping others and fighting for justice.

13. **Find lines that show Arthur's generosity toward a foe.**

    When Arthur thought that Merlin had slain the great Knight Pellinore he said, "I shall grieve my life long..." Later Arthur pardoned the knight and made him a member of the Round Table which shows Arthur's generosity towards his foe.

14. **What ideals of conduct did these stories uphold in times when might was greater than right?**

    These stories promoted service to others and justice for all in times when might was greater than right.

15. **The stories of King Arthur and his knights found in this book are modified from the version of Sir Thomas Malory; make a list of quaint expressions which show that the use of the English language has changed since the time of Malory.**

    The use of archaic words such as "thee," "thou," "ye," and "just" show how language has changed over time. Some of the phrases showing this change are:

    "She would have naught to do with him."

    "At last seemed like to die"

    "that ye obey my son"

    "Whoso can draw forth"

    "he bethought him of the sword"

    "I perceive that ye are my king and here I tender you my homage."

16. **What fine qualities of human nature, about which you read on page 104, have you noted in this story?**

    The spirit of adventure "to gain a new experience or to render some service" is the quality of human nature found in this story.

17. **Find in the glossary the meaning of: postern gate, realm, counseled, clamoring, decreed, scabbard (pp. 105-108); oppression, lurk, peasant, Christendom, Pentecost (pp. 109-110); sorceress, turret, portcullis, salutation, petition, squire, page, fain, estate, battlement, succor, vigil, vassal, behoove, mere, samite, fathom, anon, wafted, mystic (pp. 111-117).**

18. **Pronounce: bade, tournament, sovereign (pp. 107-108); courteous (p. 111); stanch (p. 115)**

### Class Reading

Arthur's adventure with the sorceress, page 111, line 7, to page 114, line 13; the finding of Excalibur, page 116, line 11, to page 117, line 20; bring to class and read the song of Arthur's knighthood in the "Coming of Arthur," Tennyson.

### Outline for Testing Silent Reading

    (a)  The birth of Arthur;

    (b)  How he became king;

    (c)  How King Arthur took a wife;

    (d)  The Order of the Round Table;

    (e)  The vows of true knighthood;

    (f)  The finding of the sword Excalibur.

### Library Reading

*The Boy's King Arthur,* Lanier, illustrated by Wyeth; *The Romance of King Arthur,* illustrated by Rackham; *The Story of King Arthur and His Knights,* Pyle.

# THE STORY OF GARETH, P. 120

## SUMMARY

### How Beaumains Came to King Arthur's Court, p. 120

King Arthur would not eat the Feast of the Pentecost until he had seen or heard a great marvel. One day some men approached the castle. One of the young men asked Arthur for three gifts. Arthur granted them. The first gift was to feast for a year in his castle and the other two gifts would be requested at the end of the year. Sir Kay and some other knights made fun of this man who would not reveal his name or rank. They named him Beaumains. He stayed in the kitchen during the course of the year. The next Pentecost arrived and a damsel came to Arthur asking that her sister, Dame Liones, be rescued from the Red Knight of the Red Lands. She asked if one of his grand knights would fight for her lady's honor. Beaumains approached requesting that he be made a knight by Sir Lancelot and be allowed to fight the Red Knight of the Red Lands. The damsel scoffed at him since he was just a kitchen boy. King Arthur, however, granted Beaumains his request. Once they left the castle, Beaumains fought with Sir Kay and overtook him. He then fought with Sir Lancelot. The two called a truce, and Sir Lancelot knighted Beaumains for showing such strength and bravery. Beaumains revealed to Sir Lancelot that he was Sir Gareth, Sir Gawain's brother. Again on their journey, Beaumains saved a knight and fought with two others.

### How Beaumains Fought with the Four Knights, p. 125

Beaumains, determined not to leave the damsel, continued on his journey. He first came to the Black Knight of the Black Lands. Beaumans fought the Black Knight and killed him. He then came upon the Green Knight. They battled, and Beaumains showed mercy to the Green Knight. Beaumains battled again with the Green Knight's brothers, the Red Knight and the Blue Knight, showing mercy to them as well.

### How Beaumains Conquered the Red Knight of the Red Lands, p. 130

Finally, the damsel and Beaumains reached the Red Knight of the Red Lands. The damsel, still being uncourteous to Beaumains, pleaded with him to retreat from the Red Knight. Beaumains, determined to win, moved forward. The two knights battled, and Beaumains took the upper hand. Beaumains said he would show him mercy on two conditions. First the Red Knight was to ask forgiveness for the wrongs he had done and, second, he was to send 600 knights to serve in King Arthur's court.

### How at the Feast of Pentecost All the Knights that Sir Gareth Had Overcome Came and Yielded Them to King Arthur, p. 133

At the next Pentecost, the Green, Red, and Blue knights came to the kingdom with all their knights. Arthur wondered who Beaumains was to have fought so bravely and valiantly. Then the Red Knight of the Red Lands appeared at the castle and made apologies for all he had done wrong. King Arthur made him a knight of the Round Table.

### How the Queen of Orkney Came to the Feast, p. 134

The queen of Orkney, Sir Gareth's mother, came to King Arthur and rebuked him for treating her son so poorly. King Arthur then learned the truth of Beaumains's identity. No one, however, knew Sir Gareth's location. King Arthur sent a messenger to Dame Liones asking the whereabouts of Sir Gareth. Sir Gareth made Dame Liones promise not to reaveal his location or identity. Dame Liones presented King Arthur with the prospect of having a tournament with all the knights. Dame Liones thought this would bring Sir Gareth out into the open without breaking her promise, so King Arthur agreed to the tournament.

**How King Arthur Went to the Tournament, p. 137**

King Arthur took all his knights to the tournament. The knights chose sides and then they battled all day. Lancelot battled with two knights, but Gareth interrupted so no "stroke would smite" him. All the knights wanted to know who the noble knight was. King Arthur sent a herald to ride near him. The herald read "Sir Gareth" on his helmet and made the announcement to King Arthur. In the meantime, Sir Gareth rode off into the forest.

**How Sir Gareth Came to a Castle Where He Was Well Lodged, p. 138**

Sir Gareth wandering in the midst of a storm in the forest came upon a castle. The lady of the castle allowed him shelter, but said her husband was an enemy of King Arthur's, and should he find Sir Gareth, he would kill him. Sir Gareth took the chance and stayed the night. The next morning he rode off and met with Duke de la Rowse, the master of the castle he just left. The two battled, and Sir Gareth again was the victor.

**How Sir Gareth and Sir Gawain Fought Each Against Other, p. 140**

Sir Gareth then came upon Sir Gawain, and the two began fighting. The damsel appeared and told Sir Gawain that he was fighting his brother. Sir Gawain then threw off his shield and asked for mercy. Sir Gareth then, too, asked for mercy, and there were many kind words between the two. King Arthur and Sir Gareth's mother went to them and rejoiced.

1. **What classes of people are mentioned in this story?**

   Kings, knights, servants (messengers, kitchen help, and heralds), ladies, and dukes are mentioned in this story.

2. **Were the people of one class on terms of equality with those of another class? Under such a system do all have equal opportunities?**

   No, the people of one class were not on the same terms as those of another class. Under such a system people do not always have equal opportunities. In the United States, however, efforts are made so that all people are able to be given equal opportunity.

3. **Upon what ideal was our government founded?**

   Our government was founded on the belief that all men are created equal and all have the right to life, liberty, and the pursuit of happiness.

4. **What reason can you give for Gareth's wish to keep his name and rank a secret?**

   Gareth possibly wanted to prove his worth through his actions rather than through his position.

5. **One who wished to become a knight must first prove himself worthy of the honor; would it be easy for a kitchen boy to give this proof?**

   It would be difficult for a kitchen boy to give proof of his worth because having the opportunity to do so would be difficult. In the story, Beaumains is able to prove his worth due to the kindness of King Arthur who grants him the adventure.

6. **If, under such circumstances, he won the honor, could he**

**feel sure that he had rightfully earned it?**

Yes, under such circumstances, he could feel sure that he had rightfully earned the honor because it would have been earned through actions and not by any other means.

7. **By what test should the conduct of a person be judged?**

The conduct of a person should be judged by his courtesy and respect of others.

8. **What knights at Arthur's court made rank their test?**

The knights at King Arthur's court who made rank their test were Sir Kay, Sir Lancelot, and Sir Gawain.

9. **Which one of these acknowledged his mistake?**

Sir Lancelot acknowledged his mistake. He saw the brave actions of Beaumains and granted him knighthood.

10. **How did Arthur, Lancelot, and Gawain judge Gareth?**

They judged him as being unworthy because he looked as if he came from a poor and humble background.

11. **Point out lines that help to portray the character of Gareth by showing:**

**(a) that he wished to win knighthood through ability, not through influence of his rank and wealth.**

"…it doth me good to feel your might. Hope you that I may any while stand a proved knight."

**(b) that he would take no reward for helping the distressed**

"I will no reward have; I was this day made knight of noble Sir Lancelot and therefore I will no reward have but God reward me."

**(c) that he was not afraid when outnumbered**

"I will not turn again if they were six more."

**(d) that he could not be turned from his purpose by ridicule or injustice**

"'If you follow me,' said the damsel, 'thou art but slain, for I see all that ever thou dost is but by chance and not by might of thy hands.' 'Well, damsel, ye may say what ye will, but wheresover ye go, I will follow you.'"

**(e) that he granted mercy to those who asked it**

"'Fair Knight,' said the Green Knight, 'save my life…' …Then Beaumains said, 'Sir Knight, I release thee at this damsel's request.'"

**(f) that he would not take an unfair advantage of an opponent**

"Ah, for shame, fair damsel, say ye so nevermore to me, for I will win honorably, or die knightly in the field."

**(g) that he was always courteous**

"Oh," said the damsel, "I marvel what manner of man ye be, for so shamefully did never a woman treat knight as I have done you, and ever courteously ye have born it."

**(h) that he was ready to forgive wrongs done to him**

"With all my heart," said he (Beaumains), "I forgive you, and now I think there is no knight living but I am able enough for him."

**(i) that he desired to help in righting wrongs in Arthur's kingdom.**

"Alas, my fair brother," said Sir Gawain, "I ought of right to honor you, if ye were not my brother, for ye have honored King Arthur and his court, for ye have sent him more honorable knights this twelvemonth than six of the best of the Round Table have done except Sir Lancelot."

12.  **What reasons had Arthur for founding such an order as the Knights of the Round Table?**

King Arthur established the Round Table so that he could create order and an alliance against enemies.

13.  **Is it necessary now to become a member of such an order if one wishes to help right wrongs?**

It is not necessary to become a member of such an order if one wishes to help right wrongs. There are many things one person can do alone to help right wrongs. However, belonging to such an order gives strength in numbers, thus more could be done to right wrongs.

14.  **Point out ways in which the laws of the Boy Scouts express in a practical way the ideals set forth in the oath of Knights of the Round Table; the third law of the Boy Scouts reads: "A Scout is helpful. He must be prepared at any time to save life, help injured persons, and to share home duties. He must do at least one good turn to somebody every day."**

The Boy Scouts learn skills that are practical in helping people. They learn such things as CPR and survival skills.

15.  **What other organizations do you know that are based upon a similar purpose?**

There are many organizations based on a similar purpose. Organizations vary from place to place. Have students research their community to find charitable organizations. National organizations such as the Girl Scouts or the Red Cross help many people.

16.  **Find the lines that tell of Gareth's love for Sir Lancelot.**

"Then made Sir Lancelot great cheer of Sir Gareth, and he of him, for there was never knight that Sir Gareth loved so well as he did Sir Lancelot, and ever for the most part he would be in Sir

Lancelot's company.

17. **Find in the glossary the meaning of: wroth, proffered, chid (pp. 122-125); manor, rebuke, pavilion (pp. 126-128); amends (p. 133)**

18. **Pronounce : alms, homage (pp. 125-126); lineage (p. 134)**

## Class Reading

The encounter with the Red Knight of the Red Lands, page 131, line 21, to page 133, line 12; the tournament, page 137, line 13, to page 138, line 16.

## Outline for Testing Silent Reading

(a)   How Beaumains came to King Arthur's court;

(b)   His request for three gifts;

(c)   How Beaumains fought with the knights, the Black Knight, the Green Knight, the Blue Knight, the two Red Knights;

(d)   How Beaumains made himself known to the damsel and Sir Persant;

(e)   How the lady that was beseiged had word from her sister;

(f)   The feast of Pentecost and how the knights whom Gareth had overcome celebrated it;

(g)   The queen of Orkney at the feast;

(h)   The proclamation of the tournament;

(i)   King Arthur at the tournament;

(j)   Sir Gareth;

(k)   The Duke de la Rowse;

(l)   Sir Gareth and Sir Gawain in battle against each other;

(m)  Gareth honored by the king, his mother, and Sir Lancelot.

## Library Reading

*Tommy Remington's Battle,* Burton E. Stevenson.

# THE PEERLESS KNIGHT LANCELOT, P. 143

## SUMMARY

### The Tournament at Winchester, p. 143

King Arthur called a great tournament that would be held in Winchester. Arthur and his knights departed for the tournament except for Sir Lancelot who left a day later. On his way Sir Lancelot stopped at Sir Bernard of Astolat's home. There he borrowed Sir Bernard's son's shield because Sir Lancelot did not want any of the knights at the tournament to know his identity. Sir Bernard's daughter offered Lancelot her red sleeve to wear as well. Sir Bernard's oldest son, Sir Lavaine, accompanied Lancelot for he was a good knight and would serve Sir Lancelot well. The two departed for the tournament. When they arrived they fought valiantly. Unfortunately, Lancelot was injured by his cousin, Sir Bors. Sir Lancelot and Sir Levaine departed for Sir Baudwin of Brittany who was a surgeon. The hermit at first was hesitant to help Sir Lancelot because Lancelot would not reveal his name and had fought against King Arthur's knights, but soon gave in and began to nurse Sir Lancelot's wounds. All the kings were saddened with the news that this noble, nameless knight had been injured. King Arthur knowing it was Sir Lancelot, sent Sir Gawain to find him. Sir Gawain went to Sir Bernard's house where he met his daughter, Elaine. She showed him Sir Lancelot's shield and he knew immediately who the nameless knight was. Gawain returned to King Arthur and revealed what he had learned. This grieved Sir Bors greatly when he discovered it was Sir Lancelot he had injured.

### Sir Lancelot at the Hermitage, p. 153

Elaine was out one day and saw her brother, Sir Lavaine, exercising his horse. She approached him and told all that had occurred with Sir Gawain. Sir Lavaine took Elaine to see Lancelot. At the hermitage, she nursed Lancelot faithfully. Lancelot asked Lavaine to find Sir Bors, his cousin, and bring him to the hermitage. Sir Bors came and stayed a month helping Lancelot recover. Then a tournament was announced. Thinking he was well, Lancelot tried to ride his horse. He fell and did more damage to his injury. The hermit convinced Sir Bors to attend the tournament, but to leave Lancelot in his care. At the tournament Sir Bors and Sir Gawain smote 20 knights and shared the prize between them. Lancelot recovered and all rejoiced except two knights—Sir Agravaine and Sir Modred.

### The Death of Elaine, p. 158

Elaine grieved over the absence of Sir Lancelot. As she was dying she wrote a letter to Lancelot and asked to be sent on a barge down the Thames with the letter in her hand. This was granted. King Arthur and Queen Guinevere saw her on the barge and went to her. They read the letter and then shared it with Lancelot. The letter asked Lancelot to give her a proper burial. This he did because he was a noble knight and her knight.

### The Tournament at Westminster, p. 160

After the death of Elaine there were justs made for a diamond. Sir Lavaine did so well, the knights thought he should be made a knight of the Round Table at the next feast of Pentecost. Then, King Arthur called another big tournament to be held at Westminster. Queen Guinevere refused Lancelot to fight unless his kinsmen knew him. She also requested he wear her gold sleeve. Lancelot then departed with Sir Lavaine to the hermitage where they rested in preparation of the Westminster tournament. The day of the tournament arrived and all the kings appeared with a hundred knights each. King Arthur, however, brought two hundred knights. The tournament commenced with King Arthur's knights faring considerably well. When

Lancelot entered the field he smote thirty knights. King Arthur called nine knights to go against Lancelot, for King Arthur knew not it was Sir Lancelot. Sir Gareth went disguised to help Sir Lancelot. They battled victoriously against King Arthur's men. Sir Gawain then advised King Arthur to call a close to the tournament. King Arthur invited Sir Lancelot to feast with him. There King Arthur gave Sir Lancelot the prize then scolded Sir Gareth for siding against him. Gareth explained why he was loyal to Sir Lancelot. King Arthur replied, "For ever it is an honorable knight's deed to help another honorable knight when he seeth him in great danger."

1. **What was Arthur's purpose in founding the Order of the Round Table?**

   The Order of the Round Table was to develop unity among the knights.

2. **What just was proclaimed by King Arthur?**

   King Arthur proclaimed there would be a just between any who would come against himself and the king of Scots.

3. **Why was a training in strength and bravery in battle necessary to these knights?**

   Training prepared the knights in case they had to fight a real battle.

4. **What way of supplying this training is described in this story?**

   Tournaments or contests were called by a king for military display. It gave the knights opportunity to practice and show their skill.

5. **Tell what you know of this custom.**

   Answers will vary.

6. **Have we any contests of skill that bear any resemblance to this in method or purpose?**

   Many sports have tournaments that are for demonstration only. For example, karate schools will hold intraschool tournaments. Football teams will divide into two teams and play one another.

7. **Give a brief account of the tournament in Westminster.**

   Refer to the summary of the Tournament in Westminster. Teachers may want to have students write a script and perform a skit of the tournament.

8. **What plan had Lancelot for disguising himself?**

   Lancelot decided to borrow the shield of someone unknown. He also wore a lady's sleeve. He was not known to have ever done this.

9. **What reasons had he for such a plan?**

   By hiding his identity, he had the opportunity to fight with other knights on his side who were valiant.

10. **How was Lancelot's personality shown in the impression he made on the baron?**

    Lancelot showed kindness and courtesy.

11. **What custom of the just is indicated by Elaine's request?**
Many knights would fight in honor of their lady. Elaine asks Lancelot to fight for her.

12. **Picture the scene as the tournament opened; where was the king? Where were the opposing knights?**
The king was probably on one side sitting in the stands looking over the battle field and the opposing knights and kings on the other side.

13. **What knightly qualities did Lancelot show in this contest?**
Lancelot showed mercy, courage, and skill.

14. **Why did Lancelot call his injury "a little hurt" when speaking to Elaine?**
Lancelot called his injury "a little hurt" because he was showing bravery to Elaine.

15. **What quality of Lancelot do you admire most?**
Answers will vary.

16. **Read again the last paragraph on page 104, and then tell how our appreciation of the fine qualities of Lancelot makes us braver and better.**
Lancelot can serve as a hero for us all.

17. **Find in the glossary the meaning of: token, burges, buffet, hermit (pp. 144-149); discomfited (p. 162).**

18. **Pronounce: grievous (p.143); jeopardy (p. 156); Thames (p. 158).**

**Class Reading**

The tournament at Winchester, page 145, line 13 to page 148, line 5, the death of Elaine, page 158, line 1 to page 159, line 35; the tournament at Westminster, page 161, line 33, to page 165, line 6; bring to class and read "The Lady of Shalott," Tennyson (The Lady of Shalott was written about Elaine)

**Outline for testing Silent Reading**

(a) The tournament at Winchester;
(b) Lancelot's disguise;
(c) The result of the encounter;
(d) The hermitage;
(e) Sir Gawain recognizes Sir Lancelot's shield;
(f) Sir Bors learns who his opponent was;
(g) Elaine meets her brother;
(h) Sir Bors finds Sir Lancelot;
(i) Sir Lancelot tries his armor;
(j) Sir Gawain, Sir Bors, and Sir Gareth at the tournament;
(k) Sir Lancelot leaves Elaine and goes to Winchester;

(l)  Elaine;

(m)  Sir Lancelot and Sir Lavaine at the tournament;

(n)  Sir Gawain's counsel to the king;

(o)  Sir Lancelot wins the prize;

(p)  King Arthur praises Sir Gareth.

## Library Reading

*The Story of Sir Lancelot,* Pyle.

## Suggestions for Theme Topics

1. Comparison of a "full noble surgeon" of King Arthur's time with a present-day surgeon.

2. The qualities most admired in the days of chivalry compared with the qualities most admired today.

3. Present-day adventures of firemen, policemen, coastguards, railway engineers, nurses, etc., compared with the kind of adventures sought by King Arthur's knights.

## *Extended Activities:*

1. A Venn Diagram is a visual way of comparing and contrasting ideas. Use any of the "Theme Topics" for this section and create a Venn Diagram.

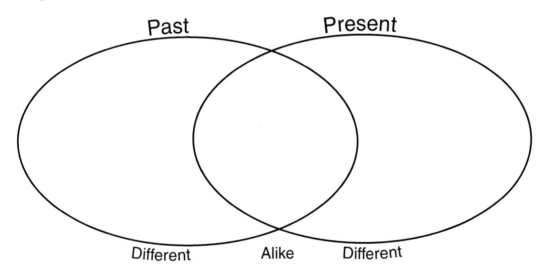

2. Invite a guest speaker to the class. Select someone who is listed in "Theme Topics" #3.

Have students create a list of questions prior to the guests' arrival.

## THE PEERLESS KNIGHT LANCELOT, p. 143

**Suggestions for Theme Topics**

    1. Comparison of a "full noble surgeon" of King Arthur's time with a present-day surgeon.

    2. The qualities most admired in the days of chivalry compared with the qualities most admired today.

    3. Present-day adventures of firemen, policemen, coastguards, railway engineers, nurses, etc., compared with the kind of adventures sought by King Arthur's knights.

**A Venn Diagram is a visual way of comparing and contrasting ideas. Use any of the "Theme Topics" above and create a Venn Diagram.**

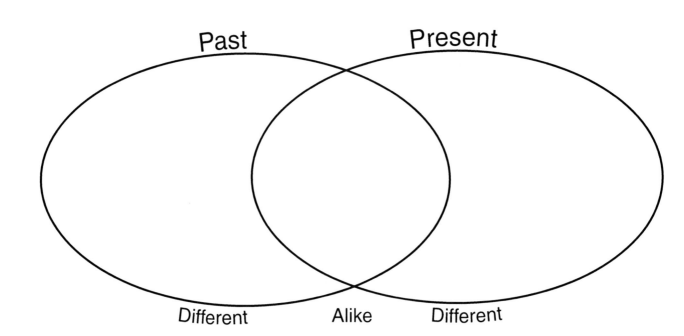

Past                     Present

Different           Alike           Different

# THE PASSING OF ARTHUR, p. 167

## SUMMARY

### How Sir Modred Plotted Against Sir Lancelot and of the Death of Sir Agravaine and Twelve Knights, p. 167

Sir Modred spoke ill of Queen Guinevere and Sir Lancelot. When King Arthur left on a trip, Modred convinced twelve knights to attack Sir Lancelot because of his treason against the king. What the twelve did not know was that Sir Lancelot had been invited to see the queen, and his visit was innocent. Sir Modred, however, felt the circumstances would not look favorably towards Sir Lancelot and used this to his advantage. Sir Lancelot fought the twelve. Only Sir Modred escaped alive. When King Arthur heard of the circumstances, he was upset.

### The Trial of the Queen, p. 168

The rumors began to spread and people became suspicious of Queen Guinevere, and eventually they wanted to see her put to death. King Arthur asked Sir Gareth, Sir Gaheris, and Sir Gawain to accompany the queen to her execution, but all three refused. When the queen was at the stake, Sir Lancelot rode in and rescued her from her death. In the confusion of Sir Lancelot's rescue, Sir Gareth and Sir Gaheris were accidentally killed. When Sir Gawain heard about the deaths, he swore revenge on Sir Lancelot and "thus began the war."

### How Sir Gawain Defied Sir Lancelot, p. 170

Rome heard about the fight between King Arthur and Sir Lancelot and sent a message that the two should try to reconcile. Sir Lancelot returned the queen to King Arthur and attempted to explain his innocence in the death of the two great knights. Sir Gawain, however, would believe none of it and counseled King Arthur to pass judgment on Lancelot. Sir Gawain called Lancelot a "liar" and a "traitor." Sir Lancelot, greatly distressed by the situation, departed for his home in France.

### How King Arthur and Sir Gawain Went to France, p. 173

Sir Gawain persuaded King Arthur to follow Sir Lancelot to France. Arthur agreed saying he would rather fight openly than for Sir Gawain to kill Sir Lancelot treacherously. They followed through on their plans and attacked France making their way to Sir Lancelot's castle. Sir Lancelot, still wanting reconciliation, sent a damsel to King Arthur asking for a truce. Again, Sir Gawain convinced the king that Sir Lancelot had been a traitor saying "the time for peace is past." Sir Lancelot then made ready for battle instructing his knights to not touch King Arthur. All the knights fought a good fight. Sir Lancelot refused to attack Sir Gawain; rather, he just did what he could to defend against him.

### Modred the Traitor, p. 176

While Arthur was away in France, Sir Modred took the opportunity to usurp King Arthur. He convinced those in the kingdom that the king had died and had Parliament pronounce him king. Queen Guinevere refused to believe King Arthur had died. She took up residence in the Tower of London for fear of the new King Modred. When King Arthur received the news, he returned to Britain where he fought with Modred's knights. Sir Gawain became mortally wounded in these battles. Before he passed, Sir Gawain wrote a letter to Sir Lancelot forgiving Lancelot for any wrongdoing.

### The Battle in the West, p. 178

Another battle at Barham Down took place, and King Arthur was successful at forcing Modred's men to retreat to Canterbury. Modred then fled to the West where he lobbied more knights to his cause. King Arthur had a dream. In the dream, Sir Gawain warned him to hold off the fights for a month. During this time Sir Lancelot would arrive to help him fight against Modred. Sir Gawain warned the king that he would die if he fought before Sir Lancelot arrived to help him. When the king awoke he met with Modred, and the two agreed to cease fighting for a month. While the two men were on the field, a knight pulled his sword trying to chase away a snake. The other knights thought there had been an attack, so the men began to battle. King Arthur was sorely wounded in the head by Modred. Sir Lucan and Sir Bedivere took the king to a little chapel on the seashore.

**The Death of Arthur, p. 180**

The king asked Sir Bedivere to take his sword Excalibur to the sea and toss it away. The sword was so beautiful, Sir Bedivere could not bring himself to toss it. Three times King Arthur asked Sir Bedivere to toss the sword. On the third time, he did as the king asked. A hand took the sword. The king then asked Sir Bedivere to put him on a barge so he could sail to the Valley of Avalon. After the king departed, Sir Bedivere went to live in a hermitage for the rest of his life.

**How Queen Guinevere Became a Nun at Almesbury and of the Death of Sir Lancelot, p. 183**

Sir Lancelot heard the news of King Arthur's death. He was grieved that Modred, a villain, would escape his sword. Lancelot then visited Sir Gawain's grave and prayed. Afterwards he went alone in search of Queen Guinevere. Finding her in a nunnery, he asked her to accompany him back to France. She refused. Depressed, Lancelot went to a hermitage. Sir Bors and other knights of the Round Table were worried about Lancelot because he had not returned to Dover. They went in search of him. In the meantime, Lancelot dreamed that the queen had died. Going back to Almesbury, he found his dream was true. He buried her in the abbey of Glastonbury where some say King Arthur's tomb can be found. Lancelot then died, as well.

1. **Were Arthur and his knights successful in restoring order in the kingdom?**

   Yes, King Arthur and his knights were, for the most part, able to unite and rid the kingdom of evil.

2. **Why were they so successful?**

   They were successful because of their strength in unity. They also had a strong leader, and they were strong fighters as well.

3. **What value have union and loyalty in any cause?**

   Union and loyalty are valuable in any cause. They keep people focused on a goal and create strength that is not easily broken.

4. **When did this union of King Arthur and his knights begin to weaken?**

   The union began to weaken when jealousy and treason began to take root in some of the knights' hearts.

5. **Whose unfaithfulness and treachery began its destruction?**

   Sir Modred's unfaithfulness and treachery began its destruction.

6. **What was the great fault in Modred that prevented him from being loyal?**

   Greed was the great fault in Modred that prevented him from being loyal.

7. **How did "true knights" regard Sir Lancelot?**

The "true knights" regarded Sir Lancelot as a noble and honorable knight.

8. **Find lines which show that Arthur did not think himself greater than the law.**

"I sit as king to be a rightful judge and keep all the law, wherefore I may not do battle for my own queen and now there is none other to defend her."  This line shows Arthur did not think himself greater than the law because he had to punish his own queen.

9. **Can good government exist without respect for the law?**

No, good government cannot exist without respect for the law.

10. **Trace the progress of disunion from its beginning in Modred's jealousy as follows: jealousy; plot; combat; deaths; vengeance; false accusation; decree of death by burning; rescue; deaths; vow of vengeance; war.**

Sir Modred became jealous of Sir Lancelot and King Arthur, so Sir Modred attempted to take over the kingdom for himself.  He plotted his usurpation by spreading rumors about the knight and the queen.  Men were killed, which spurned other men to anger.  Fighting took place, and more men were killed.  All along, the seed of jealousy and need for revenge grew until, eventually, the noble king, Sir Lancelot, Queen Guinevere, and other knights lost their lives.

11. **What proof did Sir Lancelot give of his love for the king, even while at war with him?**

As proof of Sir Lancelot's love for the king, he ordered his knights not to touch the king while in battle with him.  Lancelot said, "for never…will I see the noble king who made me knight either killed or shamed."

12. **Was King Arthur at fault when he allowed himself to be persuaded by Sir Gawain to make war on Sir Lancelot?**

Answers will vary.  Discuss with the class the concept of personal responsibility.

13. **Find lines that show the king loved Lancelot, in spite of all that had come between them.**

The king loved Lancelot.  He says, "Methinks…my joy on earth is done; for never have I loved any men as I have loved you, my nephew, and Sir Lancelot."

14. **Find lines that show how Sir Gawain's love and generosity triumphed over his desire for vengeance.**

Sir Gawain's love and generosity triumphed over his desire for vengeance when on his death bed he wrote Sir Lancelot a letter.  It read, "To Sir Lancelot, the noblest of all knights, I Gawain, send greeting before I die.  For I am smitten on the wound ye gave me before your castle of Benwick in France, and I bid all men bear witness that I sought my own death and that ye are innocent of it. I pray you, by our friendship of old, come again unto Britain and, when ye look upon my tomb, pray for Gawain of Orkney. Farewell."

15. **Over what did King Arthur grieve when he lay wounded after the "battle in the west"?**

King Arthur grieved over the death of his friend Sir Lucan.

16. **How does the fact that these old stories have lived for centuries show that we like "to become partners in all the brave deeds of the past," as told you in the "Introduction" on page 104?**

If we did not enjoy the stories they would not have been passed on from generation to generation. The fact that they have lived for centuries tells us that we like "to become partners in all the brave deeds of the past."

17. **What have the fine ideals of these legends—union for defense of the weak, mercy to all, and wrongful gain to none—had to do with making the legends live?**

The fine ideals of these legends are ideals that most people find worthy and inspiring. These ideals have helped the legends live.

18. **The last sentence on page 104 tells of the benefit we gain from reading stories of adventure. What is this benefit? In what way do you feel that your reading of the King Arthur stories has benefited you?**

Answers will vary.

19. **Find in the glossary the meaning of: leagued, churl (p. 168); reconciled, gainsay, unscathed, Dolorous (pp. 170-170); requiem, peer (p. 185).**

## Class Reading

The quarrel between Gawain and Lancelot, page 171, line 13, to page 173, line 4; the casting away of Excalibur, page 180, line 25, to page 182, line 2; the passing of Arthur, page 182, line 6, to page 183, line 5; bring to class and read "The Passing of Arthur," Tennyson, beginning with line 330.

## Outline for Testing Silent Reading

    (a) Sir Modred's jealousy;

    (b) His plot;

    (c) The combat;

    (d) Feuds;

    (e) The law in respect to treason;

    (f) The king's decree;

    (g) Plans for the execution;

    (h)  The rescue;
    (i)   The deaths of Sir Gareth and Sir Gaheris;
    (j)   Sir Gawain's vow;
    (k)  Arthur's siege of the Joyous Garde;
    (l)   The return of the queen;
    (m) The banishment of Lancelot;
    (n)  King Arthur and Gawain in France;
    (o)  The fight between Lancelot and Gawain;
    (p)  Modred, the traitor, in Britain;
    (q)  Gawain's letter;
    (r)   The battle in the west;
    (s)  King Arthur's dream;
    (t)   The adder;
    (u)  The death of Modred;
    (v)  Sir Bedivere and the sword Excalibur;
    (w) Guinevere in the nunnery;
    (x)  The death of Lancelot.

## Library Reading

*The Story of the Grail and the Passing of Arthur,* Pyle.

## Suggestions for Theme Topics

1. The method used by the knights of Arthur's court to right wrong.
2. Some methods used in our day to right a wrong.
3. The word that knights might do now in relieving suffering and in protecting the weak.
4. The story of some brave act of which you know.
5. A man you know of today who would have made a good knight in the days of King Arthur.
6. Training given to boys today to fit them for service to others.
7. Compare the brave deeds of our soldiers in World War One with those of King Arthur and his knights.

## *Extended Activities:*

1. Write a fictional story in which the hero is a knight of your own design. Follow the elements of plot when planning the story: exposition, narrative hook, rising action, climax, falling action, and resolution. Be sure the story contains an interesting conflict.

2. Select a piece of music that relates to the *mood*—the feeling one gets when reading—of the story. Allow students to play it for the class and explain in writing or in an oral presentation how the music relates to the story.

3. Have students choose a scene from the story and illustrate it. Display the artwork.

NAME_____CLASS_____DATE_____

## THE PASSING OF ARTHUR, p. 167

1.  Write a fictional story in which the hero is a knight of your own design. Follow the elements of plot when planning the story: exposition, narrative hook, rising action, climax, falling action, and resolution. Be sure the story contains an interesting conflict.
2.  Select a piece of music that relates to the *mood*—the feeling one gets when reading—of the story. Play it for the class and explain in writing or in an oral presentation how the music relates to the story.
3.  Choose a scene from the story and illustrate it. Display the artwork.

## NARRATIVES IN VERSE

### SIR PATRICK SPENS, p. 188

1. **Why did the king choose Sir Patrick Spens?**

   The king chose Sir Patrick Spens because he was the best sailor upon the sea.

2. **What did Sir Patrick say when he had read the king's letter?**

   When Sir Patrick read the king's letter he said, "O wha is this has don this deid, This ill deid don to me.  To send me out this time of yeir to sail upon the se!"

3. **What signs of a storm had been noticed?**

   The signs that a storm was approaching were a new moon with the old moon in her arms.

4. **Point out all the ways in which the ballad tells that the ship was wrecked.**

   The reader can infer that the ship was wrecked when we are told the ladies sat long waiting for their men who did not return.  The ballad also says that Patrick Spens was "50 fathoms deep." This implies he was drowned in the sea.

5. **How have the old ballads come down to us?**

   Old ballads have come to us through oral tradition.

6. **Have you read any other old ballads?**

   Answers will vary.

7. **Tell how the old ballads came into being and name a characteristic of them.**

   Old ballads came into being by being passed from generation to generation.  Characteristics of a ballad are that they tell a story, that there is not a known author, and that it was handed down orally.

8. **What do the old ballads tell us of the life of the early people?**

   Ballads tell us about the "standards, superstitions, and beliefs" of early peoples.

9. **How does a modern ballad differ from a folk, or popular, ballad?**

   A modern ballad introduces descriptions of characters and there is a known author.

10. **You will enjoy hearing phonograph records of present-day ballads, such as Kipling's "Fuzzy-Wuzzy," "Gypsy Trail," "Rolling Down to Rio," and "On the Road to Mandalay."**

**Class Reading**

Bring to class and read "The Wreck of the Hesperus," Longfellow.

**Library Reading**

Another version of "Sir Patrick Spens" (in *The Ballad Book,* Bates); *Some British Ballads,* illustrated by Rackham; Selected ballads from *English Popular Ballads,* Hart; "The Loss of the White Ship," Blaisdell (in *Stories from English History*); "Steering Without a Compass," Kobbe (in *Sea-Stories Retold from St. Nicholas*).

**Suggestions for Theme Topics**

1. A comparison of the story of Sir Patrick Spens in this ballad with the version in *The Ballad Book,* Bates.
2. A comparison of Sir Patrick Spens, the captain, with the skipper of the Hesperus, as to courage and skill.
3. A captain of a modern lake or ocean steamer, his duties and his qualifications.

## THE SKELETON IN ARMOR, p. 191

1. **With which stanza does the narrative begin?**
   The narrative begins in stanza four.

2. **What may the first three stanzas be called?**
   The first three stanzas can be called the prologue.

3. **Which of these three stanzas is descriptive?**
   Stanza two is descriptive.

4. **In which does the Viking make himself known?**
   The Viking makes himself known in the third stanza.

5. **With what line does the story end?**
   The story ends with "Skoal! to the Northland! Skoal!"

6. **Describe the scene suggested by the first stanza; who is speaking?**
   The poet is speaking in the first stanza.

7. **Describe the guest to whom the poet speaks.**
   The guest to whom the poet speaks is clad in "rude" armor with his arms outstretched.

8. **In using the word "fearful" to describe the guest, was the poet emphasizing only the outward appearance of his guest?**
   No, the poet in using the word "fearful" was not just emphasizing the outward appearance. The word "fearful" might also describe his voice and demeanor.

9. **Can you use other words equally exact and poetical for "daunt" and "haunt"?**
   Answers will vary. Have students use a thesaurus to find synonyms.

10. **Give a name to the "flashes" that are seen when the northern skies gleam in December.**
    These flashes are the Northern Lights (Aurora Borealis). They are seen different times of the year in different parts of the world.

11. **To what is the voice of the skeleton compared?**
    The voice of the skeleton is compared to "the water's flow under December's snow."

12. **Is it an apt comparison?**
    Yes, it is an apt comparison.

13. **Does the second stanza prepare us for a story of happy things? Give reasons for your answer.**
    The second stanza does not prepare us for happy things. Words such as "cavernous eyes" and "dull voice of woe" prepares us for something sad.

14. **What stanzas help you to see the kind of people the Vikings were and to imagine the life they led?**

Stanzas six through eight tell what kind of people the Vikings were. The Vikings are described as "wild," killing people, staying out late and drinking.

15. **The Viking showed his wonderful courage in going out on the "open main" in a wild hurricane; give all the other evidences of his courage found in the poem.**

The Viking also showed wonderful courage because he hunted early. He also eloped with the maiden.

16. **The "Introduction" (pp. 103-105) mentions various motives for seeking adventures; which of these motives do you think King Arthur's knights had? The Vikings?**

King Arthur seeks adventure to do a kind service to others. The Vikings seemed to seek adventure to broaden their territory and exhibit their power.

17. **How does this ballad differ from a folk ballad, such as "Sir Patrick Spens"?**

This ballad is written in more standard English whereas "Sir Patrick Spens" is colloquial.

18. **Find in the glossary the meaning of: scald, saga, gyrfalcon, corsair, cormorant.**

19. **Pronounce: daunt, haunt, armed, launched, toward.**

## Class Reading

Bring to class and read "The Three Fishers," Kingsley.

## Library Reading

"The Saga of King Olaf," Longfellow (Parts I, II, XII, XIII, XXII); *The Thrall of Leif the Lucky*, Liljencrantz.

## Suggestions for Theme Topics

1. A description of a Viking ship.
2. The Tower at Newport.
3. The rhyming scheme of this ballad.

## LORD ULLIN'S DAUGHTER, p. 198

1. **Tell briefly the story of the poem.**

   The story is about two lovers who were running from the girl's father. They went out to sea and were drowned.

2. **What picture do the first two stanzas give you?**

   The first two stanzas paint a picture of two people who are very anxious and frayed.

3. **What reason did the boatman give for saying he would row them over the ferry?**

   The boatman says, "It is not for your silver bright, but for your winsom lady" that he will row them over the ferry.

4. **What change of time do you notice in the third stanza on page 199?**

   The time change is that they have been out to sea some time when the father arrives at the shore.

5. **What does the fourth stanza on page 199 tell you?**

   The fourth stanza on page 199 tells us that on the "fatal shore" the father finds them dead.

6. **Which stanza tells you of the tragedy?**

   The last stanza tells us of the tragedy.

7. **What other poems of the sea have you read in this book?**

   Some other poems of the sea in this book are: "Spanish Waters" (p. 200), "Kilmeny" (p. 203), "Ye Mariners of England" (p. 260), "The Shipbuilders" (p. 454), "Old Ironsides" (p. 460), and "O Captain! My Captain!" (p. 477).

8. **What characteristics of the ballad has this poem?**

   This poem tells a story like the ballad.

9. **Find in the glossary the meaning of: pound, water-wraith.**

**A Suggested Problem.**

   Notice the quotation from Campbell in the "Biography"; make a list of similar "favorite lines" from selections that you have read in this book.

## Spanish Waters, p. 200

1.  **Who is addressed in the first stanza?**
    The first stanza is addressed to Spanish waters.
2.  **What comparison do you find in this stanza?**
    The comparison in this stanza is the sound of water compared to music.
3.  **Tell the story in your own words.**
    Answers will vary.
4.  **Where was the treasure secured?**
    The treasure was secured in the middle of the island. They marked it with a tree.
5.  **What marks of the ballad do you find in this poem?**
    This poem tells a story like the ballad.
6.  **What do you particularly like in the selection?**
    Answers will vary.
7.  **This poem is rich in musical quality, about which you read on page 22; can you tell what gives it this quality? Compare it with Wordsworth's "The Daffodils"; which seems to you the more musical?**
    The musical quality is produced by the rhyme. The rhyme in this poem is more complicated and not as sing-song as in Wordsworth's "The Daffodils."
    Answers will vary in regards to which poem is more musical.
8.  **What reference to Spanish treasure ships is made by Lowell in "To the Dandelion"?**
    Lowell makes reference to the buccaneers who searched for El Dorado.
9.  **Find in the glossary the meaning of: lazareet, gear, desecrated, Don, mattock, blazed, awhiles.**
10. **Pronounce: quagmire, palm.**


**Class Reading.**
> Bring to class and read: "Sea Fever," Masefield, "Forty Singing Seamen," Noyes; "Andy Battle," De la Mare (in *Peacock Pie*).

**Library Reading.**
> "The Moor's Legacy," Irving (in *The Alhambra*); "To Repel Boarders," London (in *Sea-Stories Retold from St. Nicholas*).

**Suggestions for Theme Topics.**
> 1. What I have learned from magazines about Masefield.

2. A report on *Treasure Island*, Stevenson.
3. A report on another story dealing with hidden treasures.
4. How a modern ship with a cargo of fuel or food may be as much a treasure ship as if it carried gold.

## Extended Activity:

Have students draw a treasure map and compose a short poem about their hidden treasure.

Name_____Class_____Date_____

## Spanish Waters, p. 200

**Draw a treasure map and compose a short poem about your hidden treasure.**

## KILMENY—A SONG OF THE TRAWLERS, P. 203

1. **What picture does the first stanza give you?**
   The picture in the first stanza is one of a deep, dark evening.
2. **What gives you a hint as to the work in which the trawler was engaged?**
   The hint given as to the work in which the trawler was engaged is the gun on the front and back of the ship.
3. **The ballad is rich in suggestion; which stanza suggests the result of *Kilmeny's* trip?**
   Stanza three suggests the result of *Kilmeny's* trip with the lines: "Now at sixty-four fathom a conger may come And nose at the bones of a drowned submarine."
4. **What was the magic that called *Kilmeny* to the quest?**
   The magic that called *Kilmeny* to the quest was the "Laughter of London, the boasts of Berlin."
5. **Find in the glossary the meaning of: trawler, conger, gnome.**

**Class Reading.**
   Bring to class and read what you consider the best ballad that has appeared in the magazines in recent months.

**Suggestions for Theme Topics.**
   1. How *Kilmeny* differs from any of the other ships that you have read about in this book.
   2. How the skipper of the *Kilmeny* compares in courage to Sir Patrick Spens; with the skipper of the *Hesperus;* and with the Viking.
   3. What the navy of the United States did in the world wars against the submarines of the enemy.

## *Extended Activities:*

   1. Using Theme Topic #1, have students draw pictures of the different ships.
   2. Using Theme Topic #3, have students research current naval ships and report on their functions. Where have these ships been used to secure America within the past ten years?

NAME_____CLASS_____DATE_____

## KILMENY—A SONG OF THE TRAWLERS, P. 203

1.  Using Theme Topic #1, draw pictures of the different ships.

2.  Using Theme Topic #3, research current naval ships and report on their functions. Where have these ships been used to secure America within the past ten years?

# A TALE FROM SHAKESPEARE

## THE TEMPEST, p. 205

### SUMMARY

Prospero was usurped by his brother, Antonio, and the king of Naples. They sent Prospero and his daughter, Miranda, out to sea to die. Fortunately, a loyal count loaded their boat with food, books, and other supplies. The two landed on an enchanted island where an evil witch, Sycorax, had imprisoned the good spirits into the bodies of trees. Prospero knew magic and freed these spirits who then became his loyal subjects. Ariel was the chief of these spirits and was offered freedom if he would help Prospero bring Antonio and the king of Naples to him. Ariel formed a tempest that caused the usurpers' ship to land on the island. Ferdinand, the prince of Naples, thought Antonio and his father had drowned in the storm. Ariel, singing a sweet song, lured Ferdinand to Miranda where the two fell immediately in love. Ariel also tormented Antonio and the king of Naples so badly that they thought their afflictions were the result of their evil deeds towards Prospero. Repenting of their ways, the two men were taken to Prospero where they were reunited. With Ariel providing favorable winds, they all returned home safely.

1. **Make a list of the characters mentioned in the story.**

   The characters in the story were Ariel; Prospero; Miranda; Antonio; the king of Naples; and Ferdinand, the prince of Naples.

2. **Which are the principal characters?**

   Prospero, Ariel, and Miranda are the principal characters.

3. **What was Prospero's purpose in raising a violent storm?**

   His purpose was to bring Antonio and the king of Naples to his island.

4. **What tells you that it is a magic storm?**

   The following tells you that it is a magic storm: "Having these powerful spirits obedient to his will, Prospero could by their means command the wind and waves of the sea."

5. **Tell the story that Prospero told his daughter.**

   Prospero gave his brother, Antonio, power to run the kingdom so Prospero could study, but Antonio and the king of Naples abused the power and usurped Prospero. They put Prospero and his daughter out to sea in hopes they would drown. However, a loyal count provided them with food and other supplies aboard the boat.

6. **Why is Miranda made to sleep?**

   Miranda is made to sleep so she would not hear Prospero talking to Ariel, "(As it would seem to her) [Prospero was talking] with the empty air."

7. **What is the purpose of Ariel's song?**

   The purpose of Ariel's song is to lure the men to Prospero.

8. **Tell the story of reconciliation of Antonio and Prospero.**

Ariel told Antonio and the king of Naples that what affected them was a result of their deeds against Prospero. They repented and made amends to Prospero.

9. **Repeat from memory Ariel's farewell song.**

10. **Which of the characters do you like best? Why?**
Answers will vary.

11. **Mention humorous incidents in the story.**
Answers will vary.

12. **How does this story of adventure differ from those in the group called the "Days of Chivalry"?**
This story differs from the stories in the group called the "Days of Chivalry" in that there are no battles or no bloodshed.

13. **Which do you like better, legends based partly on historical fact, such as the stories of King Arthur and his knights, or those that are pure fancy?**
Answers will vary.

14. **In what ways are the King Arthur stories and this story by Shakespeare alike?**
The King Arthur stories and this story by Shakespeare are similar in that they both tell of characters who do good service to others.

15. **Shakespeare wrote this tale merely to amuse and entertain; does it also teach a lesson, such as the King Arthur legends do?**
Yes, this story teaches a lesson as the King Arthur legends do. The lesson learned is that evil will not prevail over those who do good deeds.

16. **Read again the last paragraph of the "Introduction" on page 104, and then tell what this story has done for you.**
Answers will vary.

17. **Find in the glossary the meaning of: knell, constancy, enjoined, harpy, voracious, nuptials.**

18. **Pronounce: mischievous, heir, uncouth.**

### Class Reading:

Prospero's account of his banishment, page 207, line 11 to page 208, line 4;

Ferdinand piling logs, page 211, line 29, to page 213, line 10;

The reconciliation, page 213, line 25, to page 215 line 14.

### Outline for Testing Silent Reading.

(a) Prospero and his companions on the island;

(b) The storm at sea;

(c) The story Prospero tells Miranda;

(d) Ariel's account of the shipwreck;

(e) Ferdinand before Prospero and Miranda;

(f) The task set before Ferdinand;

(g) The reconciliation;

(h) The departure from the island.

## Library Reading.

Other stories from *Tales from Shakespeare,* Lamb, illustrated by
Rackham.

NAME_____CLASS_____DATE_____

*Story*          ***Find in the glossary the meaning of:***
*Reader p. 105*  **postern gate**_____
                 **realm**_____
                 **counseled**_____
                 **clamoring**_____
                 **decreed**_____
                 **scabbard**_____
                 **oppression**_____
                 **lurk**_____
                 **peasant**_____
                 **Christendom**_____
                 **Pentecost**_____
                 **sorceress**_____
                 **turret**_____
                 **portcullis**_____
                 **salutation**_____
                 **petition**_____
                 **squire**_____
                 **page**_____
                 **fain**_____
                 **estate**_____
                 **battlement**_____
                 **succor**_____
                 **vigil**_____
                 **vassal**_____
                 **behoove**_____
                 **mere**_____
                 **samite**_____
                 **fathom**_____
                 **anon**_____
                 **wafted**_____
                 **mystic**_____
*Reader p. 120*  **wroth**_____
                 **proffered**_____
                 **chid**_____
                 **manor**_____
                 **rebuke**_____
                 **pavilion**_____
                 **amends**_____
*Reader p. 143*  **token**_____

burgess _____

buffet _____

hermit _____

discomfited _____

*Reader p. 167*    leagued _____

churl _____

reconciled _____

gainsay _____

unscathed _____

dolorous _____

requiem _____

peer _____

*Reader p. 191*    scald _____

saga _____

gyrfalcon _____

corsair _____

cormorant _____

*Reader p. 198*    pound _____

water-wraith _____

*Reader p. 200*    lazareet _____

gear _____

desecrated _____

Don _____

mattock _____

blazed _____

awhiles _____

*Reader p. 203*    trawler _____

conger _____

gnome _____

*Reader p. 205*    knell _____

constancy _____

enjoined _____

harpy _____

voracious _____

nuptials _____

*Pronounce*:
bade, tournament, sovereign, courteous, stanch, alms, homage, lineage, grievous, jeopardy, Thames, daunt, haunt, armed, launched, toward, quagmire, palm, mischievous, heir, uncouth.

# Part III:
# Our Inheritance of Freedom

## In This Section—

*Objectives—*

By completing "Part III," the following objectives will be met.

1. The student will use effective reading strategies to construct meaning and identify the purpose of a text including:
   a. using illustrations
   b. defining unfamiliar words
   c. retelling and summarizing
   d. outlining
2. The student will determine the main idea or essential message and identify relevant supporting details and facts of a text.
3. The student will read and organize facts from the text and other sources to make a report, outline and perform an authentic task.
4. The student will prepare for writing and for an oral presentation by focusing on the topic and organizing supporting details in a logical sequence.
5. The student will draft and revise writing.
6. The student will produce final documents that have been edited for correct spelling, punctuation, and grammar.
7. The student will write for a variety of audiences and purposes.
8. The student will write in a variety of genres including narrative and expository.
9. The student will use reference materials (dictionaries, encyclopedias, maps, charts, photos, and electronic reference) to gather information.
10. The student will use speaking strategies effectively such as eye contact, gestures, and visuals that engage the audience.
11. The student will identify the development of plot and how conflicts are resolved in a story.
12. The student will identify and understand similarities and differences among the characters, settings, and events presented in various texts.
13. The student will identify the author's purpose and point of view.
14. The student will respond critically to fiction and poetry, identifying such elements as alliteration and rhyme scheme.
15. The student will recognize cause-and-effect relationships in literary texts.
16. The student will respond to a text by explaining how the motives of the characters or events compare with those in his or her own life.
17. The student will understand the qualities necessary for people to become good citizens and apply those qualities to his or her personal life.
18. The student will understand the qualities necessary to develop good character.
19. The student will analyze and evaluate motives of characters.

*S*TORIES AND *S*ONGS OF
    *L*IBERTY

**L**EONIDAS, THE **S**PARTAN, p. 225

1. **What does the second paragraph on page 221 tell you about enemies of freedom?**

   The second paragraph on page 221 tells us that the enemies of freedom want power. Some have ruled for years, but as brave men fight against these oppressors, freedom is slowly won for future generations.

2. **What do you learn from this selection about the aims of Xerxes in the invasion of Greece?**

   We learn that Xerxes wanted to expand his territory. He says: "If we subdue them and their neighbors, we shall make the Persian territory as extensive as the air of heaven."

3. **What effect on our "inheritance of freedom" do you think the success of Xerxes would have produced?**

   Xerxes would have hindered our success to gain freedom.

4. **Describe the place of defense chosen by Leonidas.**

   The place Leonidas chose for defense was Thermopylae, a pass narrower than any other.

5. **Compare the two armies in numbers and fighting ability.**

   The Greeks were small in number, 4,300, and Xerxes's armies numbered more than five million men.

6. **Tell briefly the story of the battle.**

   The men of Greece fought so valiantly that the men of Xerxes kept retreating. Xerxes sent in his "Immortals" and they, too, were run off. Xerxes then tried to go behind the mountain to attack. This strategy helped him win the battle.

7. **What impression of the courage and skill of the Greeks do you gain from this selection?**

   From this selection, one learns that the Greeks were very courageous and were very skillful.

8. **What has your reading of the story of Leonidas done for your appreciation of our "inheritance of Freedom?**

   Answers will vary.

9. **Leonidas lost his life in a vain effort to defeat the Persians. Do you think the battle was a complete failure for Greece?**

   Answers will vary, but students should recognize that the battle, while lost, provided future generations with a hero.

10. **Find in the glossary the meaning of: best-appointed,**

exile, barbarian, repel, dispatch, immortals, libation, Lacedaemonians.

11. **Pronounce: morass, memorably, scourge.**

**Outline for Testing Silent Reading:**
Make an outline to guide you in telling the story.

## *Extended Activity:*
Instruct students in the proper format for creating a formal outline.

I. Main Idea
   A. Suppporting Idea
   B. Supporting Idea
     1. Details
     2. Details
       a. Specific details
       b. Specfic details
II. Main Idea

Note: In creating a formal outline, listings must come in pairs. For example, you cannot have an A without a B, a 1 without a 2, and so on. Students should align their headings properly. The first word after a number or letter is capitalized.

NAME_____ CLASS_____ DATE_____

## LEONIDAS, THE SPARTAN, p. 225

Create an outline of this story. Make sure you align your headings properly
and capitalize where appropriate.

_____

_____

_____

_____

_____

_____

_____

_____

_____

_____

_____

_____

_____

_____

_____

_____

_____

_____

_____

_____

_____

_____

_____

_____

_____

_____

_____

_____

_____

_____

## ARNOLD WINKELRIED, p. 231

1. **Who cried, "Make way for liberty"?**
   Arnold Winkelried cried, "Make way for liberty."

2. **In what way did the Austrians resemble a wall?**
   The Austrians resembled a wall because there were so many men it was hard to distinguish them individually.

3. **What does the poet mean by comparing them to a wood?**
   A wood is thick with trees. The Austrian army was thick with men.

4. **Who were the "hovering band"? For what were they fighting?**
   The "hovering band" was the men of Switzerland. They were fighting for Swiss independence.

5. **Why do you think men are better fighters when they are fighting for freedom than for other causes?**
   Men are better fighters when they are fighting for freedom because it is freedom that allows men other rights. Freedom is the concept on which our country was founded.

6. **What tells you that the Swiss were not accustomed to war?**
   The Swiss were not accustomed to war because they did not have the manpower or weapons like the Austrians had.

7. **What lines tell you that the Austrians were well disciplined?**
   The lines that tell you that the Austrians were well disciplined are: "...the Austrians held their ground." "In arms the Austrian phalanx stood, a living wall, a human wood."

8. **What gave the Swiss courage to face so strong a foe?**
   The cause of freedom for their wives and children gave the Swiss courage to face so strong a foe: "How could they rest within their graves, To leave their homes the haunts of slaves."

9. **Find lines in the third stanza which tell that each of the Swiss felt that victory depended on him alone. What effect had this thought on their efforts?**
   The effect this thought had on their efforts was that each gave one hundred percent: "Few were the numbers she could boast, Yet every freeman was a host; And felt as 'twere a secret known That one should turn the scale alone, While each unto himself was he On whose sole arm hung victory."

10. **In what respects is the story of Arnold Winkelried like the story of Leonidas?**
    The story of Arnold Winkelried is like Leonidas in that both men stood for courage and forged ahead even though the odds were against them.

11. **Find in the glossary the meaning of: phalanx, impregnable, annihilate, trump, rumination, anticipate, instantaneous.**

## TALES OF A GRANDFATHER—ROBERT THE BRUCE, P. 235

1. **What incident made Robert Bruce leave the English army?**

    The incident that made Robert Bruce leave the English army was while he was eating he had blood on his hands. The other men made fun of him because he had his brothers' blood on his own hands signifying his treason.

2. **What qualities for leadership did he possess?**

    The qualities for leadership he possessed are mentioned in these lines: "Bruce was held the best warrior in Scotland. He was very wise and prudent, and an excellent general. He was generous, too, and courteous by nature."

3. **What happened when Comyn and Bruce met at the church in Dumfries?**

    When Comyn and Bruce met at the church in Dumfries they argued. Bruce in his anger attacked Comyn. Two men then entered, killing Comyn.

4. **What misfortunes followed Bruce after this event?**

    After this event, Bruce's castle was taken, his wife was captured by the enemy, and his brother was executed.

5. **Which did you wish Bruce to do, fight the Saracens, or fight for Scotland?**

    Answers will vary. Have students explain their reasoning.

6. **Read again the second paragraph on page 221, and then tell to whom Scotland owes her freedom. In what way is this story like the story of Leonidas?**

    Scotland owes her freedom to men like Bruce. This story is like Leonidas in that one man did great deeds and was an example to others.

7. **What did the spider show Bruce?**

    The spider showed Bruce perseverance. His seventh try was a success.

8. **How did Bruce and James Douglas meet?**

    Bruce and James Douglas met on the island of Arran.

9. **What do you know about Sir Thomas Randolph?**

    Sir Thomas Randolph's mother was the sister to King Robert.

10. **Describe the taking of Edinburgh Castle.**

    Edinburgh Castle had steep walls, but Francis had climbed a part of the wall so many times, he was very familiar with it. Francis showed Bruce's men how to climb it, and they were able to take the castle.

11. **By what stratagem was the Castle of Lithgow taken?**

    A Binnock farmer was commissioned to bring hay to the castle. So he hid his men under the hay and stationed other men near the door. The portcullis could not shut because of the cart, and the men were able to take over the castle.

12. **Read lines that show the character of the king's brother, Sir Edward.**

Lines that show Sir Edward's character are: "The king admired his (Sir Edward's) courage though it was mingled with rashness."

13. **Find in the glossary the meaning of: adherents, insurgent, mutual, persevering, reconciled, posterity.**

14. **Pronounce: patriotic, yeomanry, severity, audacious.**

**Class Reading.**

The incident of the spider, page 238, line 22, to page 239, line 18; The capture of Edinburgh Castle, page 241, line 1 to page 242, line 34.

**Outline for Testing Silent Reading.**

Make an outline to guide you in telling the story.

**Library Reading.**

*Stories from Scottish History,* Edgar; "The Rat Trap," Caball (In *Harper's Magazine,* December 1907); "Taking of Three Castles," Rolf (In *Tales from Scottish History*); *Little Journeys to Scotland and Ireland,* Whitcomb and George.

# TALES OF A GRANDFATHER—THE BATTLE OF BANNOCKBURN, p. 247

1. **Describe the two armies, the English and the Scotch.**

   The English army was well equipped, "one of the greatest armies which a king of England ever commanded." There were not fewer than 100,000 men. The Scots had 30,000 men who were poorly equipped.

2. **What stratagem did the Scotch king use?**

   The Scotch king used wisdom, not might, to defeat his enemy. He dug traps for the English army, charged the archers, and hid the servants who were then mistaken by the English as another army.

3. **What did King Robert mean when he said to Randolph, "there is a rose fallen from your chaplet"?**

   By this he meant that Randolph had lost some honor by suffering the enemy to pass where he had been stationed to hinder them."

4. **Find passages that show two fine sides of Douglas's nature.**

   Passages that show two fine sides of Douglas's nature are: "'So please you,' said Douglas to the king, 'my heart will not suffer me to stand idle and see Randolph perish—I must go to his assistance'" and "'Halt!' said Douglas to his men, 'Randolph has gained the day; since we were not soon enough to help him in the battle do not lessen his glory by approaching the field!'" These two quotes show that Douglas was eager to help a fellow citizen and to allow someone else to take the credit for deeds well done.

5. **Describe the Scotch king as he rode up and down the ranks of his army.**

   The Scotch king was "dressed in his armor and distinguished by a gold crown, which he wore over his helmet. He was not mounted on his great war horse, because he did not expect to fight that evening. But he rode on a little pony up and down the ranks of his army...."

6. **Describe the battle.**

   The battle took place with the British archers shooting bows, but the Scots rode among them killing many since they had no defense when attacked hand to hand. Horses then rode to help the archers but fell in the holes the Scots had dug. Englishmen began to fall in disorder when Scottish servants and attendants hiding over a hill came out. The English ran, for they thought these men were more of the Scottish army. Even King Edward fled.

7. **What decided the victory?**

   The servants coming over the hill decided the victory.

8. **Compare the incident that decided this victory with that of King Arthur's "Battle in the West," page 179.**

   King Arthur's battle in the West was won because of a knight who dropped his sword. The armies incorrectly thought battle had begun. The victory for the Scots was also decided on a misconception of the armies.

9. **Find passages that seem to you the most thrilling.**

   Answers will vary.

10. **Why was this such an important battle?**

    This battle was important because it gave Scotland her freedom. "The nation of Scotland was also raised once more from the situation of a distressed and conquered province to that of a free and independent state."

11. **Note that it was the English king who was trying to conquer the Scotch, not the great mass of the English people, who had nothing to say in the matter. Scotland is now a contented part of the British Empire. Compare Bruce's accomplishment for freedom with that of Leonidas and that of Arnold Winkelried.**

    Bruce and Arnold Winkelried were able to secure freedom for their countries. Leonidas was not; however, all three men fought bravely for their country.

12. **Find in the glossary the meaning of : terminated; diligence; succor; encompass; sustain; valiant; gentry ; dispersed.**

13. **Pronounce: boggy, exhorted; frontiers.**

## Class Reading.

Bring to class and read:

"How Sleep the Brave," Collins;

"Bruce and the Spider," Barton.

## Outline for Testing Silent Reading.

Make an outline to guide you in telling the story.

## BRUCE'S ADDRESS AT BANNOCKBURN, p. 253

1. **Who is supposed to speak the words?**
   Robert Bruce is supposed to speak the words.

2. **To whom are they supposed to be addressed?**
   They are supposed to be addressed to his armies.

3. **For what did Bruce contend?**
   Bruce contended against the English for Scotland's freedom.

4. **What patriot before him had fought against great odds in the same cause?**
   Sir William Wallace was the patriot who fought against great odds in the same cause.

5. **In these lines what choice does Bruce offer his army?**
   Bruce offers his armies the choice to fight or die: "Liberty's in every blow—Let us do or die."

6. **To what deep feeling does he appeal?**
   He appeals to the men's sense of honor to secure freedom for their people.

7. **Does this poem represent truly Bruce's own feeling for his country?**
   Yes, this poem represents Bruce's feeling for his country.

8. **Which are the most stirring lines?**
   Answers will vary.

9. **What was Burns's purpose in writing it?**
   Burns wrote the poem in response to his "enthusiasm on the theme of liberty and independence" "while riding on horseback over the moors of Scotland."

10. **What influence does such a poem have?**
    The poem stirs people's emotions to action.

11. **What did you read on page 222 about the service of poets in building our "inheritance of freedom"?**
    Poets "arouse men to struggle for freedom" and "work to make for us our noble inheritance of freedom."

12. **Find in the glossary the meaning of: gory, lour, servile door.**

## THE LAST FIGHT OF THE REVENGE, p. 255

1. **Describe the English fleet as it lay anchored near Flores.**
   "...with six of Her Majesty"s ships, six victualers of London, the Bark Raleigh, and two or three pinnaces riding at anchor near unto Flores..."

2. **What was the condition of the men on the *Revenge* and the *Bonaventure?***
   The *Revenge* had 90 diseased and the *Bonadventure* "not so many in health as could handle her main sail."

3. **What two things could Sir Richard do?**
   Sir Richard, when the Spanish approached, could retreat with the other ship or stay and fight.

4. **Which did he choose? Why?**
   Sir Richard chose to stay and fight because "he would rather die than dishonor himself and his country."

5. **How were the Spanish ships manned as compared with the English?**
   The Spanish ships were manned better than the English ships. They "were filled with companies of soldiers, in some two hundred besides the mariners, in some five, in others eight hundred." The English fleet of six was crippled because the men on board were very ill. "...one half of the men of every ship sick and utterly unserviceable."

6. **Describe the condition of the *Revenge* on the second day of the fighting.**
   On the second day of fighting, fifteen vessels assailed the *Revenge*. All the powder to the last barrel was gone. "All her pikes broken, forty of her best men slain, and the most part of the rest hurt."

7. **What was Sir Richard's order to the master gunner?**
   Sir Richard ordered the master gunner to sink the ship.

8. **What was the opinion of the captain and the master?**
   The captain and the master disagreed with Sir Richard. They alleged "that the Spaniard would be as ready to entertain a composition as they were willing to offer the same, and that there being divers valiant men yet living, whose wounds were not mortal, they might do their country service hereafter."

9. **What do you think of the reasons they gave?**
   Answers will vary.

10. **What was the Spaniard's offer?**
    The Spaniards offered to save all the lives aboard the *Revenge*.

11. **What did you read in the second paragraph on page 221 about dangers that threaten freedom? What "ambitious**

**men or groups of men" were opposed by Leonidas?  By Arnold Winkelried?  By Robert Bruce?  By the English sea captains like Sir Richard?**

The King of Persia, Xerxes, was against Leonidas.  The English were against the Scots and Robert the Bruce, and Arnold Winkelried was against the Austrians.  The Spanish fought against Sir Richard. Dangers that threaten freedom inspire men to do courageous acts.

12.  **Find examples of quaint expressions and uses of words such as *which* for *who,* page 255, line 15.**

"Which was otherwise had been lost"; " So that ere the morning..."; "...the ship must needs be possessed by the enemy..."

13.  **Look up in the glossary the meaning of: ordinance, divers, galleon, affirmed, several, squadron, assault, condescended, mortal.**

14.  **Pronounce: victualers, Azores, armada, wounded, dissuade.**

## YE MARINERS OF ENGLAND, p. 260

1. **Which stanzas refer to the present; which one refers to the past; which one to the future?**

   Stanzas one and two refer to the past, stanza three refers to the present and stanza four to the future.

2. **Why does the poet take this view into the past and future?**

   The poet takes this view into the past to inspire the mariners to live up to the respected reputation gained by former mariners and to remind them that their deeds will affect the future.

3. **Notice the interesting rhyme in the seventh line of every stanza.**

   The interesting rhyme in the seventh line of every stanza is called internal rhyme, rhymes that occur within a line. Words that rhyme at the end of lines are called end rhymes.

4. **Notice the pleasing effect which the poet produces by using, in one line, several words beginning with the same letter: "battle," "breeze," "loud" and "long"; find other examples.**

   This sound effect is called alliteration. Alliteration is the repetition of a consonant sound at the beginning of words. Other examples are: "field" - "fame"; "Britannia" - "bulwark"; "feast" - "flow."

5. **What service for our "Inheritance of Freedom" was done by the "mariners of England" in the struggle against the Spanish Armada?**

   The mariners helped England keep its freedom from Spain by fighting bravely.

6. **Find in the glossary the meaning of: launch, bulwark, steep, terrific.**

### Library Reading.

"On Admiralty Service," Harding (in *Harper's Magazine,* 1917); "Battle of the Baltic," Campbell.

## *Extended Activity:*

Have students rewrite the poem changing the colloquial words to standard English. Then have students compare the two poems. Which is most effective?

NAME_____CLASS_____DATE_____

## YE MARINERS OF ENGLAND, P. 260

Rewrite "Ye Mariners of England" changing the colloquial words to standard English.  Compare the two poems.  Which one is most effective?

_____

_____

_____

_____

_____

_____

_____

_____

_____

_____

_____

_____

_____

_____

_____

_____

_____

_____

_____

_____

_____

_____

_____

_____

_____

_____

_____

_____

## ENGLAND AND AMERICA IN 1782, p. 261

1. **Why does the poet think England should be proud of America?**

   The poet says "Those men thine arms withstood, Re-taught the lesson thou hadst taught, And in thy spirit with thee fought—Who sprang from English blood!" In essence, Tennyson is telling England to be proud of America because she fought with the courage that England had taught her people. Americans upheld the principles first learned from the English.

2. **Read the lines that tell, in figurative language, what England and Englishmen will do when their rights are attacked.**

   The lines that tell what Englishmen do when their rights are attacked can be found in stanza three.

3. **Notice in the last stanza how the words *harmonious, note chord, smote,* and *vibrate* all help to carry out the thought expressed in figurative language.**

4. **What was the "chord which Hampden smote"?**

   Hampden was an English Parliamentarian who was against Charles I. The "chord which Hampden smote" was the chord of freedom.

5. **Is it still "vibrating"?**

   Yes, the chord is still vibrating.

6. **On page 222 you read that George Washington "performed a double service in the cause of freedom." What was this "double service"? Which line in the second stanza shows that Tennyson understood this fact?**

   George Washington not only fought for America's freedom, but he was also the first president. Tennyson understood this fact when he writes, "Those men thine arms withstood, Re-taught the lesson thou hadst taught."

7. **On page 224 you read a prophecy by Burke; how does Tennyson's poem prove that Burke was right?**

   Burke says on page 224 "that the future would look back upon the American Revolution and see that it helped freedom not only in America but also among the English-speaking peoples everywhere." Tennyson's poem proves this when he writes in the last stanza that "The growing world assumes" the work Americans did to help spread freedom to others.

## MEN WHO MARCH AWAY, p. 263

1. **What "faith and fire" must the soldier have who freely enlists in the service of his country in war?**

   The "faith and fire" a soldier must have when freely enlisting in the service of his country in war is faith in victory and the desire and courage to fight.

2. **Whom does the poet address in the second stanza?**

   The second stanza is addressed to those who scorn or question the soldier who enlists.

3. **Use other words instead of "purblind prank."**

   "Purblind prank" can also mean an uneducated or rash decision.

4. **Explain the meaning of the fourth and fifth lines of the third stanza.**

   "England's need are we; Her distress would leave us rueing" means that England is in need of the soldiers, men willing to fight for her freedom. Not to go and serve England would be a regretful action.

5. **Why does the poet say the soldiers march to war ungrieving?**

   Soldiers march to war "ungrieving" because they have to be brave and strong, and are sure of victory.

6. **What reason is given for the "faith and fire" of the soldiers?**

   The reason for the "faith and fire" of the soldiers is their belief that the just will be victorious.

7. **In the fourth stanza, what belief does the author say the soldier has?**

   Soldiers believe "Victory crowns the just."

8. **What was said on page 222 about the service of poets in the cause of freedom?**

   Poets "arouse men to struggle for freedom."

9. **How does a poem like this cause men to volunteer to fight for their country? During what war was this poem written?**

   A poem like this can cause men to volunteer to fight for their country because it inspires them to fight for freedom. This poem was written during World War One.

10. **Find in the glossary the meaning of: musing, dolorous, pondering, dallier, rueing.**

## *Extended Activity:*

Have students compose their own poem in which they call a group of people to fight for a cause. Their cause might be for people to donate money to a charity, or give of their time for a charity. Have students also explain in a paragraph why their cause is important to them.

NAME_____CLASS_____DATE_____

## MEN WHO MARCH AWAY, P. 263

Compose your own poem in which you call a group of people to fight for a
   cause.  Your cause might be for people to donate money to a charity, or
   give of their time for a charity.  Also explain in a paragraph why your
   cause is important to you.

_____

_____

_____

_____

_____

_____

_____

_____

_____

_____

_____

_____

_____

_____

_____

_____

_____

_____

_____

_____

_____

_____

_____

_____

_____

_____

_____

## EARLY AMERICAN SPIRIT OF FREEDOM

### GRANDFATHER'S CHAIR—THE STAMP ACT, p. 265

1. **Describe the loyalty of the colonists to King George.**

   The people loved the king, and this love increased "by the dangers which they had encountered."

2. **Give two reasons why the colonies began to feel more and more independent.**

   Two reasons why the colonies began to feel more independent were: First, they were no longer afraid of the bands of French and Indians. Second, they felt they were able to protect themselves without help from England.

3. **What were some of the laws passed by the English Parliament that made the colonies wish for independence?**

   The colonists were "forbidden to manufacture articles for their own use or to carry on trade with any nation but the English."

4. **What was the stamp act?**

   The stamp act "was a law by which all deeds, bonds, and other papers of the same kind were ordered to be marked with the king's stamp, and without this mark they were declared illegal and void." People had to pay threepence to get the stamp.

5. **Would you have felt as Clara did, or as Laurence felt?**

   Answers will vary.

6. **How did these wrongs change the feelings of the colonists?**

   The wrongs done to the colonists changed their feelings for England. They "showed the grim, dark features of an old king-resisting puritan."

7. **Describe the congress proposed by the Massachusetts legislature.**

   Massachusetts "proposed that delegates from every colony should meet in congress."

8. **What did this congress do?**

   The congress sent a "petition to the king and a memorial to the Parliament beseeching that the stamp act might be repealed."

9. **Why was this congress so important?**

   This congress was important because it was the first "coming together of the American people by the representatives from the North and South."

10. **How did Liberty Tree get its name?**

    Liberty Tree "was an old elm tree…which stood near the corner of Essex street, opposite Boylston Market. Under the spreading branches of this great tree the people used to assemble whenever they wished to express their feelings and opinions."

11. **What "fruit" did it bear?**

    The fruit it bore was the liberty people had in expressing their opinions.

12. **Show that the colonists in resisting the stamp act contributed to our "inheritance of freedom."**

    The colonists in resisting the king were fighting for their freedom. They would not agree to be taxed wrongly or taxed without representation.

13. **Find in the glossary the meaning of: comprehend, dominion, tributary.**

14. **Pronounce: sagacious, Parliament, effigy.**

**Class Reading.**

Select passages to be read aloud in class.

**Outline for Testing Silent Reading.**

Make an outline to guide you in telling the story.

**Library Reading.**

Other stories from *Grandfather's Chair,* Hawthorne;

"Boston Boys," Perry (in *St. Nicholas,* July, 1876);

"Economic Freedom," McPherson (in *The Youth's Companion,* December 9, 1920)

## GRANDFATHER'S CHAIR—SOME FAMOUS PORTRAITS, p. 271

1. **Describe the family group around the fireside.**

    Grandfather, Laurence, Clara, Charlie, and little Alice, who sat on Grandfather's lap, sat around a table near the fireside looking at a book Laurence had been given as a New Year's gift.

2. **What is the center of interest?**

    The center of interest was a collection fo portraits.

3. **Contrast the pictures of Samuel Adams and John Hancock.**

    Samuel Adams was poor and earned his living through a humble occupation whereas John Hancock was born "to the inheritance of the largest fortune in New England."

4. **What is said about General Joseph Warren?**

    General Joseph Warren "was an eloquent and able patriot." No man's voice was more powerful in Faneuil Hall.

5. **Would you have been able to recognize "the illustrious Boston boy" from Hawthorne's word picture?**

    Answers will vary. Most likely students would recognize Benjamin Franklin from the line he, "snatched the lightning from the sky."

6. **How does Grandfather explain the existence of these remarkable men just when they were most needed?**

    Grandfather explains that "Providence" provided these men for a time when they were needed most.

7. **Do you know of any other time in our history when this seemed true?**

    Answers will vary.

8. **Mention the humble origin of some of the Revolutionary patriots.**

    Some of the humble origins of the Revolutionary patriots were: General Warren, physician; General Lincoln, farmer; General Knox, bookbinder; General Nathaniel Greene, Quaker/blacksmith.

9. **Why do you think they were well adapted to be founders of a great democracy?**

    Answers will vary.

10. **What suggestion was there in this for Charley?**

    The suggestion made to Charley was that in America boys and girls from any background can grow to have the opportunity to do great things.

11. **On page 222 you read that soldiers, poets, orators, and statesmen all contributed to our "inheritance of freedom"; how many of these kinds of patriots are shown in this selection?**

    In this selection soldiers, orators, and statesmen are shown.

12. **What is said on page 223 about many great Englishmen who sympathized with the American colonists in their struggle for independence?**

    Edmund Burke spoke for the Englishmen who sympathized with the colonies when he wrote in his letter to the colonies that they were not at war with the people of England.

13. **Mention several of these Englishmen who are described by Hawthorne.**

    Several men who are described by Hawthorne are the Earl of Chatham, Edmund Burke, Colonel Barré, and Charles James Fox.

14. **Why was Burke an especially valuable friend to the Americans?**

    Burke was an especially valuable friend to the Americans because his wisdom and great skill in oration worked to repeal the unjust taxation of the Americans.

15. **Find in the glossary the meaning of: distinguished, inflexible, zealous, venerable, destined, peer.**

16. **Pronounce: abhorrence, gorgeous, courtier.**

**Outline for Testing Silent Reading.**

Make an outline to guide you in telling the story.

**A Suggested Problem.**

Prepare an exhibit showing by means of pictures and brief biographies clipped from newspapers and magazines of some famous Americans who have achieved greatness from humble beginnings.

A list may include: (a) statesmen; (b) poets and prose writers; (c) editors and journalists; (d) soldiers; (e) clergymen; (f) physicians; (g) captains of industry; (h) inventors and scientists; (i) engineers and architects; (j) artists; (k) musicians; (l) nurses and social welfare workers.

## WARREN'S ADDRESS AT BUNKER HILL, P. 276

1.  **Find the lines that are an answer to those who still hoped for mercy from the British.**
    The lines that answer those who still hoped for mercy from the British are: "Hear it in that battle peal, Read it on yon bristling steel."

2.  **What lines show the striking contrast between those who fight for hire and those who fight to protect their homes?**
    The lines in stanza two show that those who fight for hire have no heart and inspire those who are saving their homes to fight valiantly. Stanza three is the call to those who are fighting to protect their homes.

3.  **Which of the appeals in the first and second stanzas seem most forceful to you?**
    Answers will vary.

4.  **Compare the spirit of Warren's address with that of Bruce at Bannockburn; what likeness do you note in the form of the poems?**
    Both poems are heart-felt calls to action for the sake of freedom.

5.  **In what ways was the Battle of Bunker Hill like the Battle of Thermopylae, where Leonidas and the Spartans fought the Persians?**
    In both battles those fighting for their freedom were out-numbered and out-equipped.

6.  **How does the Bunker Hill Monument answer the question asked in the last lines of the poem?**
    The poem asks, "O where can dust to dust Be consigned so well?" The monument immortalizes these men.

7.  **Find in the glossary the meaning of: quail, consigned.**

8.  **Pronounce: address.**

### Class Reading.

Bring to class and read, "The Old Continentals," McMaster; "Grandmother's Story of Bunker Hill Battle," Holmes.

## LIBERTY OR DEATH, p. 277

1. **What were the occasion and the purpose of Patrick Henry's speech?**

   The occasion and purpose of Patrick Henry's speech was given in congress to encourage the colonies to go to war against Britain.

2. **What reasons for presenting his views does Patrick Henry give in the beginning of his speech?**

   Patrick Henry says, "The question before the House is one of awful moment to this country. For my own part, I consider it as nothing less than a question of freedom or slavery; and in proportion to the magnitude of the subject ought to be the freedom of the debate."

3. **Do you think Patrick Henry expressed a truth for all time when he said, "In proportion to the magnitude of the subject ought to be the freedom of the debate?"**

   Yes, the truth is that without freedom one would not be able to express his opinions without fear of retribution.

4. **Find in your history some of the acts of the British Ministry against the Colonies in the ten years before 1775.**

   Encourage students to investigate this subject using their history texts.

5. **What are the arguments which Patrick Henry uses to convince the delegates of the need of immediate action?**

   To convince the men of immediate action, Patrick Henry asks the men to consider the past actions of Britain, he questions why the British have such armies stationed in their part of the world, he says God is on their side, and he says the battle has already begun.

6. **What did the next gale sweeping from the north bring to their ears?**

   The gale sweeping from the north is the "clash of resounding arms."

7. **Compare these arguments with the views of Edmund Burke, then a member of the English Parliament, about which you read in the "Introduction," page 223.**

   These arguments are more passionate and immediate than those of Edmund Burke.

8. **In this speech Patrick Henry made his language emphatic by using what we call figures of speech, such as "lamp of experience;" can you explain this and find other examples?**

   The "lamp of experience" means that as a lamp lights one's way, so experience gives him guidance.  Some other figures of speech are: "song of the sirens till she transforms us into beasts."  And "We have done everything that could be done to avert the storm which is now coming…"

9.  **Notice that the orator attacks King George and his Ministry, together with Parliament, not the English people; name some men who spoke in Parliament for the colonies and for the English people.  The "Ministry" means the British cabinet.**

One of the men who spoke for the colonies was Edmund Burke.

10.  **Show how an orator like Patrick Henry can, by making such a speech, play his part in building our "inheritance of freedom."**

An orator like Patrick Henry can inspire others to fight for freedom.

11.  **Apply the speech of Patrick Henry to the words of Lowell on page 219.  Was this a "deed done for freedom"?  How have the results of this deed "trembled from east to west"?**

The "deed done for freedom" was Henry's inspiration.  The result of this deed has "trembled from east to west" because the American Revolution affected not only the United States and Britain, but also other countries who have looked to America as a model.

12.  **Find in the glossary the meaning of:  magnitude, comport, subjugation, interposition, arrest, inviolate, cope, supinely, election.**

13.  **Pronounce:  illusion, siren, arduous, solace, insidious, inestimable, formidable.**

### Library Reading.

"Immortals" (in *The Youth's Companion,* December 9, 1920);

"Liberty or Loyalty," Dickson (in *Pioneers and Patriots in American History*).

## *Extended Activities:*

Have students prepare an oral presentation in which they convince their audience to support a cause.

NAME_____CLASS_____DATE_____

## LIBERTY OR DEATH, p. 277

Prepare an oral presentation in which you convince your audience to support
a cause.  Use this sheet for your notes.

_____

_____

_____

_____

_____

_____

_____

_____

_____

_____

_____

_____

_____

_____

_____

_____

_____

_____

_____

_____

_____

_____

_____

_____

_____

_____

_____

_____

_____

## LETTER TO HIS WIFE, p. 282

1.  **Name the fine qualities of Washington shown in this letter.**
    Encourage students to identify the qualities they notice. Sensitivity, humility, honor, service, patriotism, faith, confidence, bravery, encouragement, prudence, and foresight are some of the noble qualities General Washington expressed in his letter.

2.  **Read the sentence that tells briefly what had happened.**
    Line 6: "It has been determined in Congress that the whole army raised for the defense of the American cause shall be put under my care and that it is necessary for me to proceed immediately to Boston to take upon me the command of it."

3.  **What do you imagine was Mrs. Washington's reply to this letter?**
    Encourage students to write a letter from Mrs. Washington's perspective responding to his letter.

4.  **What did Washington mean when he said, "a kind of destiny has thrown me upon this service"?**
    Washington believes he is destined to be a leader in the fight for American's freedom from England, a fight he considers a service to his country and fellow Americans.

5.  **It has been said that "destiny" has given America great leaders in times of unusual danger. Washington was one; what other great leaders can you mention?**
    Students should explore America's great leaders through history. To name a couple: Abraham Lincoln was a great leader destined to lead America through the Civil War. John F. Kennedy also led America through the Cuban Missile Crisis.

6.  **What important part did Washington play in our "inheritance of freedom," about which you read on pages 221 to 224?**
    Page 222 reminds us that "he performed a double service in the cause of freedom: he overthrew in the American colonies the unjust rule of the English king and, by this victory, he weakened the king's despotic power over his own subjects in England. Thus Washington made it possible for liberty loving Englishmen gradually to gain a larger share in their own government."

7.  **Find in the glossary the meaning of: aggravated, capacity, designed, tenor, apprehensive, intimate, esteem.**

**Suggestions for Theme Topics.**
1. How letters were sent in colonial times.
2. Benjamin Franklin and our postal system.

## *Extended Activity:*

1. In question one, students were encouraged to identify the noble qualities that Washington expressed in his letter to Mrs. Washington. After students have brainstormed and listed the qualities they perceived, have them choose three of the qualities and define them in their own words. Students should then identify occasions when they or someone they know exhibited those same qualities.

2. In his letter, Washington makes many references to his love for Mrs. Washington. Not only does he remind her of his love and sadness at leaving her, he assures her that he will provide for her future by preparing a will for her well-being in the event that he does not return from the war. Have students freewrite on the topic, "Love Is..." From their freewriting, have students write a finished essay on the qualities of love as exhibited by Washington and how best to express it.

NAME_____ CLASS_____ DATE_____

## LETTER TO HIS WIFE, p. 282

1.  In question one, you were encouraged to identify the noble qualities that Washington expressed in his letter to Mrs. Washington. After you have brainstormed and listed the qualities you perceived, choose three of the qualities and define them in your own words.

_____

_____

_____

_____

_____

Identify occasions when you or someone you know exhibited those same qualities.

_____

_____

_____

_____

_____

_____

_____

_____

_____

_____

_____

2.  In his letter, Washington makes many references to his love for Mrs. Washington. Not only does he remind her of his love and sadness at leaving her, he assures her that he will provide for her future by preparing a will for her well-being in the event that he does not return from the war. Freewrite on the topic, "Love Is..." From your freewriting, write a finished essay on the qualities of love as exhibited by Washington and how best to express it.

## LETTER TO GOVERNOR CLINTON, p. 285

1. **Read in your history text what is said about the winter of 1777-1778 at Valley Forge.**

   Students should be acquainted with the fact that the winter of 1777-1778 was extremely miserable for Washington's troops. Without sufficient food, warm clothing, and adequate shelter, officers resigned, soldiers deserted, and many died. In spite of the severe circumstances, Washington marshaled his troops and survived the winter with renewed spirits.

2. **Compare the methods of providing food for the army in Washington's time with those of our own times.**

   In the "Historical Note," students will learn that farmers throughout the colonies were encouraged to supply cattle from their own herds to feed the soldiers, considering it a service to the cause of their country. Today, the American populace does not get personally involved in the food supply of the troops.

3. **Compare the difficulties of feeding Washington's army with those of feeding our army in France during World War One.**

   In Washington's time, food supplies for the army could be found around them in the fields and flocks of their American supporters, and transporting any supplies not readily available locally did not have to travel vast distances, although not having a large and organized central treasury made paying for supplies difficult. During World War One, the United States had a large, organized treasury and source of funds, but had to provide for its army in a foreign land and had to send food across the ocean.

4. **How did Washington hope to avert a terrible crisis?**

   He hoped that "all the energy of the Continent shall be exerted to provide a timely remedy" to the crisis of cold, starvation, and death.

5. **What debt of gratitude do we owe to the soldiers who endured even starvation to win our "inheritance of freedom"?**

   Encourage students to consider the debt of gratitude they owe, both to the soldiers and to General Washington as indicated in the following question.

6. **Washington not only carried the burden of the fighting, but also the provisioning of the army; what is our great debt to him for this service?**

   See number 5. Encourage students to discuss ways that they can show their gratitude through acts of service to others.

7. **What did you read on page 224 about the way by which we can show that we are worthy of such sacrifices as George Washington and his soldiers made?**

   "We free citizens of fortunate America owe a duty to all mankind. This duty is to value our freedom so highly that we will make free government more and more successful in our country, more and more a model that all other nations will gladly follow. Only in this way can we show that we are worthy of the sacrifices made for us by the brave men of long ago who fought that we might have this precious "inheritance of freedom."

8. **How did our soldiers in the World Wars show that they were worthy of these sacrifices?**

   They fought to extend our freedom to "other nations" as mentioned above.

9. **Find in the glossary the meaning of: zealous, conceive, dispersion, avert, magazine, precarious.**

10. **Pronounce: incomparable, catastrophe, adequate.**

## Song of Marion's Men, p. 287

1. **Who is speaking in this poem?**

   Marion's men are describing their lives as soldiers.

2. **What does the word "band" tell you about these men?**

   Students will note that in the glossary a "band" is "a company of men organized for a common purpose." Their common purpose, as seen in the "Historical Note," was to make swift attacks on the British then flee to the woods. While not a part of the organized army, their "band" helped to bring victory to the Americans in the Revolutionary War.

3. **How do seamen know their way when on the ocean?**

   Seamen know their way by following the course of the sun, moon, and stars.

4. **How do woodsmen know their way in the forest?**

   They can identify their location by the types of vegetation they travel through, the "walls of thorny vines," "reedy grass," and "safe and silent islands within the dark morass."

5. **Find the lines that picture a southern forest.**

   Lines 5 and 6: "Our fortress is the good, green wood, Our tent the cypress-tree."

6. **What does the second stanza tell you of Marion's method of attack.**

   The soldiers attack at midnight, light the enemy tents on fire, create a vast noise like "a mighty host behind," then flee back to their hiding place in the woods.

7. **Notice in the third stanza how the men spent their leisure time.**

   They "talk the battle over, And share the battle's spoil. The woodland rings with laugh and shout, As if a hunt were up." In addition, they gather flowers to crown their caps, sing merrily, and sleep sweetly.

8. **When did these hours of release occur?**

   They occurred after a night raid, before the "peep of day."

9. **Why is the moon called friendly?**

   The moon knows them and provides light for their attacks.

10. **Which lines show you that this band of men was swift in action?**

    Lines 17 and 18: "A moment in the British camp—A moment—and away."

11. **For whom were these men fighting?**

    They were fighting for the "grave men" and the "lovely ladies."

12. **Find in the glossary the meaning of: glade, deem, spoil, barb, hoary.**

**Class Reading.**

Bring to class and read, "Another of Marion's Men," Dickson (in *Pioneers and Patriots in American History*); "The Swamp Fox," Simms.

**Suggestions for Theme Topics.**

1. What can I do as a young American citizen to show that I am worthy of the sacrifices made by the patriots in the American Revolution?
2. What can I do to make our free government more and more a model for other nations to follow?
3. How public school is a part of the American government.

## TIMES THAT TRY MEN'S SOULS, P. 290

1. **Select from these paragraphs sentences that would make good mottoes.**

   Answers may vary, but should include the following: "Tyranny, like hell, is not easily conquered." "The harder the conflict, the more glorious the triumph." "What we obtain too cheap, we esteem too lightly." "'Tis the business of little minds to shrink."

2. **What political and military situation did Paine have in mind in the opening sentences?**

   Paine had in mind the battle for America's freedom from British rule. Students should read the "Biographical and Historical Notes" for more information on Paine's background and beliefs.

3. **What do you think of the argument of the tavern keeper at Amboy as compared with Paine's?**

   Encourage a classroom discussion of the two opposing views, the tavern keeper who wanted peace in his time and Paine who fought for freedom so his children could enjoy peace.

4. **If all Americans had been like this Tory at Amboy, would America today enjoy its "inheritance of freedom"?**

   America would not know freedom today if each generation had not passed on the torch of freedom to succeeding generations.

5. **What do we think today of our "remoteness from the wrangling world"?**

   Students should consider that because the world has become a global village, we can no longer be remote from "the wrangling world." However, how much should we be involved in the affairs of other countries? Students may discuss the role of America as the world's peacekeeper.

6. **What things, in the last one hundred years, have brought Europe and America closer together than they were in Paine's day?**

   Certainly the World Wars have changed our relationship with Europe. Our common interest in ridding the world of despotic leaders and terrorists have given us a common bond.

7. **Under what conditions did Paine think war justifiable?**

   Paine considered war to be justified when his house or his country came under attack whether from "a king or a common man; my countryman or not my countryman; whether it be done by an individual villain or an army of them."

8. **Find in the glossary the meaning of: crisis, celestial, Tory, dominion, induced, assigned.**

9. **Pronounce: impious, villain.**

## *Extended Activity:*

After students have identified the mottoes in question one, have them choose a motto and create a poster that depicts that motto.

# —POSTER TIPS—

### WHAT MAKES A GOOD POSTER?

Include these poster assets:

- A brief catchy message; one theme that can be read in 10 seconds
- A slogan telling the viewer to do something and making them want to do it
- Colors and white space to grab and hold attention
- Letters large enough to be easily read; words separated enough to make them quickly grasped
- Principles of good design

### AVOID THESE POSTER FAULTS

- More than one theme
- Too busy—too many and/or scattered pictures or words
- Material not relevant to topic
- Message becomes lost

### OTHER TIPS TO REMEMBER

- Illustrations and white space add emphasis and attract attention.

- Plan Ahead by sketching out your designs and ideas before you go to your final poster board; you will have a successful piece and fewer mistakes.

- Use guide lines. Pencil them lightly at the beginning and erase when finished.

- Remember Spacing. Find the center of your poster and mark it. Center the letters according to the mark. For example:

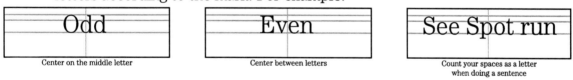

| Odd | Even | See Spot run |
|-----|------|--------------|
| Center on the middle letter | Center between letters | Count your spaces as a letter when doing a sentence |

- Small lettering is hard to read at a distance. Consider the following heights for readability from 10 feet:
  Easiest to read-1", easy to read-3/4", fairly easy to read-1/2", hard to read-1/4", and impossible to read-3/16".
- **Boldness** makes a difference.
- **Plain** lettering is more readable than *Fancy* lettering.
- Margins should be larger at the bottom——————————→ and equal on the other three sides.

## TIMES THAT TRY MEN'S SOULS, p. 290

After you have identified the mottoes in question one, choose a motto and create a poster that depicts that motto.

**N**AME_____**C**LASS_____**D**ATE_____

| *Story* | *Find in the glossary the meaning of:* |
|---|---|
| *Reader p. 225* | **best-appointed**_____ |
| | **exile**_____ |
| | **barbarian**_____ |
| | **repel**_____ |
| | **dispatch**_____ |
| | **Immortals**_____ |
| | **libation**_____ |
| | **Lacedaemonians**_____ |
| *Reader p. 231* | **phalanx**_____ |
| | **impregnable**_____ |
| | **annihilate**_____ |
| | **trump**_____ |
| | **rumination**_____ |
| | **anticipate**_____ |
| | **instantaneous**_____ |
| *Reader p. 235* | **adherents**_____ |
| | **insurgent**_____ |
| | **mutual**_____ |
| | **persevering**_____ |
| | **reconciled**_____ |
| | **posterity**_____ |
| *Reader p. 247* | **terminated**_____ |
| | **diligence**_____ |
| | **succor**_____ |
| | **encompass**_____ |
| | **sustain**_____ |
| | **valiant**_____ |
| | **gentry**_____ |
| | **dispersed**_____ |
| *Reader p. 253* | **gory**_____ |
| | **lour**_____ |
| | **servile**_____ |
| *Reader p. 255* | **ordinance**_____ |
| | **divers**_____ |
| | **galleon**_____ |
| | **affirmed**_____ |
| | **several**_____ |
| | **squadron**_____ |
| | **assault**_____ |

condescended_____

mortal_____

*Reader p. 260*   launch_____

bulwark_____

steep_____

terrific_____

*Reader p. 263*   musing_____

dolorous_____

pondering_____

dallier_____

rueing_____

*Reader p. 265*   comprehend_____

dominion_____

tributary_____

*Reader p. 271*   distinguished_____

inflexible_____

zealous_____

venerable_____

destined_____

peer_____

*Reader p. 276*   quail_____

consigned_____

*Reader p. 277*   magnitude_____

comport_____

subjugation_____

interposition_____

arrest_____

inviolate_____

cope_____

supinely_____

election_____

*Reader p. 282*   aggravated_____

capacity_____

designed_____

tenor_____

apprehensive_____

intimate_____

esteem_____

*Reader p. 285*   zealous_____

conceive_____

dispersion_____

avert_____

magazine_____

precarious_____

*Reader p. 287*  glade_____

deem_____

spoil_____

barb_____

hoary_____

*Reader p. 290*  crisis_____

celestial_____

Tory_____

dominion_____

induced_____

assigned_____

Pronounce:

morass, memorably, scourge, patriotic, yeomanry, severity, audacious, boggy, exhorted, frontiers, victualers, Azores, armada, wounded, dissuade, sagacious, Parliament, effigy, abhorrence, gorgeous, courtier, address, illusion, siren, arduous, solace, insidious, inestimable, formidable, incomparable, catastrophe, adequate, impious, villain.

# PART IV:
# LITERATURE AND LIFE IN THE HOMELAND

## In This Section—

*Objectives—*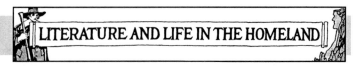

By completing "Part IV," the following objectives will be met.

1. The student will use effective reading strategies to construct meaning and identify the purpose of a text including:
   a. using illustrations
   b. defining unfamiliar words
   c. retelling and summarizing
2. The student will determine the main idea or essential message and identify relevant supporting details and facts of a text.
3. The student will read and organize facts from the text and other sources to make a report, outline, and perform an authentic task.
4. The student will prepare for writing by focusing on the topic and organizing supporting details in a logical sequence.
5. The student will draft and revise writing.
6. The student will produce final documents that have been edited for correct spelling, punctuation, and grammar.
7. The student will write for a variety of audiences and purposes.
8. The student will write in a variety of genres including narrative and expository.
9. The student will use reference materials  (dictionaries, encyclopedias, maps, charts).
10. The student will use speaking strategies effectively such as eye contact, gestures, and visuals that engage the audience through use of skits and reader's theater.
11. The student will identify the development of plot and how conflicts are resolved in a story.
12. The student will identify and understand similarities and differences among the characters, settings, and events presented in various texts.
13. The student will identify the author's purpose and point of view.
14. The student will identify and use literary terminology such as rhyme scheme, personification, alliteration, allusion, caricature, allegory, frame story, dialect, and repetition.
15. The student will respond critically to fiction, nonfiction, and poetry.
16. The student will recognize cause-and-effect relationships in literary texts.
17. The student will respond to a text by explaining how the motives of the characters or events compare with those in his or her own life.
18. The student will use context clues to understand words and ideas.
19. The student will predict events that may occur in the text, and explain the reasoning behind the prediction.
20. The student will understand the qualities necessary for people to become good citizens and apply those qualities to his or her personal life.
21. The student will understand the qualities necessary to develop good character and apply those qualities to his or her personal life.

# EARLY AMERICA

## THE CHARACTER OF COLUMBUS, P. 299

1. **Explain the comparison found in the second line.**

   The writer compares Columbus to "Moses on the Borders of the Land of Promise." Moses, an Old Testament character, was leading his people to a "new world" as Columbus was discovering "new worlds."

2. **What claims does the author make for Columbus as a scientific man?**

   "Both in theory and in practice he was one of the best geographers and cosmographers of the age. According to reliable historians, before he set out to discover new seas, he had navigated the whole extent of those already known. Moreover, he had studied so many authors and to such advantage that Alexander von Humboldt affirmed: 'When we consider his life we must feel astonishment at the extent of his literary acquaintance.'"

3. **What great inventions occurred previous to Columbus's voyage that affected his discovery of America?**

   The three great inventions were: "the printing press, which led to the revival of learning; the use of gunpowder, which changed the methods of warfare; the mariner's compass, which permitted the sailor to tempt boldly even unknown seas."

4. **Do you think the spirit of adventure had something to do with Columbus's discovery?**

   Encourage students to discuss the impact of the "spirit of adventure" on Columbus's voyages.

5. **How does the time it took Columbus to cross the ocean compare with the time required now?**

   Columbus first sailed from Spain on August 3, 1492. After sailing for 71 days, he reached land that he named San Salvador in what is known today as the Bahamas on October 12. Today the crossing is made in a few hours by airplane.

6. **What motto of an American city mentioned on page 297 expresses the spirit of Columbus in his voyage of discovery?**

   The motto is "I will." That motto certainly guided Columbus in his attempts to discover a new route to India.

7. **Find in the glossary the meaning of: facilities, Empire State, cosmographer, potent.**

8. **Pronounce: exploit, geographer.**

   See notes in the Reader, page 301.

**Class Reading.**

Bring to class and read "The Tomb of Christopher Columbus," Welch (in *St. Nicholas,* October, 1920.) *St. Nicholas* was a magazine for young people in the late 1800s and early 1900s. While a copy of "The Tomb of Christopher Columbus" could not be located, a current web site that refers to the magazine can be found at: http://home.earthlink.net/~ralphcooper/pimagc9.htm.

**A Suggested problem.**

Prepare a program for "Columbus Day" exercises in your school. Select the three best programs. Columbus Day is celebrated on October 12, to honor his first landing in the Americas. See "Extended Activity" #2 for a possible Columbus Day activity.

## *Extended Activities:*

1. Allusion in literature is the author's reference to some well-known person, place, thing, or event in history, with which he assumes the reader is acquainted. If the reader is not familiar with the thing alluded to, the connection loses its impact. In this piece, Archbishop Corrigan makes several allusions to characters in history with whom he assumes the reader is familiar. Have students identify the characters, briefly research them, and show how they relate to this story. The characters are: Moses, Washington Irving, and Jesus.

| Character | Research<br>Who, What, When, Where | Relationship<br>to Columbus |
|---|---|---|
| **Moses** | An Old Testament patriarch who led his people from slavery in Egypt to Canaan. | They both forged a path to freedom in a new country. |
| **Washington Irving** | American author who rose to fame in early 1800s. | Worked to dispel any negative images of Columbus. He wrote *The Life and Voyages of Columbus* in 1828. |
| **Christ** | The Christ of the New Testament is considered the Messiah in Catholic and Protestant belief. | One of Columbus's stated goals in discovering the New World was to introduce Christ to the natives. |

2. Have students research the life of Columbus. Research should include the following: birth and early childhood, experience at sea, how he acquired money for his first westward trip, his first trip to find India, his second, third, and fourth westward voyages, his last days, and place of death. Have students create a timeline that spans Columbus's life and indicate the major events on the timeline. The voyages should include maps of the places he landed and claimed for Spain. For added effect, students could dress in costumes of the period when they present their research.

Helpful resources for research include encyclopedias, *A History of the United States and Its People,* Lost Classics Book Company, and the Internet which may include the following sites:

http://www.jollyroger.com/xlibrary/TheLifeofHE/

http://home.vicnet.net.au/~neils/renaissance/co

http://www.rose-hulman.edu/~delacova/columbus.htm

3. The Internet resource located at rose-hulman.edu (see above) includes journals from Columbus's voyages. After reading about his life and travels, have students take on the persona of a sailor on one of Columbus's ships. Have them maintain a five-day journal that may include their reactions to any of the following: describing why they undertook the voyage, the quality of their food and ship life in general, their feelings about Christopher Columbus, and thoughts about the new land for which they are headed.

NAME_____ CLASS_____ DATE_____

## THE CHARACTER OF COLUMBUS, p. 299

1. Allusion in literature is the author's reference to some well-known person, place, thing, or event in history, with which he assumes the reader is acquainted. If the reader is not familiar with the thing alluded to, the connection loses its impact. In this piece, Archbishop Corrigan makes several allusions to characters in history with whom he assumes the reader is familiar. Identify the characters, briefly research them, and show how they relate to this story.

| Character | Research Who, What, When, Where | Relationship to Columbus |
|---|---|---|
| Moses | | |
| Washington Irving | | |
| Jesus | | |

2. Research the life of Columbus. Research should include the following: birth and early childhood, experience at sea, how he acquired money for his first westward trip, his first trip to find India, his second, third, and fourth westward voyages, his last days and place of death. Create a timeline that spans Columbus's life and indicate the major events on the timeline. The voyages should include maps of the places he landed and claimed for Spain. For added effect, you could dress in costumes of the period when you present your research.

Helpful resources for research include encyclopedias, *A History of the United States and Its People,* Lost Classics Book Company, and the Internet which may include the following sites:

> http://www.jollyroger.com/xlibrary/TheLifeofHE/
> http://home.vicnet.net.au/~neils/renaissance/co
> http://www.rose-hulman.edu/~delacova/columbus.htm

3.  The Internet resource located at rose-hulman.edu (see above) includes journals from Columbus's voyages. After reading about his life and travels, take on the persona of a sailor on one of Columbus's ships. Maintain a five-day journal that may include your reactions to any of the following: describing why you undertook the voyage, the quality of your food and ship life in general, your feelings about Christopher Columbus, and thoughts about the new land for which you are headed.

## THE LANDING OF THE PILGRIM FATHERS, p. 301

1. **What picture do the first two stanzas give you?**

   The poet describes a stormy night with crashing waves when "exiles moored their bark."

2. **Compare the coming of a conqueror with the coming of these early settlers.**

   Stanza 3 makes that comparison. "Not as the conqueror comes, They, the true-hearted, came; Not with the roll of the stirring drums, And the trumpet that sings of fame." Rather, "Amidst the storm they sang, And the stars heard and the sea; And the sounding aisles of the dim woods rang To the anthem of the free!"

3. **What different kinds of persons composed the "pilgrim band"?**

   The poet describes "men with hoary head," "woman's fearless eye," "manhood's brow serenely high, And the fiery heart of youth" that were in that "pilgrim's band."

4. **Why did they come to this new country?**

   "They sought a faith's pure shrine."

5. **Why does the poet say "holy ground"?**

   The glossary defines "holy ground" as a "place made holy by their sacrifice and ideals."

6. **What legacy have the Pilgrims left us?**

   "They have left unstained what there they found—Freedom to worship God." We enjoy that legacy to this day.

7. **What picture of early America does this poem give you?**

   Students will have a variety of responses. Have them list on the board the images they glimpsed as they read this poem.

8. **On page 298 you were told of things that will help you to gain a complete picture of what our country is, and what it means to you; what are some of these things?**

   Have students read again the first paragraph on page 298 and list all the images that are mentioned beginning with "History and legend, the knowledge of past events…" Lead a class discussion of the importance that these images of mood, activity, ideals, and hopes play and how vital they are to our national unity.

9. **How does this poem help to give you a picture of America?**

   Answers will vary but should include the concept that America was begun through sacrifice, fearlessness, and faith, not through a desire for "bright jewels," "wealth of seas, the spoils of war."

10. **How did the "Pilgrim Fathers" show the spirit indicated by the motto and statue that are mentioned on page 295?**

The motto states: "One flag, one land, one heart, one hand, One Nation evermore!" Encourage students to explain how the Pilgrims exhibited that spirit.

See notes in the Reader, page 303.

### Class Reading.

Bring to class and read:

"Damaris Goes to School," Smith (in *St. Nicholas,* September, 1920). See note on *St. Nicholas* under "The Character of Columbus."

### Library Reading.

The resources listed here were printed in *St. Nicholas* and *The Youth's Companion,* neither of which are any longer in print.

## *Extended Activity:*

As the students may recall from the "Extended Activity" in "Part I," "The Frost Spirit," end rhyme in poetry refers to the words at the ends of two or more lines that have the same sounds. Slant rhyme refers to words at the ends of lines that look similar but do not have exact rhyme, such as wall and soul. Have students identify the slant rhyme words in Hemans's poem.

Answers: coast, tossed; come, gloom; afar, war.

NAME_____CLASS_____DATE_____

## THE LANDING OF THE PILGRIM FATHERS, p. 301

As you may recall from the "Extended Activity" in "Part I," "The Frost Spirit," end rhyme in poetry refers to the words at the ends of two or more lines that have the same sounds. Slant rhyme refers to words at the ends of lines that look similar but do not have exact rhyme, such as wall and soul. Identify the slant rhyme words in Hemans's poem.

_____     _____

_____     _____

_____     _____

# THE COURTSHIP OF MILES STANDISH, p. 304

## SUMMARY

"The Courtship of Miles Standish" is the fictional poem of the marriage of John and Priscilla Alden, two of the three main characters in the poem along with Miles Standish. The story begins in Miles's house where he was reading Ceasar's battle strategies, and John Alden was writing letters to send to England via the *Mayflower* which was to sail on the morrow. As he wrote, John filled his letters with the praises of a young Pilgrim woman, Priscilla.

At length, Miles interrupted his reading to express his regret for the loss of his wife and his desire for companionship. He determined to propose to Priscilla and asked John to meet with her and make the proposal on his behalf since he considered John to be a man of words while he was just a man of war. John was crushed that Miles wanted Priscilla for his wife when John had dreams of marrying her, but for the sake of his friendship with Miles, he kept quiet about his thoughts and consented to do Miles's bidding.

Gathering his courage, John visited Priscilla with Miles's proposal which she promptly rejected, wanting, rather, the hand of John. Miles became violently angry when he learned that Priscilla had rejected him and blamed John for being a traitor. Forthwith, Miles departed with his army to quell an Indian uprising. John, in dismay over losing Priscilla and failing in his duty to Miles, determined to sail back to England on the *Mayflower* to escape the lost love of Priscilla and the lost friendship with Miles.

The following day as the *Mayflower* prepared to sail, John prepared to board until he saw Priscilla in the distance. He determined to stay in Plymouth and protect her the rest of his life.

In the course of time, a messenger brought word that Miles had been killed in battle, so John and Priscilla were free to marry. At their wedding ceremony, Miles returned from battle very much alive and repentant for his anger. He gave John and Priscilla his blessing, and they were happily married.

1. **Read the history of the Pilgrims' settlement at Plymouth.**
   Encourage students to read about the first pilgrims in an encyclopedia before they read this poem.

2. **Describe the Plymouth of the first year of the settlement.**
   The *Mayflower* landed at Cape Cod on November 20, 1620, the Pilgrims eventually settling in Plymouth. The first year was extremely difficult with little food or shelter, cold weather, illness, and death that claimed nearly half the members. After surviving the winter, those that remained learned survival skills such as fishing and gardening with the help of the Indians. The following autumn, they held a festival to celebrate their survival in the New World.

3. **How long had the Pilgrims been in their new home at the time this story opens?**
   The characters in this poem all came to America on the *Mayflower* in November, 1620. The poem describes the departure of the

*Mayflower's* return to England which occurred in April, 1621, so the events in this story took place within that time span.

4. **What tells you this?**

The poet makes reference to the death of Miles Standish's wife, Rose, and Priscilla's mother, father, and brother which occurred that first winter.

5. **Find lines that tell how hard the first winter had been.**

Page 309, lines 14-16: "She is alone in the world; her father and mother and brother Died in the winter together; I saw her going and coming, Now to the grave of the dead, and now to the bed of the dying." Page 314, lines 1-3; "He remembered that day in the winter; After the first great snow, when he broke a path from the village, Reeling and plunging along through the drifts that encumbered the doorway."

6. **What tells you that the captain had read his Caesar many times?**

Page 307, line 3-6: "Finally down from its shelf he dragged the ponderous Roman, Seated himself at the window, and opened the book, and in silence Turned o'er the well-worn leaves, where thumb marks thick on the margin, Like the trample of feet, proclaimed the battle was hottest."

7. **What principle of conduct did he learn from Caesar's victories?**

Miles Standish begins his reflections of Caesar on page 307, line 15, where he describes his respect for this "wonderful man" in the following lines. Among other things, the principle of conduct he learned is found on page 308, lines 14-15: "That's why I always say: if you wish a thing to be well done, You must do it yourself, you must not leave it to others."

8. **When did he entirely disregard this principle?**

He disregarded this principle when he asked John Alden to go to Priscilla to offer her Miles's hand in marriage. Page 309, lines 23-25: "Go to the damsel Priscilla, the loveliest maiden of Plymouth; Say that a blunt old Captain, a man not of words but of actions, Offers his hand and his heart, the hand and heart of a soldier."

9. **What excuse did he give for not acting upon it?**

Page 309, lines 27-28: "I am a maker of war, and not a maker of phrases. You, who are bred as a scholar, can say it in elegant language."

10. **Find the words in which John Alden tells why he will undertake the Captain's errand.**

Page 310, line 26: "Then made the answer John Alden: 'The name of friendship is sacred; What you demand in that name, I have not the power to deny you!'"

**11. What ideal of friendship had he?**

"Friendship prevailed over love." John gave up his love for Priscilla for his friendship with Miles. Encourage students to support or refute this ideal of friendship.

**12. What do you think of Alden's description of his friend's character?**

John's description of Miles' character can be found on page 316, line 12, to page 317, line 3. Direct a class discussion of the description. Was his description accurate? Did he believe the description himself? Whom was he trying to persuade, Priscilla or himself? How does this show his loyalty to Miles?

**13. Find the lines in which Priscilla shows her love of truth and loyalty.**

Page 331, line 4: "Let us, then, be what we are and speak what we think, and in all things, Keep ourselves loyal to truth and the sacred professions of friendship."

**14. When does Miles Standish show himself most noble?**

He is most noble when he arrives at their wedding and apologizes for his harsh behavior. Page 343, line 3: "Forgive me! I have been angry and hurt—too long have I cherished the feeling; I have been cruel and hard, but now, thank God! it is ended."

**15. Who is the real hero of this poem?**

The three main characters in the poem are Miles, John, and Priscilla. Have students define the characteristics of a hero and determine which of the main characters best displayed those traits using lines from the poem to support their answers.

**16. Commit to memory lines which seem to you to express the moral truths and the high ideals which the poem puts before us.**

Several lines express those truths and ideals. Have students identify and memorize the lines that they think best define moral truths and high ideals.

**17. Make a brief outline of the story.**

Students may want to use a topic outline using the subtitles as guides. A sample outline could include the following:

I.  Miles Standish
   A. Appearance
   B. Relationship to John Alden
   C. Love for arms and battle
II. Love and Friendship
   A. Caesar
   B. Miles's wish to marry Priscilla
   C. Request to John

   III.   The Lover's Errand
         A. Walk to Priscilla's house
         B. Message delivered
   IV.   John Alden
         A. Despair and decision to leave on the *Mayflower*
         B. Report to Miles
         C. Miles attends the council
    V.   The Sailing of the *Mayflower*
         A. Miles goes to war
         B. John's decision
         C. The *Mayflower* departs
   VI.   Priscilla
         A. Priscilla's request
         B. John's response
   VII.   The March of Miles Standish
         A. Miles meets Wattawamat
         B. Wattawamat's insults
         C. Miles's response
   VIII.   The Spinning-Wheel
         A. Alden's activities
         B. Priscilla's activities
         C. The message
   IX.   The Wedding Day
         A. The ceremony
         B. Miles returns
         C. Bridal procession

**18. You will be interested in the pictures in the edition of "The Courtship of Miles Standish," illustrated by Wyeth.**

Houghton Mifflin's 1920 edition of N. C. Wyeth's painting of "The Courtship of Miles Standish" sold for $244,500. More information on Wyeth's work can be found at:

http://www.maineantiquedigest.com/articles/barr1099.htm

Also note that the cover picture on this Guide and the Reader by Laslett John Pott depicts a part of this story.

**19. Longfellow's quiet humor is shown at its best in this poem; point out examples of it.**

Encourage students to identify the passages that they found to be humorous.

**20. This poem portrays Puritan life and character; it has historical value; and it shows the beauty of a loyalty to friendship that would make any sacrifice of self rather than sacrifice an ideal; which of these values do you think Longfellow sought most to impress upon us?**

Answers will vary. The values of honesty, loyalty, friendship, and integrity are all present in this poem. Have students identify others and discuss which ones Longfellow emphasized.

21. **In "Part III" of this Reader, you learned how we owe our "inheritance of freedom" to our forefathers. Do Americans of today owe any debt to men like Miles Standish and John Alden?**

   Their courage, honesty, and bravery contributed to the formation of our country. Americans do owe them a debt of gratitude.

22. **What ideals of freedom brought the Pilgrims to America?**

   The most obvious ideal was that of religious freedom; additional goals may have included the possibility for new opportunities and adventure. Encourage students to suggest other ideals based on the readings in this book and other research they have done.

23. **Quote lines to show that Priscilla was a thrifty homemaker.**

   Priscilla's thrift is seen throughout the section, "The Spinning-Wheel," which begins on page 337, where John praises her industry.

24. **Compare the life of the present-day homemaker with that of Priscilla, to show how far we have departed from the simplicity and thrift of early days in America.**

   Priscilla's chief activity in this poem was that of spinning which resulted in all the cloth materials required for life in the colony. Few homemakers today sew their family's supply of clothing; fewer yet spin their own thread to sew the clothing. Have students identify other comparisons between a Pilgrim homemaker's life in the 1620s and life in the twenty-first century.

25. **On page 298 you were told that we gain a knowledge of our homeland by getting a glimpse of "snapshots of our nation's childhood." Mention some of the scenes from America's "childhood" you have seen from this poem.**

   A variety of responses will surface. Snapshots of the character and values of the Pilgrims and friendship, pain in death and love, housing, warfare, bravery, and survival all appear in the poem.

26. **Find in the glossary the meaning of: arsenal (p. 305), ensign (p. 308), carded, pedigree, estates, stature (pp. 312-317), attitude, quiver (p. 321), entreaty, pallet, verge (pp. 324-328), loadstone (p. 328), parley, gigantic, trophy (pp. 334-337), apparition, adage (p. 342-343).**

27. **Pronounce: athletic, sinew (p. 304), comely, memoirs, taciturn (pp. 307-310), aerial (p. 311), stalwart, gesture (p. 322), capacious, victual (pp. 326-327), subtle (p. 328), hearth (p. 342).**

**Class Reading.**

Select passages to be read aloud in class; bring to class and read Psalm 100, The Bible, Moulton edition. Priscilla was singing Psalm 100, "the grand old Puritan anthem," when John approached her with Miles's request for marriage, page 312, line 17. Proverbs 31 is also referred to on page 338, line 21, when John describes Priscilla.

**A Suggested Problem.**

Dramatize selected scenes from the poem.

**Library Reading.**

Since these materials are no longer in print, have students research other resources on Pilgrim life. (*Mary of Plymouth*, Lost Classics Book Company, describes the first ten years of life in Plymouth.)

**Suggestions for Theme Topics.**

1. The Pilgrim Tercentenary is a three-hundred year celebration of the Pilgrims' coming to America. The original *Elson Readers* were written about 300 years after the Pilgrims first came.

2. Longfellow's knowledge of the Bible as shown in this poem. Longfellow sprinkles biblical references throughout the poem. The Bible was one of Miles's three books and appeared frequently in the poem. In addition to direct references to Psalm 100 and Proverbs 31, (see "Class Reading" above) Longfellow inserts many Biblical phrases. Have students identify the phrases and their location, remembering that the King James version of the Bible would likely have been Longfellow's source. Possible answers include: Page 309, line 8: "'Tis not good for man to be alone." Genesis 2:18; Page 313, line 12: "Let not him that putteth his hand to the plow look backwards." Luke 9:62; Page 316, line 15: "How with the people of God he had chosen to suffer affliction." Hebrews 11:25; Page 319, line 2-3: "Leading me out of the land of darkness, the bondage of error, Through the sea, that shall lift the walls of its water around me," is a reference to Moses leading the children of Israel through the Red Sea in Exodus; Page 324, line 3: "Beautiful were his feet on the purple tops of the mountain." Isaiah 52:7; Page 341, line 9: "Those whom the Lord hath united, let no man put them asunder!" Matthew 19:6.

3. Thrift in Pilgrim days compared with thrift today. Refer to question #24 above. For additional comparisons have students complete a Venn Diagram showing the comparisons.

# Extended Activities:

1. Students should note that this is a free verse poem without rhyme scheme or rhythm. It is a narrative poem, one that tells a story, in this case a romance narrative. Longfellow does not write in the typical poetic form using stanzas with an equal number of lines to divide the work. However, he uses a variety of poetic terms and figurative language throughout the work, among them simile, metaphor, allusion, alliteration, and assonance. Students should be able to readily identify these terms and locate them in the poem.

Assign each subtitle to a group of students and have them identify as many of the terms listed above as they can, guided by these definitions and their accompanying examples from the poem.

Simile—compares two unlike things saying one is like or as the other. Page 304, line 13: "Brown as a nut was his face."

Metaphor—compares two unlike things saying one is the other. Page 306, line 13: Rose Standish, Beautiful rose of love."

Allusion—the author's reference to some well-known person, place, thing, or event in history, with which he assumes the reader is acquainted. Page 304, line 19: "Whom St. Gregory saw, and exclaimed, 'Not Angles but Angels.'"

Alliteration—repeats the same beginning consonant sounds in two or more words in a line. Page 304, line 8: "Cutlass and corselet of steel."

Assonance—repeats the same vowel sounds in two or more words in a line. Page 304, line 2: "To and fro in a room of his simple and primitive dwelling."

2. Have students design a book cover for "The Courtship of Miles Standish." The cover should include: the front cover including design and title, the inside front flap containing a summary of the book, the inside back flap describing the author, and the back cover containing endorsements from the readers.

| Author Information | Back Cover | Spine | Front Cover | Summary |

Name_____Class_____Date_____

## The Courtship of Miles Standish, p. 304

1. You should note that this is a free verse poem without rhyme scheme or rhythm. It is a narrative poem, one that tells a story, in this case a romance narrative. Longfellow does not write in the typical poetic form using stanzas with an equal number of lines to divide the work. However, he uses a variety of poetic terms and figurative language throughout the work, among them simile, metaphor, allusion, alliteration, and assonance. You should be able to readily identify these terms and locate them in the poem.

    Identify in the subtitle assigned to you as many of the terms listed above as you can, guided by these definitions and their accompanying examples from the poem.

    Simile—compares two unlike things saying one is like or as the other. Page 304, line 13: "Brown as a nut was his face."

    Metaphor—compares two unlike things saying one is the other. Page 306, line 13: Rose Standish, Beautiful rose of love."

    Allusion—the author's reference to some well-known person, place, thing, or event in history, with which he assumes the reader is acquainted. Page 304, line 19: "Whom St. Gregory saw, and exclaimed, 'Not Angles but Angels.'"

    Alliteration—repeats the same beginning consonant sounds in two or more words in a line. Page 304, line 8: "Cutlass and corselet of steel."

    Assonance—repeats the same vowel sounds in two or more words in a line. Page 304, line 2: "To and fro in a room of his simple and primitive dwelling."

Simile—

_____

_____

_____

_____

Metaphor—

_____

_____

_____

_____

**Allusion—**

_____
_____
_____
_____

**Alliteration—**

_____
_____
_____
_____

**Assonance—**

_____
_____
_____
_____

2.  Design a book cover for "The Courtship of Miles Standish." The cover should include: the front cover including design and title, the inside front flap containing a summary of the book, the inside back flap describing the author, and the back cover containing endorsements from the readers.

## THE PINE TREE SHILLINGS, P. 348

1. **Describe bartering in the early colonial days.**

   Since the people had no money, they traded goods for services rendered. "For instance, if a man wanted to buy a coat, he perhaps exchanged a bearskin for it. If he wished for a barrel of molasses, he might purchase it with a pile of pine boards. Musket bullets were used instead of farthings." Indians used wampum to trade, and "fish, bushels of corn, or cords of wood instead of silver or gold" were used to pay debts.

2. **Who was the first mint master?**

   "The Captain John Hull aforesaid was the mint master of Massachusetts."

3. **Upon what conditions did he manufacture the coins?**

   He "was to have one shilling out of every twenty to pay him for the trouble of making them."

4. **Where did the silver come from?**

   To make the shillings, the people contributed all their old silver consisting of cans, tankards, buckles, spoons, buttons, and sword hilts, along with "bullion from the mines of South America."

5. **Describe the pine tree shillings.**

   "All this old and new silver being melted down and coined, the result was an immense amount of splendid shillings, sixpences, and three pences. Each had the date 1652 on the one side and the figure of a pine tree on the other."

6. **Tell the story of the wedding of Betsey Hull and Samuel Sewell.**

   Samuel Sewell requested her hand in marriage which Captain Hull gladly gave. After the ceremony, Captain Hull had his servants bring in a large scale. They put Betsey on one side and filled the other with shillings from Captain Hull's iron chest. When the scales balanced, Captain Hull told Samuel to take the shillings to care for his daughter. "It is not every wife that's worth her weight in silver."

7. **Point out humorous passages.**

   Answers will vary. Humorous passages can be found throughout the story, for example: description of the chair, Betsey, and the weigh-in, along with the final sentence that states, "If wedding portions nowadays were paid as Miss Betsey's was, young ladies would not pride themselves upon an airy figure, as many of them do."

8. **This story is taken from *Grandfather's Chair*; what other stories from this book have you read?**

"The Stamp Act," page 263, is from this book. Have students review the passage.

9. **What picture of early America do you gain from this story?**
   Students may identify various pictures. Among them, thrift in their method of furniture repair and minting money, in Hull's saving of money, honesty, and good character.

10. **You have now read all the selections of the group called "Early America." On page 298 these are spoken of as "snapshots of our nation's childhood"; mention several pictures of early America that you have gained from reading this group.**
    Have students refer to "The Landing of the Pilgrim Fathers," discussion question #8 and "The Courtship of Miles Standish," question #25, to aid them in their reflections.

11. **Find in the glossary the meaning of: venerable, bullion, diligently, ceremony, ponderous.**

12. **Pronounce: ominous, specie.**
    See notes in the Reader, page 352.

## Class Reading.

Select passages to be read aloud in class.

## Outline for Testing Silent Reading.

Make an outline to guide you in telling the story. See outline format in "The Courtship of Miles Standish," question #17, which can be used as a guide to create this outline.

## Library Reading.

"Our Colonial Coins," Mathews (in *St Nicholas*, September, 1876). *St. Nicholas*, a youth magazine in the late 1800s/early 1900s is no longer in print.

## Suggestions for Theme Topics.

1. Bartering: its advantages and disadvantages over the use of money. Hawthorne mentions some of the items used for bartering. Have students identify those items and explain why they would have been useful to the receiver. Have them brainstorm items today that could be valuable for bartering among their peers. What items would be considered equal in value? What services would be rendered to receive these items?

2. A coin collection which I have seen. Visit a coin shop or invite a coin collector to visit your class.

3. Emblems on coins. Research and illustrate the various emblems that have existed over the years.

4. What you know about our government mints today; where located; where the gold, silver, nickel, and copper come from. From the original pine tree shilling to our current coins, money has made many changes, including how it is made and designed. Have students research the manufacturing methods and designs of money today and compare it with the early money system used in the colonies that this story describes.

## *Extended Activity:*

This section, titled "Early America," provides students with a variety of viewpoints from the period including the man who "discovered" America to Pilgrims in general, as well as specific Pilgrims, and their lifestyles. These narratives, each in their own way, helping us to visualize early American life, gave us glimpses into the lives of real people. They focused on a specific event, gave the reader a clear picture of the people and action with specific details that held the reader's attention, and used a range of strategies to help the reader experience the adventure, including dialogue and suspense. Have students write a narrative story about a person or event with whom they are personally acquainted. The event should include an element of suspense and/or humor that holds the reader's attention. Like these stories, the student's writing should make clear the setting of the story, give a vivid and colorful description of the characters, and describe the event or suspense in a way that brings the story to a satisfying end. The narrative should include dialogue with use of proper punctuation to indicate speakers, as well as following the basic rules of grammar and spelling.

## THE PINE-TREE SHILLINGS, P. 348

This section, titled "Early America," provides you with a variety of viewpoints from the period including the man who "discovered" America to Pilgrims in general, as well as specific Pilgrims, and their lifestyles. These narratives, each in their own way, helped you to visualize early American life, giving you glimpses into the lives of real people. They focused on a specific event, gave you a clear picture of the people and action with specific details that held your attention, and used a range of strategies to help you experience the adventure, including dialogue and suspense.

Write a narrative story about a person or event with whom you are personally acquainted. The event should include an element of suspense and/or humor that holds the reader's attention. Like these stories, your writing should make clear the setting of the story, give a vivid and colorful description of the characters, and describe the event or suspense in a way that brings the story to a satisfying end. The narrative should include dialogue with use of proper punctuation to indicate speakers, as well as following the basic rules of grammar and spelling.

## AMERICAN SCENES
### AND LEGENDS

### MY VISIT TO NIAGARA, P. 353

1. **Why was Hawthorne at first disappointed in Niagara?**

   His high expectations of the grandeur of Niagara were about to be realized and he was "loath to exchange the pleasures of hope for those of memory so soon." He had approached the Niagara, "haunted with a vision of foam and fury, and dizzy cliffs, and an ocean tumbling down out of the sky—a scene, in short, which Nature had too much good taste and calm simplicity to realize. My mind had struggled to adapt these false conceptions to the reality, and finding the effort vain, a wretched sense of disappointment weighed me down."

2. **How did he finally come to know that it is one of the world's wonders?**

   "Gradually, and after much contemplation, I came to know, by my own feelings, that Niagara is indeed a wonder of the world, and not the less wonderful because time and thought must be employed in comprehending it."

3. **What feelings did Niagara produce in Hawthorne?**

   He felt that he "was unworthy to look at the great falls, and careless about beholding them again." But the longer he contemplated it, the more awed he became. "Night after night I dreamed of it, and was gladdened every morning by the consciousness of a growing capacity to enjoy it."

4. **What effect on the reader did he seek to produce?**

   He sought to impress upon the reader, the same sense of Niagara's power and awe that it inspired in him. "The beholder must stand beside it in the simplicity of his heart, suffering the mighty scene to work its own impression."

5. **What does Hawthorne say is necessary in order to appreciate nature?**

   He says that nature requires more than a passing glance to fully appreciate its grandeur. It requires time and stillness, using the power of the senses to absorb nature's beauty. The last day at Niagara, he sat on the Table Rock, his feet dangling over the edge, hearing the thunder, feeling the mist, seeing the foaming water. "Never before had my mind been in such perfect unison with the scene."

6. **Account for the fact that Niagara grew on Hawthorne.**

   Time, observation, and contemplation changed his perceptions of Niagara. From his initial sense of disappointment, his "enjoyment became the more rapturous, because the spot so famous through the world" was now his.

7. **What comments of other observers does Hawthorne give?**

He describes the fat English gentleman who peeks over the rock and grins, his wife who is so intent on watching her son that she doesn't see Niagara, a native American who comes and leaves "without one new idea or sensation of his own," the visitor who only notes and contests the position of Goat Island, traders who agree that the Niagara is "worth looking at," but they'd prefer the "noble stone works of Lockport," and the young man who, in his awe, dropped his staff, and it crashed on Table Rock.

8. **What do you think determines the kind of response an observer gives to a wonderful scene in nature, such as Niagara?**

Encourage students to discuss the kinds of responses that may occur.

9. **Have you ever seen Niagara? If so, tell about your feelings.**

Answers will vary.

10. **What other famous American scenes have you read about or seen?**

Answers will vary.

11. **On page 298 you were told of things that help us to picture our country; what do scenes such as Niagara add to the meaning our country has for us?**

Student responses will vary but should reflect the idea that scenes such as this help us to experience the many contrasting landscapes and natural wonders we find in our country.

12. **Find in the glossary the meaning of: cataract, native, turmoil.**

13. **Pronounce: loath, heroism, route, unwonted, minutely, reptile, tremor, abyss, tour, idea.**

See notes in the Reader, page 360.

## Library Reading.

"A Descent in to the Maelstrom," Poe.

## Suggestions for Theme Topics.

1. A description of a visit to a new building, a park, the country, or to some city.

2. A diary of an imaginary trip, based on material in your geography. Have students choose a remote location in a foreign country and research its climate and resources. Students should make a list of all the items they will need for survival in that location. They

are to design a vehicle that will carry them and their supplies to that location for a short visit.

## *Extended Activity:*

In this story of Hawthorne's visit to Niagara, he describes how his expectations of the visit differed from what he experienced when he finally saw it for himself. Have students think about an event in their lives that turned out differently than they expected. Have them complete the following chart to illustrate or write what they imagined the event would be like and what it was really like.

| **What I Expected** | **What I Experienced** |
| --- | --- |
|  |  |

NAME_____ CLASS_____ DATE_____

## My Visit to Niagara, p. 353

In this story of Hawthorne's visit to Niagara, he describes how his expectations of the visit differed from what he experienced when he finally saw it for himself. Think about an event in your life that turned out differently than you expected. Complete the following chart to illustrate or write what you imagined the event would be like and what it was really like.

| What I Expected | What I Experienced |
| --- | --- |
|  |  |

## FROM MORN TILL NIGHT ON A FLORIDA RIVER, p. 361

1. **From this selection what do you think of the author's power of description?**

   Lanier uses many sensory details, details that appeal to the five senses, to help the reader visualize his river voyage. Have students find descriptive lines and identify the senses to which they appeal.

2. **Mention instances in which he makes use of humor to add to his descriptive power.**

   Have students identify the passages that contained humor for them.

3. **Quote his words describing the Ocklawaha.**

   The best descriptions of the river can be found on page 361, lines 8-14 and page 363, lines 14-28.

4. **What does the author mean by saying, "We find it a river without banks"?**

   Page 363, line 15: "The swift, deep current meanders between tall lines of trees; beyond these, on either side, there is water also-a thousand shallow rivulets lapsing past the bases of a multitude of trees." The author suggests that the river spread out across the land and had no clear river bank.

   **Have you ever seen such a river?**

   Answers will vary.

5. **In your own words, give a description of the alligator's home.**

   The author says the alligator lives in the "handsomest residence in America." Living in a house in the cove, under the overhanging leaves of the river bank, his bed is made of moss, and lily pads serve as his apartment walls, as well as his covers. He never quarrels with his cook, and the river current maid sweeps his house. Wind cannot destroy his home, rain poses no problem, and he never sees snow. Finally, with a flip of his tail, he can change houses any time he chooses.

6. **Make a list of things Lanier saw on this trip that he would not see on a trip down a river in New England.**

   In addition to the alligator, Lanier mentions various trees, cypresses, palms, and magnolias, and birds such as the water turkey which inhabit this river bank that would not appear in colder climates.

7. **What gives this piece of prose its musical quality?**

   Lanier's appeal to the senses and his vivid descriptions of the solitude and beauty of nature give this piece its musical quality.

8. **What comparison do you find in lines 21 and 22, page 363?**

"The lilies sitting on their round lily pads like white queens on green thrones" compares lilies to queens.

9. **Point out some examples of alliteration, that is, similar sounds at the beginning of successive words, as "steamboat had started"; for what purpose does the author use alliteration?**

   The use of alliteration enhances the musical quality of the piece. Students should be encouraged to look for examples of alliteration. Possible answers include: page 362, line 13: "twisted it, twiddled it;" page 362, line 24: "clear, curves round;" page 362, line 29: "marvelous mosses for his mattress;" page 363, line 28: "became a black band."

10. **On page 298 you read that our country presents many moods; what mood does this selection portray?**

    Mood refers to the feelings the reader experiences as he reads. On 298, the author mentions moods such as stern, grave, placid, laughing, and angry. Encourage the students to explain the mood they feel as they read this piece.

11. **Does this selection make you think that the author loved his southland home? What tells you this?**

    Clearly, the author loved his home. From the first sentence, "For a perfect journey God gave us a perfect day," to the last sentence, "When you wake in the morning you will feel as new as Adam," the author expresses his love for this home through his insights and friendship with nature there.

12. **Find in the glossary the meaning of: avocation, preposterous, contortion, placid.**

13. **Pronounce: contemplative, leisurely, infinite.**

**Outline for Testing Silent Reading.**

   Make an outline to guide you in telling the story.
   A sample outline follows.
   I. The Ocklawaha River
   II. The steamboat, *Marion*
   III. The water snake
   IV. The alligator
   V. The riverbank
   VI. The night of glory

## *Extended Activity:*

This brief story of Lanier's voyage on a Florida river is a memoir, written in first person describing an event that the author personally experienced. Have the students complete the following web to list details that could only be described by the person experiencing them. After students have listed their details, have them share their details and group them into similar categories such as sensory images, types of animals and plants, and personal experiences of the author.

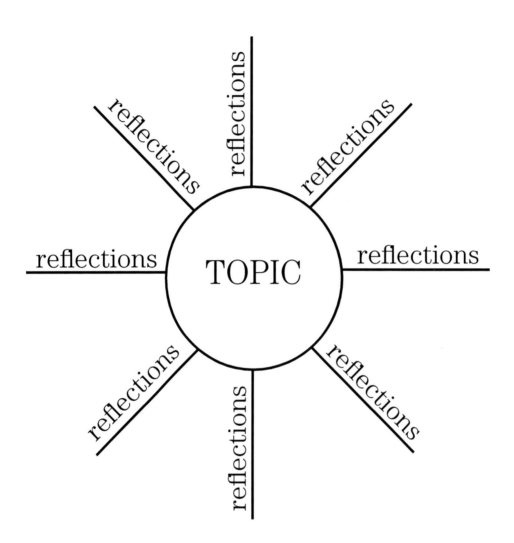

NAME_____CLASS_____DATE_____

## FROM MORN TILL NIGHT ON A FLORIDA RIVER, P. 361

This brief story of Lanier's voyage on a Florida river is a memoir, written in first person describing an event that the author personally experienced. Complete the following web to list details that could only be described by the person experiencing them. After you have listed your details, share your details and group them into similar categories such as sensory images, types of animals and plants, and personal experiences of the author.

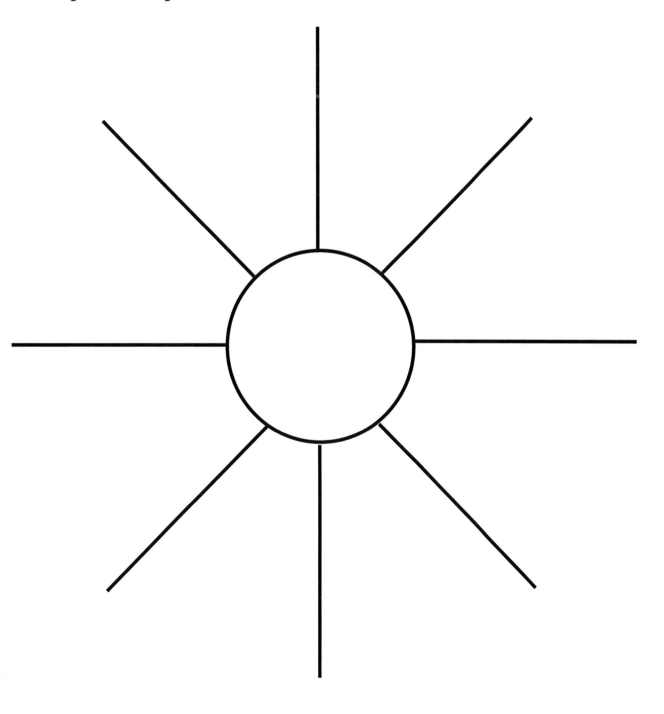

## I Sigh for the Land of the Cypress and Pine, p. 365

1. **What part of the country does the poet mean when he refers to the "land of the cypress and pine"?**
   The poet refers to the deep South where the "cypress and pine," as well as the "snowy flower of the orange" are located.

2. **Mention things named in the first stanza which characterize this land.**
   Besides the cypress and pine, the poet names the jessamine (jasmine), the woodbine, the moss on the green oak tree, and the "sun-bright land."

3. **Have you ever seen the "moss on the green oak tree"?**
   Answers will vary.

4. **What birds does the poet mention?**
   The poet mentions the hummingbird, the mockingbird, and the whippoorwill.

5. **Are these birds found only in the South?**
   No, they are found throughout the United States.

6. **Have you ever heard the whippoorwill?**
   Answers will vary. Various web sites recording a variety of bird sounds are available on the Internet. Encourage the students to locate the whippoorwill's call.

7. **Do you think the poet was right in calling its note a "moan"?**
   Answers will vary.

8. **On page 297 you were told of things that express what America means to its citizens. Love of the homeland is a condition of good citizenship; what do you love about the section in which you live?**
   Answers will vary.

9. **You will enjoy hearing the Victor record, "Mocking Bird," Gluck, with bird voices by Kellogg.**

10. **Find in the glossary the meaning of: roundelay, rugged.**

**Library Reading.**
   "The Whippoorwill," van Dyke in *The Builders and Other Poems*.

**Suggestions for Theme Topics.**
   1. Why you like your own home section best.
   2. What can you do to make it still more lovely?

## Extended Activity:

1. The preceding selections in this section are autobiographical, personal accounts that describe an event in the author's life including his thoughts, feelings, and opinions about the event. From reading his work, the reader can get a good picture of the author's character and purpose for writing. Have students complete the following web based on one of the selections: "My Visit to Niagara," "From Morn Till Night on a Florida River," or "I Sigh For the Land of the Cypress and Pine." When the web is complete have them share their observations with the class.

2. In the preceding selections, the authors visited places that held special meaning for them. Have students complete the following chart: a place to which I would like to travel, why I would choose that place, how I would get there, what I would take along, and what I would expect to see when I arrive.

NAME_____ CLASS_____ DATE_____

## I SIGH FOR THE LAND OF CYPRESS AND PINE, P. 365

1.  The preceding selections in this section are autobiographical, personal accounts that describe an event in the author's life including his thoughts, feelings, and opinions about the event. From reading his work, the reader can get a good picture of the author's character and purpose for writing. Complete the following web based on one of the selections: "My Visit to Niagara," "From Morn Till Night on a Florida River," or "I Sigh For the Land of the Cypress and Pine." When the web is complete, share your observations with the class.

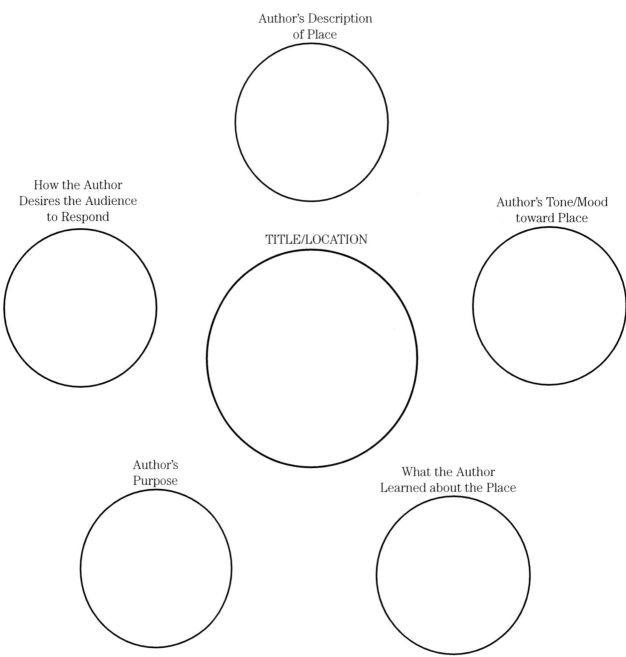

Author's Description
of Place

How the Author
Desires the Audience
to Respond

TITLE/LOCATION

Author's Tone/Mood
toward Place

Author's
Purpose

What the Author
Learned about the Place

2.  In the preceding selections, the authors visited places that held special meaning for them. Complete the following chart: a place to which you would like to travel, why you would choose that place, how you would get there, what you would take along, and what you would expect to see when you arrive.

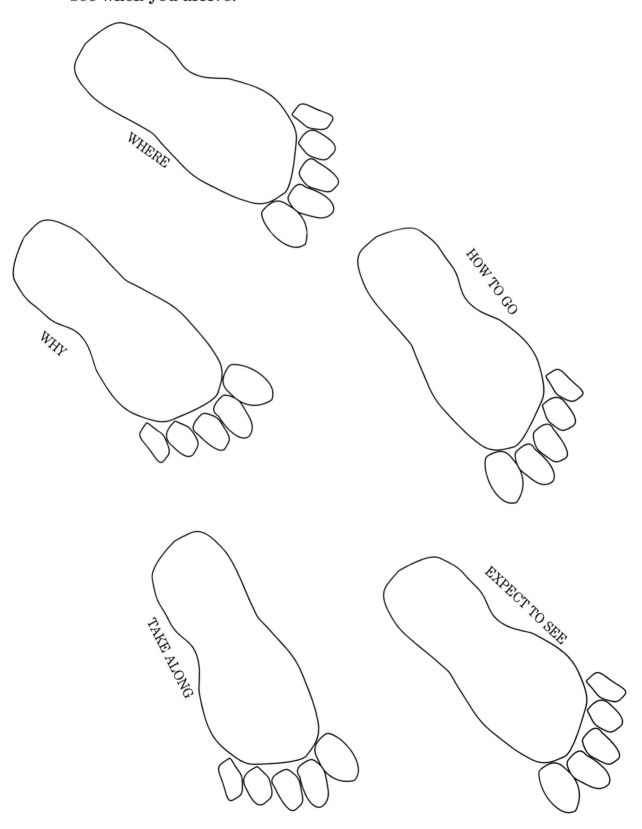

## THE LEGEND OF SLEEPY HOLLOW, p. 367

### SUMMARY

In "The Legend of Sleepy Hollow," we read the story of Ichabod Crane, a poor schoolmaster, and his encounter with the village legend, the headless horseman. Besides his role as a schoolmaster, Ichabod was a player of children's games, a singer of songs, a teller of tales, and a respected community member. In his community wanderings, he developed an interest in Katrina, a local farmer's daughter. However, Brom Bones, another local man, also had an interest in her and did everything in his power to harass and shame Ichabod in Katrina's eyes.

As the story unfolds, Katrina's father invited the village to his farm for a quilting frolic. Ichabod dismissed school to attend the event. After the feasting, dancing, and story telling, Ichabod went to Katrina to say goodnight but she rebuffed him, and he returned home disconsolate and moody.

As he approached the bridge at dead of night, he discovered a fellow traveler who had all the appearances of the headless horseman. Ichabod galloped off in terror, but the horseman followed. As he approached Ichabod, he hurled his head at Ichabod, throwing him from the horse. The horseman galloped off into the night and all that was found of Ichabod the next morning was his hat alongside a smashed pumpkin. Brom Bones married Katrina and looked "exceedingly knowing" whenever the story of Ichabod's calamity arose. Ichabod was not seen in the village again, but his encounter with the headless horseman was added to the village legend.

1.  **What was the situation of Sleepy Hollow?**

    Sleepy Hollow was located in New York on the Hudson River. "A drowsy, dreamy influence seems to hang over the land, and to pervade the very atmosphere. Some say that the place was bewitched by a high German doctor, during the early days of the settlement; others, that an old Indian chief, the prophet or wizard of his tribe, held his powwows there before the country was discovered by Master Hendrick Hudson."

2.  **Make a list of all the names Irving applies to this valley.**

    They include: little valley, lap of land, sequestered glen, Sleepy Hollow, enchanted region, sleepy region, peaceful spot, by-place of nature.

3.  **What impression do these names help to give?**

    These names give one the image of a sleepy little village bathed in mystery and superstition.

4.  **What effect upon the inhabitants had the situation of the valley?**

    It is "under the sway of some witching power that holds a spell over the minds of the good people, causing them to walk in a continual reverie. They are given to all kinds of marvelous beliefs, are subject to trances and visions, and frequently see strange sights, and hear music and voices in the air." Not only the valley inhabitants, but everybody who passes through for a short period is "sure, in a little time, to inhale the witching influence of the air, and begin to grow imaginative—to dream dreams and see apparitions."

5. **In describing this effect, what comparison does Irving use?**

   The people of Sleepy Hollow are undisturbed by migration and change around them. "They are like those little nooks of still water which border a rapid stream; where we may see the straw and bubble riding quietly at anchor, or slowly revolving in their mimic harbor, undisturbed by the rush of the passing current."

6. **Why does Irving exaggerate Ichabod's peculiarities? Find examples of exaggeration.**

   Ichabod, described in this way, leads the reader to believe he is an apt character for the peculiarities of Sleepy Hollow.

   Examples of exaggeration include: "hands that dangled a mile out of his sleeves, feet that might have served for shovels."

7. **What stories does Ichabod enjoy?**

   "His appetite for the marvelous, and his powers of digesting it, were equally extraordinary; and both had been increased by his residence in this spellbound region. No tale was too gross or monstrous for his capacious swallow."

8. **What effect did these have upon him?**

   The tales put "a mere mist before his eyes," "fluttered his excited imagination," and he "was ready to give up the ghost, with the idea that he was struck with a witch's token. His only resource on such occasions, either to drown thought, or drive away evil spirits, was to sing psalm tunes."

9. **For what is the author preparing the reader when he tells this?**

   Clearly the author is preparing the reader for Ichabod's encounter with something mysterious. Have students predict what events may occur as a result of Crane's imaginations.

10. **How do you account for Ichabod's disappearance?**

    Have students discuss what happened to Ichabod. Was he attacked by the headless horseman or Brom Bones?

11. **Make a list of all the hints throughout the story that helped you to come to this conclusion.**

    Have students support their answers to question 10 by listing the hints that led them to their conclusions.

12. **Find lines that show Irving's humor.**

    Have students identify the lines that they found humorous.

13. **In what ways does he create humor?**

    Through exaggeration and vivid imagery, Irving draws his characters with strokes that make them humorous.

14. **Find lines that show Irving's power to describe nature.**

Page 384, line 29 to page 386, line 14 provides a lengthy description of nature as Ichabod noted it on his way to the frolic.

15. **Which description do you think is the finest?**

Answers will vary.

16. **In what humorous way does Irving account for the prevalence of ghosts in a community like Sleepy Hollow?**

Page 389, line 25: "Besides there is no encouragement for ghosts in most of our villages, for they have scarcely had time to finish their first nap, and turn themselves in their graves, before their surviving friends have traveled away from the neighborhood; so that when they turn out at night to walk their rounds they have no acquaintance left to call upon." But in a village like Sleepy Hollow where change seldom occurs, there is plenty of time and room for ghost stories to flourish.

17. **On page 298 you read that legend and history help to acquaint us with our country; how does this story help you to understand America?**

Our country consists of people from many countries with many superstitions and legends. The better we understand their stories, the more we appreciate their characteristics and contributions to our country.

18. **This story gives you a picture of the farmland country of New York after the Revolutionary War; compare this picture to the poverty of country life in early New England, as shown in "The Courtship of Miles Standish."**

"The Courtship of Miles Standish" describes life in a wilderness full of death and danger with little reference to abundance. This story describes in detail the wealth of the land and its people: their food, clothing, and community life.

19. **Why is it good for a country to have its citizens familiar with "scenes and legends," such as you find in this group of selections?**

Have students discuss the value of shared "scenes and legends" that help to build common bonds and forge community.

20. **Find in the glossary the meaning of: legend, tranquility, rustic, superstition (pp. 367-368); architect, urchin, revenue, budget, goblin (pp. 370-374), hardihood, decision (p. 379); despotic, refugee (pp. 382-389).**

21. **Pronounce: inapplicable, patron, elm (pp. 370-376), Herculean, alternative (pp. 379-382), horizon, hospitable (pp. 386-388).**

**Class Reading.**

Description of Ichabod Crane, page 370, lines 1-20; description of
the Van Tassel farm and mansion, page 375, line 34, to page
378, line 21; Brom Bones, page 379, line 7, to page 380, line 8;
the quilting frolic, page 386, line 15, to page 388, line 28; the
headless horseman, page 394, line 5, to page 396, line 35.

**Outline for Testing Silent Reading.**

Make an outline for the story, using the topic headings found in the
text. A sample outline follows.

   I.   The Valley and its superstitions
     A. Location
     B. Mood
  II.  Ichabod Crane and Katrina Van Tassel
     A. Ichabod's appearance
     B. Ichabod's importance in the community
     C. Baltus Van Tassel's farm
     D. Ichabod's visions for Katrina
 III.  Brom Bones
     A. Appearance
     B. Plans for Katrina
 IV.  The quilting frolic
     A. The invitation
     B. Ichabod's ride to the frolic
     C. The dance
     D. Story time at the frolic
  V.  Ichabod's terrifying experiences
     A. The tree
     B. Ichabod's fellow traveler
     C. Ichabod disappears

**Library Reading.**

Another story from *The Sketch Book,* Irving;
A story from *Tales of a Traveller* or from *The Alhambra,* Irving.

**Suggestions for Theme Topics.**

1. Your favorite story by Washington Irving.
2. A description of "Sunnyside" from personal observation or from
   pictures.
3. A dialogue that you imagine might have taken place between
   Ichabod and the old farmer who had been to New York.
4. A comparison of an American school of long ago with my school.

## *Extended Activity:*

1. A caricature is an illustrated drawing of a character with exaggerated or distorted features that make him appear funny or ridiculous. Irving gives vivid and humorous descriptions of several characters in this story: Ichabod Crane, Katrina Van Tassel, Brom Bones, Ichabod's horse, the headless horseman. Have the students choose one character, reread Irving's descriptions, and create a caricature of the character based on Irving's imagery of him or her.

2. The plot line tells the events as they occur in the story. It follows the design of a pyramid and usually consists of five main parts: the exposition explains the background and setting of the story including any of the following: who, what, when, where; the rising action introduces the conflicts and action in the story; the climax is the turning point, the highest part of the pyramid from which the reader can begin to make accurate predictions about the story's end; the falling action wraps up the conflicts; the resolution is the satisfying end of the story when all the problems are solved. Have the student tell the plot line of "The Legend of Sleepy Hollow" by completing the pyramid.

**STORY: The Legend of Sleepy Hollow**

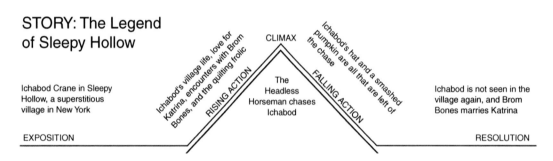

Ichabod Crane in Sleepy Hollow, a superstitious village in New York

EXPOSITION

Ichabod's village life, love for Katrina, encounters with Brom Bones, and the quilting frolic

RISING ACTION

CLIMAX

The Headless Horseman chases Ichabod

FALLING ACTION

Ichabod's hat and a smashed pumpkin are all that are left of the chase

Ichabod is not seen in the village again, and Brom Bones marries Katrina

RESOLUTION

NAME_____CLASS_____DATE_____

## THE LEGEND OF SLEEPY HOLLOW, p. 367

1.  A caricature is an illustrated drawing of a character with exaggerated or distorted features that make him appear funny or ridiculous. Irving gives vivid and humorous descriptions of several characters in this story: Ichabod Crane, Katrina Van Tassel, Brom Bones, Ichabod's horse, the headless horseman. Choose one character, reread Irving's descriptions, and create a caricature of the character based on Irving's imagery of him or her.

2. The plot line tells the events as they occur in the story. It follows the design of a pyramid and usually consists of five main parts: the exposition explains the background and setting of the story including any of the following: who, what, when, where; the rising action introduces the conflicts and action in the story; the climax is the turning point, the highest part of the pyramid from which the reader can begin to make accurate predictions about the story's end; the falling action wraps up the conflicts; the resolution is the satisfying end of the story when all the problems are solved. Tell the plot line of "The Legend of Sleepy Hollow" by completing the pyramid.

STORY:

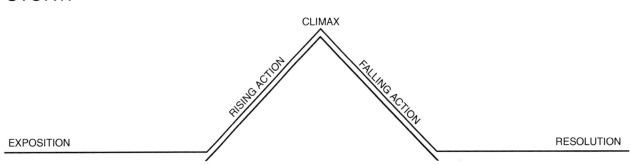

# THE GREAT STONE FACE, p. 402

## SUMMARY

"The Great Stone Face" describes the education of one young boy who lived under the watchful eye of a great face etched in the mountain stone that overlooked his valley. Ernest believed the village prophecy that one day a man with the same noble features and generous spirit as that of the great stone face would appear in the valley. Eagerly he awaited the arrival of that man and was thrilled to learn that soon a man was to arrive. However, Mr. Gathergold, the stone face's likeness, turned out to be stingy and self-centered, so Ernest knew he could not be the one. Next came another man, a great warrior, who claimed to be the face's image. But Old Blood-and-Thunder was stern and hard, not warm and gentle like the stone face on the mountain. In time, the third man came to the valley whose image the village people declared to be that of the stone face. Eagerly Ernest watched for his arrival, but Old Stony Phiz, a great statesman, lacked the stateliness and sympathy portrayed in the stone face, and once again, Ernest was disappointed.

The years progressed and daily Ernest watched the great stone face, learning from its wisdom and kindness. He read, studied, and assumed the characteristics of true greatness he had seen in the great stone face. One day, while reading the poetry of a gifted poet, Ernest was visited by the poet himself who had arrived in the village to meet Ernest whose wisdom and simplicity of life had become famous. Thinking the poet might be the man who wore the likeness of the stone face, Ernest greeted him with delight only to find that even the poet whose great works Ernest admired, lacked the beauty of the face he so loved. As Ernest spoke, the poet recognized the image of the stone face in Ernest and knew that the prophecy had been fulfilled. By mirroring the goodness in the face, Ernest had become the living replica of the great stone face carved in the mountain.

1. **What old prophecy did Ernest hope to see fulfilled?**

   "The purport was, that, at some future day, a child should be born hereabouts, who was destined to become the greatest and noblest personage of his time, and whose countenance, in manhood, should bear an exact resemblance to the Great Stone Face."

2. **What did he see in the Great Stone Face that influenced him?**

   He saw kindness, encouragement, nobility, and an expression "at once grand and sweet, as if it were the glow of a vast, warm heart that embraced all mankind in its affections, and had room for more."

3. **What did Gathergold care most for?**

   Gathergold cared most for his amassed wealth of gold.

4. **For what did he use his wealth?**

   He used his wealth to build an elaborate mansion complete with "magnificent furniture" and "a whole troop of black and white servants."

5. **The "Introduction" on page 298 closed with the question,**

"What is America to me, and what can I do to make her happy?" How would Ernest have answered this question?

Ernest showed kindness, sympathy, and service to his fellow citizens. Encourage students to discuss Ernest's response to that question.

6. **Ernest was seeking all his life for the ideal American citizen. The village folk at first thought that Gathergold was such a man; what did he represent?**

He represented wealth and the end of suffering and poverty in the village.

**Why did he fail?**

His money could not buy his happiness nor did it reduce the poverty of those around him.

7. **How may a wealthy man show himself an ideal citizen of his homeland?**

A wealthy man can invest in the welfare of the community by contributing to local charities, hospitals, libraries, museums, and schools.

8. **Mention some very wealthy men who have used their riches to help their fellow men (founding libraries, etc.).**

In the late 1800s Andrew Carnegie used his wealth to benefit education and public libraries. John Rockefeller founded a university and established foundations to benefit the public. Today the Bill Gates Foundation benefits education and health organizations around the world.

9. **Next, the village folks looked upon Old Blood-and-Thunder as the ideal citizen; what did he represent?**

As a warrior, he represented military strength and safety.

10. **Why did he fail to measure up to the ideal?**

With all his warfare skills and iron will, he lacked the wisdom to bring peace.

11. **Mention some great soldiers who have proved ideal American citizens; tell what they did for our country.**

Students could mention a variety of early American soldiers such as George Washington, as well as current great soldiers such as Colin Powell.

12. **Why did Old Stony Phiz fail to meet the standard?**

While he was considered a great politician and statesman, he lacked the ability to challenge and inspire the people. "He had no other object than to shake hands with his fellow citizens, and neither thought nor cared about any effect which his progress through the country might have upon the election."

**Compare him with Patrick Henry and Abraham Lincoln.**

Both Hale and Lincoln are remembered for their patriotism and their ability to match words with action.

13. **Why did the poet fail? Compare him with Longfellow.**

The poet failed because as he told Ernest, "My life, dear Ernest, has not corresponded with my thought. I have had grand dreams, but they have been only dreams, because I have lived—and that, too, by my own choice—among poor and mean realities. Sometimes even—shall I dare say it?—I lack faith in the grandeur, the beauty, and the goodness which my own works are said to have made more evident in nature and in human life." Refer students to Longfellow's brief biography on page 345. After they have read about Longfellow's impact on culture, have them compare the two poets.

14. **Read again what is said in the "Introduction" on page 22 about what the poets do for us; also what is said in the "Introduction" on page 222 about the part poets have played in the struggle for freedom.**

Page 22: Poets "enrich your appreciation of nature by awakening your powers of imagination and fancy. These men and women interpret for you the deeper meaning of the life about you-things that the eye alone, no matter how keen, can never reveal."

Page 222: "For great poets have played an important part when they wrote patriotic poems that aroused men to struggle for freedom."

15. **How did Ernest show by his simple life that he was himself the ideal citizen?**

"His words had power because they accorded with his thoughts; and his thoughts had reality and depth because they harmonized with the life which he had always lived. It was not mere breath that this preacher uttered; they were the words of life, because a life of good deeds and holy love melted into them." Through these traits he showed himself an ideal citizen.

16. **How does a legend such as this help us to understand what America is, and how we can help to make her happy?**

Answers will vary but should reflect the concept that words and deeds must be in harmony. Like Ernest, our walk should match our talk.

17. **This selection is taken from Hawthorne's "Tales of the White Hills," in *The Snow Image and Other Twice-Told Tales*. In the White Mountains of New Hampshire there is a cliff that resembles a human face. It was this rugged profile, known as "The Old Man of the Mountain," that gave Hawthorne the suggestion for this story.**

18. **Why do you think this is a typical short story?**

A typical short story should include: believable characters, a setting in which the events occur, a problem or conflict that drives the story, and a satisfactory ending. "The Great Stone Face" has all of those items.

19. **On page 298 you read that you can become acquainted with your homeland partly through "snapshots" of the scenes that show her "infinite variety of moods," and partly through her legends. Mention some "moods" and legends found in the five selections you have just read in the group called "American Scenes and Legends."**

"Mood" is the feeling the readers get from the stories, feelings such as laughter, anger, gravity, or calm. Legends include the spirit of laughter, labor, and loyalty among American citizens. Students will experience a variety of moods and see a variety of legends as they read these selections. Encourage student discussions on mood and legend.

20. **Find in the glossary the meaning of: spacious, perpendicular, Titanic, visage, prophecy, ardor, pensive, commodity, portico (pp. 402-406), sordid, mediate, ignoble, clangor, verdant, epaulet (pp. 408-411), truculent, illustrious, spectacle, array, despondent, grandeur (pp. 413-417), utterance (p. 419).**

21. **Pronounce: benign (p. 403), harbinger, beneficence, wound (pp. 407-409), buoyantly (p. 414), obliquely, draught, (pp. 421-422).**

## Class Reading.

Gathergold's wealth and his mansion, page 405, line 7, to page 407, line 4;

The festival for Old Blood-and-Thunder, page 410, line 13, to page 412, line 12;

Ernest addresses the assemblage, page 421, line 10, to end of story.

(*St. Nicholas,* a youth magazine, is no longer in print.)

## Outline for Testing silent Reading.

(a) The Great Stone Face;

(b) The prophecy;

(c) The story of Gathergold;

(d) The story of Old Blood-and-Thunder;

(e) The story of Old Stony Phiz;

(f) The meeting of Ernest and the poet;

(g) The poet's discovery.

**Library Reading.**

> Other stories from the *Snow Image and Other Twice-Told Tales*, Hawthorne;
> A story from *Twice-Told Tales*, Hawthorne;
> *Will o' the Mill*, Stevenson.

**Suggestions for Theme Topics.**

1. Apply to Washington and Lincoln the principle that the life we live is reflected in our features, spirit, and actions.
2. My favorite hero or heroine.
3. The kind of boy or girl you should like to be.
4. How ideals can be realized.
5. How a study of Hawthorne may help you to increase your vocabulary. (Note the different names Hawthorne uses in referring to the face.)

**Extended Activity:**

1. Allegory in literature has meaning beyond what appears on the surface. For example, an author may assign a name to a character that describes his personality or behavior. Have students list the names of each of the characters in this story and explain the allegory.

Possible answers: Ernest's name reflects his earnest, serious, approach to life; Mr. Gathergold spent his life gathering gold but did not use it to help his fellowmen; his nickname, Scattercopper, reflects the copper coins that he threw from his carriage window; General Blood-and-Thunder with the iron will and battle scars lacked human tenderness and sympathy; Old Stony Phiz reflects the exuberant, verbal statesman whose great orations fizzled out before they produced results. His "life, with all its high performances, was vague and empty, because no high purpose had endowed it with reality."

2. Allusion in literature refers to a well-known event or person in history with which the writer assumes the reader is acquainted. Hawthorne makes two allusions in this story: Page 407, line 24, he refers to the Midas-hand; page 416, line 2, he refers to a heroic Titanic model. Have students research Midas and Titan to help them understand Hawthorne's allusion. (A story of King Midas and his golden touch can be found in *The Elson Reader, Book Five*, Lost Classics Book Company.) See Extended Activity #1 in "Part IV," "The Character of Christopher Columbus," for an allusion chart.

3. Students may be acquainted with another set of stone faces carved out of mountain stone found in South Dakota—Mt. Rushmore. Have students research the history of the carvings, identify the names of the faces carved in stone, why they were chosen, and explain how those lives impacted America.

4. Both "The Legend of Sleepy Hollow" and "The Great Stone Face" are short stories with distinct plot lines that follow the pyramid used to identify short stories. (See "Extended Activity" #2 under "The Legend of Sleepy Hollow.") Have students create a short story using the pyramid as a guide to plot development. The students should consider the following guidelines as they develop their short stories: make the characters and their actions and words believable; create a problem that affects the main character and that can be solved in a short story; keep the actions and conversations relevant to the story; keep the readers guessing about the outcome; the climax should occur close to the end and come to a natural ending. Students should share their stories with the class and identify the elements of a story: exposition, rising action, climax, falling action, resolution.

NAME_____CLASS_____DATE_____

## THE GREAT STONE FACE, p. 402

1. Allegory in literature has meaning beyond what appears on the surface. For example, an author may assign a name to a character that describes his personality or behavior. List the names of each of the characters in this story and explain the allegory.

Character: _____

_____

_____

_____


Character: _____

_____

_____

_____


Character: _____

_____

_____

_____


Character: _____

_____

_____

_____


Character: _____

_____

_____

_____

2. Allusion in literature refers to a well-known event or person in history with which the writer assumes the reader is acquainted. Hawthorne makes two allusions in this story: Page 407, line 24, he refers to the Midas-hand; page 416, line 2, he refers to a heroic Titanic model. Research Midas and Titan to help understand Hawthorne's allusion. (A story of King Midas and his golden touch can be found in the *Elson Reader, Book Five,* Lost Classics Book Company.)

_____

_____

_____

_____

_____

_____

_____

_____

_____

_____

_____

_____

_____

3. You may be acquainted with another set of stone faces carved out of mountain stone found in South Dakota—Mt. Rushmore. Research the history of the carvings, identify the names of the faces carved in stone, why they were chosen, and explain how those lives impacted America.

_____

_____

_____

_____

_____

_____

_____

_____

4. Both "The Legend of Sleepy Hollow" and "The Great Stone Face" are short stories with distinct plot lines that follow the pyramid used to identify short stories. Create a short story using the pyramid as a guide to plot development. You should consider the following guidelines as you develop your short stories: make the characters and their actions and words believable; create a problem that affects the main character and that can be solved in a short story; keep the actions and conversations relevant to the story; keep the readers guessing about the outcome; the climax should occur close to the end and come to a natural ending. Share your stories with the class and identify the elements of a story: exposition, rising action, climax, falling action, resolution.

## STORY:

CLIMAX

RISING ACTION     FALLING ACTION

EXPOSITION     RESOLUTION

_____

_____

_____

_____

_____

_____

_____

_____

_____

_____

_____

_____

_____

_____

_____

_____

_____

_____

AMERICAN LITERATURE OF
LIGHTER VEIN

## THE CELEBRATED JUMPING FROG, P. 425

1.  **What paragraphs in this selection relate the circumstances under which Simon Wheeler's reminiscences of Jim Smiley were told?**

    The first three paragraphs and the last five paragraphs provide the setting for Simon Wheeler's reminiscences. Students should be aware that this is a frame story which contains a story within a story. The first and last paragraphs provide a frame for the inner story.

2.  **What were these circumstances?**

    The frame: the author has been asked by his friend in the east to contact Simon Wheeler and ask about a certain Leonidas W. Smiley. The author visits Mr. Wheeler in an old tavern and asks about Mr. Smiley; inner story: so begins the tale of Mr. Smiley according to Mr. Wheeler who tells his story with "earnestness and sincerity."

3.  **Are all parts of these introductory paragraphs to be taken seriously?**

    Mark Twain probably intends that the reader question Mr. Wheeler's serious manner and reflections.

4.  **Does Mark Twain intend to convince his readers that they will find Simon Wheeler's narrative "monotonous" and "interminable"?**

    Encourage students to explain why they were or were not convinced by Twain's description of Mr. Wheeler's narrative.

5.  **Why does he call it so?**

    Twain probably attempts to rouse the reader's curiosity regarding Mr. Wheeler's tone.

6.  **What paragraphs in these reminiscences lead up to the story of the jumping frog?**

    Paragraphs four to six set the stage for the story of the frog.

7.  **In whom do these paragraphs serve to interest the reader?**

    The reader's interest is drawn to Jim Smiley.

8.  **What is this person's most marked characteristic?**

    He is "the curiosest man about always betting on anything that turned up you ever see, if he could get anybody to bet on the other side; and if he couldn't, he'd change sides."

9.  **What illustrations of this characteristic are given?**

He mentions Jim's bets on a dogfight, a catfight, a chicken fight, birds, a parson, a straddle-bug, the parson's wife, a horse, and Jim's bull pup; all leading up to the bet on the frog.

10. **Did you enjoy reading this selection?**
   Answers will vary.

11. **Can you tell what made it enjoyable?**
   Encourage students to support their answers to question ten using support from the selection.

12. **How does the author make his story humorous?**
   The author uses exaggeration and local dialect to add humor to the story.

13. **This selection is a humorous description of a certain type of lazy character found in many rural communities; have you ever known such a man as the rambling storyteller, Wheeler? As the shiftless Jim Smiley?**
   Answers will vary. If the students are acquainted with such persons, have them describe them as Twain described Mr. Wheeler and Jim.

14. **What other selections have you read in this book that are enriched by touches of humor?**
   Answers will vary. If the students have read the book, they may mention the humor of "Moti Guj," and "The Pine-Tree Shillings" along with other stories they found humorous.

15. **What is the value of humor in literature?**
   Humor in literature adds interest and helps the reader identify with the characters in the story.

16. **This is a typical short story; can you point out the introduction, the climax, and the other parts of the story? (See "Note," p. 422.)**
   The note on page 422 identifies the basic structure of a short story: "introduction, a main incident, a point of highest interest (called the climax), and a conclusion. In this tale, the introduction or setting includes Mr. Wheeler sitting in a tavern preparing to describe Jim Smiley. A point of high interest is Jim's frog-training antics. The climax describes the frog race, and the conclusion describes the author's farewell to Mr. Wheeler.

17. **Find in the glossary the meaning of: compliance, garrulous, append, conjectured, dilapidated, commissioned, initial, interminable, transcendent, finesse.**

18. **Pronounce: infamous, tedious, inquiries, exquisitely, fellow, amateur.**

**Class Reading.**
   Select passages to be read aloud in class.

**Outline for Testing Silent Reading.**
Make an outline to guide you in telling the story.

**Library Reading.**
*A Literary Nightmare,* Mark Twain;
Tales of Laughter, Wiggin; in *Life Magazine,* 1921;
"In Mark Twain Land," Milbank (in *St. Nicholas,* August, 1919).

**A Suggested Problem.**
Prepare a program for "Humor Day" in your school. Bring to class humorous selections—stories, poems, clippings, etc.—that have been enjoyed in your family. A committee of pupils may plan interesting ways for presenting this material. Let the class artist give a talk illustrated by his own drawings.

**Suggestions for Theme Topics.**
1. A humorous monologue: A Boy Scout telling a humorous incident that occurred on a hike; A Girl Scout describing camp life humorously; A Camp Fire girl telling a humorous incident of a ceremonial meeting; A sailor spinning a funny yarn, etc.
2. A book review of *Tom Sawyer,* pointing out particularly humorous incidents, such as how Tom Sawyer whitewashed the fence (add interest to your report by reading selected passages to the class).

## *Extended Activities:*

1. Twain uses local dialect, the way people in a certain region speak, to add humor to his story. In dialect, words or phrases are spelled and/or pronounced differently from standard English. Have students rewrite in standard English each of the following dialect sentences.

A. "There couldn't be no solitry thing mentioned but that feller'd offer to bet on it." (p.426, line 35.)

B. "If he ever seen a straddle-bug start to go anywheres, he would bet you how long it would take him to get to wherever he was going to, and if you took him up, he would foller that straddle-bug to Mexico but what he would find out where he was bound for and how long he was on the road." (Page 427, line 9.)

C. "Lots of the boys here has seen that Smiley, and can tell you about him. Why it never made no difference to him—he would bet on *any* thing—the dangedest feller." (Page 427, line 14.)

D. "And he had a little small bull pup, that to look at him you'd think he wan't worth a cent but to set around and look onery and lay for a chance to steal something." (Page 428, line 2.)

E. "I know it, because he hadn't had no opportunities to speak of, and it don't stand to reason that a dog could make such a fight as he could under them circumstances if he hadn't no talent." (Page 428, line 31.)

F. "Well, thish-yer Smiley had rat-terriers, and chicken cocks, and tomcats, and all them kind of things, till you couldn't rest, and you couldn't fetch nothing for him to bet on but he'd match you." (Page 429, line 1.)

G. "He ketched a frog one day, and took him home, and said he cal'klated to edercate him; and so he never done nothing for three months but set in his back yard and learn that frog to jump." (Page 429, line 4.)

H. "Well, I don't see no p'ints about that frog that's any better'n any other frog." (Page 430, line 12.)

I. "Dan'l gave a heave, and hysted up his shoulders-so-like a Frenchman, but it wan't no use—he couldn't budge." (Page 431, line 2.)

J. "And then he see how it was, and he was the maddest man—he set the frog down and took out after that feller, but he never ketched him." (Page 431, line 19.)

2. Have two students prepare a reader's theater presentation between the stranger and Jim beginning on page 429, line 35 to page 431, line 7. Students should note carefully the use of dialogue, the italicized words for emphasis, and the gestures of the characters in order to present the scene as it was meant to be viewed.

3. "The Celebrated Jumping Frog" is considered a tall tale. Through humor, exaggeration, and use of local dialect in conversation, the reader is drawn into the story. Have the students create a tall tale using Twain's tools of humor, exaggeration and local dialect, to describe the "yaller one-eyed cow that didn't have no tail" that Mr. Wheeler wanted to tell next.

NAME_____CLASS_____DATE_____

## THE CELEBRATED JUMPING FROG, p. 425

1. Twain uses local dialect, the way people in a certain region speak, to add
humor to his story. In dialect, words or phrases are spelled and/or
pronounced differently from standard English. Rewrite in standard
English each of the following dialect sentences.

    A. "There couldn't be no solitry thing mentioned but that feller'd offer
to bet on it."

_____

_____

    B. "If he ever seen a straddle-bug start to go anywheres, he would bet
you how long it would take him to get to wherever he was going to, and
if you took him up, he would foller that straddle-bug to Mexico but
what he would find out where he was bound for and how long he was
on the road."

_____

_____

_____

    C. "Lots of the boys here has seen that Smiley, and can tell you about
him. Why it never made no difference to him—he would bet on *any*
thing—the dangedest feller."

_____

_____

    D. "And he had a little small bull pup, that to look at him you'd think
he wan't worth a cent but to set around and look onery and lay for a
chance to steal something."

_____

_____

    E. "I know it, because he hadn't had no opportunities to speak of, and it
don't stand to reason that a dog could make such a fight as he could
under them circumstances if he hadn't no talent."

_____

F. "Well, thish-yer Smiley had rat-terriers, and chicken cocks, and tomcats, and all them kind of things, till you couldn't rest, and you couldn't fetch nothing for him to bet on but he'd match you."

G. "He ketched a frog one day, and took him home, and said he cal'klated to edercate him; and so he never done nothing for three months but set in his back yard and learn that frog to jump."

H. "Well, I don't see no p'ints about that frog that's any better'n any other frog."

I. "Dan'l gave a heave, and hysted up his shoulders—so—like a Frenchman, but it wan't no use—he couldn't budge."

J. "And then he see how it was, and he was the maddest man—he set the frog down and took out after that feller, but he never ketched him."

2.  Prepare a reader's theater presentation between the stranger and Jim beginning on page 429, line 35 to page 431, line 7. Note carefully the use of dialogue, the italicized words for emphasis, and the gestures of the characters in order to present the scene as it was meant to be viewed.
3.  "The Celebrated Jumping Frog" is considered a tall tale. Through humor, exaggeration, and use of local dialect in conversation, the reader is drawn into the story. Create a tall tale using Twain's tools of humor, exaggeration and local dialect to describe the "yaller one-eyed cow that didn't have no tail" that Mr. Wheeler wanted to tell next.

## THE HEIGHT OF THE RIDICULOUS, p. 433

1. **What is it that is described by the poet as being the "height of the ridiculous"?**
   The humorous lines he wrote were the "height of the ridiculous."

2. **What incidents are related that seem to show him to be right in this estimate?**
   The poet, after reading them, said he "laughed as I would die." When his servant read them, he broke into a roar of laughter, popping off his buttons, and falling in a fit.

3. **What opinion of the poet does the poem give you?**
   The poet displays a sense of humor.  Encourage students to describe the poet as they see him.

4. **In what state of mind do you think of him as writing it?**
   Answers will vary.

5. **What is the "trifling jest" referred to in the fourth stanza?**
   The glossary defines a "trifling jest" as a "little joke."
   **What are the duties of a "printer's devil"?**
   A "printer's devil" was a "printer's assistant."

6. **This poem is pure nonsense for the sake of a hearty laugh; of what use is a poem like this?**
   Many poems are of a serious nature that express a writer's deep feelings about life and encourage readers to respond with equally serious thoughts.  Nonsense poems for the sake of a hearty laugh free the reader from the task of determining deeper meanings and reflections, allowing them to laugh at life.

### Library Reading.

*The Nonsense Book,* Lear;
"Just Nonsense," (in *The Home Book of Verse for Young Folks,* Stevenson).

### Suggestions for Theme Topics.

1. A discussion of present-day humor as seen in the funny pictures of the newspaper.
2. The tendency of the modern newspaper reader to get his humor through pictures rather than words.
3. Some well-known cartoonists and the characters they have created.
4. The joke column of the newspaper which you are in the habit of reading; its title and its editor.
5. Limericks
6. Movies as sources of humor.

# Extended Activities:

1. In the "Suggestions for Theme Topics" in the Reader (see above), students are encouraged to consider humor in comic strips. Have them create a comic strip of this poem by Holmes, paying close attention to Holmes's description of the characters' appearance and actions.

2. In "Suggestions for Theme Topics" (see above), number five mentions limericks as a source of humor. A limerick consists of five lines: lines one, two, and five rhyme and have three stressed syllables; lines three and four rhyme and contain two stressed syllables. Have students write a limerick following those guidelines, remembering to make it humorous.

NAME_____CLASS_____DATE_____

## THE HEIGHT OF THE RIDICULOUS, p. 433

1. In the "Suggestions for Theme Topics" in the Reader, you are encouraged to consider humor in comic strips. Create a comic strip of this poem by Holmes, paying close attention to Holmes's description of the characters' appearance and actions.

2.  In "Suggestions for Theme Topics," number five mentions limericks as a source of humor.  A limerick consists of five lines: lines one, two, and five rhyme and have three stressed syllables; lines three and four rhyme and contain two stressed syllables.  Write a limerick following those guidelines, remembering to make it humorous.

_____

_____

_____

_____

_____

_____

_____

_____

_____

_____

_____

_____

_____

_____

## THE GIFT OF THE MAGI, p. 436

1. **Has this story an interesting beginning?**
   Answers will vary.  Have students explain what interests them in the introduction.

2. **How does it arouse your curiosity?**
   Answers will vary.

3. **Throughout the story find other instances where the author arouses your curiosity, but does not immediately tell you what you wish to know.**
   Encourage students to identify the parts that aroused their curiosity.

4. **When did a plan for obtaining money first suggest itself to Della?**
   When she looked in the "pier glass" and saw her reflection, she thought of the plan.

5. **Where did you first begin to suspect what the plan is?**
   Answers will vary.

6. **Does Jim's behavior, when he is told that Della has cut off her hair, puzzle you as well as Della?**
   Answers will vary.

7. **O. Henry's stories usually have a surprise at the end; is there a surprise in this one?**
   O. Henry surprises the reader at the end when he says that Jim sells his watch to buy combs for Della.

8. **What reason do you see for calling Jim and Della "the magi"?**
   In the glossary the magi are defined as "the three wise men who brought gifts to the Christ child."  See Matthew II.
   Encourage students to explain why Jim and Della were called "the magi."  In the sense that they sacrificed to give the best gifts they had to each other, they may be considered "magi."

9. **In this story humor is used to enrich a high moral lesson; what is the lesson?**
   Encourage students to explain the moral lesson they perceive in the story.  Gifts of love and sacrifice may be considered some aspects of the moral lesson in the story.

10. **How does the humor of this story differ from that of the other selections in the group?**
    This story has a moral; the other two stories were humorous without a moral emphasis.

11. **What have the humorists done for the world?**
    They have helped us to laugh at our humanity and perhaps not take ourselves so seriously.

12. **What have you gained from the selections in this group?**
    Answers will vary.
13. **How do such selections help to make the "spirit of laughter in America," mentioned on page 298?**
    Encourage students to explain how these selections contribute to the "spirit of laughter in America."
14. **In Holmes's time and even in Mark Twain's, pictures were not widely used to provide humor for the readers of newspapers and magazines; what present-day cartoonists can you name?**
    Answers will vary.
15. **Find in the glossary the meaning of: magi, appertaining, agile, meretricious, peculiar, coveted.**

**Class Reading.**
    Select passages to be read aloud in class.

**Outline for Testing Silent Reading.**
    Make an outline to guide you in telling the story.

**Library Reading.**
    Another story from *The Four Million*, O. Henry;
    *Christmas Tales and Christmas Verse*, Field.

**A Suggested Problem.**
    Make a collection of "funny pictures" for "Cartoon Day" in your school, dividing them into three groups, (1) those that are merely silly, (2) those that are clever, and (3) those that drive home a truth in the form of a joke.

## *Extended Activity:*

1. As seen in the "Extended Activities" in "The Great Stone Face" in the previous section, allusion in literature refers to a well-known event or person in history with which the writer assumes the reader is acquainted. O. Henry makes several allusions in this short story. Have the students identify these characters and explain why O. Henry refers to them: Queen of Sheba, King Solomon, and a Coney Island chorus girl.

2. Have students write short paragraphs describing the best gift they ever received and the best gift they ever gave.

NAME_____CLASS_____DATE_____

## THE GIFT OF THE MAGI, p. 436

1.  As seen in the "Extended Activities" in "The Great Stone Face" in
    the previous section, allusion in literature refers to a well-known
    event or person in history with which the writer assumes the reader
    is acquainted.  O. Henry makes several allusions in this short story.
    Identify these characters and explain why O. Henry refers to them.

    **Queen of Sheba**

    _____

    _____

    _____

    _____

    _____

    _____

    **King Solomon**

    _____

    _____

    _____

    _____

    _____

    _____

    **A Coney Island chorus girl**

    _____

    _____

    _____

    _____

    _____

    _____

2. **Write short paragraphs describing the best gift you ever received and the best gift you ever gave.**

The Best Gift I Ever Received Was:_____

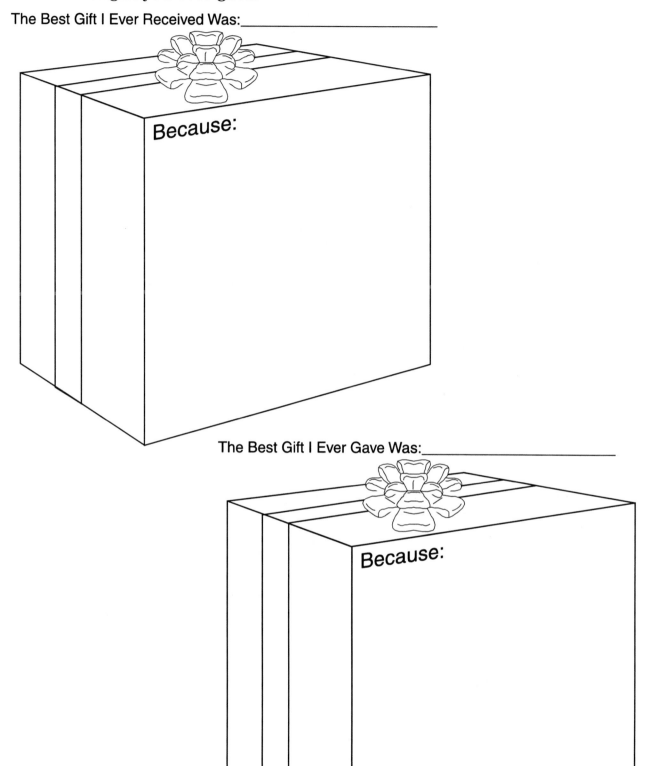

Because:

The Best Gift I Ever Gave Was:_____

Because:

## AMERICAN WORKERS AND THEIR WORK

### MAKERS OF THE FLAG, P. 443

1.  **Why did the Flag greet the author as "Mr. Flag Maker"?**

    The Flag considered all "beneficent individuals," people who worked for the good of humanity, to be flag makers.

2.  **Why are the Georgia boy, the mother in Michigan, and the school teacher in Ohio makers of the Flag?**

    They each contributed in some way to the welfare of the country.

3.  **Tell in your own words some of the things that Mr. Lane says the Flag is.**

    Answers will vary but should reflect the Flag as a belief, a dream, mood and passion, pride, ego, and hope.  It is a song, a day's work, the Constitution, a battle, a mystery, and an idea.

4.  **What does the Flag mean by saying, "I am all that you hope to be and have the courage to try for"?**

    Our dreams and hopes, along with the dreams and hopes of our forefathers, are reflected in the Flag.  It was designed to symbolize our courage.

5.  **How is the Flag a "symbol of yourself"?**

    The Flag is a symbol for our actions, hopes, and dreams.

6.  **Do you think that you are a maker of the Flag?**

    Answers will vary.  Encourage students to explain why they consider themselves a flag maker.

7.  **In your opinion who are the greatest makers of the Flag?**

    Answers will vary.

8.  **Read again what is said in the first paragraph on page 298, and tell how this address shows the "infinite activities" of America.**

    This address evokes images of the activities in which Americans engage—battles, dreams, ideas, changing moods, "song, fear, struggle, and panic, and ennobling hope."  America is a "many-sided personality."

9.  **What great activities are symbolized in the picture on page 443?**

    The activities of hard work, whether in fields or factories, by hand or with machines, are symbolized.

10. **Find in the glossary the meaning of: peon, statute, reasoned.**

11. **Pronounce: cordial, garish.**

**Library Reading.**

*The Story of Great Inventions,* Burns;
*The Boys' Book of Inventions,* Baker;
*Stories of Useful Inventions,* Forman;
*The Boys' Airplane Book,* Collins;
*The Book of Wireless,* Collins.

**Suggestions for Theme Topics.**

1. A school boy or girl flag maker.
2. An interesting account of some particular service rendered by a doctor that I know; a policeman; a fireman; a nurse; a milkman; a postman; a newsboy; a soldier.

## *Extended Activity:*

1. Writers use repetition to emphasize an idea or point. Lane repeats key words to draw attention to the Flag's message. Have students list all the responses to the following repetitive phrases.

"Yesterday ...,"

"I am ...,"

"Sometimes I ...,"

2. Have the students find and read a copy of Martin Luther King, Jr.'s speech, "I Have A Dream" and identify his repetitive phrases.

They include, but are not limited to:

"I have a dream…"

"With this faith…"

"Let freedom ring…"

"When we let freedom ring…"

"We will be able to…"

Name_____Class_____Date_____

## Makers of the Flag, p. 443

1.  Writers use repetition to emphasize an idea or point.  Lane repeats key
    words to draw attention to the Flag's message.  List all the responses
    to the following repetitive phrases.
    "Yesterday...,"

    _____

    _____

    _____

    _____

    "I am...,"

    _____

    _____

    _____

    _____

    "Sometimes I...,"

    _____

    _____

    _____

    _____

2.  Find and read a copy of Martin Luther King, Jr.'s speech, "I Have A
    Dream" and identify his repetitive phrases.

    _____

    _____

    _____

    _____

    _____

    _____

    _____

    _____

## I HEAR AMERICA SINGING, p. 446

1. **Who is it that the poet hears singing?**
   The poet hears "America singing."

2. **In line 1, what "varied carols" does he hear?**
   He hears the "varied carols" of America's workforce, singing as they labor.

3. **What do you think was the poet's underlying idea in writing this poem?**
   Answers will vary but may reflect the idea that everyone has a song to sing, and everyone's song must be heard.

4. **Do you think he meant to point out that the road to happiness is the road to work?**
   Encourage students to discuss Whitman's intentions in writing this poem.

5. **When the worker is interested in his work he enjoys it, for he puts his heart into it; can you give an instance from your own experience?**
   Answers will vary.

## *Extended Activity:*

As noted in the "Extended Activity" in "Makers of the Flag" writers use repetition to emphasize an idea. Like Lane, Whitman uses repetition in his poem to focus on his theme of America's greatness. Have students identify all the laborers that were singing in this poem. Have them choose one laborer and illustrate him or her using Whitman's details in their drawing.

NAME_____CLASS_____DATE_____

## I HEAR AMERICA SINGING, P. 446

As noted in the Extended Activity in "Makers of the Flag" writers use repetition to emphasize an idea. Like Lane, Whitman uses repetition in his poem to focus on his theme of America's greatness. Identify all the laborers that were singing in this poem. Choose one laborer and illustrate him or her using Whitman's details in your drawing.

_____

_____

_____

_____

_____

## PIONEERS! O PIONEERS!, p. 448

1. **Whom does the poet address in the first stanza?**
   The poet addresses the "tan-faced children."
2. **What does he ask the pioneers to have ready?**
   He asks them to have ready their weapons—pistols and axes.
3. **Why cannot they "tarry here"?**
   They must face the dangers that lie ahead; "all the rest on us depend."
4. **How does the poet characterize the "Western youths"?**
   They are "impatient, full of action, full of manly pride and friendship."
5. **Why must the pioneers "take up the task eternal"?**
   "The burden and the lesson" of our freedoms will always be with us. We must never quit fighting for them.
6. **What new world do they enter upon?**
   They enter "upon a newer mightier world, varied world, Fresh and strong."
7. **Mention some of the tasks that the pioneers must do?**
   The pioneers must go forward "Conquering, holding, daring, venturing," felling forests, stemming rivers, piercing mines, surveying surfaces, and upheaving soil.
8. **Where do these pioneers come from?**
   They come from Colorado, Nebraska, Arkansas, Missouri, "all the Southern, all the Northern."
9. **Why does the poet mourn and yet exult?**
   Perhaps Whitman mourns for the labor of those who have died for our freedom as he exults with love for those who continue to labor. Encourage students to discuss how one can both mourn and exult at the same time.
10. **Why would the motto mentioned on page 297 be a good one for the pioneers?**
    The motto is "I will." It expresses the pioneers' attitude about working for America's development.
11. **Find in the glossary the meaning of: pioneer, primeval, vexing, sierras.**

### Library Reading.
*America at Work,* Husband;
*The Boys' Book of New Inventions,* Manle;
*The Land We Live In,* Price.

### Suggestions for Theme Topics.
1. In an imaginary conversation with Walt Whitman tell him what

America is doing today to carry out the ideals he expressed in the fourth and fifth stanzas.

2. Pioneers of today: the aviator, the submarine seaman.

3. Luther Burbank, a pioneer.

4. Marconi, a pioneer.

5. Thomas A. Edison, a pioneer.

## *Extended Activity:*

As noted in Whitman's biography on page 447, he rarely uses the common poetic device of rhyme in his poems. Much of his poetry is free verse, having no particular rhyme scheme. After reading "Suggestions for Theme Topics," have students discuss current "pioneers" in technology, science, space, or medicine, describing the qualities they possess, the difficulties they experience, and the tasks they face in modern America, writing class ideas on the board. Then have students create a free verse poem about current pioneers, modeling Whitman's poem by ending each stanza with his phrase, "Pioneers! O pioneers!"

NAME_____ CLASS_____ DATE_____

## PIONEERS! O PIONEERS!, P. 448

As noted in Whitman's biography on page 447, he rarely uses the common poetic device of rhyme in his poems. Much of his poetry is free verse, having no particular rhyme scheme. After reading "Suggestions for Theme Topics," discuss current "pioneers" in technology, science, space, or medicine, describing the qualities they possess, the difficulties they experience, and the tasks they face in modern America, writing class ideas on the board. Then create a free verse poem about current pioneers, modeling Whitman's poem by ending each stanza with his phrase, "Pioneers! O pioneers!"

_____

_____

_____

_____

_____

_____

_____

_____

_____

_____

_____

_____

_____

_____

_____

_____

_____

_____

_____

_____

_____

_____

_____

## THE BEANFIELD, p. 450

1.  **Why did Thoreau wish to earn some extra money?**
    He wanted to "meet my unusual expenses."

2.  **What seeds did he plant?**
    He planted "about two acres and a half chiefly with beans, but a small part with potatoes, corn, peas, and turnips."

3.  **The author likens the hoeing of the beans to a "Herculean labor"; explain this reference.**
    "Herculean labor" is a reference to the mighty Hercules, a powerful hero of Greek mythology. Students can read about some of his exploits in *The Elson Readers, Book Six,* "The Three Golden Apples."

4.  **What were Thoreau's auxiliaries?**
    Thoreau's auxiliaries were "the dews and rains which water this dry soil."
    **His enemies?**
    His enemies were "worms, cool days, and, most of all, woodchucks" who nibbled "a quarter of an acre clean."

5.  **According to the author, what is the best time to work in the garden?**
    The best time was in the morning "while the dew was on—I would advise you to do all your work if possible while the dew is on."

6.  **How did he come "to know beans" so well?**
    He learned to know beans through "planting, and hoeing, and harvesting, and thrashing, and picking over, and selling them."

7.  **Explain the metaphor that refers to the weeds as Trojans.**
    "A long war, not with cranes, but with weeds, those Trojans who had sun and rain and dews on their side." Trojans were the inhabitants of ancient Troy who worked with energy and endurance to defend their country against the Greeks. Like the Trojans, the weeds fought valiantly, appearing every morning to threaten the beans. (*The Elson Readers—Book Six* includes the stories of the Greeks and Trojans.)

8.  **How much did the author clear on his garden?**
    He cleared $8.71 and one-half cents on the garden.

9.  **What encouragement to thrift in gardening was given during the World Wars?**
    Victory Gardens were encouraged to help with the food shortage. Many men went to war so the production of food was limited. People would plant gardens in their back yard or in vacant lots. Victory Gardens were used in both world wars.

10. **Find in the glossary the meaning of: copse, tendrils.**

**Library Reading.**

*Young People's Story of American Literature* (Chapter XXII), Whitcomb;

"The Habit of Thrift," Herrick (in *The Youth's Companion,* January 2, 1919);

*My Summer in a Garden,* Warner.

**A Suggested Problem.**

If your school is interested in gardening, you may wish to become members of our national school board organizations. Write to the Bureau of Education, Washington, DC, for information relating to "The United States School Garden Army" and for Home Gardening for City Children and A Manual for School-Supervised Gardening; or to the Department of Agriculture for Circular 48 of the "Boys' and Girls' Club Work."

**Suggestions for Theme Topics.**

1. An experience with a garden.
2. How you planned a garden.
3. Canning Clubs, Corn Clubs, etc.
4. Farming on a large scale, with "improved implements of husbandry."

## *Extended Activity:*

Thoreau mentions several threats he faced to successful gardening. In "A Suggested Problem" (above) students are encouraged to research farming with "improved implements of husbandry." Have students write a letter to the United States Department of Agriculture or visit their web site at http://www.usda.gov/ to find information on modern farming methods that combat weeds, disease, and predators of crops. Have students research some of those current methods and write to explain how they may have helped a gardener like Thoreau. Students should present a thesis, organize their information, and summarize and paraphrase the information they find.

NAME_____CLASS_____DATE_____

## THE BEANFIELD, p. 450

Thoreau mentions several threats he faced to successful gardening.   In "A Suggested Problem" you are encouraged to research farming with "improved implements of husbandry."   Write a letter to the United States Department of Agriculture or visit their web site at http://www.usda.gov/ to find information on modern farming methods that combat weeds, disease, and predators of crops.   Research some of those current methods and write to explain how they may have helped a gardener like Thoreau.   You should present a thesis, organize your information, and summarize and paraphrase the information you find.

_____

_____

_____

_____

_____

_____

_____

_____

_____

_____

_____

_____

_____

_____

_____

_____

_____

_____

_____

_____

_____

_____

_____

## THE SHIPBUILDERS, p. 454

1. **What does the title tell us?**
   The title, "The Shipbuilders," prepares the reader for a story about shipbuilding.

2. **Make an outline that shows what each stanza tells us of the shipbuilders, for example: Stanza 1-Morning; time for work. Stanza 2-The smithy; work of the smith, etc.**
   Answers will vary but may reflect the following generalizations: Stanza 3-Workers bring in the logs. Stanza 4-Workers build the ship. Stanza 5-The ship responds to the seamen. Stanza 6-The ship's great strength. Stanza 7-The ship sails. Stanza 8-The ship's importance. Stanza 9-The ship—a world traveler.

3. **What do the first four lines tell us of the time?**
   "The sky is ruddy in the east, The earth is gray below, And, spectral in the river-mist, The ship's white timbers show." These lines describe the early morning when the rising sun begins to color the eastern horizon and mists rise from rivers.

4. **Note how much else they tell; what pictures do they give? What comparison do they suggest?**
   The lines paint a picture of an early morning seascape, contrasting the colors of sky and earth. The reference to "spectral" river-mists contrasted with the "white timbers" suggest the ship's ghostlike appearance in the early morning.

5. **What line in the second stanza adds to the picture in the first stanza?**
   Line 12 describes the fire-sparks "fading with the stars" as the sun appears.

6. **In what sense is the smith working "for us"?**
   The smith is designing the metal used by "us," the shipbuilders.

7. **What does the "panting team" bring from the "far-off hills"?**
   The "panting team" is felling the great trees used to build the ship.

8. **With whose labor does the work of shipbuilding really begin? Read the lines that tell this.**
   Nature provides the trees with which we build the ships. Line 27: "We make of Nature's giant powers The slaves of human Art."

9. **Which line in the third stanza do you like best?**
   Answers will vary.

10. **What comparison does the poet make between shipbuilding and other kinds of labor?**
    The poet says shipbuilding is the most noble labor. "In nobler toil than ours No craftsmen bear a part."

11. **Is the "master" the only one responsible for making the ship obey the helm?**

    The shipbuilders must build a ship that will answer the helm.

12. **What is the subject of "may peel," page 455, line 14?**

    "The vulture-beak Of Northern ice" "may peel" the "oaken ribs" of the ship.

13. **What dangers to the ship are pointed out?**

    In addition to the Northern ice, the poet mentions "sunken rock and coral peak" and "wind and wave."

    **How may the shipbuilders guard against these dangers?**

    The shipbuilders must know "well the painted shell" and work to protect her from these dangers by building her strongly.

14. **Read the stanzas that urge honest workmanship.**

    Stanza 4 encourages the builders to create a ship without "faithless joint nor yawning seam." Stanza 6 says if the ship has been well-built, it "Must float, the sailor's citadel, Or sink, the sailor's grave."

15. **At what point in the building of a ship are the "bars and blocks" struck away?**

    When the ship is ready to sail, they "strike away the bars and blocks."

16. **In what sense does this "set the good ship free"?**

    It is no longer moored to land; it is free to sail the sea.

17. **Find the lines that tell of the ship's work?**

    Page 456, line 5: "She helps to wind the silken chain Of commerce round the world!"

18. **In what sense can the "Prairie's golden grain" "be hers"?**

    She may transport the "Prairie's golden grain" to distant lands.

19. **What is meant by the "Desert's golden sand"?**

    She may carry the spices and wares around the world that reach the coast from across the "Desert's golden sand."

20. **What poetic name is given to the Far East?**

    "Morning-land" describes the Far East from which direction the sun rises in the morning.

21. **Find the lines that express the poet's wish for the ship.**

    Page 456, line 11: "Her pathway on the open main May blessings follow free, And glad hearts welcome back again Her white sails from the sea!"

22. **Select the lines in this poem that give the most vivid pictures.**

    Answers will vary.

23. **What picture of America at work mentioned in the "Introduction," page 298, does this poem give you?**

    This poem pictures American workers from the builders who design and build the ship to the farmers who grow "food for the world" that the great ships transport.

24. **What consequences would result from faulty or dishonest work in shipbuilding?**

    Have students consider the stages of shipbuilding: choosing quality trees, finding dependable smiths, hiring capable builders. How would failure or dishonesty in any of those areas affect the final result?

25. **Discuss pride in workmanship as a test of good citizenship.**

    Have students brainstorm their ideas of good citizenship on the chalk board. Have them identify how pride in workmanship would contribute to a stronger America.

26. **Find in the glossary the meaning of: spectral, craftsmen, treenail, spar, reeling, citadel, Hindustan, mart, main.**

27. **Pronounce: sooty, scourge, Hebrides, helm, coral.**

**Suggestions for Theme Topics.**
1. American shipbuilding during the World Wars.
2. Why America should have a large number of ships of commerce.

## *Extended Activity:*

1. Have students identify and illustrate all the tools and machinery used by various laborers to build the ship in this poem. They should identify: saw, broadax, mallet, bellows, forge, anvil, rafts, barges, ax, oak, and treenails. In addition have them locate in a detailed picture of a ship the ribs, beams, joint, seam, keel, spars, helm, deck, shell, prow, and sails.

Be sure to check the glossary for definitions of ship terms with which students are unfamiliar.

2. Assign each student or pairs of students one stanza from the poem to illustrate. When the illustrations are complete, hang them in the order in which the poem is written to help students get a visual image of the process used in building this ship.

## THE SHIPBUILDERS, p. 454

1. Identify and illustrate on separate paper all the tools and machinery used by various laborers to build the ship in this poem. In addition locate in a detailed picture of a ship the ribs, beams, joint, seam, keel, spars, helm, deck, shell, prow, and sails.
2. Choose one stanza from the poem to illustrate. When your class's illustrations are complete, hang them in the order in which the poem is written to help get a visual image of the process used in building this ship.

**Stanza:** _____

# THE BUILDERS, p. 457

1. **Tell in your own words what the first stanza means to you.**

   Answers will vary, but should reflect the concept that our actions determine the kind of "building," or life, we create.

2. **Find the line which tells what we must build whether we wish to do so or not.**

   Line 1: "All are architects of Fate."

3. **Upon what does the beauty of the "blocks" depend?**

   The beauty of the "blocks" depends on the "materials" with which we fill our "Time."

4. **Explain the meaning of the fourth stanza.**

   No part of our lives is inconsequential; each plays a role whether seen or unseen.

5. **By whom are "massive deeds" performed?**

   "Massive deeds" may be notable acts of courage by heroes.

6. **By whom are "ornaments of rime" made?**

   In the glossary, students will note that "ornaments of rime" refers to poetry written by poets.

7. **Explain the meaning of the "elder days of Art," and mention some works that belong to that time.**

   In the glossary, "elder days of Art" are "ancient times which produced the pyramids, some of the beautiful Greek temples still standing, and statues such as the Venus de Milo." Have students look up these art forms and explain why they are still considered as the wonders of the world today.

8. **Tell in your own words the meaning of the last stanza.**

   Answers will vary.

9. **How do the selections in the group called "American Workers and Their Work" help you to realize how infinite are the activities of our country, about which you read in the "Introduction" on page 298?**

   The "Introduction" refers to the workers who contribute to our country. These selections identify many of those workers. Have students review the selections and list all the laborers mentioned in this section.

10. **How does a poem such as this one help you to see how much the character of the workman determines the quality of his work?**

    Honest work builds a strong foundation, a metaphor of life, for a house that is "beautiful, entire, and clean." Shoddy, incomplete work builds "Broken stairways" that cause us to fall in our climb through life.

11. **Read again the last paragraph of the "Introduction," page 298; how does this poem help you to answer the question, "What is America, and what can I do to make her happy"?**

   Encourage students to respond with actions they can take to make America "happy."

12. **In the second stanza Longfellow expresses the thought that the task that we have in hand, whatever it may be, is important, and "supports the rest." Apply this thought to situations in everyday life: (a) To the stenographer who carelessly misdirects an important letter. (b) To the horseshoer who carelessly shoes a horse. (c) To the mechanic who carelessly repairs an automobile.**

   Assign the topics to groups of students and have them identify how these roles "support the rest."

13. **What do you think was Longfellow's purpose in writing this poem?**

   Answers will vary.

**Library Reading.**

   *Heart, A Schoolboy's Journal,* De Amicus;
   *With the Men Who Do Things,* Bond;
   *All About Engineering,* Knox;
   *The Romance of Labor,* Twombly and Dana;
   *The Romance of Modern Manufacture,* Gibson.

## *Extended Activities:*

1. Have students read "The Shipbuilders" and "The Builders." After reading, have them complete the Venn diagram explaining the images that are similar and those that are different.

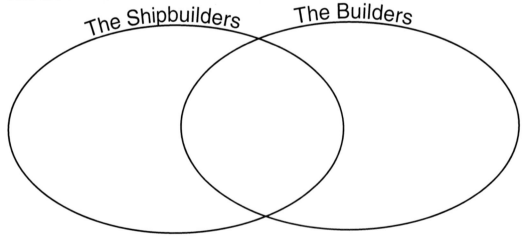

2. Henry Wadsworth Longfellow wrote another poem entitled "A Psalm of Life." The poem can be located in *The Elson Readers, Book Six,* published by Lost Classics Book Company. Have students read and explain in what ways these two poems express the same concepts.

### A PSALM OF LIFE

Tell me not, in mournful numbers,
  "Life is but an empty dream!"
For the soul is dead that slumbers,
  And things are not what they seem.

Life is real! Life is earnest!
  And the grave is not its goal;
"Dust thou art; to dust returnest"
  Was not spoken of the soul.

Not enjoyment and not sorrow
  Is our destined end or way;
But to act that each tomorrow
  Find us farther than today.

Art is long, and Time is fleeting,
  And our hearts, though stout and brave,
Still, like muffled drums, are beating
  Funeral marches to the grave.

In the world's broad field of battle,
  In the bivouac of Life,
Be not like dumb, driven cattle
  Be a hero in the strife!

Trust no Future, howe'er pleasant!
  Let the dead Past bury its dead!
Act—act in the living Present!
  Heart within, and God o'erhead!
Lives of great men all remind us
  We can make our lives sublime,
And, departing, leave behind us
  Footprints on the sands of time;

Footprints, that perhaps another,
  Sailing o'er life's solemn main,
A forlorn and shipwrecked brother
  Seeing, shall take heart again.

Let us, then, be up and doing,
  With a heart for any fate;
Still achieving, still pursuing,
  Learn to labor and to wait.

NAME _____ CLASS _____ DATE _____

## THE BUILDERS, P. 457

1. Read "The Shipbuilders" and "The Builders." After reading, complete the Venn diagram explaining the images that are similar and those that are different.

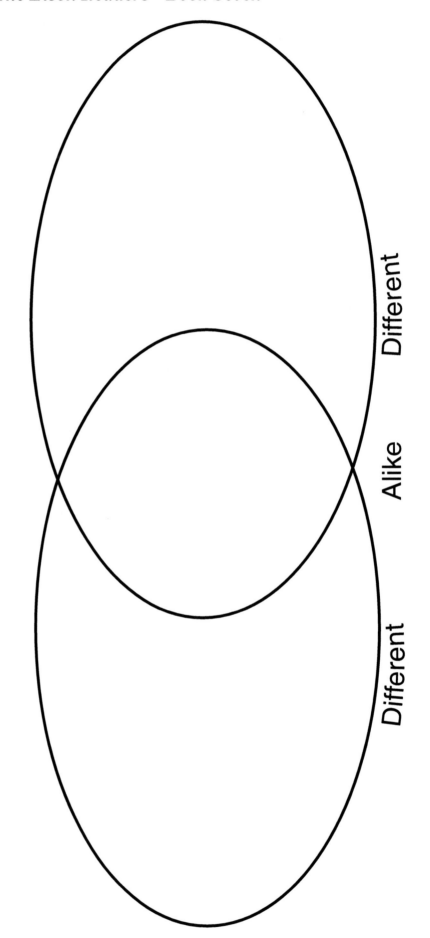

Different      Alike      Different

**2. Henry Wadsworth Longfellow wrote another poem entitled "A Psalm of Life." The poem can be located in *The Elson Readers, Book Six,* published by Lost Classics Book Company. Read and explain in what ways these two poems express the same concepts.**

A PSALM OF LIFE

Tell me not, in mournful numbers,
    "Life is but an empty dream!"
For the soul is dead that slumbers,
    And things are not what they seem.

Life is real! Life is earnest!
    And the grave is not its goal;
"Dust thou art; to dust returnest"
    Was not spoken of the soul.

Not enjoyment and not sorrow
    Is our destined end or way;
But to act that each tomorrow
    Find us farther than today.

Art is long, and Time is fleeting,
    And our hearts, though stout and brave,
Still, like muffled drums, are beating
    Funeral marches to the grave.

In the world's broad field of battle,
    In the bivouac of Life,
Be not like dumb, driven cattle
    Be a hero in the strife!

Trust no Future, howe'er pleasant!
    Let the dead Past bury its dead!
Act—act in the living Present!
    Heart within, and God o'erhead!
Lives of great men all remind us
    We can make our lives sublime,
And, departing, leave behind us
    Footprints on the sands of time;

Footprints, that perhaps another,
    Sailing o'er life's solemn main,
A forlorn and shipwrecked brother
    Seeing, shall take heart again.

Let us, then, be up and doing,
    With a heart for any fate;
Still achieving, still pursuing,
    Learn to labor and to wait.

## LOVE OF COUNTRY

### OLD IRONSIDES, p. 460

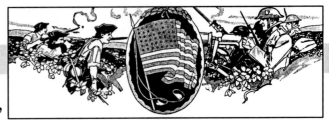

1. **This group of selections is called "Love of Country." Why is this poem a good one to introduce such a group?**

   "Old Ironsides" represents the battles and blood that bought our freedom.

2. **As you read this poem, do you think of the frigate as an inanimate object or does it seem personified?**

   Holmes's use of personification, giving human actions to non-human objects, gives the reader the impression of a warrior, a person directly involved in the battle.

3. **What does the poet say would be better than to have the ship dismantled?**

   "O better that her shattered hulk Should sink beneath the wave; Her thunders shook the mighty deep, And there should be her grave."

4. **Do you think this a fitting end for a ship of war?**

   Answers will vary.

5. **Read the story of the fight between the *Constitution* and the *Guerriere* given in your history and be prepared to tell it in class. Why did the nation have particular pride in this achievement?**

   Have students research the battle of the *Constitution* after which "Old Ironsides" was named. Briefly, navy buildup had been neglected while the army was promoted. Therefore, the navy was ill equipped to face enemy ships. However, while the army struggled under weak inferior officers, the navy's *Constitution* captured and conquered the *Guerriere,* an English frigate. The nation took particular pride in that achievement since the defeat of the powerful English navy, considered "the mistress of the seas," was unheard of at that time.

6. **In the "Introduction" on page 271, you read that history— the knowledge of past events—"must acquaint us with our country"; can you mention some other past events that are a source of pride to patriotic Americans?**

   Encourage students to research historical events that Americans celebrate such as July 4, Memorial Day, and Labor Day.

**Suggestions for Theme Topics.**

   1. "Old Ironsides," the forerunner of the steel battleship.
   2. Compare "Old Ironsides" with a modern battleship.

## *Extended Activity:*

Meter in poetry refers to the pattern of stressed and unstressed syllables that create the rhythm in the poem. Stressed or accented syllables are indicated with a ('); unstressed or unaccented syllables are indicated with a (ˇ). While Holmes's rhyme scheme is not precise in this poem, he employs a distinct meter or rhythm that can be heard in the regular rise and fall of the reader's voice as he reads aloud. Have students recopy the poem, then above each syllable mark a ' or a ˇ to indicate the meter of the poem. When completed, have them read the poem following the natural flow of the stressed syllables to feel the rhythm of this poem.

NAME_____CLASS_____DATE_____

## OLD IRONSIDES, p. 460

Meter in poetry refers to the pattern of stressed and unstressed syllables
that create the rhythm in the poem. Stressed or accented syllables are
indicated with a ('); unstressed or unaccented syllables are indicated
with a ( ˘ ). While Holmes's rhyme scheme is not precise in this poem,
he employs a distinct meter or rhythm that can be heard in the regular
rise and fall of the reader's voice as he reads aloud. Recopy the poem,
then above each syllable mark a ' or a ˘ to indicate the meter of the
poem. When completed, read the poem following the natural flow of
the stressed syllables to feel the rhythm of this poem.

_____

_____

_____

_____

_____

_____

_____

_____

_____

_____

_____

_____

_____

_____

_____

_____

_____

_____

_____

_____

_____

## THE AMERICAN FLAG, p. 462

1. **What may be seen in a nation's flag by a thoughtful mind?**
   "A thoughtful mind, when it sees a nation's flag, sees not the flag only, but the nation itself."

2. **Of what is the American flag a symbol?**
   It is a symbol of "the government, the principles, the truths, the history, which belong to the nation which sets it forth."

3. **What are the stars of the flag compared to?  The stripes?**
   "The stars upon it were to the pining nations like the morning stars of God, and the stripes upon it were beams of morning light."

4. **What do people see in the "sacred emblazonry" of the flag?**
   They see "only LIGHT, and every fold significant of liberty."

5. **Tell something of the history of this banner.**
   Washington rode under it, Burgoyne surrendered to it, Arnold's treachery was driven away by it; it cheered our army, streamed over Valley Forge and Morristown, crossed at Trenton, brought hope to our nation, and waved over Washington as Yorktown surrendered and the Revolutionary War ended.

6. **What does it mean to "stand by the stars and stripes"?**
   To "stand by the stars and stripes" means we will "resolve, come weal or woe...in life and in death, now and forever" to defend and protect our flag.

7. **Do you think the men who fought for us in the World Wars lived up to the ideals given to us in this poem?**
   Encourage students to explain their responses.

8. **Did our flag mean the same in the World Wars that the author, in the third paragraph, says it means?**
   The flag may well have had the same meaning to our soldiers in the World Wars.

9. **In the second paragraph the author speaks of the Hungarian flag; find out all you can about Hungarian liberty resulting from World War One.**
   Students should be encouraged to research Hungary's liberty in encyclopedias or on the Internet.  Briefly, in 1867 Austria and Hungary formed a dual monarchy and shared a peaceful collaboration on financial, military, and foreign affairs.  At the turn of the twentieth century, Hungarian national groups demanded self-rule, and in 1914, a Serb killed the heir to the Austrian-Hungarian throne.  Suspecting Serbia was responsible, Austria-Hungary declared war on Serbia, which led to World War One.  Austria-Hungary was defeated, signing an armistice in 1918, and the Hungarian government declared itself a

republic.  Eventually, Admiral Horthy came to power, bringing a conservative government, which was operative at the time mentioned in "The American Flag."  (See the "Appendix" for a more thorough description of this war.)

10. **Find in the glossary the meaning of: symbol, tricolor, emblazonry, luminous.**

11. **Pronounce: insignia, rampant.**

**Class Reading.**

Bring to class and read: "The Stars in Our Flag," Clary (in *St. Nicholas,* July, 1918).  As noted in the teacher's guide in the notes after "The Character of Columbus," *St. Nicholas* was a magazine for young people in the late 1800s and early 1900s.  This poem may no longer be in print.

## *Extended Activity:*

Beecher mentions a variety of people, places, and events that were important in American history.  Have students make a list of these people, places, and events and research their importance.  Possible topics include: Washington and his army, Burgoyne, West Point, Fort Montgomery, Arnold, the army's pilgrimage through New Jersey, Valley Forge, Morristown, Trenton, and Yorktown.  Have students display their research in a map and timeline showing the dates and places of each event.

## THE AMERICAN FLAG, p. 462

Beecher mentions a variety of people, places, and events that were important in American history. Make a list of these people, places, and events and research their importance. Display your research in a map and timeline showing the dates and places of each event.

## THE FLAG GOES BY, p. 464

1.  **What feeling inspires the cry "Hats off!"?**
    The sound of "a blare of bugles, a ruffle of drums, a flash of color" inspires a feeling of patriotism. "The flag is passing by!"

2.  **What does the poet mean by "more than a flag is passing"? Compare with Beecher's expression of the same thought.**
    The flag represents "sea fights and land fights," "weary marches and sinking ships," "days of plenty and years of peace," "equal justice, right, and law, stately honor and reverend awe." Beecher also expresses the concept of the flag as a symbol of "the principles, the truths, the history, which belong to the nation which sets it forth."

3.  **Name historical events that illustrate the different references in the third stanza.**
    The third stanza refers to sea and land fights, "weary marches and sinking ships; Cheers of victory on dying lips." If students have researched the events listed in the "Extended Activity" under "The American Flag," they will readily identify the historical events of which this poem speaks.

4.  **How many of the things mentioned by the poet do you see when the flag goes by?**
    Answers will vary.

5.  **Do you think the poem will help you to see more?**
    Answers will vary.

6.  **How did the flag "ward her people from foreign wrong" in the World Wars?**
    The flag was a "Sign of a nation great and strong." It commanded respect and instilled fear in the hearts of foreign entities that sought to harm the nation for which the flag stood. Therefore, the flag served to "ward her people from foreign wrong."

## THE FLOWER OF LIBERTY, p. 466

1. **What line in the first stanza answers the question with which the poem opens?**

   The poem opens with the question, "What is this flower that greets the morn?" The last line of the stanza answers the question; the flower is "The starry Flower of Liberty."

2. **Explain the metaphor of the "burning star" and the "flaming band," etc.**

   Students will find in the glossary that "the stars and stripes of the flag are called 'burning' and 'flaming' to bring out their great power and beauty."

3. **How many "burning stars" does our flag contain? How many "flaming bands"?**

   Our flag now contains 50 "burning stars" and thirteen "flaming bands."

4. **How far back in history must we go to find the seed time of the Flower of Liberty?**

   "In savage Nature's far abode," noted in the glossary as the "uninhabited part of the world," the seed was sown. Humankind has always and in every place sought the Flower of Liberty.

5. **Did the Flower of Liberty come to full bloom in a time of strife or a time of peace?**

   It came to bloom in a time of strife. "The storm-winds rocked its swelling bud; Its opening leaves were streaked with blood, Till lo! earth's tyrants shook to see The full-blown Flower of Liberty."

6. **What were the "storm-winds"?**

   The glossary refers to the "storm-winds" as the "troubles met in the founding of the nation—wars, etc."

   **What blood streaked the opening leaves of the Flower of Liberty?**

   The blood of humankind fighting for liberty streaked the opening leaves of the Flower.

7. **How does the poet show that the North and South unite as one in the flag?**

   "The red that fires the southern rose, With spotless white from northern snows, And spangled o'er its azure, see The sister Stars of Liberty!"

8. **How did the American army in the World Wars show that all parts of our country are equally devoted to the flag?**

   We fought as a united country, North and South, East and West, to keep our country free.

9. **How do the "blades of heroes fence" the flag?**

The glossary identifies the "blades of heroes" as the "swords which have won great victories." To fence is to "protect," so the heroes who have fought for their country have protected the flag.

10.  **Why is the Flower of Liberty thrice holy?**

In stanza three, "The red that fires the southern rose, With spotless white from northern snows, And, spangled o'er its azure," each of the colors of the flag—red, white, and blue—are represented and emphasize the sacrifices that made our country great. "To all their heavenly colors true, In blackening frost or crimson dew And God love us as we love thee, Thrice holy flower of Liberty!"

11.  **Find in the glossary the meaning of: flaming, dome, sentry, blackening.**

## *Extended Activity:*

Holmes uses the metaphor of the flower to describe liberty. Have students brainstorm what liberty means to them. Have them identify a metaphor of their choosing that best expresses their image of liberty and create a poem showing that metaphor.

NAME_____CLASS_____DATE_____

## THE FLOWER OF LIBERTY, P. 466

Holmes uses the metaphor of the flower to describe liberty. Brainstorm what liberty means to you. Identify a metaphor of your choosing that best expresses your image of liberty and create a poem showing that metaphor.

_____

_____

_____

_____

_____

_____

_____

_____

_____

_____

_____

_____

_____

_____

_____

_____

_____

_____

_____

_____

_____

_____

_____

_____

## CITIZENSHIP, p. 468

1. **Who are the citizens of this country?**

   The citizens of this country are those who, by birth or naturalization, work to preserve and protect their nation and who benefit from its government.

2. **What is the duty of a citizen to his country?**

   He "shall be obedient to the law, shall be kindly to his neighbors, shall regard the rights of others, shall perform his duties as juror, shall, if the hour of peril come, yield his time, his property, and his life to his country."

3. **What is the duty of a country to its citizens?**

   The country "shall protect him in every right which the Constitution gives him."

4. **What incident illustrates the difficulties one country overcame in order to protect a citizen?**

   England sent troops to Abyssinia who traveled "more than four hundred miles through swamp and morass under a burning sun," marched up mountains, scaled walls, broke down iron gates, entered the dungeon, and took back a British citizen held there as a prisoner.

5. **In the "Introduction" on page 298 you read that the book closes with "some expressions of love for our country that sum up what America means to patriotic citizens." What did America mean to Senator Frye?**

   Senator Frye believed that America was a land of opportunity. "Oh, this blessed Republic of ours stretches its hand down to men, and lifts them up, while despotism puts its heavy hand on their heads and presses them down." Encourage students to discuss examples of America stretching "its hand down to men."

6. **What does the career of Garfield prove about America?**

   It proves that with hard work, integrity, and motivation every citizen can improve his or her life, as well as those around him.

7. **Mention some other famous Americans who rose from humble beginnings to high honor.**

   In addition to historical figures like Abraham Lincoln, students may want to identify current famous Americans with which they are familiar who have risen from humble beginnings to positions of honor.

8. **Why should these instances increase your "love of country"?**

   Encourage students to define what they love about America and explain why.

9. **Find in the glossary the meaning of: incarcerated, Sepoy, debarked, impose.**

## Library Reading.

"Better Speech for Better Americans," Willett (in *St. Nicholas,* June, 1918).

## Suggestions for Theme Topics.

1. What our country does for the education of its citizens.
2. What protection it gives to the life and property of its citizens.
3. What protection to public health it gives.
4. What pensions our government gives to its war veterans.

## *Extended Activity:*

Senator Frye mentions that the Constitution was designed to give its citizens various rights. Four principles designed to provide those rights are: popular sovereignty, separation of powers, federalism, and limited government. Divide students into groups and assign each group one of the principles. Have them research and prepare a class presentation in the form of a skit that portrays that principle as it affects their lives as students.

NAME_____CLASS_____DATE_____

## CITIZENSHIP, p. 468

Senator Frye mentions that the Constitution was designed to give its citizens various rights. Four principles designed to provide those rights are: popular sovereignty, separation of powers, federalism, and limited government. Divide into groups. Research and prepare a class presentation on one of the principles in the form of a skit that portrays that principle as it affects your lives as students.

## THE CHARACTER OF WASHINGTON, p. 471

1. **What peculiarly fitted Jefferson to describe the character of Washington?**

   He "knew General Washington intimately and thoroughly."

2. **What conflict gave Washington an opportunity to show his greatness?**

   As commander of the Continental Army, Washington led his country to freedom from Britain.

3. **How had Washington's life prepared him to take advantage of his opportunities?**

   Washington's colonial background provided him with hard work, noble character, and faith. Those aspects prepared him to step into public service.

4. **Name the qualities, as given by Jefferson, that made Washington so great a leader.**

   Jefferson mentions a great mind, bravery, prudence, integrity, justice, and honor. "On the whole, his character was, in its mass, perfect, in nothing bad, in few points indifferent."

5. **How did he show prudence? Integrity? Justice?**

   Washington showed prudence, "never acting until every circumstance, every consideration, was maturely weighed; refraining if he saw a doubt, but, when once decided, going through with his purpose whatever obstacles opposed." He showed integrity and justice with "no motives of interest or consanguinity, of friendship or hatred, being able to bias his decision. He was, indeed, in every sense of the words, a wise, a good, and a great man."

6. **From your readings can you give any instance in which he showed fearlessness?**

   Answers will vary.

7. **How did he show sureness in judgment?**

   He was "slow in operation, being little aided by invention or imagination, but sure in conclusion...he selected whatever was best; and certainly no general ever planned his battles more judiciously."

8. **What, in Jefferson's opinion, was the strongest feature of Washington's character?**

   "Perhaps the strongest feature in his character was prudence." See number 5 for his explanation of prudence.

9. **How did Jefferson summarize his estimate of Washington?**

   "On the whole, his character was, in its mass, perfect, in nothing bad, in few points indifferent; and it may truly be said that never did nature and fortune combine more perfectly to make a man great, and to place him in the same constellation with whatever worthies have merited from man an everlasting remembrance."

10. **Give a summary of the things Washington accomplished.**

He led his country through a war for independence, he conducted the government of the birth of our nation, and obeyed the laws throughout his entire career, "civil and military."

11. **What part of this characterization of Washington impressed you most?**

Answers will vary.

12. **Which of the qualities mentioned would you most wish to possess?**

Answers will vary.

13. **In the "Introduction," page 298, you read that history and legend acquaint us with our country; how do the stories of the lives of great leaders such as Washington aid us in understanding the spirit and ideals of the country?**

They help us to see that the character qualities of honor, integrity, and responsibility to our fellow citizens lead to a strong country with strong ideals.

14. **What "double service" did Washington render in the Revolutionary War, about which you read on page 222?**

"He overthrew in the American colonies the unjust rule of the English king and, by this victory, he weakened the king's despotic power over his own subjects in England. Thus Washington made possible for liberty loving Englishmen gradually to gain a larger share in their own government."

15. **Find in the glossary the meaning of: delineate, judiciously, deranged, prudence, integrity, colloquial, mediocrity, fluency, constellation, destiny, arduous.**

## THE TWENTY-SECOND OF FEBRUARY, p. 474

1. **How does the poet describe a day in February?**
   "Pale is the February sky And brief the midday's sunny hours; The wind-swept forest seems to sigh" for spring.

2. **Why "has no month a prouder day"?**
   This month "Brings, in its annual round, the morn when greatest of the sons of men" was born.

3. **Whose birthday occurs on the twenty-second of February?**
   "Our glorious Washington was born" on February twenty-second.

4. **Do you know any other great man whose birthday comes in February?**
   Abraham Lincoln's birthday is February 12.

5. **Give in your own words the comparison of "the mighty Hudson" and the fame of Washington?**
   Just like "the wildest storm" can "raise no ripple" on the face of "the mighty Hudson," Washington's fame remains "unmarred, undimmed" in spite of "the wreck of thrones."

6. **Tell of some interesting incident in Washington's life.**
   Answers will vary.

7. **In the last stanza the poet speaks of wrecked thrones; what thrones can you name that were wrecked during the World Wars?**
   Encourage students to research the effects of the wars, especially in Europe where many countries were reshaped.

8. **Why is it a good thing for a country to celebrate the birthdays of its great citizens?**
   It provides an opportunity to reflect on their contribution to our country. The birthday of another great citizen, Martin Luther King, Jr., is now a national holiday. In addition to great citizens, we also celebrate important events such as the Declaration of Independence which unite our country and make us a stronger nation.

## *Extended Activity:*

President's Day, held in February, now recognizes both Washington and Lincoln for their leadership and courage. Have students plan and prepare a birthday party honoring Washington and/or Lincoln. Include skits of some of their acts of courage, their words of wisdom, and why they are considered among America's leading presidents.

NAME_____CLASS_____DATE_____

## THE TWENTY-SECOND OF FEBRUARY, p. 474

President's Day, held in February, now recognizes both Washington and Lincoln for their leadership and courage. Plan and prepare a birthday party honoring Washington and/or Lincoln. Include skits of some of their acts of courage, their words of wisdom, and why they are considered among America's leading presidents.

## ABRAHAM LINCOLN, p. 475

1. **Tell what you can of the author, noting anything in his life that was common to that of Lincoln.**

   Have students read the author's biography on page 476. They will note that both the author and Lincoln lost a parent in their youth, both had a limited education, and both were devoted to reading.

2. **Name the qualities that the poet says made Lincoln "one of Nature's masterful great men."**

   Lincoln possessed "strong arms" with which he won victories, he was "direct of speech, and cunning with the pen," he had a sense of humor, and he was wise.

3. **What does "homely" mean as used in the first line?**

   The glossary defines "homely" as "plain; strong."

4. **From your study of pictures of Lincoln what other words can you suggest to describe his features?**

   Answers will vary. Provide the students with a thesaurus to find exact and expressive descriptions of Lincoln's features.

5. **Explain the meaning of "cunning with the pen."**

   "Cunning with the pen" refers to his ability to express himself well; "he had the art Of winning with his humor, and he went Straight to his mark, which was the human heart."

6. **Repeat any of Lincoln's sayings that you know.**

   Answers will vary.

7. **What does the eighth line tell you of Lincoln's character?**

   He was a wise man, "for what he could not break, he bent."

8. **How did his humor help him to win?**

   His humor made a mark on the human heart.

9. **Why was the "burden of the commonwealth" so great, and why was it laid on his shoulders?**

   In the glossary, the "burden of the commonwealth" is defined as the "responsibilities of the whole country." It was laid on his shoulders as the president of the Union.

10. **Toward what did the road tend "suddenly downward," and how did Lincoln meet the situation created by Secession?**

    The road tended "suddenly downward" to secession, and Lincoln, as a new president, fought to unite the country. Encourage students to review the events that led to the declaration of war and Lincoln's efforts to unite the states.

11. **What reasons can you give for calling him a "Benefactor of the Race"?**

A benefactor is "one who does great good" according to the glossary. We are a richer nation because of the great good he did to unite our country.

12. **Compare the achievements of Lincoln with those of Washington.**

Have students research the careers of Lincoln and Washington and discuss their contributions to America.

13. **Explain the last two lines.**

"Hold, warriors, councilors, kings!  All now give place To this dead Benefactor of the Race."  Though Lincoln no longer lives, his heroic role in American history is remembered by "warriors, councilors, kings."

14. **Which do you think the better description, that written by Stoddard or that by Jefferson?**

Answers will vary.

15. **Find in the glossary the meaning of: masterful, councilor, benefactor.**

**Class Reading.**

Bring to class and read "Lincoln, the Man of the People," Markham.

**Library Reading.**

"A New Lincoln Statue and a Lincoln Story" (in *The Outlook,* September 29, 1920);

*The Boys' Life of Abraham Lincoln,* Nicolay;

*He Knew Lincoln,* Tarbell.

## *Extended Activity:*

One of Lincoln's most famous speeches was the Gettysburg Address, given in 1863, at the dedication of the battlefield where many soldiers died.  Have students read that address and write a reflective journal entry as if they had been present when it was read.  (The Gettysburg Address can found in *The Elson Readers—Book Eight,* published by Lost Classics Book Company.)

NAME_____ CLASS_____ DATE_____

## ABRAHAM LINCOLN, P. 475

One of Lincoln's most famous speeches was the Gettysburg Address, given in 1863, at the dedication of the battlefield where many soldiers died. Read that address and write a reflective journal entry as if you had been present when it was read. (The Gettysburg Address can found in *The Elson Readers—Book Eight*, published by Lost Classics Book Company.)

_____

_____

_____

_____

_____

_____

_____

_____

_____

_____

_____

_____

_____

_____

_____

_____

_____

_____

_____

_____

_____

_____

_____

_____

## O CAPTAIN! MY CAPTAIN!, p. 477

1. **Tell what you know of the poet that fitted him to write of Lincoln's character and achievements.**

   Have students read the biography of Whitman on page 447. They will learn that he was a volunteer nurse in Washington, D.C. during the Civil War and was acquainted with Lincoln. Like Lincoln he was against slavery and sympathized with Lincoln's efforts to free the slaves.

2. **In this poem the Union is compared to a ship; who is the captain of the ship?**

   Lincoln is the captain of the ship.

3. **What fate befalls the captain, and at what stage of the voyage?**

   Death befalls the captain as the ship nears the port and the people prepare to celebrate.

4. **What "port" has been reached?**

   The "port" is the the end of the Civil War and the reunification of the country.

5. **What is "the prize we sought and won"?**

   The union of the North and South is "the prize we sought and won."

6. **Point out words of rejoicing and of sorrow in the last stanza.**

   Rejoicing: "safe and sound," "closed and done," "victor ship," "object won," "Exult, O shores! and ring, O bells!"

   Sorrow: "pale and still," "no pulse nor will," "fearful trip," "mournful tread," "cold and dead."

7. **What parts of the poem impress you with the deep personal grief of the poet?**

   Answers will vary.

8. **This poem put into words the nation's deep grief at the time of Lincoln's death; do you think this accounts for the wide popularity of the poem?**

   Answers may reflect that, in part, this does account for the poem's popularity, but in addition, Whitman's expressions of sympathy and loss make the poem timeless in its appeal to everyone who loses a hero.

9. **Find in the glossary the meaning of: weather'd, rack, exulting.**

10. **Pronounce: bouquet.**

**Class Reading.**

Bring to class and read:

"When Lilacs Last in the Dooryard Bloomed," Whitman, describing the journey of the train bearing the body of the martyred president from Washington to Springfield, Illinois;

"A 'Lost' Portrait of Lincoln" (in *The Youth's Companion,* November 25, 1920).

## *Extended Activity:*

1. In Whitman's biography, page 447, students will see that Whitman was noted for writing "chants" rather than paying careful attention to rhyme. Through repetition of words and phrases, Whitman's poems convey his intense emotions. Have students find and list all the examples of repetition of words and/or phrases in this poem. They should include: O Captain! My Captain!, heart, the deck, Fallen cold and dead, For you.

2. Abraham Lincoln was assassinated in 1865. Have students brainstorm other world figures that have died at the hands of assassins such as John F. Kennedy, Martin Luther King, Jr., and Mohandas K. Ghandi. After they have chosen and researched their figure, have them create a tribute in the form of a poem to that leader, using Whitman's "chant" style to convey deep emotions.

NAME_____CLASS_____DATE_____

## O CAPTAIN! MY CAPTAIN!, p. 477

1.  In Whitman's biography, page 447, you will see that Whitman was noted for writing "chants" rather than paying careful attention to rhyme. Through repetition of words and phrases, Whitman's poems convey his intense emotions. Find and list all the examples of repetition of words and/or phrases in this poem.

_____

_____

_____

_____

_____

_____

_____

2.  Abraham Lincoln was assassinated in 1865. Brainstorm other world figures that have died at the hands of assassins such as John F. Kennedy, Martin Luther King, Jr., and Mohandas K. Ghandi. After you have chosen and researched your figure, create a tribute in the form of a poem to that leader, using Whitman's "chant" style to convey deep emotions.

_____

_____

_____

_____

_____

_____

_____

_____

_____

## IN FLANDERS FIELDS, p. 478

1. **Tell in your own words the scene which the poet describes in the first five lines.**

   The poet describes the quiet beauty of blowing poppies and singing larks among the rows of crosses that mark the graves of fallen soldiers.

2. **The poppy is an emblem of sleep; what significance does it have in this poem?**

   It symbolizes the eternal "sleep" of the soldiers who have died in battle.

3. **What does the poet bid us do?**

   He bids us to "Take up our quarrel with the foe! To you from falling hands we throw the torch. Be yours to hold it high!"

4. **What was the "torch" mentioned in the second stanza?**

   The torch is the flame of liberty for which the soldiers died.

5. **What do you think was the motive which inspired Lieutenant-Colonel McCrae to write this poem?**

   Encourage students to visualize the setting that may have given rise to this poem. What events were occurring in the world at this time? Where was Lieutenant McCrae when he wrote it? What images did he see?

6. **On page 22 you were told that some poems are treasured "for their musical rhythm and the charm of their language;" point out the qualities that make this poem pleasing to you.**

   Answers will vary but may include the rhyme, rhythm, and visual images that McCrae inserts in this poem.

7. **What do you notice that is unusual about the rhyme in this poem?**

   The rhyme scheme is somewhat irregular: AABBAAABC AABBAC

## *Extended Activity:*

"Class Reading" under "O Captain! My Captain!" suggests bringing to a class and reading Whitman's "When Lilacs Last in the Dooryard Bloomed." The poem can be located on the Internet at http://www.liglobal.com/walt. Have students read the poem and compare it to McCrae's tribute. What images do they share?

NAME_____CLASS_____DATE_____

## In Flanders Fields, p. 478

The "Class Reading" note under "O Captain! My Captain!" suggests bringing to a class and reading Whitman's "When Lilacs Last in the Dooryard Bloomed." The poem can be located on the Internet at http://www.liglobal.com/walt. Read the poem and compare it to McCrae's tribute. What images do they share?

_____

_____

_____

_____

_____

_____

_____

_____

_____

_____

_____

_____

_____

_____

_____

_____

_____

_____

_____

_____

_____

_____

_____

_____

## AMERICA'S ANSWER, p. 479

1.  **Why does the poet say that the "Flanders dead" may now rest in peace?**

    They can rest in peace because "the fight that ye so bravely led We've taken up."

2.  **Who took up the struggle?**

    Those who continue to fight for freedom have taken up the struggle.

3.  **Why does the poet say that the heroes of Flanders have not "died for naught"?**

    They have not "died for naught" because "The torch ye threw to us we caught."

4.  **Do you think that this answer is a fitting response to the stirring poem that precedes it? Give reasons.**

    Answers will vary, but students should support their answers with reasons.

5.  **In the "Introduction" to "Part III," page 221, you read that we owe much to those who gave their lives to leave us our "inheritance of freedom"; will future generations of Americans owe a similar debt to those who gave their lives in the World Wars to uphold the "torch" mentioned in this poem?**

    Future generations of Americans will always owe a debt of gratitude for those men and women who have sacrificed their lives to uphold our country's freedoms.

6.  **From your reading of the selections in this group called "Love of Country," mention several ideas you have gained that show why you should love your homeland.**

    Have students brainstorm and list on the board the reasons they love their country.

## Class Reading.

Bring to class and read:

"America, A Beacon Light of Peace," D'Annunzio;

"A Sight in Camp in the Daybreak Gray and Dim," "As Toilsome I Wandered Virginia's Woods," "Ashes of Soldiers," and "For You, O Democracy," Whitman.

Copies of these poems may be found at http://www.liglobal.com/walt

## *Extended Activities:*

Throughout this section, students have been encouraged to reflect on their love for America and what it means to them. Have them identify a particular concept that sums up America for them and draw a symbol of that image on plain paper. As a class, combine the images to create a quilt of America.

NAME_____ CLASS_____ DATE_____

## AMERICA'S ANSWER, P. 479

Throughout this section, you have been encouraged to reflect on your love for America and what it means to you. Identify a particular concept that sums up America for you and draw a symbol of that image on plain paper. As a class combine the images to create a quilt of America.

| *Story* | *Find in the glossary the meaning of:* |
|---|---|
| *Reader p. 299* | **facilities**_____ |
| | **Empire State**_____ |
| | **cosmographer**_____ |
| | **potent**_____ |
| *Reader p. 304* | **arsenal**_____ |
| | **ensign**_____ |
| | **carded**_____ |
| | **pedigree**_____ |
| | **estates**_____ |
| | **stature**_____ |
| | **attitude**_____ |
| | **quiver**_____ |
| | **entreaty**_____ |
| | **pallet**_____ |
| | **verge**_____ |
| | **loadstone**_____ |
| | **parley**_____ |
| | **gigantic**_____ |
| | **trophy**_____ |
| | **apparition**_____ |
| | **adage**_____ |
| *Reader p. 348* | **venerable**_____ |
| | **bullion**_____ |
| | **diligently**_____ |
| | **ceremony**_____ |
| | **ponderous**_____ |
| *Reader p. 353* | **cataract**_____ |
| | **native**_____ |
| | **turmoil**_____ |
| *Reader p. 361* | **avocation**_____ |
| | **preposterous**_____ |
| | **contortion**_____ |
| | **placid**_____ |
| *Reader p. 365* | **roundelay**_____ |
| | **rugged**_____ |
| *Reader p. 367* | **legend**_____ |
| | **tranquility**_____ |
| | **rustic**_____ |
| | **superstition**_____ |

architect_____

urchin_____

revenue_____

budget_____

goblin_____

hardihood_____

decision_____

despotic_____

refugee_____

*Reader p. 402* spacious_____

perpendicular_____

Titanic_____

visage_____

prophecy_____

ardor_____

pensive_____

commodity_____

portico_____

sordid_____

mediate_____

ignoble_____

clangor_____

verdant_____

epaulet_____

truculent_____

illustrious_____

spectacle_____

array_____

despondent_____

grandeur_____

utterance_____

*Reader p. 425* compliance_____

garrulous_____

append_____

conjectured_____

dilapidated_____

commissioned_____

initial_____

interminable_____

transcendent_____

finesse_____

*Reader p. 436* magi_____

appertaining_____

agile_____

meretricious_____

peculiar_____

coveted_____

*Reader p. 443*  peon_____

statute_____

reasoned_____

*Reader p. 448*  pioneer_____

primeval_____

vexing_____

sierras_____

*Reader p. 450*  copse_____

tendrils_____

*Reader p. 454*  spectral_____

craftsmen_____

treenail_____

spar_____

reeling_____

citadel_____

Hindustan_____

mart_____

main_____

*Reader p. 462*  symbol_____

tricolor_____

emblazonry_____

luminous_____

*Reader p. 466*  flaming_____

dome_____

sentry_____

blackening_____

*Reader p. 468*  incarcerated_____

Sepoy_____

debarked_____

impose_____

*Reader p. 471*  delineate_____

judiciously_____

deranged_____

prudence_____

integrity_____

colloquial_____

mediocrity_____

fluency_____

constellation_____

destiny_____

arduous_____

*Reader p. 475* masterful_____

councilor_____

benefactor_____

*Reader p. 477* weather'd_____

rack_____

exulting_____

*Reader p. 478* flaming_____

*Pronounce:*

exploit, geographer, athletic, sinew, comely, memoirs, taciturn, aerial, stalwart, gesture, capacious, victual, subtle, hearth, ominous, specie, loath, heroism, route, unwonted, minutely, reptile, tremor, abyss, tour, idea, contemplative, leisurely, infinite, inapplicable, patron, elm, Herculean, alternative, horizon, hospitable, benign, harbinger, beneficence, wound, buoyantly, obliquely, draught, infamous, tedious, inquiries, exquisitely, fellow, amateur, cordial, garish, sooty, scourge, Hebrides, helm, coral, insignia, rampant, bouquet.

# APPENDIX I
## INSTRUCTIONAL AIDS

The first section of this appendix, "Silent and Oral Reading," appears in the original *Elson Readers, Book Seven* and offers the teacher and/or parent a useful method of assisting the student(s) in attaining the objectives in this guide. The remaining aids have been written specially for this guide by the authors as additional resources for the teacher and parent.

### SILENT AND ORAL READING

**Silent Reading.** This book includes abundant material for both silent and oral reading. Some stories and poems must be read thoughtfully in order to gain the author's full meaning; such reading cannot be done rapidly. In other selections the meaning can be grasped easily, and the reading can be rapid; in such cases we read mainly for the central thought, for the story element.

You read silently more often than you read aloud to others; you should, therefore, train yourself in rapid silent reading, concentrating your mind on the thought of the selection. You will soon discover that as you give closer attention to a story you will not only understand it better, but you will also remember more of it. In previous grades your training in silent reading has enabled you to gather facts from individual paragraphs and to hold in mind the thread of the narrative in shorter selections. But you are to extend this power steadily until you can gather facts and follow the unfolding plot in selections of considerable length. A number of stories in this book are long enough to train you to read with intelligence a newspaper, a magazine article, or a book. And this is precisely the ability you most need, not only in preparing lessons in history and other school subjects, but in all your reading throughout life. As you train yourself to grasp swiftly and accurately the meaning of a page, you increase your capacity to enjoy books—one of the most pleasurable things in life. Theodore Roosevelt trained himself to be such a rapid reader that he was able to grasp the central thought of a page almost as quickly as he could turn the leaves of the book.

In preparing lessons in geography and history and in the use of geographical and historical stories, you have a splendid opportunity to increase your ability to gather facts quickly from the printed page. These informational studies, however, do not take the place of the reading lesson in literature. They merely offer additional opportunity for you to increase your ability in rapid silent reading.

Notice that the rapid silent readers in your class generally gain and retain from their reading more facts than the slow readers do. Notice, too, that you read more rapidly when you are looking for the answer to some particular question or looking for a certain passage than you do when you read merely to follow the thread of the story. Moving your lips or pointing to the words with your finger retards your speed. In the selections in this book suggested for silent reading you may test your ability at thought-getting in any of the following ways:

1. By using a list of questions covering the most important ideas of the selection (see "Questions for Testing Silent Reading," p. 42).
2. By telling the story from a given outline (see "Outline for Testing Silent Reading," p. 42).
3. By making a list of questions yourself, allowing some classmate to use them to test his or her ability at thought-getting, while you make similar use of his or her questions.
4. By telling the story from an outline that you have made. Telling the substance of the story from your own outline is an excellent kind of test because you test not only your understanding of the story, but also your memory and your power to express the thought of what you have read.

In all your reading, both at home and at school, you should read as rapidly as you can, but not so fast that you fail to get the thought. In preparing your lessons on selections in this book, test yourself by seeing how many of the questions, under "Discussion," that develop the most important thoughts of the story, you can answer after one reading. You may have to read parts of the story more than once in order to gain the full meaning. If, from time to time, you record your reading speed and your thought-getting ability, comparing your standing with that of your classmates and with the standard for seventh grade pupils, you will be able to see whether or not you are making satisfactory progress. The standard for seventh grade boys and girls is 250 words per minute, with the ability to reproduce after one reading 50% of the ideas in a 400-word passage.

The following form will suggest a way to record the results of your test:

### INDIVIDUAL RECORD

| DATE | TITLES | SPEED | | COMPREHENSION |
|---|---|---|---|---|
| | | No. of minutes required to read story | No. words per minute | Ten points for each of ten test questions* |
| | Hunting the Grizzly Bear | | | |
| | Total No. Words, 1957 | | | |
| | The Great Stone Face... | | | |
| | Total No. Words, 7475 | | | |

*Questions to be selected by the teacher.

### CLASS RECORD

| DATE | SPEED | | | COMPREHENSION | | | |
|---|---|---|---|---|---|---|---|
| | No. words per minute | | | Ten points for each of ten test questions | | | |
| | Lowest | Highest | Median | Lowest | Highest | Median | |
| | | | | | | | |
| | | | | | | | |

**Oral Reading.** In the prose selections suggested for silent reading, you will wish to read aloud certain passages because of their beauty, their dramatic quality, or the forceful way in which the author has expressed his thoughts. In these selections, "Class Readings" are listed for this purpose. Sometimes these readings are intended for individual pupils; sometimes, particularly in dialogue, they are intended for groups. "Class Readings" include also supplementary poems and stories suggested for oral presentation.

In general, all poetry should be read aloud, for much of the beauty of poetry lies in its rhythm. The voice, with its infinite possibilities of change, is an important factor in interpreting a poem. As you listen to your teacher or some other good reader, you will appreciate how much pleasure one who has learned the art of reading is able to give others. Oral reading trains the ear of the listener to become sensitive to a pleasing voice, to correct pronunciation, and to distinct articulation. The sympathetic reading of many of the poems in this book will reveal to you the beauty of the language that we speak and by which we express our thoughts. Longfellow says, "Of equal honor with him who writes a grand poem is he who reads it grandly."

## OUTLINE FOR ORAL PRESENTATIONS

The following rubric is a general guideline to consider when critiquing student oral presentations. As the teacher, you may want to assign a point value to each of the items which you consider to be pertinent to the assignment.

## General Guidelines

| | Points Possible | Points Earned |
|---|---|---|
| **Completed on time** | | |
| **Fulfilled the guidelines of the assignment** | | |
| **Message:** <br> **Clear and pertinent** | | |
| **Appealing and detailed** | | |
| **Research:** <br> **Current and varied** | | |
| **Properly cited** | | |
| **Technology:** <br> **Used technical materials,** <br> **i.e., computer, puppets,** <br> **tools appropriately** | | |
| **Used art materials i.e. wood,** <br> **paint, paper creatively** | | |
| **Presentation:** <br> **Good posture** | | |
| **Eye contact with the audience** | | |
| **Voice control, volume, rate and expression** | | |
| **Body language shows enthusiasm** | | |

PRESENTATION CHECKLIST:

The following checklist is designed to assist the student in gathering materials and information for an oral presentation. The student should be encouraged to complete the proposal and review it with the teacher to insure a well-organized presentation.

## Proposal

**Topic on which I'll speak**

_____

**Supporting facts I plan to use**

_____

_____

_____

**Supporting anecdotes or stories to interest my listeners**

_____

_____

_____

**Visual aids to enhance my speech**

_____

**Musical background to accompany my speech**

_____

**Technological equipment I will need**

_____

**What do I want my listeners to learn from this presentation**

_____

_____

**My conclusion**

_____

## THE STAGES OF THE WRITING PROCESS

Throughout the Reader, students are encouraged to write essays on a variety of topics for a variety of audiences and purposes. The following general guideline for the stages of the writing process will assist the student in producing a meaningful, well-organized, well-crafted essay. The writing process includes four stages: prewrite, draft, edit/revise, final copy.

**PREWRITE PLANNING GUIDE:**

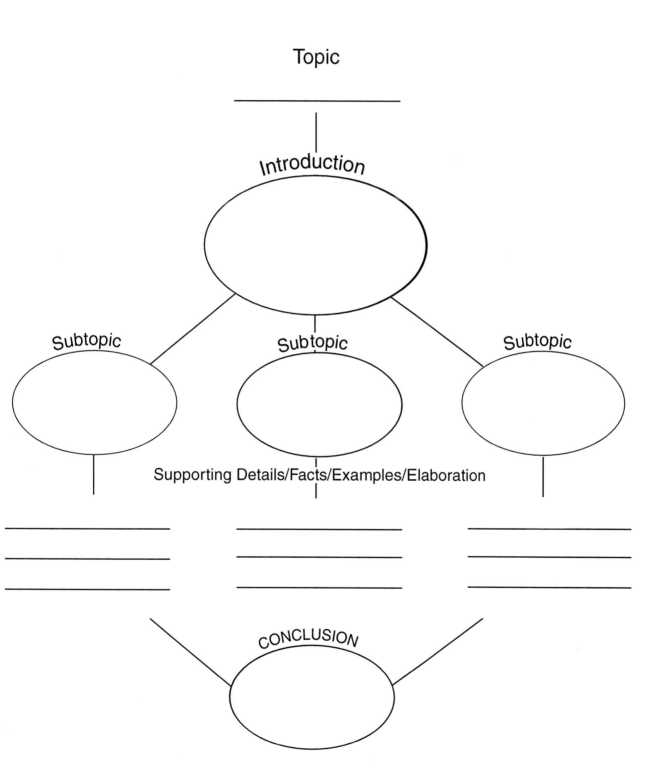

**1. Introduction:**

Students should develop their paper with the following elements:

    I. Introduction:

        A. Hook sentence—This sentence hooks "the interest of the reader." A hook sentence can be a quote, a question, an interesting fact, or anecdote.

        B. Thesis sentence—This sentence must include the subject about which the paper is written and an opinion. For example: Those living near the Mississippi River need to be prepared for floods. NOT: I'm going to write about floods along the Mississippi River.

        C. Map sentence—This sentence lists the three main points of the body of the paper.

**2. Body:**

Develop the main reasons, one paragraph for each reason, using vivid sensory details. As appropriate, use statistics, quotations, stories, and examples to support the reason. Use transitions appropriately at the beginning and within each body paragraph.

        **TREEES paragraphs**
          Topic
          Reason
             Elaboration
          Example
             Elaboration
          Summary

**3. Conclusion:**

Restate the thesis and summarize your main reasons. Challenge the reader with a closing thought, action, or recommendation. In the conclusion, do not use exact words or phrases from the introduction.

**Edit/Revise:**

Review the essay to make sure it is organized with vivid details and examples that support the thesis, the tone is appropriate for the audience, and word choice is precise and lively. Sentences should be complete and varied in length and structure. Grammar should be appropriate, and spelling and punctuation are generally correct.

**Final Draft:**

Rewrite the essay to include the revisions made in the editing stage.

**Evaluation Rubric (Checklist):**

At right.

| | Points Possible | Points Earned |
|---|---|---|
| **Planning:** | | |
| **Draft:** | | |
| **Revision/ Editing:** | | |
| **Final Copy:** **Conventions** spelling, punctuation, grammar | | |
| **Supporting Details** | | |
| **Neatness** | | |
| **Introduction** | | |
| **Conclusion** | | |
| **Organization** | | |

# APPENDIX II

## A BRIEF DESCRIPTION OF WORLD WAR ONE
### BY ANDY JAMESON

World War One had ended just a few years before the original *Elson Readers* appeared. This event was fresh in the mind of Americans and profoundly changed the way they looked at themelves and their role in the world. This changed outlook is reflected in *The Elson Readers,* in both the literature that was included and in the study questions. This brief description of that great event is provided as both a source of background information and a starting point for parents, teachers, and students to begin discussions on this turning point in American history.

World War One (also known as the Great War) lasted for four years—from 1914 to the end of 1918. The war was fought between Germany and its allies (Austria-Hungary of the Hapsburg Empire and Turkey of the Ottoman Empire) known as the Central Powers (or the Triple Alliance), and Great Britain, France, Russia, Italy, Japan, and, from 1917, the United States called the Allies. Germany was forced to fight the war on two fronts: the Western Front against the Allies and the Eastern Front against Russia. It was the first international conflict in which the United States participated.

The leading causes of the war were the alliance system of the late nineteenth century, which divided European states into two contending camps; the German victory over France in the Franco-German War (1870-71); the unification of Germany under Chancellor Otto von Bismarck and its rapid industrialization; the nationalist and ethnic agitation in the Balkans; and the fact that by 1900, European states were engaged in an escalating arms race and building vast military and naval forces in peacetime. The alliance system was symptomatic of the tension in European society between the growth of an international economy—the competition for goods and markets—and the political outlook of European states based on their own narrow national interests.

Bismarck set out to build a German empire based on the nationalistic premise that Germany also deserved a "place in the sun"—which meant an international political, economic, and military position like that of the British Empire. In Europe, the Germans claimed that they were being encircled by France and Russia. The entrance of Germany into the world scene exacerbated the intense rivalry for power and colonial markets in Africa, the Near East, and the Far East, as well as control of the seas. When the Germans decided to build a navy in 1891, they began the Anglo-German naval race.

The "race for empire" led to crises in Morocco, where Germany sent a gunboat to protect German interests, and in the Balkans, where Germany supported its Austrian ally against the national liberation movements which threatened the integrity of the Austro-Hungarian Empire. The three Balkan Wars (1912-1913), which were a prelude to World War One, also involved the Turks, whose Ottoman Empire had been disintegrating under the liberation movements of the Greeks and the southern Slavic peoples (Serbs, Croats, Bulgarians), and the Russians, who intervened in the Balkans as the "big Slavic" protectors of the Orthodox Christians—thus posing a threat to the Central Powers.

It was the nationalist movements in the Balkans which provided the "spark" that began World War One. On June 29, 1914, the heir to the Hapsburg Empire, Archduke Franz Ferdinand, was assassinated in Sarajevo (the capital of Bosnia). The Germans supported their Austrian ally, while the French supported the Russians. Protected by their navy, the British tried to maintain their policy of "splendid isolation," but the threat to the British naval forces in the North Sea from the German fleet, and with the French coast of the Channel open to German naval attack, the British were forced to protect their sea lanes and defend their French ally. When the Russians refused a German demand to stop their mobilization on the eastern border, Germany declared war (August 1, 1914), and France followed with its declaration (August 3). And when the Germans launched their Schlieffen Plan—a military strategy which involved a rapid thrust through Belgium to crush the French forces (in violation of the treaty which guaranteed the neutrality of Belgium)—Great Britain also declared war on Germany (August 4).

To supply their Russian ally, the British and French launched a disastrous naval attack on Turkey via the Dardanelles (1915), but the campaign was called off when the Allies lost 143,000 killed or wounded in the Gallipoli campaign.

On the Eastern Front, the early Russian offensive of 1914, which had driven into German territories in Prussia, Poland, and Galicia, was stopped and driven back by the Austro-German offensive of 1915.

By 1916, the war of maneuver on the Western Front ground to a halt, and it became a war of position and attrition—the massive armies were deadlocked in trench warfare. The machine gun—a new weapon—immobilized the troops which could advance only with staggering losses, while the tank, which was to become the antidote to the machine gun, and the airplane, the future antidote to the tank, were still in the experimental stages of development as weapons of war. The stalemate on the Western Front, however, ended when the Russians withdrew from, and the Americans entered, the war. The imperial Russian armies, plagued by poor military leadership and inadequate supplies, collapsed, and Czar Nicholas II was forced to abdicate from the internal pressure of the socialists (Marxists), especially from the leader of the Bolsheviks, the extreme faction of the Russian Marxists, V. I. Lenin (who formed the Communist party). When the czar abdicated, Lenin seized power in November, 1917, and the Bolsheviks signed the treaty of Brest-Litovsk with the Germans (December 3, 1917). At this point the war shifted to the Western Front, where the German High Command, under its Generals Hindenburg and Ludendorff, planned an offensive against the Allies. The Germans moved their army from the Russian front to the west via the railroad.

The German policy of unrestricted submarine warfare led United States President Woodrow Wilson to break off diplomatic relations with Germany, and when the British ship Lusitania was sunk with American passengers on board, and American ships were lost to U-boat action, he asked Congress for a declaration of war "to make the world safe for democracy,"(April 2, 1917). But it would be one year before the American military force and industrial production were prepared for war, and American soldiers arrived on the Western Front. With conscription administered by a Selective Service system, the armed services built a force of over four million. The government undertook the massive task of converting producers in the lumber, steel, automobile, and other industries to war production. Shipping tonnage increased from one million to ten million tons. The war effort encouraged citizens to conserve food (sugar was rationed and meatless Tuesdays were introduced) and fuel (daylight-saving time was adopted to save coal), and to purchase government Liberty bonds—the Treasury Department staged rallies at which Hollywood stars appeared to promote bond sales. At the same time, farmers were induced to grow more crops, and the production of civilian goods was cut (75,000 tons of tin were diverted to military production from children's toys and 8,000 tons of steel from the manufacture of women's corsets to munitions). The United States also provided loans to the Allies, which they used to purchase food and supplies.

While American military and economic power were geared up, the French and British suffered great losses in holding the line on the Western Front. When asked about an allied offensive, French General Pétain said, "I am waiting for the Americans and the tanks." In June, 1918, American troops under the command of General John J. Pershing, engaged the Germans at the Battles of Château-Thierry, Belleau Wood, and the Argonne, as 250,000 Americans were landing in France each month. Faced with this allied buildup, the German command realized that Germany could not win the war, and the government of Kaiser Wilhelm II began peace negotiations. By the time the armistice was signed (November 11, 1918), there were two million American soldiers in France and another million were heading for Europe. The Allies suffered ten million killed and twenty million casualties in the war, and the United States lost 115,000 dead and 315,000 casualties. While the allied losses far surpassed those of the Americans, it was the specter and the reality of American military and economic power that were decisive in ending the war.

In military history, World War One is notable for the brutal conditions under which the war was fought and for the incompetent leadership of the commanders—and the effect on the morale and discipline of the troops. The idea that soldiers were "manipulated from above" subject to the traditional military concept of obedience based on punishment resulted in revision of the military code of conduct.

Among the legacies of the war, which affected the course of the twentieth century, were the creation of the League of Nations (an international consortium), the rise of totalitarianism, and the imperial partition of the Near East (which resulted in the future states of Iraq, Syria, and Jordan).

# GLOSSARY

| | | | |
|---|---|---|---|
| a as in m<u>a</u>t | ə as in b<u>a</u>nana | ä as in f<u>a</u>ther | Ø as in s<u>i</u>de |
| e as in b<u>e</u>d | ər as in f<u>urther</u> | aủ as in l<u>ou</u>d | ŋ as in si<u>ng</u> |
| i as in t<u>i</u>p | ā as in d<u>a</u>y | ē as in n<u>ee</u>d | ō as in sn<u>o</u>w |
| ȯ as in s<u>aw</u> | ȯi as in c<u>oi</u>n | ü as in r<u>u</u>le | ủ as in p<u>ull</u> |
| | ° as in eat<u>e</u>n | th as in hea<u>th</u>er | |

## A

**abandoning their post** leaving their position

**a base ment** (ə-'bā-smənt) humiliation

**ab bess** ('a-bəs) head of a convent

**Ab er deen shire** (a-bər-'dēn-shər)

**ab hor rence** (əb-'hȯr-ənts) hatred

**a bide** (ə-'bØd) wait; live

**a bode** (ə-'bōd) lived; home

**a bodiless spec tral il lu sion** ('spek-trəl; i-'lü-zhən) a ghost

**abroad** away from home

**ab rupt** (ə-'brəpt) steep; sudden; hurried

**absolute property** thing owned entirely by one

**a bu sive** (ə-'byü-siv) insulting

**a byss** (ə-'bis) great depth

**Ab ys sin i a** (a-bə-'si-nē-ə) a country in East Africa

**ac cess** ('ak-ses) admission

**ac com pa nied** (ə-'kəmp-nēd) went with

**accord** agree

**accorded into one strain** harmonized perfectly

**account** consider

**ac cu mu la tion** (ə-kyü-myə-'lā-shən) collection

**ac cu rate** ('a-kyə-rət) exact

**a chieve your adventure** (ə-'chēv) perform the knightly deed you have requested

**a chieve ment** (ə-'chēv-mənt) deed; accomplishment

**A chil les** (ə-'ki-lēz) one of the heroes in the Iliad

**ac quire** (ə-'kwØr) gain

**ac tu at ed** ('ak-chə-wā-təd) inspired

**a cute** (ə-'kyüt) deep; sharp

**ad age**  ('a-dij)  old or wise saying

**ad a mant**  ('a-də-mənt)  hardest stone known

**ad a man tine**  (a-də-'man-tēn)  hard as the hardest stone

**a dapt**  (ə-'dapt)  fit

**ad der**  ('a-dər)  poisonous snake

**ad dress**  (ə-'dres)  speech; speak to; write to

**ad e quate**  ('a-di-kwət)  suitable; sufficient

**ad her ent**  (ad-'hir-ənt)  follower

**a dieu**  (ə-'dü)  good-bye

**ad ja cent**  (ə-'jā-sᵊnt)  near by

**ad just**  (ə-'jəst)  arrange

**administered justice with dis crim i na tion**  (dis-kri-mə-'nā-shən)  in punishments he used judgment

**ad mi ral**  ('ad-mə-rəl)  naval officer of the highest rank

**a do**  (ə-'dü)  trouble

**ad ven tur ous**  (əd-'ven-chə-rəs)  bold

**ad ver sa ry**  ('ad-vər-ser-ē)  foe

**ad ver si ty**  (ad-'vər-sə-tə)  misfortune

**ad vert**  (ad-'vərt)  refer

**ad vo ca cy**  ('ad-və-kə-sē)  support; favor

**ad vo cate for an im pos tor**  ('ad-və-kət; im-'päs-tər)  are you one who pleads the cause of a deceiver

**ae ri al**  ('ar-ē-əl)  in the air

**af firm**  (ə-'fərm)  declare

**afflicted**  unhappy

**affliction**  misfortune

**afford**  give

**af front ed**  (ə-'frən-təd)  offended

**a full noble surgeon**  a man who knew how to care for the wounded or sick

**against the red west**  with the sunset sky behind them

**Ag a siz**  ('ag-ə-sē)  famous naturalist

**ag gra vat ed**  ('a-grə-vā-təd)  magnified

**a ghast**  (ə-'gast)  amazed

**ag ile**  ('a-jəl)  lively; quick-moving

**ag i tat ed**  ('a-jə-tā-təd)  frightened; excited

**Ag ra vaine**  ('ag-rə-vān)

**aide-de-camp**  (ād-di-'kamp)  a general's assistant

**a kind of destiny**  necessity which has forced me to do this

**a lert**  (ə-'lərt)  watch; watchful

**Al giers**  (al-'jērz)  African seaport

**al ien** ('ā-lē-ən) foreign; strange

**al lay** (ə-'lā) quiet

**al lege** (ə-'lej) declare

**all hor rent** ('hor-ənt) bristling all over

**al lit er a tion** (ə-li-tə-'rā-shən) repetition of the same letter or sound at the beginning of two or more words in succession

**al lot ment** (ə-'lät-mənt) share

**all that here could win us** everything that would keep us here

**al lude** (ə-'lüd) refer

**Almes bury** ('ämz-bər-ē)

**alms** ('älmz) charity

**al ter nate ly** ('ol-tər-nət-lē) by turns; first one, then the other

**al ter na tive** (ol-'tər-nə-tiv) choice

**am a teur** ('a-mə-tər) careless; beginner

**am bush** ('am-bush) hiding; trap

**a mend** (ə-'mend) correct; change

**a mends, to make** (ə-'menz) do all he can to make up for his sins; be forgiven by; give reward for injustice

**am o rous og lings** ('a-mə-rəs; 'ō-gliŋz) loving looks; "making eyes"

**amour** (ə-'mur) love-affair

**am ple** ('am-pəl) large; full

**ample base** strong foundation

**Am ster dam** ('am-stər-dam) in Holland, the only place where printing of religious pamphlets could be done

**a nat o my** (ə-'na-tə-mē) science which treats of the structure of the body

**ancient ice** thick ice which has been there unmelted so many years

**Andre, Major** ('än-drā) a British spy

**an gel ic kin dred** (an-'je-lik; 'kin-drəd) a relationship to heaven

**An gles** ('aŋ-gelz) old English

**an guish of spirit** ('aŋ-gwish) mental agony

**an gu lar** ('aŋ-gyə-lər) uneven

**an i mate** ('a-nə-māt) inspire

**animate the people's hearts** stir the people and fill them

**an ni hi late** (ə-'nØ-ə-lāt) wipe out

**An noure** (a-'nur)

**au di tor** ('o-də-tər) listener

**aught** ('ot) anything

**aus tere** (o-'stir) stern

**au then tic** (ə-'then-tik) correct

**authentic records** correct history

**au thor i ta tive** (ə-'thär-ə-tā-tiv) commanding

**aux il ia ry**  (ȯg-ˈzil-yǝ-rē)  helper

**a vail**  (ǝ-ˈvāl)  help

**avail themselves of their numbers**  make use of their greater force

**A val on**  (ˈa-vǝ-län)  an imaginary earthly paradise where heroes were carried after death

**a venged upon you**  (ǝ-ˈvenjd)  made you suffer for

**a vert**  (ǝ-ˈvǝrt)  prevent; turn away

**av o ca tion**  (a-vǝ-ˈkā-shǝn)  occupation which one has for pleasure

**a vow al**  (ǝ-ˈvau̇-ǝl)  declaration

**awful moment**  tremendous importance

**a whiles**  (ǝ-ˈhwØlz)  sometimes

**ay**  (ˈØ)  alas; yes

**Ay mer de Va lence**  (ā-mǝr-dǝ-ˈvä-läns)

**Azores**  (ˈā-zōrz)  islands near and belonging to Portugal

**az ure**  (ˈa-zhǝr)  sky-blue

# B

**Ba al**  (ˈbā-ǝl)  Phoenician god of love

**Bacon, Sir Francis**  English philosopher and statesman (1561-1626)

**bade**  (ˈbād)  ordered; commanded

**badge of his au thor i ty**  (ǝ-ˈthär-ǝ-tē)  sign of his power

**baf fled**  (ˈba-fǝld)  defeated

**bal lad**  (ˈba-lǝd)  a kind of short, narrative poem suitable for singing

**balm**  (ˈbälm)  fragrance; balms, herbs used to preserve bodies

**Bal tic's strand**  (ˈbȯl-tiks; ˈstrand)  shore of the Baltic Sea

**band**  (ˈband)  company of men organized for a common purpose

**barb**  (ˈbärb)  fast horse; point

**bar bar i an**  (bär-ˈber-ē-ǝn)  foreigner; here, a Persian

**bard**  (ˈbärd)  a poet and singer

**bare**  (ˈbār)  carried

**barge**  (ˈbärj)  boat elegantly furnished and decorated; large flat bottomed boat

**Bar ham Down**  (ˈbär-am)

**bark**  (bärk)  boat; ship

**bar on**  (ˈbar-ǝn)  a nobleman

**ba rouche**  (bǝ-ˈrüsh)  open carriage

**Bar re, Colonel**  (ba-ˈrā)

**bar ri er**  (ˈbar-ē-ǝr)  obstacle

**bars and blocks**  fastenings which hold a ship on shore while it is being worked on

**bars ef ful gent**  (i-ˈfül-jǝnt)  shining streaks

**bar ter** ('bär-tər) trade

**barter their com mod it ies** (kə-'mä-də-tēz) trade what they had for other things they wanted

**base** ('bās) unworthy; disgraceful

**base less** ('bā-sləs) false

**base ness** ('bā-snəs) disgrace

**Bath she ba** (bath-'shē-bə) *see* David's transgression

**battlements** high towers

**battle peal** noise of cannon, etc.

**Baud win** ('bōd-win)

**bear him** conduct himself

**bear himself meetly** behave properly

**bear sway** ('swā) rule

**bear the brunt of** ('brənt) face the most serious

**bear witness** hear me state

**Beau mains** ('bō-mānz)

**beautiful were his feet** *see* Isaiah LII:7

**be daubed** (bi-'dȯbd) covered; coated

**be deck** (bi-'dek) decorate

**Bed i vere** ('be-də-vir)

**bee tling** ('bē-t°l-iŋ) projecting

**be fits the scene** (bi-'fits) fits the spring day

**be get that golden time again** (bi-'get) recall the wonderful experience you gave me

**beggar description** make any description of it seem poor compared with how bad it really was

**be guiled** (bi-'gꭓld) led

**be hest** (bi-'hest) command

**be hoove** (bi-'hüv) be proper for; befit

**be lab o ring** (bi-'lā-bə-riŋ) beating

**Bell i cent** ('bel-i-sent)

**bel lig er ent** (bə-'lij-rənt) warlike

**bel lows** ('be-lōz) an instrument for blowing fires

**beneath** (bi-'nēth)

**ben e dic tion** (be-nə-'dik-shən) blessing

**ben e fac tor** ('be-nə-fak-tər) one who does great good

**be nef i cence** (bə-'ne-fə-sənts) doing good

**be nef i cent** (bə-'ne-fə-sənt) kind

**ben e fits forgot** ('be-nə-fitz) kindness to others not appreciated by them

**be nev o lent** (bə-'nev-lənt) kind

**be nign** (bi-'nꭓn) kind; loving

**be nig nant** (bi-'nig-nənt)  kind

**bent**  determined

**berserk** (bə-'zərk)  one of the wild warriors of heathen times in Scandinavia

**Bertha**  a legendary queen

**best-appointed**  having the best equipment

**be stirs him well** (bi-'stərz)  moves about briskly, or busily

**be thy man**  serve you

**be trayed with a kiss** (bi-'trād)  deceived by pretended friendship. *See* Matthew XXVI:48

**be troth al** (bi-'trō-thəl)  marriage ceremony (the word usually means *engagement*)

**bev y** ('be-vē)  flock

**beyond per ad ven ture** ('pər-əd-ven-chər)  without doubt

**be zoar** ('bē-zōr)  a mineral matter found in certain animals, once used as a remedy to counteract the effects of poison

**bi as** ('bØ-əs)  influence

**bite so nigh** ('nØ)  hurt so much

**bite the dust**  die in defeat

**biv ouac** ('bi-və-wak)  encampment of soldiers prepared for fighting

**blackening**  making black; killing

**blades of heroes**  swords which have won great victories

**Blake, Robert**  a British admiral

**blared across the shal lows** ('blard; 'sha-lōz)  called across the river

**blast ed** ('blas-təd)  withered

**blazed** ('blāzd)  marked by having a piece of bark cut away

**bla zon** ('blā-zᵊn)  coat of arms

**bleached**  whitened by the sun

**blessed** ('blest)  much loved

**bliss of sol i tude** ('sä-lə-tüd)  great comfort in lonely moments

**blithe** ('blØth)  happy; joyous

**block ad ed** (blä-'kā-dəd)  kept

**bloom**  time of greatest happiness

**blossom into melody**  break into song

**blow** ('blō)  blossom

**board**  table

**bod ed ill** ('bō-dəd)  foretold misfortune

**boding** ('bō-diŋ)  warning

**bog gy** ('bä-gē)  marshy; having swamps

**bold peas an try** ('pe-zᵊn-trē)  brave farmers whose land belonged not to themselves, but to their lords

**Bon a ven ture** (bōn-ə-ven-'tür)

**bon dage** ('bän-dij) slavery

**bondage of error, the** mistaken view which keeps me from doing right (lines 1-4 refer to the story of God leading the Israelites through the Red Sea. *See* Exodus XIV)

**bon ny bird** ('bä-nē) fair lady

**bookstall** a small book-shop

**boon** ('bün) jovial

**boor ish** ('bùr-ish) rude

**border** *see* frontier, second meaning

**bore** went

**boundless reach** endless stretch

**boun te ous** ('baùn-tē-əs) generous

**boun ti ful** ('baùn-ti-fəl) generous

**bou quet** (bō-'kā) mass of flowers

**bour geois** (bùrzh-'wä) head man

**bow** ('baù) forward part of a vessel

**bow er** ('baù-ər) apartment

**Bra bant** ('brä-bənt) Belgian province

**brack ish** ('bra-kish) salty; distasteful

**brag gart** ('bra-gərt) boaster

**braided light** light from the red, white, and blue intermingled

**brand from the burning** ('brand) piece of burning wood from the midst of the fire—that is, out of the midst of great danger

**Brath wick** ('brath-ik)

**braved** ('brāvd) courageously met

**brawl** ('bròl) quarrel; rush

**bra zen** ('brā-zᵊn) brass

**breach** ('brēch) opening

**break faith** fail to carry on the great work we have died doing

**breast ing** ('brest-iŋ) forcing their way through

**breast plate** ('brest-plāt) armor

**breast work** ('brest-wərk) fortification

**bred** ('bred) brought up

**bridge** platform over the forward deck of a ship

**brim stone** ('brim-stōn) sulphur

**bring him to knowledge** recognize him

**bringing weary thought home** making me discontented

**brist ling steel** ('bris-liŋ) spears pointed in the air

**Brit an ni a** (bri-'tan-yə) poetic name for Great Britain

**broader sig ni fi ka tion** (sig-nə-fə-'kā-shən) deeper meaning

**broadside** with his side facing me

**bron co** ('bräŋ-kō)  small wild horse

**brood**  sit on eggs to hatch; lie

**brought to bay**  cornered so that escape seems impossible

**brute forms**  wild creatures

**Bru tus** ('brü-təs)  a Roman who was one of Caesar's slayers

**buc ca neer** (bə-kə-'nir)  adventurer

**Buch an** ('bək-ən)

**bud get** ('bə-jət)  collection

**buf fet** ('bə-fət)  blow

**built in an age**  in process of building for many years

**bul lied** ('bù-lēd)  irritated and injured

**bul lion** ('bùl-yən)  silver which has not been coined or made into objects

**bul rush** ('bùl-rəsh)  a large rush growing in water

**bul wark** ('bùl-wərk)  fortification

**buoy ant ly** ('bȯi-ənt-lē)  joyfully

**burden of the commonwealth**  responsibilities of the whole country

**bur gess** ('bər-jəs)  freeman who could vote

**Bur goyne** (bər-'gȯin)  the English general who surrendered to Washington

**burning star**  the stars and stripes of the flag are called "burning" and "flaming" to bring out their great power and beauty

**bur nish** ('bər-nish)  polish

**bur row** ('bər-ō)  hole dug in the ground

**bur then** ('bər-thən)  burden

**butte** ('byüt)  steep hill

**by mortal means**  by bringing him to great danger through someone else


## C


**Caer le on** (kär-'lē-ən)

**Ca ius** ('kā-yəs)

**Cal i ban** ('kal-ə-ban)

**calm, spoken to a** ('kälm)  quieted

**cal trop** ('kal-trəp)  spike driven into the ground, having four crossed points projecting at the head

**Cam el iard** ('kam-əl-yärd)

**Cam e lot** ('ka-mə-lät)  the legendary seat of Arthur's palace and court

**cam paign** (kam-'pān)  war

**Camp bell, Thomas** ('ka-məl)

**can ter** ('kan-tər)  easy gallop

**ca pa cious** (kə-'pā-shəs)  holding a great deal

**capacity** (kə-'pa-sə-tē)  ability

**ca price** (kė-'prēs)  fickleness

**ca pri cious** (kə-'pri-shəs)  changeable

**captives whom St. Greg o ry saw** ('greg-ə-rē)  young fair-haired boys of Britain were seen in the slave market of Rome by St. Gregory, a monk of the sixth century

**car cass** ('kär-kəs)  dead body

**carded**  prepared for spinning by combing

**card of prudent lore** ('lōr)  wise advice

**Car lisle** ('kär-lØl)

**car ol so madly** ('kar-əl)  sing so merrily

**carried away the palm** ('pälm)  took all  the honor

**cascade**  waterfall

**case ment** ('kās-mənt)  hinged window

**caste** ('kast)  any of the classes into which the society of India is divided. Deesa belonged to the lowest caste

**cat a ract** ('ka-tə-rakt)  large waterfall

**ca tas tro phe** (kə-'tas-trə-fē)  calamity

**caught the loom** ('lüm)  saw the outline far away

**cause way** ('kȯz-wā)  paved road

**cav al cade** ('ka-vəl-kād)  procession

**cav a lier** (ka-və-'lir)  knight

**cav al ry** ('ka-vəl-rē)  horsemen

**cav ern ous** ('ka-vər-nəs)  hollow; dark, like a cave

**ca vort ing** (kə-'vȯr-tiŋ)  prancing

**ce les tial** ('sə-les-chəl)  heavenly

**cen sure** ('sen-shər)  find fault with

**century-cir cled oak** ('sər-kəld)  oak 100 years old.  Each year a tree grows a circle

**cer e mo ny** ('ser-ə-mō-nē)  wedding; words by which a marriage is made lawful

**ce ru le an** (sə-'rü-lē-ən)  sky-blue

**chafed** ('chāft)  raged; chafed his hands, rubbed to start circulation

**chaf fer** ('cha-fər)  bargain

**chaf ing** ('chā-fiŋ)  excited; washing against

**cham pi on** ('cham-pē-ən)  defender

**chair of state**  seat used only by officials or honored guests

**chan ti cleer** (chan-tə-'klir)  rooster

**cha ot ic** (kā-'ä-tik)  disordered

**chap let** ('chap-lət)  wreath of honor

**char ac ter ize** ('kar-ik-tə-rØz)  describe

**charm** ('chärm)  small, decorative object

**chaste** ('chāst) dignified

**chas tise ment** (chas-'tŏz-mənt) punishment

**Chat ham** ('cha-təm)

**Cha til lon** (shä-tē-'yōn)

**cher ish** ('cher-ish) admire; love; hold; care for

**chid** ('chid) found fault

**chide** ('chŏd) scold

**chiv al rous** ('shi-vəl-rəs) gallant

**chiv al ry** ('shi-vəl-rē) courtesy and heroism

**chol er ic** ('kä-lə-rik) hot-tempered

**chord which Hampden smote** John Hampden, an Englishman, by refusing to pay an unjust tax in 1637 roused the patriotism of the people as a musician stirs his audience

**chosen for large designs** the kind of man to manage great affairs

**Chris ten dom** ('kri-sᵊn-dəm) parts of the world where Christianity is practiced

**chron i cle** ('krä-ni-kəl) history; tale

**chrys o lite** ('kri-sə-lŏt) yellow or green gems

**churl** ('chərl) common man; rude fellow

**cinch** ('sinch) *see* packing cinch

**cinque foil** ('siŋk-fȯil) a common plant with a five-parted leaf

**cir cuit, making a** ('sər-kət) moving in circle

**cir cum stan tial** (sər-kᵊm-'stant-shəl) realistic

**cit a del** ('si-tə-dᵊl) fort

**City of God** *see* Revelation XXI:10-27

**civil war** war between different parties of the same country

**clam or** ('kla-mər) shout

**clan gor** ('klaŋ-ər) ringing sound

**cleave** ('klēv) cut

**clem ents** ('kle-mənts) nature

**clois ter** ('klȯi-stər) convent

**close-reefed vessels** ('rēft) vessels or boats with their sails folded tightly

**cloud ves ture** ('ves-chər) dress of clouds

**clutch of an idea** ('kləch) first inspiration to do something great

**Clyde** ('klŏd) river in Scotland which has shipbuilding yards on its banks

**cocked** ('käkt) turned up

**cog no men** (käg-'nō-mən) last name

**coir swab** ('kȯir-swäb) mop or cloth made from outer fiber of the coconut

**col lapsed in proportion** (kə-'lapst) the other side caved in as far as the one side puffed out

**col lat ing** (kə-'lā-tiŋ) comparing

**col lo qui al** (kə-'lō-kwē-əl)  conversational

**col um bine** ('kä-ləm-bØn)  dainty flower which grows on a tall branching stalk

**combed** ('kōmd)  with the fleshy crest on its head

**come ly** ('kəm-lē)  good-looking

**Come weal or woe** ('wēl; 'wō)  whether in prosperity or in trouble

**comforts of the cup board** ('kə-bərd)  good things they had to eat

**com mend me** (kə-'mend)  take my regards

**Commentaries of Cae sar** ('sē-sər)  history of the seven years of the Gallic War, written by Julius Caesar

**com min gled** (kə-'miŋ-gəld)  combined

**com mis sion** (kə-'mi-shən)  appoint

**com mit** (kə-'mit)  to intrust

**com mod i ty** (kə-'mä-də-tē)  article

**com muned** (kə-'myünd)  thought over things

**com mun i cat ed electricity** (kə-'myü-nə-kā-təd)  gave enthusiasm

**companion meet**  a suitable friend

**com pass** ('käm-pəs)  an instrument for determining directions

**com pe ten cy** ('käm-pə-tənt-sē)  supply

**com pet i tor** (kəm-'pe-tə-tər)  rival

**com pli ance** (kəm-'plØ-ənts)  accordance

**com po nent** (kəm-'pō-nənt)  a part

**com port** (kəm-'pōrt)  agree

**com posed** (kəm-'pōzd)  made up

**composure** (kəm-'pō-zhər)  calmness

**com pre hend** (käm-pri-'hend)  understand

**com press** (kəm-'pres)  condense

**Com yn** ('kə-mən)

**con** ('kän)  memorize

**con ceive** (kən-'sēv)  imagine

**con cen tric** (kən-'sen-trik)  having a common center

**con cep tion** (kən-'sep-shən)  understanding; idea

**conch shell** ('känk)  sea shell

**con cise** (kən-'sØs)  brief

**con clude** (kən-'klüd)  think

**con de scend** (kän-di-'send)  lower oneself; consent

**con fer ence** ('kän-frənts)  meeting for discussion

**confession in the countenance, makes**  shows its sorrow in its face

**con fid ing** (kən-'fØ-diŋ)  trusting

**con fined** (kən-'fØnd)  imprisoned; limited

**confusion alone was supreme**  disorder reigned everywhere

**con gen ial**  (kən-'jē-nē-əl)  sympathetic

**con ger**  ('käŋ-gər)  a large eel

**con gest ed**  (kən-'jes-təd)  stopped

**con gre gate**  ('käŋ-gri-gāt)  assemble

**con gre ga tion**  (käŋ-gri-'gā-shən)  gathering

**con ject ure**  (kən-'jek-chər)  guess

**con nois seur**  (kä-nə-'sər)  one well versed in any subject; expert

**con san guin i ty**  (kän-san-'gwi-nə-tē)  blood relationship

**con scious ness of its,** etc.  ('känt-shəs-nəs)  knowledge that it is a task

**con se crat ed**  ('kän-sə-crā-təd)  made sacred

**con se quent exercise**  ('kän-sə-kwənt)  use which naturally follows

**con serv a tor ies**  (kən-'sər-və-tōr-ēz)  greenhouses

**con signed**  (kən-'sØnd)  given; laid him aside

**consigned to, dust to dust be**  lives be given up, *see* Genesis III:19

**con sol a to ry**  (kən-'sō-lə-tōr-ē)  comforting

**con stan cy**  ('kän-stən-sē)  loyalty; steadfastness; devotedness

**con stel la tion**  (kän-stə-'lā-shən)  stars; class of honored men

**con strain**  (kən-'strān)  force

**con tem plat ing**  ('kän-təm-plā-tiŋ)  looking at thoughtfully

**con tem pla tion**  (kän-təm-'plā-shən)  thought

**con tem pla tive**  (kən-'tem-plə-tiv)  thoughtful

**con temp tu ous**  (kən-'temp-chə-wəs)  scornful

**contend**  fight; argue; struggle

**con ti nen tal blood,** etc.  (kän-tᵊn-'en-tᵊl)  blood of East and West mingled

**con tor tion**  (kən-'tȯr-shən)  twisting

**con tra band**  ('kän-trə-band)  forbidden

**con tract ed**  (kän-'trak-təd)  gone into

**con trib ute**  (kən-'tri-byət)  furnish

**con tri tion**  (kən-'tri-shən)  repentance

**con trive**  (kən-'trØv)  plan

**con ven tion al**  (kən-'vench-nəl)  formal; customary

**con verse**  ('kän-vərs)  conversation

**con vey**  (kən-'vā)  carry

**con vic tion**  (kən-'vik-shən)  belief

**con vo lut ed**  ('kän-və-lü-təd)  twisted

**con voy**  ('kən-'vȯi)  take

**con voy**  ('kän-vȯi)  protection

**con vul sive**  (kən-'vəl-siv)  violent

**cope**  ('kōp)  struggle with successfully

**co pi ous ness**  ('kō-pē-əs-nəs)  large number of; abundance

**copse** ('käps) grove

**co quette** (kō-'ket) flirt

**cor al** ('kȯr-əl) skeletons of certain small sea-animals which have been deposited during the ages and form islands

**Cor bi tant** ('kȯr-bə-tənt) Indian chief

**cord age** ('kȯr-dij) ship-ropes

**cor dial sal u ta tion** ('kȯr-jəl; sal-yə-'tā-shən) hearty greeting

**Cor do van** ('kȯr-də-vən) from Cordova, a city in Spain, famous for leather

**cor mo-rant** ('kȯrm-rənt) a large fish-eating sea bird

**cor rod ed** (kə-'rō-dəd) rusted and worn

**cor rup tion** (kə-'rəp-shən) wickedness

**cor sair** ('kȯr-sar) pirate-ship

**corse let** ('kȯr-slət) armor for the body

**cos mog ra pher** (käz-'mä-grə-fər) one who has made a study of the earth and the heavens

**cou lee** ('kü-lē) deep bed of a stream

**coun ci lor** ('kaȯn-sə-lər) statesman

**coun sel** ('kaȯn-səl) advise

**coun sel or** ('kaȯn-sə-lər) adviser

**coun te nance** ('kaȯn-tᵊn-ənts) face

**coun ter part** ('kaȯn-tər-pärt) likeness

**count the risk** fear the consequences

**cou ri er's feet delayed** ('kȯr-ē-ərz) messenger detained on his errand

**cours er** ('kȯr-sər) war horse

**courted peril for its own sake** sought danger because of his love of adventure

**cour te ous** ('kər-tē-əs) polite

**cour tier** ('kōr-tē-ər) attendant on a king

**court ly** ('kōrt-lē) elegant; courteous

**cove** ('kōv) inlet

**cover** protection; **thick cover**, dense woods

**cov ert** ('kō-vərt) covering

**cov et ed** ('kə-və-təd) longed for

**cow er** ('kaȯ-ər) hide in fear

**cox comb** ('käk-skōm) noisy fellow

**crab bed ly hon est** ('kra-bəd-lē; 'ä-nəst) honest but in a disagreeable manner

**crafts men** ('krafts-men) skilled workmen

**crafty** ('kraf-tē) skillful

**crane** ('krān) wading bird

**cra ni um** ('krā-nē-əm) head

**crave a boon of your chivalry** ask that you use your bravery and gallantry in doing me a favor

**cre du li ty** (kri-'dü-lə-tē) childishness

**creeper** red-flowered vine

**crest** ('krest) top; head

**crest-waving Hec tor** ('hek-tər) tall weed. Hector, a Trojan warrior, was represented with a waving plume

**cri sis** ('krø-səs) time of trouble

**crisis must en sue** (in-'sü) state of affairs will result

**crit i cal a cu men** ('kri-ti-kəl; ə-'kyü-mən) thoughtful judgment

**crone** ('krōn) old woman who knew nothing but work

**cross** interfere with; sorrow

**cross hilt ed** ('kròs-hil-təd) with a handle in the shape of a cross

**cud gel** ('kə-jəl) beat

**cu li na ry** ('kə-lə-ner-ē) for the kitchen

**cul ling his phrases** ('kə-liŋ; 'frā-zəz) choosing his words with care

**curd ling awe** ('kərd-liŋ; 'ò) fright that made his blood run cold

**cur lew** ('kər-lü) long-billed bird

**cur rent** ('kər-ənt) circulating; **current coinage**, money in use at that time

**cut lass** ('kət-ləs) heavy, curved sword

**cyn i cal ly I play,** etc. ('si-ni-klē) I become selfish and act like a coward

**cy press** ('sø-prəs) dark evergreen tree

# D

**dal li er** ('da-lē-ər) shirker

**Da mas cus** (də-'mas-kəs) a city of Syria, famous for its silks and steel

**dangerous disposition** desperate state of mind

**danger's troubled night** war, England had just had two naval battles with France

**daunt** ('dònt) frighten

**David, King** *see* II Samuel VI:1

**David's trans gres sion** ('trans-gre-shən) because he loved Bathsheba, David sent Uriah, her husband, to the front of the battle to be killed. *See* II Samuel XI

**deal** give

**death without quarter** merciless death

**de barked** (dē-'bärkt) landed

**de bouch** (di-'baủch) march out

**de cease** (di-'sēs)  death

**de cis ion** (di-'si-zhən)  settlement

**de cis ive** (di-'s∅-siv)  important; positive

**de cliv i ty** (di-'kliv-ət-ē)  steep hill

**de co rum** (di-'kōr-əm)  fitness; modesty

**de cree** (di-'krē)  order

**ded i cate** ('de-di-kāt)  give up

**deem** ('dēm)  imagine; think

**deem more sacredly of**  be more reverent toward

**de fect** (di-'fekt)  fault

**de fi ance** (di-'f∅-ənts)  challenge

**de fi ant** (di-'f∅-ənt)  bold

**de fraud ed** (di-'frȯ-dəd)  cheated

**deign** ('dān)  be kind enough

**de ject ed** (di-'jek-təd)  sad

**de lec ta ble** (di-'lek-tə-bəl)  delightful

**de lib er ate** (di-'li-bə-rət)  for deliberately, slowly

**de lib er at ed to enter** (di-'li-bə-rā-təd)  decided to go on board

**de lib er a tion** (di-li-bə-'rā-shən)  care

**de lin e ate** (di-'li-nē-āt)  describe

**deliver**  rescue it from evil

**de lu sions** (di-'lü-zhənz)  deceptions

**de lu sive phan tom** (di-'lü-siv; 'fan-təm)  false expectation

**delve** ('delv)  dig; work

**Dem a ra tus** (de-mə-'rä-təs)

**de mean or** (di-'mē-nər)  manner

**de mol ish** (di-'mä-lish)  destroy

**de mor a lized** (di-'mȯr-ə-l∅zd)  cast into disorder

**de mure** (di-'myu̇r)  modest

**de nom i nat ed** (di-'nä-mə-nā-təd)  called

**de port ment easy** (di-'pōrt-mənt)  manner of carrying himself ; graceful

**de pose** (di-'pōz)  take the throne from

**de pre ci ate** (di-'prē-shē-āt)  cheapen

**de ranged** (di-'rānjd)  disturbed

**de rived** (di-'r∅vd)  gained

**de scried** (di-'skr∅d)  beheld

**de se crat ed** ('de-si-krā-təd)  which had had their sacredness disregarded and had been dug up that the Spaniards might get the riches buried with them

**Desert's golden sand**  products, as spices, ivory, dates, etc., carried by camels across the desert

**de sign** (di-'zØn)  plan; intend

**de spite** (di-'spØt)  in spite of

**de spond en cy** (di-'spän-dən-sē)  discouragement

**de spond ent** (di-'spän-dənt)  discouraged

**des pot ic** (des-'pä-tik)  tyrannical

**des pot ism** ('des-pə-ti-zəm)  tyranny

**des tined** ('des-tənd)  intended; fated

**des ti ny** ('des-tə-nē)  fate

**de tach** (di-'tach)  send

**de tach ments** (di-'tach-m'nts)  armies

**dev a stat ing** ('de-və-stā-tiŋ)  terrible

**de vic es** (di-'vØ-səz)  tricks

**de vi ous** ('dē-vē-əs)  winding

**de void** (di-'vȯid)  destitute

**de vout** (di-'vaủt)  pious

**dex ter ous** ('dek-stə-rəs)  clever

**did but speak**  was speaking only

**di et** ('dØ-ət)  food

**dif fuse** (di-'fyüz)  spread

**dif fuse ly** (di-'fyüs-lē)  too much at length

**di lap i dat ed** (də-'la-pə-dā-təd)  ruined

**di late** ('dØ-lāt)  grew large; broad

**di lat ing powers of an an a con da** ('dØ-lā-tiŋ; a-nə-'kän-də)  ability to stretch like the big snake which can eat things twice its size

**dil i gence** ('di-lə-jənts)  care

**dil i gent** ('di-lə-jənt)  careful; industrious

**dil i gent ly** ('di-lə-jənt-lē)  hard

**dint of much effort** ('dint)  by means of much trouble

**dire ful** ('dØr-fəl)  terrible; frightful

**dire struck** ('dØr-strək)  terrorized

**dis ad van tage of situation** (di-səd-'van-tij)  weakness in position

**dis ad van ta geous** (dis-ad-van-'tā-jəs)  unfavorable

**dis card ed** (dis-'kär-dəd)  refused

**dis cern** (di-'sərn)  see

**dis charge** (dis-'chärj)  pay

**dis com fit ed** (dis-'kəm-fə-təd)  driven back and almost defeated

**dis course** (dis-'kōrs)  conversation; talk

**discovered himself**  made himself known

**dis cred it ed** (dis-'kre-də-təd)  no longer believed in

**dis creet** (dis-'krēt)  polite; wise

**disk** ('disk)  flat circle; surface

**dis lo cat ed by sudden circumstances** (ˈdis-lō-kā-təd)  forced to be changed by unexpected happenings

**dis mayed** (dis-ˈmād)  discouraged

**dis or der ly rab ble** (di-ˈsȯrd-ər-lē; ˈra-bəl)  crowd of men in confusion

**dispatch**  send quickly; kill

**dis pelled** (di-ˈspeld)  driven away

**dis perse** (di-ˈspərs)  scatter

**dis per sion** (di-ˈspər-zhən)  running away; scattering

**dis posed** (di-ˈspōzd)  occupied; anxious; inclined

**disposed of...how**  what he had done with

**dis sec tion** (di-ˈsək-shən)  cutting in pieces

**dis sem bled** (di-ˈsem-bəld)  pretended he noticed nothing

**dis si pat ed** (ˈdi-sə-pā-təd)  given to the drinking of intoxicating liquors

**dis suade** (di-ˈswād)  persuade; win

**dis taff** (ˈdis-taf)  staff for holding the flax to be spun into thread

**distant pros pect** (ˈprä-spekt)  uncertain chance

**dis temp er** (dis-ˈtem-pər)  illness

**dis tinc tive** (dis-ˈtiŋk-tiv)  unusual

**dis tin guished** (di-ˈstiŋ-gwisht)  been so strong in; marked; made out

**di verge** (də-ˈvərj)  leave; separate

**di vers** (ˈdØ-vərz)  several

**di vine** (də-ˈvØn)  foretell; guess

**Dof fue Mart ling** (ˈdä-fyü; ˈmärt-liŋ)

**dog ged** (ˈdȯ-gəd)  sullen

**dol ing out** (ˈdō-liŋ)  telling

**dol or ous** (ˈdō-lə-rəs)  very sad

**Dolorous Garde** (ˈgärd)  sorrowful castle

**do mains** (dō-ˈmānz)  lands; round of affairs

**dome**  large, rounded roof

**do mes tic creatures** (də-ˈmes-tik)  tame animals, as the dog, cat, etc.

**domestic emotions**  tenderness for home things; family ties

**dom i ciled** (ˈdä-mə-sØld)  living

**dom i nant** (ˈdä-mə-nənt)  chief; haughty

**do min ion** (də-ˈmi-nyən)  province; possession; rule

**do my en deav or** (in-ˈde-vər)  try; do my best

**Don Cos sacks** (ˈdän; ˈkä-saks)  warlike Russian horsemen

**donned the serge gown** (ˈdänd)  became a monk

**Dons** (ˈdänz)  Spaniards

**doom** (ˈdüm)  destruction; fate

**double-reefed try sail** (ˈtrØ-sāl)  sail taken in so the wind cannot catch it

**doub let** (ˈdəb-lət)  close-fitting coat

**dou bloon** (də-'blün)  a Spanish gold coin, no longer used

**draft** (draft)  draw up

**drain our dearest veins**  give up our lives

**draught** (draft)  drink.  Cleopatra is said to have drunk a glass of wine in which she had dissolved a pearl

**draughts that lead nowhere**  drinks that did not satisfy him

**draw bridge** ('drȯ-brij)  a bridge which is made to be raised over a ditch of water around a castle

**dread disturbance** ('dred)  serious change from the usual rule

**dread me**  fear

**dread naught** ('dred-nȯt)  battleship

**dressed their shields**  held their shields ready

**drew our sad dle girths** ('sa-dəl-gərths)  tightened the straps around the horses' bodies

**drew the Spanish prow** ('prau̇)  led the ships of the Spanish gold-seekers

**drinking horn**  horn of an animal used as a cup

**driving**  very fast, on horseback

**drone** ('drōn)  lazy fellow

**due** ('dü)  proper; suitable

**dues** ('düz)  rights

**Duke de la Rowse** ('dük də lə 'rau̇z)

**duke dom** ('dük-dəm)  land controlled by the dukes

**dulse** ('dəls)  coarse, red seaweed

**Dum fries** (dəm-'frēs)

**durst** ('dərst)  dare

**du ties as ju ror** ('dü-tēz; 'ju̇r-ər)  duty of being on a jury, the body of men who decide whether or not one is guilty in a trial

# E

**each unto himself**  every man thought that he would be the one

**eagle of the sea**  warship

**earth's ample round**  surface of the globe

**easier un du la tions** (ən-jə-'lā-shənz)  gentler slopes; smaller hills

**e co nom ic** (e-kə-'nä-mik)  practical

**ec stat ic** (ek-'sta-tik)  joyful

**ed dy** ('e-dē)  revolve

**ed i fice** ('e-də-fəs)  house

**ef fect ed** (i-'fek-təd)  carried out

**ef fec tu al** (i-'fek-chə-wəl)  powerful

**ef fi gy** ('e-fə-jē)  image

**ef ful gence**  (i-'fül-jənts)  brilliance

**e go that blasts judgment**  ('ē-gō)  self conceit which makes people selfish and narrow

**e lapsed**  (i-'lapst)  passed

**e late**  (i-'lāt)  joyous

**elder days of Art**  ancient times which produced the pyramids, some of the beautiful Greek temples still standing, and statues such as the Venus de Milo

**el dern**  ('el-dərn)  elderly

**elder races**  older civilizations

**El Do ra do**  (el-də-'rä-dō)  vast riches; El Dorado is an imaginary South American city of great wealth

**e lec tion**  (i-'lek-shən)  choice

**e lec tion eer**  (i-'lek-shə-'nir)  to work for a person or party in an election

**elements**  ('e-lə-mənts)  nature

**elm**  ('elm)

**el o quent**  ('e-lə-kwənt)  forceful in his way of speaking

**e man ci pa tion**  (i-man-sə-'pā-shən)  freedom

**em barked**  (im-'bärkt)  on shipboard

**em bel lish the theme**  (im-'be-lish)  use elegant language

**em bla zon ry**  (im-'blā-zᵊn-rē)  design

**em bos omed**  (im-'bu̇-zəmd)  sheltered

**e mer gen cy**  (i-'mər-jənt-sē)  necessity; crisis

**em i nent ly**  ('e-mən-nənt-lē)  especially

**e mit**  (ē-'mit)  give out

**Em pire State**  ('em-pØr)  New York

**em u la tion**  (em-yə-'lā-shən)  imitation

**en com pass**  (in-'kəm-pəs)  surround

**en coun ter**  (in-'kau̇n-tər)  meet face to face; meeting; fight

**en cum bered**  (in-'kəm-bərd)  covered

**en dowed**  (in-'dau̇d)  gifted

**endowed it with re al i ty**  (rē-'a-lə-tē)  made it of real use to mankind

**enemy in station**  hostile army encamped

**enemy to stock**  bears often kill cattle

**en force those of Se ville, etc.**  (in-'fōrs; sə-'vil)  make the Spanish ships allow him to pass through

**en forc ing his careful remembrance**  (in-'fōr-siŋ)  reminding him of their many messages to those in England

**engaging to restore**  promising to give back

**en joined**  (in-'jȯind)  laid upon

**en meshed**  (in-'mesht)  caught

**en mi ty** ('en-mə-tē) ill-will

**en rap tured** (in-'rap-chərd) delighted

**en sign** ('en-sən) standard; flag

**en ter prise** ('en-tər-prØz) plan

**enterprising** ('en-tər-prØ-ziŋ) energetic

**entertain a composition** stop the battle and talk over terms of peace

**entertaining** holding

**enter the lists against him** fight with him for a lady's favor, as knights of old

**en ti tled, is** (in-'tØ-t°ld) does deserve

**en treat ed admittance** (in-'trē-təd) asked to be let in

**en treat y** (in-'trē-tē) beseeching; begging

**e nu mer ate** (i-'nü-mə-rāt) mention

**ep au let** ('ep-ə-let) a shoulder ornament showing rank

**Eph i al tes** (ef-i-'al-təz)

**ep ic** ('e-pik) long narrative poem dealing with the history of a race, written in a dignified and beautiful style

**e pis tle** (i-'pi-səl) letter

**ep i taph** ('e-pə-taf) inscription on a tombstone

**equal agency** equal share

**equal justice** fairness for everyone in the country

**e quipped** (i-'kwipt) fitted out with necessities

**e ra** ('ir-ə) period of time

**er rant knight** ('er-rənt) man looking for adventure

**er u di tion** (er-ə-'di-shən) learning

**Esh col** ('esh-kəl) *see* Numbers XIII:23

**es pous al** (is-'pau̇-zəl) marriage

**es sayed** (e-'sād) tried

**es tate** (is-'tāt) lands and castles

**esteem** self-respect; value; respect

**E ter nal Rainbow** (i-'tər-n°l) rainbow which is always there

**e ther** ('ē-thər) sky

**e the re al** (i-'thir-ē-əl) spiritual

**e the re al ize** (i-'thir-ē-ə-lØz) change

**Eu phra tes** (yü-'frā-tēz)

**every freeman was a host** each citizen had the strength of many soldiers

**e vinced** (i-'vinst) showed clearly

**ewe neck** ('yü) hollowed-out neck

**ex ag ger at ed ap pre ci a tion, an** (ig-'za-jə-rā-təd; ə-prē-she-'ā-shən) too high an opinion

**ex alt** (ig-'zȯlt) praise

**ex cess of sen sa tion** ('ik-ses; sen-'sā-shən) too much feeling

**execute** carry out; put to death

**ex ec u tor of his estate** (ig-'ze-kyə-tər) one who looks after the things he left behind

**ex empt ed from pardon** (ig-'zemp-təd) intentionally not pardoned

**ex er tion** (ig-'zər-shən) effort

**ex ha la tion** (eks-hə-'lā-shən) breath

**ex haust ed** (ig-'zȯs-təd) used again and again

**ex hort** (ig-'zȯrt) encourage

**ex hort er** (ig-'zȯr-tər) preacher

**ex ile** ('eg-zȯl) one who may not, or does not wish to, live in his own country

**expanse** strength; extent of space

**ex pert** ('ek-spərt) skillful

**ex ploit** ('ek-splȯit) an adventure; achievement

**ex pos ing my char ac ter, etc.** (ik-'spō-ziŋ; 'kar-ik-tər) causing criticism that

**ex press** (ik-'spres) positive

**express its summer thought in** make its best effort in growing

**ex press ly** (ik-'spres-lē) only

**ex qui site ly** (ek-'skwi-zət-lē) perfectly

**ex ten u ate the matter** (ik-'sten-yə-wāt) act as if this were of small importance

**external things** all he came in contact with not of the spirit or character

**ex trem i ty** (ik-'stre-mə-tē) great need

**ex ult ing** (ig-'zəl-tiŋ) rejoicing

**ex ul ta tion** (ek-səl-'tā-shən) emotion

**eyes are in the heart, etc.,** power of the imagination to see things of other times and other lands

# F

**fa cil i ties** (fə-'si-lə-tēz) easy ways; means

**factors of civilization** helps to the world's progress

**fac ul ties** ('fa-kəl-tēz) talents

**fag ot** ('fa-gət) sticks

**fain** ('fān) gladly

**fain entreat** like to ask

**fair con quest** ('kän-kwest) territory which had been honorably won

**faith and fire within us** belief in the right, and enthusiasm we feel

**faith I owe to knighthood** pledge which I took when I was made a knight

**faith's pure shrine**   place where they could be free to worship as they wished

**Fal kirk**  ('fȯl-kərk)

**fall within your province**   come under your authority

**fal ter**  ('fȯl-tər)  hesitate

**Fan euil Hall**  ('fa-nᵊl)  a public hall in Boston used for meetings during the Revolution

**fang**  ('faŋ)  long, sharp tooth

**fan tas tic**  (fan-'tas-tik)  queer-shaped

**fare**  ('far)  treated

**fared**  ('fard)  spent

**far thing**  ('far-<u>thi</u>ŋ)  English coin worth one-quarter cent

**fashion of that creature**   habit of all spiders

**fast by**   close-by

**fasten a quarrel**   give your reasons why he is to blame in this matter

**fas tid i ous**  (fa-'sti-dē-əs)  hard to please; particular

**fast ness**  ('fast-nəs)  place of defense

**fa tal**  ('fā-tᵊl)  tragic

**fatal shore**   bank of the lake which caused his daughter's death

**fat ed**  ('fā-təd)  fortunate

**fath om**  ('fa-thəm)  measure; six feet

**fa tigued**  (fə-'tēgd)  tired

**fearful**   dreadful; ghostly

**Feast of the Holy Trin i ty**  ('tri-nə-tē)  the eighth Sunday after Easter

**fea ture**  ('fē-chər)  characteristic

**feign**  ('fān)  pretend

**fell**  ('fel)  cut; marsh

**fel low**  ('fe-lō)  man

**fellowship**   company

**fel on**  ('fe-lən)  villain

**felon knight**   wicked knight

**fen**  ('fen)  marsh

**fence**   protect

**fe roc i ty**  (fə-'rä-sə-tē)  fierceness

**fer rule**  ('fer-əl)  heavy ruler

**fer ry, o'er the**  ('fer-ē)  over the river in a ferry-boat

**fer vent**  ('fer-vənt)  earnest; strong

**fer vor**  ('fer-vər)  earnestness

**fes toon**  (fes-'tün)  wreath

**feud**  ('fyüd)  quarrel

**fi ber**  ('fꝋ-bər)  root

**fi del i ty**  (fə-'de-lə-tē)  loyalty

**fie**  ('fØ)  shame

**field of fame, their**  place where they died and became heroes

**fierce ar ti fi cer**  (är-'ti-fə-sər)  harsh workman; here, the wind

**fight not so sore**  do not fight so hard

**files**  ('fØlz)  rows

**fil ly**  ('fi-lē)  young horse

**fi nan cial pan ics**  (fə-'nan-shəl; 'pa-niks)  unusual condition in business because of lack of money

**fi nesse**  (fə-'nes)  cleverness

**fit ful**  ('fit-fəl)  starting and stopping suddenly; now showing, now behind a cloud

**flail**  ('flāl)  tool for thrashing grain

**flaming**  bright red

**Flan ders**  ('flan-dərz)  an ancient European country, now part of France, Belgium, and Holland

**flank**  ('flaŋk)  the side of an animal, between the ribs and the hip

**flashes**  northern lights

**flash of fluttering drapery**  sight of her dress blowing about

**flaunt ing**  ('flȯn-tiŋ)  waving

**flaw**  ('flȯ)  gust of wind

**flax**  plant from which linen is made

**Flemish**  of Flanders, which *see*

**fleshless palms**  ('pälmz)  skeleton hands

**flinched**  ('flincht)  drew back

**Flo res**  ('flō-rəz)

**flout ed**  ('flau̇-təd)  insulted

**flowing bowl**  height of happiness paradise

**flu en cy**  ('flü-ənt-sē)  smoothness

**flume**  ('flüm)  channel of water used to obtain gold by "washing"

**flush**  pale pinks and lavenders; level with water

**fo'castle**  ('fōk-səl)  forecastle, a short, upper deck forward

**fo li age**  ('fō-lē-ij)  leaves

**fools cap**  ('fül-skap)  large sheets of paper for writing

**for ay**  ('fȯr-ā)  raid

**for bore**  (fōr-'bōr)  held off

**ford**  shallow place in a river

**fore bod ing**  (fōr-'bō-diŋ)  fears

**fore go**  (fōr-'gō)  give up

**fore head**  ('fär-əd)

**for eign yoke**  ('fȯr-ən)  English oppression

**for feit ed** ('fȯr-fə-təd) lost

**forge** ('fōrj) make; furnace

**for mi da ble** ('fȯr-mə-də-bəl) strong; terrifying (because of the whips that came from it); important; powerful

**forth with** (fōrth-'with) without delay

**fort night** ('fōrt-n∅t) two weeks

**for tune** ('fȯr-chən) luck

**forward** help to accomplish

**fos ter father** ('fȯs-tər) man who acted as father

**foun der** ('faủn-dər) sink

**fowl ing piece** ('faủ-liŋ) light gun

**frail ten e ment** ('te-nə-mənt) poorly built house

**fraught with much danger** ('frȯt) accomplished by much risk

**fresh ar ray** (ə-'rā) new grass

**friendship is feign ing** ('fā-niŋ) friends only pretend to be friends

**frig ate** ('fri-gət) large sailing vessel

**frol ic ar chi tec ture** ('frä-lik; 'är-kə-tek-chər) the beautiful structures built in a merry mood by the wind

**from the press** out of the crowd

**fron tier** (frən-'tir) land bordering on a foreign land; borderland, that part of a country bordering on an unsettled region

**fruitless** useless

**fu gi tive sov er eign** ('fyü-jə-tiv; 'sä-vrən) ruler who was fleeing

**fulfilling your be hest** (bi-'hest) carrying out your order

**fulfillment** coming

**full** very; full hard, with difficulty

**fur bish ing** ('fər-bi-shiŋ) freshening

**fur long** ('fər-lȯŋ) forty rods

**fur ther ance** ('fərth-rənts) accomplishment

**fu til i ty** (fyủ-'ti-lə-tē) uselessness

**fu tur i ty** (fyủ-'tủr-ə-tē) the future


# G


**Ga her is** ('gā-hə-rəs)

**gain say** (gān-'sā) contradict; question

**gait** ('gāt) manner of walking or running

**Gal a had** ('ga-lə-had)

**gale** ('gāl) wind; strong wind

**gal le on** ('ga-lē-ən) a large sailing vessel

**gam bol** ('gam-bəl) trick; game

**garbed** ('gärbd) dressed

**Gar eth** ('gar-əth)

**garish** ('gar-ish) showy

**gar nered** ('gär-nərd) gathered

**gar ri son** ('gar-ə-sən) troops on duty in a fort; furnish with soldiers

**gar ru lous** ('gar-ə-ləs) talkative

**gashed** ('gasht) cut

**gather cherries in Kent** he means that he, so much older than Priscilla, could not win her love

**gaud** ('god) an ornament; brightness

**gaud y** ('go-de) showy

**gaunt** ('gont) lean

**Ga wain** (gə-'wān)

**ga zette** (gə-'zet) a newspaper

**gear** ('gir) clothing; materials; treasure; armor

**gen ius of fam ine** ('jēn-yəs; 'fa-mən) spirit of hunger

**gen tian** ('jən-shən)

**gently in sin u a ting** (in-'sin-yə-wā-tiŋ) little by little

**gen try** ('jen-trē) people of education and culture

**ge og ra pher** (jē-'ä-grə-fər) one who has studied the earth

**ges ture** ('jes-chər) movement

**gi gan tic** (jø-'gan-tik) very large, like a giant

**glade** ('glād) open place in a forest

**glar ing** ('glar-iŋ) straight up and down

**glazed** ('glāzd) of glass

**glaz ing breath** ('glā-ziŋ) a breath possessing the power to make like glass

**glebe** ('glēb) soil

**glen** ('glen) valley

**glib ly** ('glib-lē) easily

**glint ed** ('glin-təd) darted

**gloat ed** ('glō-təd) gazed at enviously

**gnarled** ('när-əld) knotted

**gnome** ('nōm) tiny being with magic powers

**gob lin** ('gäb-lən) mischievous spirit

**golden-cui rassed** (kwi-'rast) having a yellow body like a breastplate; golden time, his youth

**Go li ath of Gath** (gə-'lø-əth; 'gath) the giant slain by David. *See* I Samuel XVII

**Gon za lo** (gən-'zä-lō)

**good brand Ex cal i bur** (ek-'ska-lə-bər) fine sword called Excalibur

**good ly** ('gud-lē) handsome; worthy

**gor geous** ('gȯr-jəs) elaborate; showy

**gor get** ('gȯr-jət) collar

**gor y** ('gȯr-ē) bloody

**got to horse** mounted

**gran deur** ('gran-jər) look of splendor

**gran ite** ('gra-nət) stone

**grate** grating; crossed bars

**grave** engrave; serious

**gray, forgotten years** dimly remembered past

**great torrent of mi gra tion** (mᶦ-'grā-shən) constant moving of people

**greener graves** easier way to die

**green sward** ('grēn-swȯrd) grass

**grew loud a pace** (ə-'pās) was fast becoming worse

**griev ance** ('grē-vənts) complaints

**griev ous** ('grē-vəs) severe; sad

**Grif let** ('grif-lət)

**grim** ('grim) fierce; horrible

**grooves** ('grüvz) hollows by means of which the ship slides down into the water

**gross** ('grōs) exaggerated

**grottoes** ('grä-tōz) caves

**grounding his musket** dropping one end of his gun to the ground firmly

**grow brave by reflection** gain courage from his own strength of mind

**Guay a quil** (gwᶦ-ə-'kēl) city in Ecuador

**guer ril la** (gə-'ri-lə)

**Gui an a** (gē-'a-nə) region of South America

**guinea** ('gi-nē) an English gold coin worth about $5. 11 [1921]; a kind of fowl

**Guin e ver** ('gwi-nə-vir)

**guise** ('gᶦz) manner

**gules** ('gyülz) red color

**gul ly** ('gə-lē) deep, dry river-bed

**gun wale** ('gə-nᵊl) upper edge of a boat

**Gur net** ('gər-nət) point north of Plymouth Bay

**gut tur al** ('gə-tə-rəl) hoarse

**gyr fal con** ('jər-fal-kən) a large hawk found in cold countries


# H


**hab i ta tion** (ha-bə-'ta-shən) home

**hab it u al as cend an cy** (ha-'bit-chə-wəl; ə-'sen-dən-sē) constant control

**habitual breadth of view, an** his usual kind way of looking at all sides of a question

**haft** ('haft) handle

**Hai nault** (ā-'nō) Belgian province

**halter** strap used to lead an animal

**hand gre nade** (grə-'nād) explosive to be thrown by hand

**hand i work** ('han-di-wərk) work of God's hands, that is, the world God had made

**hanging him in ef fi gy** ('e-fə-gē) hanging a figure of someone to show hatred

**happy me di um** ('mē-dē-əm) that which is better than either of the before-mentioned

**har ass** (hə-'ras) annoy

**har bin ger** ('här-bən-jər) announcer; one who goes before

**hard** close

**hard i hood** ('här-dē-hu̇d) endurance

**hard i ness** ('här-dē-nəs) vigor

**hardy Highland wight** ('wØt) fearless Scotchman

**har mo nies of law** ('här-mə-nēz) friendship among all the nations

**har pies of the shore** ('här-pēz) men who care only for gain; in mythology the harpy is pictured as a thieving monster with a woman's head and upper body, and the wings, tail, and claws of a bird

**harpy** *see* harpies of the shore

**har ried** ('ha-rēd) annoyed

**hashed met a phor** ('me-tə-fȯr) incorrect comparison. Wings cannot "trip"

**haunt** ('hȯnt) come to, again and again; home; place he haunted

**Hav i lah** ('hä-vi-lä) a land rich in gold and precious stones. *See* Genesis II:11

**haw thorne** ('hȯ-thȯrn) flowering tree

**haz ar dous** ('ha-zər-dəs) dangerous

**haz ard their lives** ('ha-zərd) risk their lives in battle

**head-waters** upper part of a stream

**hearth** ('härth) fireside

**heart's chamber** depths of his chest

**heated** forced to a hard struggle

**heathen hosts** ('hōsts) great armies of men who were not Christians

**heave** ('hēv) raise

**Heb ri des** ('he-brə-dēz) islands off the west coast of Scotland

**height en his glory** ('hØ-tⁿn) increase his power (by winning the war)

**heir** ('ar) child to inherit the title

**heir loom** ('ar-lüm)  any piece of personal property owned by a family for generations

**Hek la** ('hek-lə)  a volcano in Iceland held, considered

**helm** ('helm)  helmet; steering wheel

**He mans, Fel i cia** ('he-mənz; fə-'lē-shä)

**her ald** ('her-əld)  messenger

**Her cu le an** (hər-kyə-'lē-ən)  powerful, like Hercules, a mighty hero of Greek mythology

**he ret i cal** (hə-'re-ti-kəl)  positive hermit, man who lives alone, giving his time to prayer and good deeds

**her mi tage** ('hər-mə-tij)  hermit's home

**her o ism** ('her-ə-wi-zəm)  courage

**her on** ('her-ən)  a wading bird

**Hes sian trooper** ('he-shən)  German soldier hired by England to fight the colonists in the Revolution

**hie** ('hØ)  hasten

**high-hearted buc ca neers** (bə-kə-'nirz)  joyous pirates

**Hildebrand** ('hil-də-brand)

**hilt** ('hilt)  handle

**Hin du stan** ('hin-dů-stan)  India

**hoard** ('hōrd)  keep secretly

**hoar y** ('hōr-ē)  white; gray

**hobbled**  having the legs tied

**Ho bo mok** ('hō-bō-mäk)

**hoist**  raise

**holding con verse** ('kän-vərs)  talking

**holy ground**  place made holy by their sacrifice and ideals

**hom age** ('ä-mij)  loyalty; service

**home ly** ('hōm-lē)  plain; strong

**hood wink** ('hůd-wiŋk)  deceive

**hopelessly in volved** (en-'välvd)  caught so they could not get out

**ho ri zon** (hə-'rØ-zən)  line where the earth and sky seem to meet; western sky

**hos pi ta ble** (hä-'spi-tə-bəl)  making them welcome to his home

**host** ('hōst)  very large number; army

**hos tile** ('häs-təl)  warlike

**hours are numbered, his**  he has not much longer to live

**hour that brings re lease** (ri-'lēs)  time when we rest

**hous ings of the horses** ('haů-ziŋz)  saddle, bridle, blanket, etc.

**hove** ('hōv)  appeared

**hov er** ('hə-vər)  stay close

**hovering band** ('hə-və-riŋ) Swiss patriots.  Hovering hero means "watchful"
**how itz er** ('haủ-ət-sər) cannon
**hue** ('hyü) color
**hulk** ('həlk) body
**hum ble** ('həm-bəl) modest
**Hum boldt, von** ('həm-bōlt) German scientist and statesman
**humor** ('hyü-mər) fancy
**hunted for the boun ty** ('baủn-tē) killed to get a small reward
**hus band man** ('həz-bənd-mən) farmer
**husbandry** ('həz-bən-drē) farming

# I

**I be ri an** (∅-'bir-ē-ən) Spanish
**Ich a bod** ('ik-ə-bäd)
**I charge thee** I earnestly command you
**icy bridge** ice that never melts, connecting the Atlantic and Pacific
**icy shield** protection of ice
**i de a** (∅-'dē-ə) thought
**idle** foolish; useless
**I doubt** ('daủt) I think
**I dyl** ('∅-dᵊl) poem giving a picture
**ig no ble** (ig-'nō-bəl) not noble; base
**ignoble yoke** slavery which had bound them down, as a yoke weighs down
the neck of an ox
**I graine** (i-grān')
**ill coun sel** ('kaủn-səl) bad advice
**il le gal** (i-'lē-gəl) not lawful
**ill starred** ('stärd) unlucky
**il lum i nat ed** (i-'lü-mə-nā-təd) explained; illuminated fog, haziness
**il lu sion** (i-'lü-zhən) dream; imagination; fancy; false delusion
**il lus trate** ('i-ləs-trāt) make clear
**il lus trat ed** ('i-ləs-trā-təd) with magic-lantern slides
**il lus tri ous** (i-'ləs-trē-əs) famous
**im bibe** (im-'b∅b) adopt; receive
**im bued** (im-'byüd) filled
**imbued with dem o crat ic principles** (de-mə-'kra-tik) filled with desire
for a government of the people
**im mor tal date** (i-'mȯr-t ᵊl) date in history which will never be forgotten
**im mor tal ized** (i-'mȯr-t ᵊl-∅zd) described so that it will never be forgotten

**immortal Prov i dence** ('prä-və-dənts) heavenly powers

**Immortals** (i-'mȯr-t³lz) so called because of their bravery; immortal means undying

**immovable as a setter** as still as a hunting dog when he scents game

**im pas sa ble** (im-'pa-sə-bəl) which could not be crossed

**im ped i ment** (im-'pe-də-mənt) hindrance

**im pen e tra bly** (im-'pe-nə-trə-blē) thickly, so they could hardly get through

**im per a tive** (im-'per-ə-tiv) commanding

**im per cep ti ble** (im-pər-'sep-tə-bəl) very slight

**im per il** (im-'per-əl) endanger

**im pet u os i ty** (im-pe-chə-'wä-sə-tē) force

**im pet u ous** (im-'pech-wəs) violent

**im pi ous** ('im-pē-əs) unholy; wicked

**im pla ca ble** (im-'pla-kə-bəl) endless

**implacable cla mor** ('kla-mər) noise which seemed as though it would never stop

**im ple ment** ('im-plə-mənt) tool

**implements of hus band ry** ('həz-bən-drē) farm tools

**im ply** (im-'plØ) suggest

**im por tu nate** (im-'pȯr-tyu̇-nət) insistent

**im pose** (im-'pōz) place upon; lay down

**im prac ti ca ble** (im-'prak-ti-kə-bəl) impassable

**im preg na ble** (im-'preg-nə-bəl) unconquerable

**im pulse** ('im-pəls) feeling; desire

**im pul sive** (im-'pəl-siv) without thinking

**im pu ni ty** (im-'pyü-nə-tē) safety

**im pu ta tion** (im-pya-'tā-shən) suggestion

**in alien able rights** (i-'nāl-yə-nə-bəl) rights that cannot be taken away

**in ap pli ca ble** (i-'na-pli-kə-bəl) unsuitable

**In ca** ('iŋ-kə) a South American Indian tribe which attained unusual culture

**in can ta tion so serene** (in-kan-'tā-shən) magic song sung so clearly and calmly

**in car cer ate** (in-'kär-sə-rāt) imprison

**in com pa ra ble** (in-'käm-prə-bəl) matchless; remarkable

**in con se quen tial** (in-kän-sə-'kwen-shəl) unimportant

**in con sid er able in ter val** (in-kən-'si-dər-ə-bəl; 'in-tər-vəl) small space of time

**in cor po rate** (in-'kȯr-pə-rāt) unite; combine into one body

**in cred i ble** (in-'kre-də-bəl) hard to believe

**in cum brance** (in-ˈkəm-brənts)  hindrance
**in curred** (in-ˈkərd)  brought on oneself
**in cur sion** (in-ˈkər-zhən)  attack
**Indian file**  one behind another
**in dif fer ent** (in-ˈdi-fərnt)  unconcerned; ordinary
**in duced** (in-ˈdüst)  persuaded
**in dulge in** (in-ˈdəlj)  allow himself to have; indulgent, kind
**in es ti ma ble** (i-ˈnes-tə-mə-bəl)  priceless
**in ev i ta ble** (i-ˈne-və-tə-bəl)  unavoidable; sure
**in ex o ra ble** (i-ˈneks-rə-bəl)  merciless
**in ex press i ble concern** (i-nik-ˈspre-sə-bəl)  greatest anxiety
**in fa mous** (ˈin-fə-məs)  base; horrible
**in fect** (in-ˈfekt)  affect
**in fest** (in-ˈfest)  fill
**in fi del** (ˈin-fə-dᵊl)  Mohammedan
**in fi nite** (ˈin-fə-nət)  endless
**in flex i ble** (in-ˈflek-sə-bəl)  strong-willed; stubborn; honorable
**in fused** (in-ˈfyüzd)  poured
**In gel ram de Um phra ville** (ˈiŋ-gəl-rəm; ˈəm-frə-vil)
**in gen ious** (in-ˈjēn-yəs)  clever
**in gra ti at ing** (in-ˈgrā-shē-ā-tiŋ)  agreeable
**in i tial** (i-ˈni-shəl)  beginning
**in i ti a tive** (i-ˈni-shə-tiv)  energy
**inkhorn**  inkwell of an animal's horn
**in league with e vil** (ˈlēg; ˈē-vəl)  in partnership with the devil
**in noble heat**  in a righteous revolt
**in no va tion** (i-nə-ˈvā-shən)  style
**in nu mer a ble** (i-ˈnüm-rə-bəl)  too many to count
**in qui ry** (in-ˈkw∅-rē)  question; investigation
**in scru ta ble** (in-ˈskrü-tə-bəl)  mysterious
**inscrutable faculty**  talent which is not understood
**in sid i ous** (in-ˈsi-dē-əs)  deceitful
**in sig ni a** (in-ˈsig-nē-ə)  mark by which it is known
**in sig nif i cant** (in-sig-ˈni-fi-kənt)  little
**in sip id** (in-ˈsi-pəd)  stupid
**in so lent ly** (ˈin-sə-lənt-lē)  disrespectfully
**in spi ra tion** (in-spə-ˈrā-shən)  brilliant thought
**in stan ta ne ous** (in-stən-ˈtā-nē-əs)  at the exact moment of
**in sti gates the moral reflection** (ˈin-stə-gāts)  suggests the wise thought
**in stinct** (ˈin-stiŋkt)  feeling

**in stru ment** ('in-strə-mənt)  servant

**in su lat ed** ('in-sə-lā-təd)  isolated

**in sur gent** (in-'sər-jənt)  rebel

**in sur rec tion** (in-sə-'rek-shən)  rebellion

**in teg ri ty** (in-'te-grə-tē)  honesty

**in tel li gence** (in-'te-lə-jənts)  news

**in tent on** (in-'tent)  busy with

**intently**  closely; earnestly

**in ter com mu ni ca tion** (in-tər-kə-myü-nə-'kā-shən)  hearing from all parts of the country

**in ter course** ('in-tər-kōrs)  conversation

**in ter mi na ble** (in-'tərm-nə-bəl)  seeming endless

**in ter po si tion** (in-tər-pə-'zi-shən)  coming between to help

**in ter pret** (in-'tər-prət)  tell the meaning of

**in ter pre ta tion** (in-tər-prə-'tā-shən)  explanation

**in ter pre ter** (in-'tər-prə-tər)  one who knew both languages

**in ter val** ('in-tər-vəl)  brief time

**in ter vene** (in-tər-'vēn)  come between

**in the crude and fashioned** ('krüd)  both ore and silver made into things

**in the scowl of heaven**  under the terrible storm cloud's shadow

**in the sunless, etc.**  the sun shines a short time, and the nights are very long

**in ti mate** ('in-tə-mət)  suggest; familiar

**in tox i ca tion gave way** (in-täk-sə-'kā-shən)  excitement died down and changed

**in tri ca cies** ('in-tri-kə-sēz)  confusing windings

**in ured** (i-'nürd)  accustomed

**in val u a ble** (in-'val-yə-bəl)  very desirable; precious

**in vest** (in-'vest)  clothe

**in vet er ate** (in-'və-tə-rət)  old; incessant

**inveterate pro pen si ty** (prə-'pen-sə-tē)  incurable habit

**in vin ci ble** (in-'vin-sə-bəl)  courageous; unconquerable

**in vi o late** (in-'vØ-ə-lət)  uninjured

**in vis i ble tearing** (in-'vi-zə-bəl)  beating of the wind and snow, which they could not see, against the house

**in vol un ta ri ly** (in-vä-lən-'ter-ə-lē)  without realizing it

**in vol un ta ry** (in-'vä-lən-ter-ē)  unexpected

**involuntary fer vor** ('fər-vər)  feeling so strong he could not control it

**inward eye**  power of imagination which can recall past happiness

**iron hail**  small shot falling thick

**i ron y** ('i-rə-nē)  saying the opposite of what one means, to emphasize it

**ir re sist i ble** (ir-i-'zis-tə-bəl)  undeniable; uncontrollable
**ir res o lu tion** (i-re-zə-'lü-shən)  doubt
**is sue** ('i-shü)  come forth; consequence; result
**i tin er ant** (Ø-'ti-nə-rənt)  wandering
**it is meet I should**  I ought to

# J

**jas per** ('jas-pər)  dark green stone
**jaunt** ('jȯnt)  short pleasure excursion
**jeop ard y** ('je-pər-dē)  risk; danger
**joc und** ('jä-kənd)  merry
**john's-wort** ('wərt)  St. John's-wort, a small yellow-flowered plant
**John the A pos tle** (e-'pä-səl)  Revelation was written by St. John
**journalist**  newspaper writer
**journalizing**  keeping a daily record of
**ju di cious ly** (jü-'di-shəs-lē)  wisely
**just** ('jəst)  combat on horseback between two knights with spears
**jus ti fy** ('jəs-tə-fØ)  cause

# K

**keel** ('kēl)  ridge extending along the middle of the bottom of a ship
**keep**  fortress
**Kil drum mie** (kil-'drə-mē)
**Kil men y** (kil-'me-nē)
**kin ni kin nick** (kə-nē-kə-'nik)
**knave** ('nāv)  rascal
**knee-haltered**  tied at the knees
**knell** ('nel)  funeral bell
**knight er rant of yore** ('er-rənt; 'yōr)  knight who used to go about seeking adventure
**knightly exercise**  training necessary to become a knight knocked down, sold at auction

# L

**Lab ra dor** ('la-brə-dȯr)  in Canada
**lab y rinth of whims** ('la-bə-rinth; 'hwimz)  many queer notions
**Lac e dae mo ni ans** (las-ə-də-'mō-nē-ənz)  Spartans
**lad ing** ('lā-diŋ)  load; cargo

**la goon** (lə-'gün) pond

**laid a board the ship** (ə-'bōrd) brought our boat to the ship's side

**laid waste to** ruined

**Lam o rak** ('la-mə-rak)

**lamp of experience** past experience which helps us to see our way in the future

**Lan ca shire** ('laŋ-kə-shər)

**Lan ce lot du Lac** ('lan-sə-lät; 'läk)

**lanc es in rest** ('lan-səz) spears aside

**land of cy press** ('si-prəs) southern United States. Dickson was born in South Carolina

**land office** a government office where sales of public land are registered

**lan guid** ('laŋ-gwəd) making one feel as if he could scarcely move

**lan guor** ('laŋ-gər) dullness

**La nier** (lə-'nēr)

**lar gess** (lär-'jes) gift

**lar i at** ('lar-ē-ət) rope with a long noose used to lasso cattle or horses

**lashing** beating down; rope

**lat er al** ('la-tə-rəl) sidewise

**lat tice box** ('la-təs) box made of a network of strips to let in air

**laud** ('lȯd) praise

**laud able** ('lȯ-də-bəl) praiseworthy

**launch** ('lȯnch) start out in a boat; set afloat; let fly

**lau rel** ('lȯr-əl) a tree whose leaves are used as a sign of honor

**la ver** ('lā-vər) vessel for washing, used by priests

**lav ish** ('la-vish) generous

**lay** ('lā) song

**laz a reet** (la-zə-'rēt) for *lazeretto*, in sailor's language, a place near the stern of a merchant vessel, used as a storehouse

**leaden rain** bullets falling like rain

**league** ('lēg) about three miles

**leagued** ('lēgd) united in a plot

**lean and ef fete** (e-'fēt) poor and worn-out

**lee** ('lē) sheltered side

**leg a cy** ('le-gə-sē) inheritance

**leg end** ('le-jənd) story that has been handed down

**leg ion** ('lē-jən) large number; army

**le git i mate ly descended, be** (li-'ji-tə-mət-lē) actually come

**leisurely** comfortable; slow

**Le Morte D'Arthur** ('lə 'mȯrt 'där-thər) French for *the death of Arthur*

**Le od o gran** (lā-'ä-də-grən)

**Le on i das** (lā-'än-ə-dəs)

**let slip their ca bles** ('kā-bəlz) drop the ropes, leaving their anchors behind

**level the ranks** tear up

**li ba tion** (lØ-'bā-shən) wine offered as sacrifice to the gods

**like li est knights** ('lØ-klē-əst) best men engaged in chivalry

**lily's breezy tent** bell-shaped blossom open to the summer wind

**lin e age** ('lØ-nij) descent; family

**Lin lith gow** (lin-'lith-gō)

**lin net** ('li-nət) singing-bird in the same family as the swallow

**lin sey-wool sey** ('lin-zē-'wül-zē) coarse cloth of linen and wool

**Li o nes** ('lē-ə-nəs)

**lists** ('lists) field of knightly combat

**lit ter** ('li-tər) stretcher to carry a sick or wounded person on

**little aided by invention** without much power to meet new situations and act quickly

**liv er y** ('li-və-rē) dress; appearance

**living pages of God's book** wonders of life and nature we see about us

**living sunbeam** as quick, as shining, and as beautifully colored as a ray of sun

**load stone** ('lōd-stōn) magnet

**loath** ('lōth) unwilling

**Loch gyle** (läk-'gØl)

**Locke, John** English philosopher

**lodgepole pine** small tree of hard wood

**lolled** ('läld) hung

**long mesh es of steel** ('me-shəz) steel nets used to entangle the submarine

**loom** ('lüm) appear

**loosed storm breaks furiously** ('lüst) storm suddenly let out from the clouds where it has been kept locked

**lose the tide** be too late to take advantage of the flowing out of the tide

**Los Mu er tos** (mü-'er-tōs)

**lost his coun te nance** ('kaün-t°n-ənts) turned white and expressionless, because of grief and shock

**lou is d'or** ('lü-ē 'dȯr) French gold coin

**lour** ('laü-ər) threaten

**luckless forms** unfortunate creatures

**luckless starr'd** born under an unlucky star; unfortunate

**lu di crous** ('lü-də-krəs) ridiculous

**lu mi nous** ('lü-mə-nəs) shining

**lurid** ('lür-əd)  like glowing fire seen through cloud or smoke
**lurk** ('lərk)  hide
**lurking** ('lər-kiŋ)  secret
**Lu ther, Martin** ('lü-thər)  German translator of the Bible


# M


**made but jest**  only made fun
**mag a zine** ('ma-gə-zēn)  storehouse
**Ma gi** ('mā-jⵁ)  the three wise men who brought gifts to the Christ child. *See*
    Matthew II
**mag nan i mous** (mag-'na-nə-məs)  unselfish
**mag ni tude** ('mag-nə-tüd)  greatness
**mag no li a** (mag-'nōl-yə)  tree with large fragrant blossoms
**ma hout** (mə-'haut)  keeper and driver of an elephant
**maimed** ('māmd)  broken
**main** ('mān)  sea
**main te nance** ('mānt-nənts)  support
**ma jes tic playfulness** (mə-'jes-tik)  amusing herself in her dignified way
**ma lev o lent** (mə-'le-və-lənt)  destructive
**Ma lis** ('mā-ləs)
**Mal or y, Sir Thomas** ('ma-lə-rē)
**mam moth** ('ma-məth)  difficult
**man**  make up the crew
**manfully abide battle**  bravely wait for the attack
**man gle** ('maŋ-gəl)  spoil
**man i fest** ('ma-nə-fest)  visible
**man i fes ta tion** ('ma-nə-fə-'stā-shən)  proof
**manifold aspects of nature**  flowers, trees, sky, water, animals, etc.
**man or** ('ma-nər)  dwelling house of a large estate
**ma raud** (mə-'ród)  raid; steal
**ma raud er** (mə-'ró-dər)  thief
**mar gin** ('mär-jən)  edge
**mar i ner** ('mar-ə-nər)  sailor
**market, full**  forenoon
**mar shal** ('mär-shəl)  general
**mart** ('märt)  market
**mar tial** ('mär-shəl)  warlike
**martial array**  warlike outfit of ships and troops
**mask his dismay**  hide his surprise
**Mas sa soit** ('ma-sə-sō-wit)

**mas ter ful** ('mas-tər-fəl)  powerful
**match lock** ('mach-läk)  an old style gun
**ma te ri al** (mə-'tir-ē-əl)  noticeable
**Math er, Cotton** ('ma-<u>th</u>ər)  American clergyman and author; he took an active interest in witchcraft
**mat tock** ('ma-tək)  tool for digging and smoothing the ground
**ma ture ly** (mə-'tu̇r-lē)  carefully
**mau ger** ('mȯ-gər)  in spite of
**max im** ('mak-səm)  proverb
**Mc Crea, John D.** (mə-'krā)
**mead** ('mēd)  meadow
**me an der** (mē-'an-dər)  wind
**meas ured in cups of ale** ('me-zhərd)  knew the length by the number of cups drunk
**measured stroke**  sound of the ax falling regularly
**Medes** ('mēdz)
**me di oc ri ty** (mē-dē-'ä-krə-tē)  the ordinary
**meditate**  think over and over
**me di um** ('mē-dē-əm)  substance to look through
**mel an cho ly** ('me-lən-kä-lē)  mournful; sad; sadness
**mem oirs** ('mem-wärz)  recollections
**mem or a ble** ('mem-rə-bəl)  remarkable
**mem or a bly** ('mem-rə-blē)  so remarkably well that it would long be remembered
**me mo ri al** (mə-'mōr-e-ēl)  statement of facts with a petition
**men ace** ('me-nəs)  threat; threaten
**men di can cy squad** ('men-di-kənt-sē; 'skwäd)  company of beggars that is, if it did not exactly "beggar description," it almost did
**Mer cu ry** ('mər-kyə-rē)  in Roman mythology, the messenger of Jupiter
**mercy des pots feel** ('des-pəts)  kindness that can be expected from tyrants
**mere** ('mir)  lake
**mere stead** ('mir-sted)  farm
**mer e tri cious** (mer-ə-'tri-shəs)  gaudy
**me see meth** (mi-'sēm-əth)  it seems to me
**met a phor** ('me-tə-fȯr)  figure of speech in which one thing is called another
**me te or** ('mē-tē-ər)  strange appearance in the sky
**meteor flag**  flag that flies above the ship like a bright star
**meteor of the ocean air**  the flag which had waved over the ocean for so long
**met tle** ('me-t<sup>ə</sup>l)  energy

**Mid i an ites** ('mi-dē-ə-nØts) Arabian tribe that made war on the Israelites

**midships** against the middle of her side

**'mid the wreck of thrones** democracy having triumphed over kings

**might not serve him there to** (thar-'tü) would not let him do it

**mighty prow ess** ('praủ-əs) great deeds of courage

**mi grate** ('mØ-grāt) move

**Mi lan** (mə-'lan) in Italy

**mi li tia** (mə-'li-shə) military reserve

**milky way** the faintly white streak across the night sky made up of millions
  of stars

**mil let** ('mi-lət) kind of grain

**mim ic in slow structures** ('mi-mik) attempt to do in a long time

**Mi nor ites** ('mØ-nə-rØts) an order of monks

**mi nute** (mØ-'nüt) very small

**mi nute ly** (mØ-'nüt-lē) carefully; exactly

**mi nut est** (mØ-'nüt-əst) slightest

**mire** ('mØr) mud

**mis ad ven ture** (mi-səd-'ven-chər) disaster; luck

**mis chie vous** ('mis-chə-ves) naughty in a gay way

**mis giv ing** (mis-'gi-viŋ) fear

**mis sile** ('mi-səl) weapon

**Mme So fro nie** (mə-'dam; sə-'frō-nē) Mme is the abbreviation for madame,
  French for Mrs.

**Mo dred and his array** ('mō-dred) the fine showing made by Modred and
  his men

**mold ered** ('mōl-dərd) crumbled

**mo les ta tion** (mō-ləs-'tā-shən) harming; annoyance

**mo men ta ry** ('mō-mən-ter-ē) brief

**mo men tum** (mō-'men-təm) force

**mo not o nous** (mə-'nä-t°n-əs) dull

**mon te ro** (män-'ter-ō) hunting cap

**Mon te zu ma** (män-tə-'zü-mə) chief of the Aztecs, Indians of ancient
  Mexico

**moored their bark** ('mürd) anchored their ship

**mo rass** (mə-'ras) deep swamp

**more than the flag** all that the flag stands for goes with it

**Morning-land** far East, Asia

**mortal** causing death; deadly; human

**mortal war** battle till one is killed

**Mo ses** ('mō-zəz) *see* Exodus I

**mos sy** ('mȯ-sē)
**Mo ti Guj** ('mo-tə; 'güzh)
**mounted on pil lions** ('pil-yənz)  climbed up on to cushions
**Mow bray** ('mō-brā)
**moy dore** ('mȯi-dōr)  old gold coin of Portugal
**much affected by learn ed men** ('lər-nəd)  in which wise men were much interested
**Muertos** (mü-'er-tōs)
**mul ti tu di nous** (məl-tə-'tü-də-nəs)  many different kinds of
**mus ing** ('myü-ziŋ)  thoughtful; thinking
**mus ter** ('məs-tər)  gather
**must needs be possessed**  would certainly be taken
**mu ta ble** ('myü-tə-bəl)  changing
**mute** ('myüt)  silent
**mu tin eer** (myü-tᵊn-'ir)  rebel
**mu tu al** ('myü-chə-wəl)  common; which they both had; to each other
**my heart giveth unto you**  my liking for you tells me
**Myn heer** (m∅n-'hār)  Dutch for *Mister*
**myr i ad-handed** ('mir-ē-əd)  manyhanded
**mystery of an eelpot**  trap that is easy to get into but impossible to get out of
**mys tic** ('mis-tik)  mysterious
**mys ti cal Ar a bic sentence** ('mis-ti-kəl; 'ar-ə-bik)  mysterious words in the Arabic language


# N


**na tive feeling** ('nā-tiv)  natural enthusiasm; nature, natural
**Nelson, Ho ra tio** (hə-'rā-shē-ō)  great English admiral (1758-1805)
**Newcastle's best**  finest kind of gun made in the city famous for guns
**new-found strength**  power they had never before realized
**Newton, Sir Isaac**  English philosopher and mathematician (1642-1727)
**Nigel** ('n∅-jəl)
**nig gard ly** ('ni-gərd-lē)  stingy
**nine fold**  numerous offspring
**noised abroad**  told all over the country
**nor faithless joint**  no badly made fastening
**norther**  storm from the north
**North ga lis** (nȯrth-'gā-ləs)
**northwind's ma son ry** ('mā-sᵊn-rē)  things the north wind has built of snow

**nup tials** ('nəp-shəlz)  marriage

# O

**ob lique ly** (ō-'blēk-lē)  slantingly
**ob sti nate ly maintained** ('äb-stə-nət-lē)  stubbornly kept up
**obstinately pa cif ic system** (pə-'si-fik)  method of continuous peace
**obtained an audience of**  was allowed to see
**Ock la wa ha** (äk-lə-'wä-hä)  branch of the St. John's River in Florida
**ode** ('ōd)  poem suitable to be sung
**of fen sive war** (ə-'fen-siv)  war started by the colonies
**of ill coun sel** ('kaùn-səl)  because you have taken bad advice
**of weight and au thor i ty** (ə-'thär-ə-tē)  of influence and power
**Og, King of Ba shan**  ('äg; 'bā-shən)  giant defeated by the Hebrews. *See*
  Deuteronomy III
**Old French War**  French and Indian war, between Great Britain and France
  in America, ending 1763
**old order was changing**  way of doing things was being improved
**oly koek** ('äl-ē; 'kùk)  kind of doughnut
**om i nous** ('ä-mə-nəs)  expressive; suggestive
**on er ous** ('ä-nə-rəs)  burdensome
**on tiptoe for a flight**  looking as though they were ready to fly
**openly disclosed**  told the secret
**oph thal mi a** (äf-'thal-mē-ə)  inflammation of the membrane of the eye
**op pres sion** (ə-'pre-shən)  cruelty
**oppression's woes** (ə-'pre-shənz)  unhappiness of not being free
**oppressive op u lence** ('ä-pyə-lənts)  great riches
**orderly train**  well worked-out system
**ord nance** ('ôrd-nənts)  cannon balls
**or gy** ('ôr-jē)  drunken merrymaking
**original divinity in tact** (in-'takt)  purity which is born in every man
  revealed
**Ork ney** ('ôrk-nē)  county in Scotland
**ornaments of rime**  poetry
**or ni thol o gy** (ôr-nə-'thä-lə-jē)  study of birds
**ort a gues** ('ôr-tə-gwäs)  Spanish coins
**or tho dox** ('ôr-thə-däks)  according to law
**overcame his scru ples** ('skrü-pəlz)  conquered his objections
**overruling Prov i dence above** ('prä-və-dənts)  a Power which foresaw
  and guided

# P

**pace** ('pās) walk upon

**packing cinch** strap to fasten pack to saddle

**packing it out** taking it on his horse

**page** boy in training for knighthood

**painted shell** the ship

**pal frey** ('pȯl-frē) lady's saddle-horse

**pal ing** ('pā-liŋ) fence

**pal let** ('pa-lət) small bed

**pal lid** ('pa-ləd) pale

**palm** ('pälm) tropical tree, the coco-palm bears coconuts

**Pal om i des** (pəl-'ōm-ə-dēz)

**Pa ri an** ('par-ē-ən) from Pares, an Island in the Aegean Sea from which beautiful white marble came in ancient times

**par ley** ('pär-lē) talk

**Par lia ment** ('pär-lə-mənt) body of men from different parts of England who make the laws

**par ried** ('pa-rēd) worked off

**par si mo ny** ('pär-sə-mō-nē) stinginess

**pass** narrow passage in mountain

**pass by the offered wealth with unrewarded eye** do not notice the beauty of common things

**pas sion** ('pa-shən) eagerness; sin; emotion

**pass sentence on** judge

**pas tor al ages** ('pas-tə-rəl) time when there were no cities; everyone lived a simple life out of doors

**pat ent** ('pa-tᵊnt) plain

**pa tri o tic** (pā-trē-'ä-tik) loyal to their own country

**pa trol** (pə-'trōl) go the rounds of

**pa tron** ('pā-trən) employer and host

**pa vil ion** (pə-'vil-yən) tent; realm

**peas ant farmer** ('pe-zᵊnt) who worked the land of his lord

**Peck su ot** ('pek-sü-wət)

**pe cul iar** (pi-'kyül-yər) strange

**peculiar portion, his** all his own

**pe cu ni a ry consideration** (pi-'kyü-nē-er-ē) thought of money

**ped a gogue** ('pe-də-gäg) teacher

**ped i gree** ('pe-də-grē) line of ancestors

**peer** companion; equal; nobleman

**peer age** ('pir-ij) rank of titled men in England

**peer less** ('pir-ləs)  without an equal

**pelt** ('pelt)  skin

**pel tries** ('pel-trēz)  skins and furs

**Pendleton, Colonel Edmund**  American statesman and patriot

**pen ny-roy al** ('pen-ē 'rȯi-əl)  mint

**pensive**  thoughtful

**pensive mood**  thoughtful state of mind

**Pen te cost** ('pen-ti-kȯst)  seventh Sunday after Easter

**pent up**  hidden

**pe on** ('pē-än)  laborer

**per ad ven ture** ('pər-əd-ven-chər)  perhaps

**per am bu la tion** (pə-ram-byə-'lā-shən)  walk

**per cep ti ble weak en ing** (pər-'sep-tə-bəl; 'wēk-niŋ)  noticeable change
  for the better

**perpendicular**  straight up and down

**per se ver ing** (pər-sə-'vi-riŋ)  trying over and over again

**per son a ble** ('pərs-nə-bəl)  handsome

**per son i fy** ('pər-'sä-nə-f∅)  to speak of or represent anything as if it
  were a person

**per ti na cious** (pər-tᵊn-'ā-shəs)  constant

**per verse** (pər-'vərs)  obstinate

**perverse ep i cur ism** ('e-pi-kyu̇r-i-zəm)  obstinate appetite

**pe ti tion** (pə-'ti-shən)  request

**petty em bas sies** ('em-bə-sēz)  unimportant errands

**pha lanx** ('fā-laŋks)  closely massed lines of infantry soldiers

**phe nom e non** (fi-'nä-mə-nän)  marvel

**phi lan thro pist** (fə-'lan-thrə-pist)  one who spends his time or money
  for others

**Phi lis tines** ('fi-lə-stēnz)  people frequently at war with the Hebrews

**phi los o phy** (fə-'lä-sə-fē)  thoughts on the meaning of life

**Pho cians** ('fō-shənz)

**phys i og no my** (fi-zē-'äg-nə-mē)  face

**picket**  fasten with stakes; place where he usually worked and was fed;
  **picketing**  tying

**pier-glass** ('pir)  full-length mirror

**pil grim** ('pil-grəm)  traveler

**pil grim age** ('pil-grə-mij)  journey

**pil lage** ('pi-lij)  captured treasure

**pil lion** ('pil-yən)  cushion behind a man's saddle for a woman to ride on

**pi lot house** ('p∅-lət)  shelter on upper deck where steering is done

**pin na cle** ('pi-ni-kəl)  top

**pi o neer** (pī-ə-'nir)  one who leads the way for others
**pipe** ('pīp)  sing
**piper**  common climbing shrub
**piqued** ('pēkt)  prided
**pitch es** ('pi-chəs)  points and peaks
**plac id** ('pla-səd)  quiet; calm
**plague** ('plāg)  disease
**plain tive** ('plān-tiv)  sorrowful
**plants an em pire** ('em-pīr)  forms a colony of its country
**plash y tramp** ('plash-ē)  footsteps in a wet place
**plas tic artist** ('plas-tik)  sculptor
**pledge of blithe some May** ('blīth-səm)  sign of the happy month of May
**pli a bil i ty** (plī-ə-'bi-lə-tē)  changeableness
**plied** ('plīd)  worked out
**plight** ('plīt)  condition
**plow share** ('plaù-sher)  *see* share
**poem of the air**  snowflakes, an expression of beauty from the clouds as a poem comes from "cloudy fancies"
**poet lau re ate** ('lòr-ē-ət)  title given a poet by the king of England.  His duty is to write poems on historical events
**point for as sault** (ə-'sòlt)  a weak spot to attack
**pole-man**  man who pushes boat off shallows with a long pole
**pom mel** ('pə-məl)  knob at the front of a saddle
**pomp** ('pämp)  splendor
**pom pous** ('päm-pəs)  magnificent
**pon der ing** ('pän-də-riŋ)  thinking
**pon der ous** ('pän-də-rəs)  heavy
**pop u lous** ('pä-pyə-ləs)  thickly inhabited
**port**  end of the war
**port cul lis** (pōrt-'kə-ləs)  grating over gate
**por tend** (pòr-'tənd)  foretell
**por ten tous** (pòr-'tən-təs)  foretelling a calamity
**por ti co** ('pōr-ti-kō)  large porch with pillars
**portion**  money her father would give her
**port ly** ('pōrt-lē)  stout
**post**  mail
**post ed** ('pōs-təd)  on guard; placed
**posted down from London**  hastened, by fast stagecoach, from London
**pos ter i ty** (pä-'ster-ə-tē)  descendants
**pos tern-gate** ('pōst-tərn)  rear gate
**po tent** ('pō-tᵊnt)  strong; powerful

**po ten tate** (ˈpō-t°n-tāt)  ruler

**po tent ly** (ˈpō-t°nt-lē)  strongly

**pound, silver**  English money, $4.87 [1921]

**pow wow** (ˈpau̇-wau̇)  celebration; medicine man

**prayed him for suc cor** (ˈsə-kər)  begged him for aid

**pre ca ri ous** (pri-ˈkar-ē-əs)  uncertain

**pre cept** (ˈprē-sept)  order

**pre cep tor** (pri-ˈsep-tər)  teacher

**precious leg a cies** (ˈle-gə-sēz)  America's inheritance of freedom

**pre cip i tate** (pri-ˈsi-pə-tət)  throw

**pre con ceived** (prē-kən-ˈsēvd)  already thought out

**pre dom i nat ing** (pri-ˈdä-mə-nā-tiŋ)  chiefly

**pre em i nent** (prē-ˈe-mə-nənt)  most prominent

**prel ate** (ˈpre-lət)  a high officer of the church

**pre pos ter ous** (pri-ˈpäs-tə-rəs)  ridiculous

**pres er va tion** (pre-zər-ˈvā-shən)  saving

**pre sides over the des ti nies** (pri-ˈzØdz; ˈdes-tə-nēz)  watches over the fortunes

**press**  throng

**press we to the field**  we hasten to battle

**pretensions to the throne**  claims that he should be made king

**pre vail** (pri-ˈvāl)  succeed; conquer; upon, persuade; prevailed, was decided on; were common

**prev a lence** (ˈpre-və-lənts)  large number

**pri me val** (prØ-ˈmē-vəl)  which had never been cut before

**primeval hush**  stillness of a place where man has never been

**prim i tive** (ˈpri-mə-tiv)  roughly built

**printer's devil**  printer's assistant

**prison bars**  his body

**pri va tion** (prØ-ˈvā-shən)  suffering

**prize we sought is won**  winning of the war is accomplished

**proc la ma tion** (prä-klə-ˈmā-shən)  notice

**procure its repeal**  have it recalled

**prod i gal** (ˈprä-di-gəl)  spendthrift

**pro di gious** (prə-ˈdi-jəs)  terrible

**prod uce** (ˈprä-düs)  result

**prof fer** (ˈprä-fər)  offer

**pro file** (ˈprō-fØl)  outline

**pro fuse ly** (prə-ˈfyüs-lē)  thickly

**proj ect** (ˈprä-jekt)  plan

**pro ject ed** (prə-ˈjekt-əd)  raised; extended

**prone** ('prōn) inclined

**pro pen si ty** (prə-'pen-sə-tē) habit

**proph e cy** ('prä-fə-sē) prediction of what is to happen; their hopes

**proph e sy** ('prä-fə-sØ) expect; foretell

**pro phet ic** (prə-'fe-tik) expected

**pro por tion** (prə-'pōr-shən) size

**pros per ous gales** ('präs-pə-rəs) favorable winds

**pro tem po re** (prō-'tem-pə-rē) for the time being; temporarily

**prouder summer-blooms** flowers which are usually more admired than dandelions are

**proud u sur pers** (yu̇-'sər-pərz) rulers who have no right to the powers they claim

**proved not themselves right** the people of the Middle Ages believed that a man who won against heavy odds did so because of divine help, and so was proved in the right

**Prov i dence** ('prä-və-dənts) heaven

**prov in cial** (prə-'vin-shəl) narrow-minded

**prov o ca tion** (prä-və-'kā-shən) cause

**pru dence** (prü-d°nts) judgment; common sense; carefulness

**prudence dictates** reason gives warning

**Psalm ist** ('säl-mist) David

**psalm o dy** ('säl-mə-dē) singing psalms

**pulse** ('pəls) plant that could be eaten; here, beans

**pur blind prank** ('pər-blØnd) an act the seriousness of which we do not realize

**purp ling east** ('pər-pliŋ) sunrise sky

**pur port** (pər-'pōrt) meaning

**purpose of res o lu tion** (re-zə-'lü-shən) decision to carry out the idea

**pursue his principles** fight for the things he believes in

**put everything at stake** risked life and liberty

**put his person in adventure** took risks

# Q

**quaffed** ('kwäft) drank

**quag mire** ('kwag-mØr) marsh land which draws things under its surface

**quail** ('kwāl) tremble; fall back; bird

**Quak er** ('kwā-kər) gray-clothed

**quar ry** ('kwȯr-ē) object of the hunt; pit, from which building stone is obtained

**quarter** mercy; back

**quarter an army**  have the soldiers camp
**quartering to me**  coming toward me in a zigzag manner
**Queen of She ba**  ('shē-bə)  a famous queen of old.  *See* I Kings X:1- 3
**quer u lous**  ('kwər-yə-ləs)  complaining
**queued**  ('kyüd)  plaited into pigtails
**quin tal**  ('kwin-tᵊl)  hundred pounds
**quiv er**  ('kwi-vər)  case for arrows

# R

**Rach rin**  ('rak-rən)
**rack**  ('rak)  wreck
**ra di ant**  ('rā-dē-ənt)  glowing
**raging white**  white-capped and growing fiercer
**rak ing**  ('rā-kiŋ)  shooting through the entire length of
**ral lied unto**  ('ra-lēd)  continued to fight as hard as they could with
**ramp ant**  ('ram-pənt)  furious
**ran dom**  ('ran-dəm)  chance
**ranging forward**  changing its course
**rant i pole**  ('ran-tə-pol)  wild young
**rapt**  ('rapt)  overcome
**rav age**  ('ra-vij)  ruin
**rave**  ('rāv)  blow furiously
**rav en ous**  ('ra-və-nəs)  greedy
**ra vine**  (rə-'vēn)  steep valley
**rav ish ment**  ('ra-vish-mənt)  rapture
**rawboned proportions**  gaunt, or having little flesh upon its forms
**re ad just ment**  (rē-ə-'jəst-mənt)  knowing how to meet the new situation
**realm**  ('relm)  kingdom
**rear'd**  ('rērd)  raised
**rea soned**  ('rē-zᵊnd)  well-thought-out
**reason to the root of things**  think of the right and wrong of the question
**Rebecca and I saac**  ('∅-zik)  *see* Genesis XXIV
**rebuke**  scold; blame; criticism
**re ced ing**  (rē-'sē-diŋ)  disappearing: stepping back
**re cep ta cle**  (ri-'sep-ti-kəl)  case
**re cess**  ('rē-ses)  a short play time
**re coil**  (ri-'kȯil)  draw back
**rec on ciled, be**  ('re-kən-sØld)  become friends again
**rec on cil i a tion**  ('re-kən-si-lē-'ā-shən)  reunion
**re deem**  (ri-'dēm)  make right

**re doubt a ble** (ri-'daủ-tə-bəl)  dangerous; honorable

**re duced** (ri-'düst)  saddened; brought

**reel** ('rēl)  fall from side to side; fall; holder; unsteady

**ref u gee** (re-fyủ-'jē)  runaway

**ref use** ('re-fyüs)  left over

**refused to execute** (rə-'fyüzd)  not carried out

**rel a tive** ('re-lə-tiv)  between the two

**re lent less** (ri-'lent-ləs)  without pity

**re lieved** (ri-'lēvd)  softened

**re lin quish** (ri-'liŋ-kwish)  give up

**re luc tant** (ri-'lək-tənt)  hesitating

**re ly** (ri-'lØ)  depend

**rem i nis cence** (re-mə-'ni-s°nts)  story

**re mon strance** (re-'män-strənts)  protest

**re mon strat ed** ('re-mən-strā-təd)  argued

**ren der** ('ren-dər)  give; make; leave

**ren dered me account** ('ren-dərd)  given me satisfaction; been punished by me

**rent** ('rent)  torn

**re pel** (ri-'pel)  hold back; drive out

**re pose** (ri-'pōz)  rest

**rep tile** ('rep-tØl)  snake

**re pute** (ri-'pyüt)  character

**re qui em** ('re-kwē-əm)  funeral hymn, service for the dead

**re search** (ri-'sərch)  study

**re sist the u surp er** (ri-'zist; yủ-'sər-pər)  fight against the man who had wrongly seized the power to rule

**re sort** (ri-'zȯrt)  turn

**re sourc es of the earth** ('rē-sȯr-səz)  natural wealth, such as minerals, waterways, forests, farm lands

**re spond to** (ri-'spänd)  return

**responsive to**  answering

**rest**  attachment on front of armor to hold handle of spear

**res ur rect ed Italy** (re-zə-'rek-təd)  Italy was changed from a number of small separate kingdoms to a united country in 1870

**retaught the lesson**  reminded England, by fighting for freedom, of her teachings of liberty

**re tire ment** (ri-'tØr-mənt)  being alone; privacy

**rev el** ('re-vəl)  merrymaking

**rev e nue** ('re-və-nü)  income

**re vere** (ri-'vir)  respect

**reverend awe** ('ȯ)　respect
**rev er ie** ('re-və-rē)　daydream
**rev o lu tion ize** (re-və-'lü-shə-nØz)　make great changes in
**re volved his discomfort** (ri-'välvd)　thought over his troubles
**re vul sion** (ri-'vəl-shən)　change of feeling
**rhyth mic pul sa tions** ('ri<u>th</u>-mik; pəl-'sā-shənz)　regular beating
**rib bing the ho ri zon** ('ri-biŋ; hə-'rØ-z°n)　streaking the sky
**ribs of steel**　steel framework
**rich as Li ma Town** ('lē-mə)　Lima is the capital of Peru, a country noted
　for its gold mines
**rig id** ('ri-jəd)　strict; severe
**Rio** ('rē-ō)　**Rio de Ja nei ro** (rē-ō-dā-zhə-'ner-ō)　city in Brazil
**riv et** ('ri-vət)　fasten firmly
**riv u let** ('ri-vyə-lət)　small stream
**ro bust** (rō-'bəst)　healthy-looking
**roist er ing blade** ('rȯi-stə-riŋ)　conceited fellow
**roun de lay** ('raůn-də-lā)　lively tune with a repeated strain
**rout** ('raůt)　disorderly flight
**route** ('rüt)　way
**roy al ist** ('rȯi-ə-list)　man on the king's side
**rue ing** ('rü-iŋ)　ashamed
**ruf fi an-like** ('rə-fē-ən)　like a cruel, brutal fellow
**ruf fle** ('rə-fəl)　muffled beat
**rug ged** ('rə-gəd)　with rough bark
**ru mi nate** ('rü-mə-nāt)　graze
**ru mi na tion** (rü-mə-'nā-shən)　meditation; thought
**ru ral** ('růr-əl)　country
**rushy**　banks with plants and weeds along the shores
**rus set** ('rə-sət)　reddish brown
**rus tic** ('rəs-tik)　farmer; countrified
**Ruth and Bo az** ('bō-az)　*see* Ruth IV
**ruth less ly** ('rüth-ləs-lē)　without pity

## S

**Saar dam** ('zär-däm)
**sa ber** ('sā-bər)　curved sword
**sa ble** ('sā-bəl)　black
**sa chem** ('sā-chəm)　chief
**sacked** ('sakt)　collected all the treasures of
**sacred professions**　faithful promises

**saddle-girth** ('gərth)  band encircling body of horse to hold saddle on

**safe conduct**  promise of a journey without danger of attack

**Sa fere** (sə-'fēr)

**sa ga** ('sä-gə)  Scandinavian legend

**sa ga cious** (sə-'gā-shəs)  wise

**sag a more** ('sa-gə-mōr)  Indian chief

**sage** ('sāj)  wise man; wise; serious

**sage ly observed** ('sāj-lē)  wisely remarked

**sa laam** (sə-'läm)  low bow

**sal lied** ('sa-lēd)  rushed

**sal low** ('sa-lō)  willow tree

**sal ly** ('sa-lē)  rush

**sal u ta tion** (sal-yə-'tā-shən)  greeting

**sal ving** ('sal-viŋ)  treated with ointment

**sa mite** ('sa-mØt)  kind of heavy silk

**Sam o set** ('sa-mō-set)  Indian chief

**sanc tion of earth** ('saŋk-shən)  permission of the law

**sanc tu a ry** ('saŋk-chə-wer-ē)  place of protection

**sandbar**  ridge of sand under water

**San tee** (san-'tē)  river of South Carolina

**sap ling** ('sap-liŋ)  slim young tree

**sap phire** ('sa-fØr)  bright-blue gem

**Sar a cens** ('sar-ə-sənz)  Mohammedans who held the Holy Land

**sat u rat ed** ('sa-chə-rā-təd)  soaked

**sau ri an** ('sȯr-ē-ən)  reptile; snake

**savage Nature's far abode**  uninhabited part of the world

**sa vor y** ('sā-və-rē)  appetizing

**Sax on** ('sak-sən)  English; blond

**scab bard** ('ska-bərd)  cover for a sword

**scald** ('skȯld)  ancient Scandinavian poet who sang of the heroic deeds of his people

**scan** ('skan)  examine; look at

**scanty gleam of heaven**  small share of perfection which everyone has

**scathed** ('skāt͟hd)  struck

**scoff of all men, the** ('skäf)  mocked by everyone

**score** ('skōr)  twenty

**scourge** ('skərj)  whip; strike

**scour ing** ('skau̇-riŋ)  race

**scout** ('skau̇t)  spy

**scribe** ('skrØb)  writer

**scru ples** ('skrü-pəlz)  delicate feelings; hesitation

**scru pu lous ly** ('skrü-pyə-ləs-lē)  carefully; conscientiously

**scru ti nized** ('skrü-t°n-Øzd)  examined

**scru ti ny** ('skrü-t°n-ē)  examination

**scut tling** ('skət-liŋ)  running swiftly

**sea mew** ('sē-myü)  sea-gull

**seamless dome** ('dōm)  the gray sky without a break anywhere

**seg ment** ('seg-mənt)  part

**self-con dem na tion** (kän-dem-'nā-shən)  guiltiness

**self-vaunt ing** ('vȯn-tiŋ)  conceited

**sem blance** ('sem-blənts)  likeness; disguise

**sensibly**  sharply

**sen tries** ('sen-trēz)  guards

**Se poy** ('sē-pȯi)  native of India

**se quence of lon gi tu di nal strips** ('sē-kwənts; län-jə-'tüd-nəl)  change from one part to another

**se ques tered** (si-'kwes-tərd)  secluded

**se rene ly high** (sə-'rēn-lē)  of noble aspect

**ser ried** ('ser-ēd)  one after another

**served his ap pren tice ship** (ə-'pren-tə-ship)  learned his trade

**ser vile** ('sər-vØl)  which bind them to an unjust king

**set**  hardened (by worry); rushed

**sev er al** ('sev-rəl)  separate

**se ver i ty** (sə-'ver-ə-tē)  harshness; cruelty

**Se ville** (sə-'vil)  province of Spain

**shad** ('shad)  fish

**share** ('shar)  sharp part of plow that turns up the ground

**shattered hulk**  worn-out body

**sheathed** ('shēthd)  covered

**Sheba, Queen of**  *see* Queen

**sheer** ('shir)  straight; pure

**shift** ('shift)  act

**shriek of the baf fled Fiend** ('ba-fəld)  angry howling of the wind because of his failure to get at the warm fireside

**shrine** ('shrØn)  altar

**si er ra** (sē-'er-ə)  ridge of mountains

**sig nif i cant** (sig-'ni-fi-kənt)  full of the meaning

**silent ghosts in misty shrouds** ('shraůdz)  like noiseless ghosts dressed in garments of mist

**silent syllables**  snowflakes which fall so quietly

**si mil i tude** (sə-'mi-lə-tüd)  likeness

**sin ew** ('sin-yü)  cord which connects muscle to body

**sinewy** ('sin-yə-wē) powerful

**single reflection well applied** one thought (just stated) if rightly understood

**sin gu lar i ty** (siŋ-gyə-'lar-ə-tē) peculiarity

**sin is ter** ('si-nəs-tər) evil

**sin u ous** ('sin-yə-wəs) curving

**si ren** ('sØ-rən) hope, deceiving us, as the sirens beguiled the sailors in the Odyssey

**Skaw** ('skȯ) north point of Jutland, Denmark

**skein** ('skān) quantity of thread

**skip per** ('ski-pər) captain

**skir mish** ('skər-mish) minor fight

**skirt ing the brink** ('skər-tiŋ) running along the edge

**Skoal** ('skōl) Scandinavian for *Hail*

**slab** ('slab) tombstone

**slack en his ma jes tic course** ('sla-kən; mə-'jes-tik) change the flowing of the dignified river

**slat y-blue** ('slā-tē) dark bluish-gray

**slaves of human Art** wonderful forces which serve mankind

**sledge-hammers** large heavy hammers

**sleeping-bag** long bag of skins used by hunters to sleep in

**slew him knightly** killed him in fair battle

**sloop** ('slüp) sail-boat

**small-bore** with a small opening

**smallclothes** knee breeches

**smith** workman who hammers metals into shape

**smith y** ('smi-thē) workshop

**smit ten the leaves** ('smi-tᵊn) withered them with his touch

**snare** ('snar) trap

**snipe** ('snØp) bird with long, straight beak

**so journed** ('sō-jərnd) dwelt for a while

**sol ace** ('sä-ləs) comfort

**solid esteem pro por tioned to it** (prə-'pōr-shənd) respect he deserved

**so lil o quy** (sə-'li-lə-kwē) mutterings to himself

**sol i tude** ('sä-lə-tüd) being alone

**sons of thine** Englishmen who had founded the American colonies

**soot y** ('su̇-tē)

**sor cer ess** ('sȯr-sə-rəs) woman magician

**sor did** ('sȯr-dəd) mean; selfish; narrow-minded

**sore vexed** much troubled

**sor rel** ('sȯr-əl) plant with sour juice

**sorrowing beyond measure**  overcome with grief

**souls that sped**  men who were killed

**Sound**  strait between Seeland (Denmark) and Sweden

**sounding aisles**  ('Ølz)  echoing depths; the trees formed long aisles

**sounding wing**  noise made by the wind as it passes

**sound of sinister o men**  ('ō-mən)  noise which suggested the coming troubles

**sov er eign**  ('sä-vrən)  ruler

**spa cious**  ('spā-shəs)  large

**spar**  ('spär)  mast

**Sparks, Jared**  American historian

**spas mod ic, becoming**  (spaz-'mä-dik)  dying out for a little while, then starting up suddenly

**spawn**  ('spȯn)  bring forth

**spe cie**  ('spē-shē)  money

**spec ta cle**  ('spek-ti-kəl)  sight

**spec tral**  ('spek-trəl)  ghostly; shadowy

**spec u la tion**  (spe-kyə-'lā-shən)  opinion; wondering

**sped**  ('sped)  got along

**speed**  fight (that is, win)

**spindle**  rod on spinning wheel which holds thread

**spi ral ly**  ('spØ-rə-lē)  round and round

**spoil**  lands and riches seized by the victors; captured treasures

**spon ta ne ous ly**  (spän-'tā-nē-əs-lē)  naturally

**spouse**  ('spaůs)  wife

**spright ly**  ('sprØt-lē)  lively; gay

**squad ron**  ('skwä-drən)  division of the fleet

**squal id**  ('skwä-ləd)  dirty; fowl; filthy

**Squan to**  ('skwän-tō)

**squib**  ('skwib)  short, witty editorial

**squire**  ('skwØr)  title of dignity next below that of knight

**stag nant**  ('stag-nənt)  foul

**stain the heath er**  ('he-th̲ər)  color the grass and plants red

**stalk ing**  ('stȯ-kiŋ)  walking haughtily

**stal wart**  ('stȯl-wərt)  strong

**stanch**  ('stȯnch)  true; stop the bleeding of

**stand ard**  ('stan-dərd)  flag; side

**star board**  ('stär-bərd)  right hand of a ship to one facing the front

**stark**  ('stärk)  stiff

**starve ling**  ('stärv-liŋ)  lean

**stat ure**  ('sta-chər)  figure; height

**stat ute** ('sta-chüt)  law

**stave** ('stāv)  note

**stayed**  held back

**steel-tipped ordered lines**  military parade of soldiers with swords

**steep**  high shore

**stem**  make headway against; dam

**ster ling** ('stər-liŋ)  genuine

**stern** ('stərn)  back of a ship

**stew ard** ('stü-ərd)  overseer of the kitchen and supplies; cook

**stim u lat ed** ('stim-yə-lā-təd)  inspired

**stock saddle** ('stȯk)  saddle with high knob in front, used by cowboys

**stom ach er** ('stə-mi-kər)  ornamental covering for the front of the waist

**storm-winds**  troubles met in the founding of the nation—wars, etc.

**stout-hearted men**  brave, hopeful men

**strad dle-bug** ('stra-dᵊl)  long-legged beetle

**strain** ('strān)  song

**strat a gem** ('stra-tə-jəm)  cleverness

**stretching to lee ward** ('lē-wərd)  like a line before us

**strip ling** ('stri-pliŋ)  youth: boy

**strong land's swift increase**  growth of a prosperous country

**strong mother of a Lion-line**  England, which has produced such strong men

**stu pe fied their senses** ('stü-pə-fØd)  dulled their feelings

**stu pen dous** (stü-'pen-dəs)  large

**stur geon** ('stər-jən)  large fish covered with tough skin

**sub jec tion, into** (səb-'jek-shən)  under my power

**subject of the Crown**  loyal citizen of England

**sub ju ga tion** (səb-ji-'gā-shən)  conquest

**sub lim i ty** (sə-'bli-mə-tē)  nobility

**sub merged** (səb-'mərjd)  underwater

**sub or di nate** (sə-'bȯr-dᵊn-ət)  adjoining

**sub se quent** ('səb-si-kwənt)  later

**sub stan tial** (səb-'stan-shəl)  wealthy

**sub ter ra ne an** (səb-tə-'rā-nē-ən)  underground

**sub tle** ('sə-tᵊl)  mysterious

**subtle  de cep tions** (di-'sep-shənz)  his mistaken idea of his feeling for Priscilla

**suc ces sion** (sək-'se-shən)  history

**succession, rapid**  quickly one after the other

**suc cor** ('sə-kər)  help

**succors...thrown into** ('sə-kərz)  troops forcing their way

**suffer**  permit

**suffer me**  allow me

**suffering worth**  one who has suffered a great deal and deserves a happier life

**suit**  ('süt)  request

**suit a ble ex trav a gance**  ('sü-tə-bəl; ek-'stra-və-gənts)  act of insanity which would have fitted the occasion

**sul phur ous**  ('səl-fə-rəs)  like burned matches

**sul try**  ('səl-trē)  hot and moist

**summer soldier**  soldier who brags about fighting when there is none to do

**sum mons**  ('sə-mənz)  service

**summon your whole for ti tude**  ('fȯr-tə-tüd)  be as brave as you can

**sump tu ous promise**  ('səmp-shə-wəs)  wonderful prospect

**sumptuous time**  season when there are so many good things to eat

**sunburn on our breasts, to the**  nearly to our armpits

**sun der**  ('sən-dər)  cut

**sun-il lu mined**  (i-'lü-mənd)  with the sunlight on it

**sunset land**  America is in the western hemisphere.  The sun seems to set in the West

**sunshine pa tri ot**  ('pā-trē-ət)  man who is loyal to his country only when it is not in trouble

**su per nu mer a ry**  (sü-pər-'nü-mə-rer-ē)  extra

**su per sti tion**  (sü-pər-'sti-shən)  untrue beliefs about mysterious things

**su pine ly**  (sú-'pØn-lē)  helplessly

**sup plant ed**  (sə-'plan-təd)  taken my place

**sup ple-jack**  ('sə-pəl-jak)  shrub with a tough, easily bent stem

**supplicating attitude**  begging manner

**supply by ad dress**  (ə-'dres)  make up for by skillful management

**sup po si tions**  (sə-pə-'zi-shənz)  hopes

**sup pressed**  (sə-'prest)  low

**sure ty**  ('shúr-ə-tē)  guarantee of character

**surge**  ('sərj)  waves

**sur mount ed**  (sər-'maủn-təd)  topped

**sur vey ing**  (sər-'vā-iŋ)  science of measuring land

**sus tain**  (sə-'stān)  meet with; assist; bear; support

**swain**  ('swān)  beau

**swel ter of yesterday**  ('swel-tər)  yesterday's heat

**swerved**  ('swərvd)  turned aside

**Syb a ris**  ('si-bə-rəs)  ancient city of Italy, famous for wealth and luxury

**syc a more**  ('si-kə-mōr)  kind of maple tree

**Syc o rax** ('si-kə-raks)

**syl van** ('sil-vən) forest

# T

**tac i turn** ('ta-sə-tərn) quiet

**tack le** ('ta-kəl) ropes

**tale of vi sion ary hours** ('vi-zhə-ner-ē) suggestions of imaginary happiness

**tamed by human cunning** put under control by men's invention

**tank ard** ('tan-kərd) covered mug

**ta per** ('tā-pər) delicately pointed

**tap es try** ('ta-pə-strē) ornamental hangings

**Tap pan Zee** ('ta-pən; 'zē)

**tar nish** ('tär-nish) dishonor

**tar ry** ('tar-ē) stay; wait; loiter

**Tar tar** ('tär-tər) wild Asiatic tribe famous for horsemanship

**task e ter nal** (i-'tər-nᵊl) endless labor of doing service for others

**taunt** ('tȯnt) sneering

**te di ous** ('tē-dē-əs) tiresome

**teemed with life** ('tēmd) was filled with animals of many kinds

**temporal concerns** business affairs

**temporal salvation** happiness on earth

**tempt** ('tempt) explore

**te nac i ty of life** (tə-'na-sə-tē) being so hard to kill

**ten ant less man sion** ('te-nənt-ləs; 'man-shən) lonely existence

**tender you my hom age** ('ä-mij) offer you my loyalty

**ten dril** ('ten-drəl) little coiling attachments to the stem

**ten or** ('te-nər) tone; character

**ter mi nat ed** ('tər-mə-nā-təd) ended; bounded

**ter mi na tion** (tər-mə-'nā-shən) ending

**ter rif ic** (tə-'ri-fik) brilliant; threatening

**tete-a-tete** (tet-ə-'tet) private talk

**Thames** ('temz) river in England

**thatch** ('thach) roof of straw

**the charm's complete** the one thing that was missing has appeared

**the o ry** ('thē-ə-rē) his idea

**there fore** (thar-'fȯr)

**Ther mop y lae** (thər-'mä-pə-lē)

**the troubled heart, etc.** the sorrows one feels can be seen in the face

**thick cover** *see* cover

**thine arms withstood**  resisted your army

**thinking no mar vel**  ('mär-vəl)  not considering it anything wonderful

**this day twelvemonth**  a year from today

**thros tle**  ('thrä-səl)  song thrush

**thunders from her native oak**  the cannon roar as they shoot their balls
   through the portholes of the ships built of wood grown in England

**thwart**  ('thwȯrt)  oppose; rower's seat across the boat

**tile**  ('tØl)  thin piece of baked clay for building purposes; here, the snow

**tiller**  handle used to steer boat

**tim ber**  ('tim-bər)  woods

**time dried the maiden's tears**  gradually she grew happier

**tim o thy**  ('ti-mə-thē)  hay

**tin y**  ('tØ-nē)  very small

**'tis life**  it is glorious

**Ti tan**  ('tØ-tᵊn)  in mythology, a god of great size and strength

**Ti tan ic**  (tØ-'ta-nik)  enormous

**to be your champion**  to fight for you

**tod dy**  ('tä-dē)  hot sweet drink

**Tok a ma ha mon**  (tä-kə-mə-'hä-mən)

**to ken**  ('tō-kən)  keepsake; sign; distinguishing mark

**tolerable degree of tran quil li ty**  (tran-'kwi-lə-tē)  fair amount of hap
   piness

**toll**  ('tōl)  tax

**tooth**  sting

**to paz**  ('tō-paz)  a yellow gem

**torch**  ideal we were fighting for

**tor pid touch**  ('tȯr-pəd)  touch which can deaden or freeze it

**To ry**  ('tōr-ē)  man on the king's side

**to the Highlands bound**  on his way to the northern part of Scotland

**touch of trans mu ta tion**  (trans-myu̇-'tā-shən)  ability to turn things into
   gold

**tour**  ('tu̇r)  journey

**tour na ment**  ('tu̇r-nə-mənt)  combat between mounted armed knights

**to ward**  ('tōrd)

**trace his footsteps now**  see where he has been

**trac ta ble**  ('trak-tə-bəl)  easily controlled

**trai tor knave**  ('trā-tər; 'nāv)  unfaithful soldier

**trance**  ('trants)  doze

**tran quil li ty**  (tran-'kwi-lə-tē)  calmness

**tran scend ent**  (tran-'sən-dənt)  extraordinary

**trans fig ured**  (trans-'fi-gyərd)  beautified

**trans gres sion** (trans-'gre-shən) sin
**tran sient** ('tran-zē-ənt) temporary
**trans mut ed** (tranz-'myü-təd) changed
**trawl er** ('tro-lər) vessel that fishes by dragging nets
**treach er ous** ('tre-chə-rəs) unfaithful
**tread le** ('tre-dᵊl) pedal
**treated it with rid i cule** ('ri-də-kyül) made fun of it
**treenail** wooden peg for fastening the planks of a vessel
**tre mor** ('tre-mər) quivering
**trem u lous** ('trem-yə-ləs) trembling
**trench ant** ('tren-chənt) sharp
**trib u ta ry** ('tri-byə-ter-ē) branch; country paying a tax to another
**tribute of our conscience** devotion of our better nature
**tricolor** French flag, blue, white, red
**trifling jest** little joke
**Tro jans** ('trō-jənz) people of Troy
**tro phy** ('trō-fē) thing won by effort and preserved as a remembrance
**tropics** warm countries
**troth** (ēträth) promises
**troubled sky** stormy sky
**truc u lent** ('trə-kyə-lənt) savage
**true and tried** has proved itself faithful
**trump** ('trəmp) call
**trump er y** ('trəm-pə-rē) goods
**trumpets of the sky** loud winds
**trussed** ('trəst) with wings fastened to the body
**tryst ing-place** ('tris-tiŋ) meeting place
**tu mul tu ous pri va cy** (tu-'məl-chə-wəs; 'prØ-və-sē) shelter from the noisy storm outside
**turf** ('tərf) grassy sod
**turn the scale** win the battle
**tur ret** ('tər-ət) tower
**Tus ca ro ra** (təs-kə-'rōr-ə)
**twofold shout** shout and its echo
**Ty ler, Wat** ('tØ-lər; 'wät) English rebel
**typ i fied by** ('ti-pə-fØd) likened to

# U

**Ul lin, Lord** ('ə-lin)
**Ul va** ('əl-və)

**un af fect ed** (ən-ə-ˈfek-təd)  sincere

**un as sum ing** (ən-ə-ˈsü-miŋ)  humble

**unbroken line of lances**  row of spears which left no opening

**un cour te ous to rebuke** (ən-ˈkər-tē-əs)  impolite to find fault with

**un couth** (ən-ˈküth)  strange; ugly; rough

**un daunt ed** (ən-ˈdȯn-təd)  bold; fearless

**under native rule, if India**  had been ruled by its own people

**under pain of a fearful curse**  threatening them with terrible punishment

**under surety of my word**  with a promise from me

**undertake he will do great marvels**  am sure he will do very unusual
things

**un du la tion** (ən-jə-ˈlā-shən)  motion

**un feigned regard** (ən-ˈfānd)  sincere affection

**unfought victories won**  difficulties of poverty, lack of education, etc.,
overcome

**ungentle knight**  one who does not deserve the title

**u ni son** (ˈyü-nə-sən)  harmony

**united crosses**  one cross on the other

**unlocks a warmer clime** (ˈklØm)  makes me feel as if I were in a warmer
climate

**unmarked**  unnoticed

**un ob tru sive** (ən-əb-ˈtrü-siv)  modest

**un re dressed** (ən-ri-ˈdrest)  not righted

**un re served** (ən-ri-ˈzərvd)  frank

**un sa vo ry** (ən-ˈsā-və-rē)  unpleasant to smell

**un scathed** (ən-ˈskāthd)  unharmed

**unscorched wing**  untouched by fire; *see Hekla*

**unseen quar ry** (ˈkwȯr-ē)  hidden bed of stone (tile) where the north wind
gets his building material

**un sub stan tial** (ən-səb-ˈstan-shəl)  unreal

**un taint ed ears** (ən-ˈtān-təd)  ears that have heard no wickedness

**un wield y** (ən-ˈwēl-dē)  fat

**un wont ed** (ən-ˈwȯn-təd)  unusual: rare

**un world ly** (ən-ˈwərl-dlē)  unselfish

**unworthy in nu en does** (in-yə-ˈwen-dōz)  undeserved suggestions

**up braid** (əp-ˈbrād)  reproach

**upper work altogether razed** (ˈrāzd)  sails, masts, etc., all shot away

**up tears** (əp-ˈtarz)  uproots

**ur chin** (ˈər-chən)  boy

**u surped** (yu̇-ˈsərpt)  seized without any right

**U ther Pen drag on** (ˈü-thər; pen-ˈdra-gən)

**ut ter ance** ('ə-tə-rənts) expression

# V

**vacant** not thinking of anything

**vague pre mo ni tion** ('vāg; prē-mə-'ni-shən) a strange, undefinable warning

**vale** ('vāl) valley

**val iant** ('val-yənt) brave

**van** ('van) front

**va ried** ('ver-ēd) different

**var ie gat ed** ('ver-ē-gā-təd) mixed

**var let** ('vär-lət) coward

**vas sal** ('va-səl) slave

**vast congregation** large gathering

**vast ex pec ta tions** ('vast; ek-spek-'tā-shənz) prospects of future riches

**vaunt ing** ('vȯn-tiŋ) boasting

**veer** ('vir) turn

**veg e tat ing** ('ve-jə-tā-tiŋ) living quietly and simply, like plants

**ve he ment ly** ('vē-ə-mənt-lē) furiously

**ven er a ble** ('ve-nər-ə-bəl) dignified, old

**ven er a tion** (ve-nə-'rā-shən) reverence

**ver dant** ('vər-dᵊnt) green

**verge** ('vərj) edge

**ver mil ion** (vər-'mil-yən) red paint

**vi brate to the doom** ('vØ-brāt) the movement started by Hampden will influence men until the end of the world

**vi cious ness** ('vi-shəs-nəs) bad temper

**vi cis si tude** (vi-'si-sə-tüd) comedown

**vict ual** ('vi-tᵊl) food

**vict ual er** ('vi-tᵊl-ər) provision ship

**vig il** ('vi-jəl) wakefulness

**vig i lant** ('vi-jə-lənt) watchful

**vi king** ('vØ-kiŋ) a Northman pirate

**vil lain** ('vi-lən) scoundrel

**vir gin** ('vər-jən) new

**virtue has been ac quired** (ə-'kwØrd) the Greeks had to work to gain their good qualities

**vis age** ('vi-zij) the face

**vi sion a ry** (vi-zhə-ner-ē) dreamy

**visionary pro jects** ('prä-jekts) doubtful plans

**vis ta** ('vis-tə) opening

**vo ca tion** (vō-'kā-shən) occupation

**vo cif er ous** (vō-'si-fə-rəs) noisy

**void** ('vȯid) useless

**vo ra cious** (vȯ-'rā-shəs) greedy

**vouch for** ('vaùch) swear to

**vows were plight ed** ('plØ-təd) pledges of love were made

**vul ner a ble** ('vəl-nə-rə-bəl) weak

**vul ture-beak** ('vəl-chər) dangerous point of the icebergs.  Vultures are large flesh-eating birds

## W

**waft** ('wäft) carry; blow

**wam pum** ('wäm-pəm) shell beads

**wandering shadow** dead skipper's ghost

**wandering voice** voice of a hidden bird

**wane** ('wān) pass; get shorter

**want** lack **want breath** lack energy

**ward** ('wȯrd) guard; keep

**warded off tyr an ny** ('tir-ə-nē) kept away an unjust ruler

**warlike gear** ('gir) armor

**warm ten e ment** ('te-nə-mənt) comfortable home

**war rant** ('wȯr-ənt) declare

**wa ry** ('war-ē) cautious

**was sail-bout** ('wä-səl-baùt) drinking revel

**waters fast pre vail ing** (pri-'vā-liŋ) waves breaking over the boat

**waters warp** freeze the streams

**water-wraith** ('rāth) spirit of the water

**Wat ta wa mat** (wä-tə-'wä-mət)

**wat tled** ('wä-tᵊld) having fleshy growths hanging from its neck

**ways of na tive dom** ('nā-tiv-dəm) habits of the poorer classes

**weath er'd** ('we-thərd) lasted through

**we find it a river** the banks are so marshy it seems as though they were a continuation of the river

**weighed** ('wād) pulled in anchors

**weigh their anchors** raise the anchors

**well-considered** thoughtful

**well-ruled and fair-languaged** man of good conduct and pleasant speech

**were wolf** ('wir-wŭlf) in old superstition, a human being turned into a wolf

**whatever promised util i ty** (yü-'ti-lə-tē)  whatever seemed to do actual
   good

**what sig ni fies it** ('sig-nə-fØz)  what does it matter

**whelm him o'er**  ruin his life

**whet ting** ('hwe-tiŋ)  rubbing to try its sharpness

**whi lom** ('hwØ-ləm)  once

**whim si cal** ('hwim-zi-kəl)  freakish

**white bas tions** ('bas-chənz)  fortifications of snow

**wholesale merchants**  men who sell large quantities to smaller stores

**wider field of ac tiv i ty** (ak-'tiv-ə-tē)  larger territory in which to work

**wight** ('wØt)  person

**wild little poet**  untamed songbird

**willfulness**  disobedience

**wince** ('wints)  shrink

**wind lass** ('wind-ləs)  machine for pulling up anchor

**windward**  on the side from which the wind is blowing

**Win kel ried** ('wiŋ-kəl-rēd)

**wise** ('wØz)  a way; case

**wit** ('wit)  humorist

**witch er y** ('wi-chə-rē)  magic

**withe** ('with)  flexible, slender twig

**withheld by re morse ful misgivings** (ri-'mòrs-fəl)  kept back by his doubt
   as to whether it was right

**with his fellowship**  accompanied by his following of knights

**with respect to fu tu ri ty** (fyù-'tùr-ə-tē)  in the future

**wit ting ly** ('wi-tiŋ-lē)  knowingly

**wont** ('wònt)  habit

**wood bine** ('wüd-bØn)  honeysuckle

**woods are greening**  trees are budding

**world ly ef fects** ('wərld-lē; i-'fekts)  possession

**worldly ends**  actual problems, such as trying to gain wealth or power

**worming his way**  crawling slowly

**wormwood**  common weed

**wor ship** ('wər-shəp)  high rank

**wor sted** ('wùs-təd)  wool

**wor thies** ('wər-<u>th</u>ēz)  great men

**wound** ('wünd)  injury

**wound ed** ('wün-dəd)  hurt

**wrapt in a vision pro phet ic** (prə-'fe-tik)  a dream of the future coming
   to him

**wrench'd of ev'ry stay** ('rencht)  every assistance is taken away

**wrench'd their rights from** gained liberty by fighting
**wroth** (ˈròth) angry
**wroth the tempest rushes** the storm becomes worse and worse
**wrought** (ˈròt) worked
**wrought together** both worked
**wrought upon and molded** influenced and shaped

## X

**Xer xes** (ˈzərk-sēz)

## Y

**yard** mast to hold the sail
**yeo man ry** (ˈyō-mən-rē) land owners
**yeo men** (ˈyō-mən) farmers
**yield thee as recreant** (ˈyēld) surrender to me, coward!
**yoke of ser vi tude** (ˈsər-və-tüd) rule of a conqueror
**yon** (ˈyän) over there
**your warrant** the witness, who will prove what you have done

## Z

**zeal** (ˈzēl) eagerness; enthusiasm
**zeal ous** (ˈze-ləs) enthusiastic; active
**zest** (ˈzest) enjoyment

## Books Available from
### Lost Classics Book Company
### American History

### Biography

### English Grammar

(*Teacher's Guides available for each of these texts*)

### Elson Readers Series

(*Teacher's Guides available for each reader in this series*)

### Historical Fiction

## To Order or Request a Catalog
### Telephone:
Retail Sales and Schools Call: (888) 611-BOOK (2665)

**Mail to**: Lost Classics Book Company, P. O. Box 1756, Ft. Collins, CO  80522

**For more information visit us at: http://www.lostclassicsbooks.com**

9 781890 62